CONVICTION

JENNIFER BLACKSTREAM

SKELETON KEY PUBLISHING

CONVICTION
A Blood Trails Novel, Book 9

USA Today Bestselling Author
JENNIFER BLACKSTREAM

To join my mailing list, visit
www.jenniferblackstream.com

Conviction
©Copyright Jennifer Blackstream 2020, Skeleton Key Publishing
Edited by Michelle
Cover Art by Covers by Juan © Copyright 2020

Other Books by Jennifer Blackstream

Blood Trails Series (Urban Fantasy):

DEADLINE
MONSTER
TAKEN
CORRUPTION
MERCENARY
CAGED
BETRAYAL
THRALL
CONVICTION
MISDIRECTION
SACRIFICE
SHROUD

Blood Prince Series (Paranormal Romance)

BEFORE MIDNIGHT
ONE BITE
GOLDEN STAIR
DIVINE SCALES
BEAUTIFUL SALVATION
THE PIRATE'S WITCH

The Blood Realm Series (Paranormal Romance):

ALL FOR A ROSE
BLUE VOODOO
THE ARCHER
BEAR WITH ME
STOLEN WISH

Join my mailing list on my website www.jenniferblackstream.com to be alerted when new titles are released.

It's never too late for a fresh start in a new direction.

ACKNOWLEDGMENTS

To my writer's group. Without our Zoom writing sprints, I don't think this book would have made its release date. Special thanks to Kate Danley, who organized the sprints, and Yasmine Galenorn, who ran additional sprints with me.

"Those who clearly recognize the voice of their own conscience usually recognize also the voice of justice." -

— ALEKSANDR SOLZHENITSYN

CONVICTION

JENNIFER BLACKSTREAM

CHAPTER 1

"Shade, I've been arrested for murder."

Andy's words sent a shock wave through my system, his calm tone doing nothing to soften that last, crucial word. I clutched my cell phone tighter, fighting not to press it too hard to my face lest I mash the end call button by mistake. Across the cozy cafe's dinner table, Liam tensed, the hand holding his coffee going still before lowering the mug to the table with a grim thud.

Arrested for murder. Andy had been arrested for murder. But why call me? Why not a lawyer, or a coworker from the FBI? Unless...

"What murder?" My voice didn't shake. Yea for me.

Andy took a deep breath. "They said I shot a kelpie. Someone named Raichel."

My gaze locked onto Liam's. Thirty seconds ago, I'd been appreciating how handsome he looked in his forest green flannel shirt and the dark jeans that made his midnight eyes look even more blue. I'd been basking in the warmth of his smile, the promise I could see in his eyes that had built the longer we lingered after we'd finished our meals.

Now I was appreciating other things about him. The fact that he was a detective sergeant of the Cleveland Metropark Police with a flashing light he could smack on top of his truck for speedy travel. The fact that he was a werewolf, and he'd already heard what Andy said without my having to repeat it. And the fact that he was an alpha, and he knew the difference between the time to talk, and the time to act.

"Where are you?" I asked, already standing as Liam dug out his wallet and left enough money to cover our meal, dessert, post-dinner coffees, and a tip.

"I'm on a boat tied up at a bar." He cleared his throat. "It's the place you and Flint dragged me out of when we were working that artifact case. It's called Something Fishy."

Something Fishy. I'd have laughed if I had the breath to spare. If my memory wasn't prickling with images of the night he'd mentioned so casually. When he'd almost died after going after a group of kelpies.

I snagged my red trench coat off the back of my chair. "Andy, whose boat is it?" I asked, even though I already knew the answer.

"I haven't seen ownership papers, but if I had to guess? Siobhan's."

Bile splashed the back of my throat. Siobhan. Sister of the kelpie Andy had shot. Killed. "Are you all right?" I didn't bother to put my coat on as I bolted for the door, my burger and fries sitting significantly less comfortably as anxiety stirred my stomach.

"I'm fine. Vincent woke me up and told me he healed me a little. He and Kylie are here processing the crime scene."

"What do you mean, he *woke you up*? And why did you need healing?"

Liam's hand on my arm drew me to a halt before I touched the front door, and he wordlessly tugged my coat out of my grasp and helped me into it. I would have told him the cold didn't bother me, but Andy was talking again and I didn't want to miss anything.

"I was unconscious for a while. I'm not sure how long. What time is it?"

"It's just after ten."

Andy swore under his breath. "I was out for a couple hours then."

"Out for a couple of *hours?*" An injury that knocked him out that long meant moderate to severe brain injury.

"Not from my injury," he said, brushing off my panic. "I was unconscious when Vincent got here. He woke me up and healed me, but he said healing isn't his specialty, and he didn't want to take a risk with a head injury where I lost consciousness. So he put me to sleep and called a healer. She just woke me up."

"You shouldn't sleep with a possible brain injury," I said uneasily.

"He didn't call it sleep. He called it 'stasis.'"

"Oh. Fine, that makes sense. Who is she? The healer?"

"She introduced herself as Justiciar Evelyn, from the Ministry of Deliverance?"

I relaxed, slightly. I'd met her before, and if Vincent had called her for healing, she must be good.

I shoved the door open and a gust of October wind tried to shove me back into the restaurant. I gritted my teeth and held my coat closed with my free hand as I made my way toward Liam's truck.

"If Evelyn and Vincent and Kylie are all there, then you're safe. And I'm on my way with Liam." I tilted my head to find an angle that wouldn't let the wind steal Andy's words before I could make them out. "Tell me what happened."

Voices in the background caught my attention, and in that moment I would have given anything for Liam's extra-sensitive hearing. Unfortunately, he was already at the truck, unlocking the doors and getting the engine started. I felt a little better when he pulled out the flashing light and stuck it to the top of the vehicle.

"I have to go. Apparently my phone time is up."

"Liam and I will be there in less than ten minutes." I jerked open the passenger door, and Liam started to pull out before I'd even gotten it all the way closed. Bless him.

The call ended, leaving me holding a silent phone and trying to swallow past a sudden lump in my throat.

"I'm not familiar with Something Fishy," Liam said, handing me his GPS.

"It's not far from my apartment. It's on the east side of the Cuyahoga, right before the West Basin." I punched the address into the GPS.

Liam nodded. "What do we know?"

I put the phone in the side pocket of my waist pouch, suddenly grateful I'd worn it on the date despite feeling a little silly about it. I unzipped the flap and lifted it open. "Peasblossom? Come out, I need you." I looked over at Liam. "I don't want to tell this story more than once."

There was movement in the enchanted confines of the pouch, and suddenly Peasblossom's voice came from far away. "Is the date over? It's awfully early, do we need chocolate? We could stop for ice cream?"

"Andy's been arrested for the murder of a kelpie. Siobhan is holding him on her boat."

"What?!"

I jerked back as my pixie familiar launched herself out of the pouch like a tiny pink bottle rocket, her multifaceted eyes wide as she looked back and forth between me and Liam.

"What happened?"

"I don't have any details yet," I said calmly. "We're heading there now."

"You said Kylie and Vincent are already there," Liam clarified.

"Yes, so Andy's fine. They won't let anything happen to him."

Liam flexed his grip on the steering wheel. "Kylie and Vincent are independent contractors connected to the Cuyahoga County Coroner's office. They're called in for task force cases, and anything that might be Other. I didn't call them in, so if they're at the scene, it means someone called the Vanguard."

Peasblossom squeaked in alarm.

The Vanguard. The Otherworld's answer to Interpol.

I didn't look at Peasblossom. I couldn't. Not when I knew we were both having the same thought.

This wasn't the first time the Vanguard had been called in after Andy had a run in with the kelpies. And even without knowing the details, I knew the Vanguard would raise an eyebrow at a second confrontation between Andy and the kelpies in which the human walked away and the kelpie didn't. Another incident with a gun.

The Vanguard didn't like coincidences.

"Tell me about the kelpies." Liam's firm, neutral tone meant he was in full cop mode. It wasn't an order, as such, but his manner said he expected an answer. "I remember when we interrogated Stavros, he taunted you over something between the kelpies and Andy. What happened?"

I pressed my hands flat against my thighs, rubbing them along the black, blue, and white geometric pattern of my leggings. "Earlier this year, Andy and I attended an art auction at the home of a *leannan sidhe*. Only it turns out, paintings weren't the only things being auctioned off—the artists were on the block as well. Young artists that the *leannan sidhe's* agent sought out at local homeless shelters. One of them, Grayson, was sold to the kelpies."

"Kelpies are waterhorses. What would they want with a human artist?"

I clenched my jaw. "Kelpies used to eat humans. They don't do it as much now, because these days when someone goes missing, there's an investigation, and too many missing people at the water's edge is bound to draw attention. Possibly on a scale large enough to force the Vanguard to act. But the kelpies didn't just eat people. They *terrified* them."

"The stories about wild rides over—and eventually under—the water," Liam noted.

"Yes. I think the kelpies found a way to merge their desire to instill fear with the desire to get more of a presence in land-based society. I think they bought Grayson with the intention of scaring the daylights out of him and seeing what kind of art he turned out."

Liam glanced at me. "You're serious?"

"I wish I wasn't. But you should have heard the crowd at that auction. The people who bought the artists." My mind drifted back to that night, taking me to a dark place I'd never wanted to go again. "There was a woman there, one of the *leannan sidhe*. She stood over the body of a dead girl, one of their victims who'd committed suicide and made her body part of the art. If you could have heard this *sidhe* speak. Not about the loss of life, not about despair... But what that *pure emotion* had done for the artist's work. How it—"

I stopped. I couldn't talk about it anymore. I couldn't help Andy if I went in with a hot head, and there were few things that upset me as much as the thought of those *leannan sidhe*. People who could talk about art as if it mattered more than someone's well being. Someone's *life*. It was a common failing of creatures who lived for centuries at a time. They started to value abstract concepts more than a single life. In some cases, more than many lives.

"So this artist the kelpies...purchased," Liam prompted quietly.

I stared out the windshield at the night sky, the stars trying their best to shine on a city with too much artificial light. "We went down to the lake to talk to him about a murder, but when Andy saw what was happening, how frightened Grayson was of the kelpies, he refused to walk away. Grayson was underage, and Andy refused to acknowledge the validity of any contract he'd signed that let the kelpies take him." I took a deep, slow breath. "When all was said and done, he'd shot two kelpies."

"He killed them?"

"One of them. Bradan. Rowyn lived."

"And the kelpies just let him walk away after that?"

"I made a deal with Marilyn—the *leannan sidhe* in charge of the auction—to offer myself to be bid on, and in exchange, she didn't contest Andy's assertion that the kids were too young to enter into a legal contract. The kelpies' ownership was deemed null and void. Therefore, Grayson wasn't their property, and Andy's actions constituted defense of a minor. The Vanguard was there to witness the deal, so there was nothing the kelpies could do."

"But they tried," Peasblossom told him.

I nodded. "Siobhan, Bradan's sister, kidnapped Andy while we were on another case. They'd been spying on him. When he got shot while we were dealing with a demon's acolytes, they took advantage of his injuries to claim they were 'trying to help him.'"

Liam tapped one finger against the steering wheel. "On the phone, he told you he was near the place where you and Flint 'dragged him out' last time."

I'd really hoped he wasn't going to pick up on that one. My appreciation for his cop side wilted a little. "A few months ago we went to the Cleveland Museum of Art for a case and we ran into Morgan—a fey woman who was at Marilyn's the night Andy shot Bradan and Rowyn. She's not a *leannan sidhe*, but she is part of the Unseelie Court."

I gripped the door handle. "I thought she was egging Andy on that night. Encouraging him to take action in Grayson's defense while I was trying to calm him down. Then when we ran into her at the museum, she brought up the kelpies again."

"And you thought she was goading Andy again?"

"Morgan made some comment about working at the art museum Marilyn runs to make up for her behavior the night of the auction. Andy brought up Grayson and said Morgan had done nothing wrong. Morgan took the opening to mention in passing that there are always kelpies in Cleveland, hanging around waterfront bars, and said they aren't 'eating people on a *regular* basis.'"

Liam's eyebrows shot up. "Yeah, that sounds like a push."

"And it worked. Later Flint and I tailed Andy to Something Fishy and found him confronting a group of kelpies on their boat. I had to pull him out of the water."

"You tailed your partner?"

In light of what was going on right this minute, now was not the time I would have chosen to talk to him about my concerns for Andy's recent change in behavior. "Andy had been acting... strangely. But it was Flint who caught him following a kelpie and warned me we'd better check in on him."

I could almost hear the wheels turning in Liam's head. Andy had shot two kelpies, killed one. Andy viewed them as predators, a natural consequence to his experience with them thus far. Now Andy had been arrested for another kelpie murder.

Even I couldn't fail to connect those dots.

Liam took one hand off the steering wheel, groping for my free hand. He squeezed it. "I'm sorry."

I jerked my hand away without meaning to. "Don't say that. We don't know what happened. It's too soon for—"

"I didn't say I'm sorry because I think he did it," Liam interrupted calmly. He held out his hand, but didn't try to take mine again. "I'm sorry because I know what it's like when someone you care about is caught up in something like this."

Understanding dawned. "Brenna."

Liam nodded. "If you'd looked only at the evidence at the scene, it would have been easy to jump to the conclusion that my sister was guilty of murder. But I didn't make that jump, and neither did you. You were calm, and you considered all the evidence. And that's what we're going to do for Andy."

My shoulders gave up some of their tension, and I took Liam's offered hand, squeezed it. Shifters ran warmer than humans by a few degrees with an average temp between one hundred and one hundred and two degrees. I hadn't realized my hands were cold until I touched Liam, and I squeezed his hand again, taking as much warmth as I could get.

He made no move to let go. "Do you remember when we first met?"

"Yes." I tilted my head. "You didn't like me very much."

"And do you remember why?"

A hint of a blush rose to my cheeks. "Because I kept leaning against you?"

The corner of his mouth twitched. "No."

"Of course not, because he'd have liked that," Peasblossom scoffed.

I ignored her and guessed again. "Because you didn't want me interfering in your investigation."

"Not just any investigation. A member of my pack had been found eating the body of a murder victim. Stephen and I had our problems, but he was still pack. He was mine to protect. I wanted to believe he was innocent, but he wasn't doing himself any favors. He didn't talk to me, didn't trust me enough to tell me what was going on with him." He slowed before rolling through a stop sign, the blue flashing lights on top of the truck casting weird shadows on the dark buildings around us. "The most important thing you need to do to help Andy is to convince him to let you help. To be honest with you."

"It's a good sign that he called me," I said hopefully.

"It is. But remember, we all have things we'd rather not share. Andy doesn't strike me as someone who likes to talk about himself, and it might be harder than you'd think to convince him that opening up is necessary."

I considered his words as he drove. After a minute, he glanced at me again. "Do you want me to stop at your place first, get Scath?"

I shook my head. "No time. I'll text her later, after we know what we're dealing with." I didn't add that it was just as likely the feline *sidhe* would find me on her own. She had a sixth sense for when I was in trouble, and some method of finding me that she refused to divulge.

We were all silent for a long time. Liam drove carefully, even with the light on his truck, probably out of respect for the fact that an accident was much more likely to kill any humans involved than us. And as much as I wanted to get to Andy as quickly as possible, I couldn't lie to myself that I wasn't also terrified.

I couldn't quit thinking about Andy's behavior lately. His temper. I didn't know if it was the fact he'd seen Grayson begging for his life that had left such a big impression on him, or if something about the kelpies struck a more personal note. But if there was one thing I knew for sure, it was that anger grew from fear. The kelpies terrified Andy.

And that made them both dangerous.

CHAPTER 2

THE LAST TIME I'd been to Something Fishy, I hadn't noticed the name on the sign. In my defense, there was enough grime covering the cracked paint that even if I'd been of a mind at the time to look for it, I might have missed it. But tonight, I couldn't help noticing.

The crime scene floodlights helped.

Peasblossom snorted. "Why not just call it 'Food Poisoning' and be done with it?"

I managed a half smile at her joke as I fortified myself for the coming task. Andy had guessed the boat he was being held on was Siobhan's, which probably meant he'd seen her. If she was here I had to be ready to face her, and I needed to be my witchiest self when I did.

Liam parked his truck in the sea of broken asphalt that passed for a parking lot, careful not to get too close to the crime scene tape marking off the section closest to the front door. There was a van parked near the entrance, the words "Cuyahoga County Coroner" emblazoned on the side in blocky blue letters. I nodded in satisfaction at the reminder that I wasn't Andy's only ally here. Kylie and Vincent were the best at what they did. Together, they would figure out what really happened.

"Headache?" Liam asked.

I paused, realizing that I'd subconsciously reached up to touch my forehead. On my last case, the killer had used a psychic-attack-by-proxy to stab me in the third eye, shredding the extrasensory organ and leaving me magically blind. It would heal, eventually, but for now, pain greeted my fingertips, pulsing in a dull ache. A warning not to try opening that sense.

"A little." I lowered my hand. "My third eye still hasn't healed. It's a good thing Vincent is here, because I couldn't use his forensic spell if I tried."

"And you'd better not try," Peasblossom warned. "Last time you tried to open your third eye—after I *told* you not to—we had to hang blackout sheets over all the windows for two days. I wasn't meant to live like a vampire."

She wasn't wrong, so I didn't argue.

I got out of Liam's truck with my head held high, my back straight. If Siobhan spotted me first, I wanted her to see my confidence. In an investigation like this, confidence was key.

A blue vinyl tent had been set up in front of the bar's front doors. The floodlights centered around that area, illuminating the scene in harsh artificial light.

"That's where the body is, isn't it?" Peasblossom asked, her voice coming from somewhere close to my ear.

"I'd imagine so. They'll want to block the body from the road."

Just then, Vincent appeared around the tent. The wizard, as usual, looked like a physics professor who'd just wandered off some college campus. His tweed suit was dark brown today, with tan elbow patches and a pale peach shirt underneath. His wild brown hair reached for the sky, as if each strand fought to get a better look at a different star. His eyes were unfocused, and I knew he was using his forensics spell, the one that sought out DNA to create ghostly shapes of whatever creature had left the evidence. I took a step forward, but shut my mouth before I could call out to him. I didn't want to interrupt.

Liam's nostrils flared. "Kelpies are out back."

"Then that's where Andy will be." The yellow crime scene tape prevented entrance to the bar, so I nodded toward the alley beside the building. "We can go around that way so we don't mess up Vincent's crime scene."

Another cold wind swept over the area, brushing my long, dark hair away from my face. Liam walked as close to me as he could without actually touching, letting me benefit from the warm pulse of his aura. The fact that his energy was still at this pleasant level made me relax a little more. If Liam were really worried, that warmth would be less warm and fuzzy and more hot and sizzling, crackling like a campfire made with fresh pine.

The brackish smell of the Cuyahoga River wrapped around me as I circled the building. It wasn't the best smell, this part of the river tucked as it was between restaurants, not far from Cleveland's club district. But I'd smelled worse. And the main body of Lake Erie was within sight, offering a cold wind to blow away any lingering foul aromas.

The pier that stretched out from the back patio of the bar was every bit as dangerous as the building itself. I didn't know what kept it standing, but it wasn't dedication to timely repair and upkeep.

My thoughts on the safety issues surrounding the property faded as I looked ahead to see a single boat tied to the pier. And standing on board that boat were two figures.

Siobhan.

And Rowyn.

Blood and bone.

"Mother Renard. So glad you could join us."

Despite her sickly sweet tone Siobhan's voice drove into me like a stab of frigid air through a broken window. A chill settled at the base of my spine. I'd expected anger, or accusation, something sharp like a weapon. This smugness was worse.

Much worse.

The lights from the boat illuminated the brown highlights in her dark hair. Her eyes were a pearlescent white, the sort of shining orb that made humans think of underwater treasure, lured them to the water's edge and encouraged them to lean forward, look deeper. Like most of her kind, she had very little body fat, all her bulk packed into thick corded muscle that shifted under her pale green-tinted skin.

"I'm here to see Andy," I said, summoning my best witchy look.

"Of course you are. Come aboard."

The boat she stood on looked...expensive. This wasn't some cheap second-hand fishing boat, this was new. It *smelled* new. Of course, anything would smell new in comparison to the rotting building behind me, but still.

"You like it?" Siobhan asked, noticing my stare. She drew a hand over the bulwark, tapping her fingernails against the smooth white fiberglass. "My fortunes have improved since the last time you managed to save Agent Bradford from the consequences of his actions." She bared her large flat white teeth in a grin. "This time, the facts and the law will favor me."

I looked past her, unwilling to engage in this conversation when only one of us had the facts of the night's events. "I trust he's come to no harm since I talked to him?"

"Didn't take long to get to the accusations, did it?" Rowyn said, disgust thick in his voice. "Have you ever considered the possibility that the reason your partner hunts us down with such dedication is because *you* have such a low opinion of our kind?"

The male kelpie had skin that was more blue than white, and his eyes were the opposite of Siobhan's, shiny black obsidian instead of pearls. It made him look alien and cold. The fact that he was built like a brick outhouse didn't make him any more comforting.

"I think my partner holds you in the estimation he does because he watched you and Bradan torture a kid," I said honestly. "Andy frowns on such things. As do I."

"We acted in good faith that night," Rowyn said tightly. "Bradan purchased Grayson. Legally. The fact that the contract was declared void because you managed to buy Marilyn's goodwill doesn't change what we did."

"No, it doesn't," I said icily. "You still bought a child. Will you stand there and tell me you intended him no harm?"

"I'm saying we had the right to harm him. By virtue of his own signature."

No one was going to win this argument. The differences were cultural. Kelpies had already given up eating humans—at least, officially. In their minds, giving up the rest of it, the fear, the wild rides, that was just asking them to lie down and die.

I gestured at Liam. "I've neglected to make introductions. Siobhan, Rowyn, this is Detective Sergeant Liam Osbourne. Liam, meet Siobhan and Rowyn."

"Charmed." Siobhan tilted her head at me. "Bring all the backup you want. He's guilty. And this time, his guilt will count for something."

I climbed up the ladder leading to the deck of the boat, ignoring the way Rowyn crowded me so I had to brush past him. It was petty, but there was no point in calling him out for it.

I noticed he didn't pull the same trick with Liam.

"Agent Bradford is down there," Siobhan said, gesturing to a door that led deeper into the boat. "Go right in."

The thought occurred to me that being on someone else's

boat—especially *inside* someone else's boat where no one could see me—was an extraordinarily vulnerable position to put myself in. Although having Liam with me improved my odds considerably, regardless of what Siobhan might have waiting.

"Don't worry, Mother Renard," Siobhan said with a smile. "The Vanguard's agent has stayed with Agent Bradford the whole time, and she can protect you too."

I stared at her long enough to let her know what I thought of her insinuation that she or her boat could scare me, then proceeded down the steps into the belly of the ship. I was grateful Andy had mentioned Evelyn on the phone. Otherwise, Siobhan's offhand mention of the Vanguard might have worried me.

The inside of the boat was as nice as the outside, and looked just as expensive. The seats that went around the perimeter were all padded with luxurious leather, and warm gold light lit the area from intricate wall sconces. It was bigger inside than I'd been expecting, almost roomy. But I didn't give a damn about Siobhan and her pretty new boat. My reason for being here was sitting in the corner.

Andy looked awful. His brown hair was mussed—and Andy's hair was *never* mussed. There were dark bags under his eyes, and even his clothes seemed to droop with exhaustion. I was guessing Vincent had taken the clothes he'd been wearing for evidence, because the grey sweatpants and hoodie he was wearing said "Turning Tides" on the front, with a picture of a racehorse. Definitely not Andy's.

He looked up as I came in. In the second our eyes met, I learned something very important. Something conveyed in the way his shoulders relaxed ever so slightly, and the lines around the corners of his eyes and mouth faded.

Andy *trusted* me.

Whatever his thoughts and fears about the Otherworld,

whatever friction had been between us lately, I'd given him hope just by being here. A weight lifted from my heart, and I found myself standing straighter, revitalized by his confidence in me.

"Andy, are you all right?"

"I'm fine."

He couldn't quite maintain eye contact. His gaze kept flicking to the side, to the other person in the room.

I followed his gaze to the woman standing a few feet away. I didn't know exactly what Evelyn was, but I knew she was at least part *deva*—a semi-divine Persian spirit. Since our last meeting I'd also learned that her formal rank at the Ministry of Deliverance was Justiciar but she rarely used it. She was taller than me, as most people were, but something about her excellent posture made her seem even taller. A quality I'd found to be common in paladins. She wore the same white robes I'd seen her in before, the plain white cloth contrasting with her exotic blue skin and gold tattoos.

"Evelyn, isn't it?"

The woman smiled, pleased I'd remembered. "Yes. And you are Mother Renard." Her smile wilted at the corners, as if remembering the night we'd met. Retrieving a demonbound was never easy, but it was much harder when innocents were involved. Especially innocents with demon-given gifts and a firm conviction that their murderous mistress didn't belong in jail. "It's good to see you again. Though of course I wish it could be under different circumstances."

"So true." I gestured at Liam. "This is Detective Sergeant Liam Osbourne. Liam, this is Evelyn. She works with the Vanguard."

I glanced over my shoulder at Andy. He stared at Evelyn as if he were waiting for her to sprout the fiery halo she'd worn the night she came for the demonbound. I couldn't blame him for being nervous. A holy warrior in full battle mode was an intimidating sight for anyone, and it definitely stayed with you.

"I'll give you some privacy," Evelyn said, taking a step toward the door. "I know giving a statement can be emotional, and I dare say Agent Bradford would feel more comfortable telling you himself." She paused. "Mac Tyre assumed you'd be taking the lead in the investigation."

"I will," I confirmed.

She nodded. "Mac Tyre has no problem with that, as you've worked for the Vanguard before. You'll still have to present the results of your investigation to him when it's over for them to be certified, but until then, proceed as you see fit." She hesitated. "I should be present when the forensic team is finished and you go in to look around and speak to the witnesses. Siobhan has concerns—"

"She's been insinuating that I might tamper with evidence," I said flatly. "I assumed she would."

"I don't believe you would, despite your close working relationship with Agent Bradford," Evelyn said. "But you understand our actions must be above all reproach."

"I understand completely." I kept the edge out of my voice, tamped down on my temper. Evelyn wasn't my enemy.

The effect of Evelyn's exit on Andy's demeanor was instantaneous. He pushed his shoulders back, and his eyes cleared, focusing on me with renewed intensity. Some part of my brain could almost picture his suit shimmering into place as if he could conjure it like a comic book superhero.

"They took my coat, and it had all my things in it. Do you have a notebook and a pen I could use?"

The request was so welcome, I couldn't help giving him a huge smile. I unzipped my waist pouch and peered inside. "Bizbee, could I have a small notepad and a pen? And the suit."

The grig that lived inside the pouch popped up with the

requested items with his usual efficiency, fuzzy-tipped antennae bobbing merrily. He passed over the notepad and pen, then reached inside with his lower insectoid legs to drag out the tip of a hanger.

I snagged the curved plastic and lifted, pulling out the suit. I'd purchased it on a whim a month ago after having Peasblossom sneak a glimpse at Andy's jacket tag on one of the few occasions he'd removed it. Liam had helped me with the sizing for the shirt. The jacket and pants were a deep navy blue, and the shirt was a white so bright it was almost a shade of blue itself. It still smelled faintly of dry cleaning chemicals.

Bizbee had freshened it up. I beamed at him and he blinked, looking slightly embarrassed.

Andy accepted the suit with quiet reverence. "Thanks."

I turned my back to give him some privacy, and Liam strode to the side of the room to peer out the windows, studying what he could see of the bar.

"I didn't kill anyone."

I turned at Andy's announcement, taking it as my cue that it was safe to turn around again. Andy stood in the same spot, but putting on the suit had reestablished the look of confidence and control that I'd come to associate with him.

I followed him back to the bench and sat beside him as he resumed his corner seat.

"Tell me what happened," I prompted.

Andy opened his jacket and tucked the pen and notepad inside, considering his words carefully before speaking. "All right. So I've been coming to Something Fishy for a while. Every Thursday for the past few months." He paused, probably expecting an outburst from me.

I didn't disappoint.

"You've been coming back here for *months?*" I stared at him. "After what happened last time, you came back?"

"Of course I came back," Andy said, his voice harder than it had been. "You heard Morgan. The kelpies—"

I held up a hand, cutting him off. "We will discuss Morgan later, I promise you. For now, tell me about tonight."

"I come here on Thursday nights, because I noticed that the kelpies are always here Thursday nights. And they always have kids with them. Teenagers, never anyone over the age of eighteen."

"And you know they aren't eighteen because...?" Liam asked.

"Because I ask."

Liam arched an eyebrow. "You ID them."

Tension pushed Andy to sit a little straighter. "This is a bar. I have every reason to ID them."

I waited for Liam to point out FBI agents don't generally cruise bars for underage drinkers, but he didn't. Instead, he took a slow step away from the window, studying Andy with an expression I couldn't quite read.

"I'm guessing these kids generally hung out on a boat, which would be private property?" Liam suggested. "They never came inside the building?"

"It's not private property when they walk down the pier to get to the boat," Andy interjected. "And that's when I card them." He waved a hand. "It doesn't matter. When I realized it was a weekly thing, I had to keep coming. I had to make sure they were okay."

I don't know what expression he wanted to see on my face, but obviously he didn't find it.

"I've seen predators before, Shade. And I'm not just talking about sexual predators. I'm talking about bullies. People who need to feel in control, and the only way they can is if they're tormenting someone else." His brown eyes darkened. "And I did my research on kelpies. They are every bit the predators I saw that night."

"He's not wrong," Peasblossom said, flopping down on my shoulder and swinging her feet.

Andy pressed his back against the wall and stared into space. "I will never forget the look on Grayson's face. That terror in his voice." He shook his head. "I'm telling you, there's something going on here. They were earning these kids' trust, and that's always the first step down a very bad road."

Something in his voice reminded me of another detail from that night at Something Fishy with the kelpies. Andy had climbed out of the lake, tearing off his shirt in a panic after getting caught up in a hydrophobia spell I'd leveled at our enemies. I'd seen scars all over his back and upper arms.

I thought of the folder Flint had tried to give me that night. The file on Andy. All his secrets.

I hadn't read it. Not just because it would have been a betrayal of Andy's trust, but because deep, deep down, I just didn't want to know the story behind those scars. I didn't want the images and details in my head.

"So tonight I came here, like I do every Thursday," Andy continued. "I sat at the bar where I had a view of the pier out back and the front door. Then around seven-thirty, I saw a kid standing outside. He didn't move toward a boat or the bar. Then I saw Siobhan." The muscle in his jaw twitched, and his stare into nothingness intensified, as if it were all happening all over again. "She started talking to him. He tried to walk away from her, but she grabbed his arm, tried to drag him out of sight."

He continued, his hands moving as if re-enacting the events. "I ran out and drew my gun. And I swear it was Siobhan. I could see her plain as day. I remembered her face, leaning over me in that rocking boat, and feeling that gunshot wound burning a hole in my side while she tried to trick me into 'accepting her help.' I warned her to let him go, but she just stared at me like I'd lost my mind. Like she didn't know who I was." His brow furrowed. "I remember telling her to get away from the kid."

I waited for him to continue, but he didn't. He just sat there, frowning.

My nerves broke before he did. "Then what?"

Andy shook his head slowly. "That's just it." He met my eyes. "I can't remember."

CHAPTER 3

"YOU DON'T REMEMBER?" I echoed, my voice rising.

Andy put his hand to his head, digging his fingers in as if he could reach inside and pull the memories free. "Someone tackled me, and I hit my head. Next thing I remember, I'm waking up here," he gestured around him at the room, "and that wizard is leaning over me saying something about trying to heal me and a possible concussion."

"You mean Vincent Aegis," Liam supplied. "He's a good man, you can trust him."

Andy looked at me, and I read the question in his eyes.

"Healing isn't as easy as I make it look," I told him honestly. "You can't just throw a healing spell at someone, you have to guide the magic, tell it what to heal, how to heal it. I studied medicine for a long time to get to where I am. A lot of magic users can do basic healing—stop bleeding, ease pain, things like that—but if you had a concussion, that means a possible brain injury. Vincent wouldn't know how to heal that."

Andy relaxed a little. "Okay. That explains it then. When he brought me around, I was still in a lot of pain, and I could still feel the wound at the back of my head."

"You thought he was lying about the healing?" Liam guessed.

"Waking up in a strange place to a strange man poking at your head can be disorienting," Andy said dryly.

"Especially if it's Vincent," Liam agreed with a small smile.

"Anyway, he asked me what happened." He closed his eyes. "And it wasn't until then that I realized I couldn't remember."

"So the very last thing you remember," Liam prompted, "is what?"

Andy opened his eyes and stared into space again. "Like I said, I remember aiming my gun at Siobhan and telling her to get away from the kid. After that it's all...garbled. Like a painting that was still wet and someone smeared the colors around." He dropped his elbows to his knees, cradling his head in his hands.

Peasblossom fanned her wings as she stood, holding on to a lock of my hair for balance. "Did Vincent tell you anything about what happened? Try to fill in the blanks?"

"He told me the person I thought was Siobhan was some kelpie named Raichel." His words came more hesitantly if recounting events he didn't want to believe. "He said there was no kid. And he said... He said I shot her. And she's dead."

Suddenly he looked up at me, and the ferocity in his eyes startled me. "I did not come here to kill anyone. I know that's what they think. I know it's what Siobhan thinks." He stopped. "I was just here to make sure nothing happened to the kids."

I shared a look with Liam and mouthed "Kids?" I hadn't seen any kids out front, or on the back patio. Liam shook his head. He hadn't seen any kids either.

"I'm going to find out what happened here tonight," I said, putting that thought aside and focusing on Andy. "I won't stop until I know everything that happened."

"I know." He shifted in his seat, concentrating hard on the floor before looking up at my face again. "Siobhan made it sound pretty damning. Witnesses, physical evidence." He made a sound that was probably meant to be a laugh, but was too strained. "She almost has *me* believing I did it."

Dread seized my stomach, but I shoved the sensation down, viciously stamping it out of existence before it could show in my face. "It's in her best interest to convince you that you did it. But I, for one, find your loss of memory very suspicious."

Andy shifted in his seat again. "So did Vincent. But he didn't find any trace of magic on me. And Evelyn said she didn't find any of the damage that usually accompanies the brute force of someone trying to manipulate memories."

"There are only signs of force if the person was inexperienced or making no effort to be careful," I insisted. "Otherwise it would take someone who specializes in memory manipulation to find the signs. Let me talk to the witnesses. Find out who—and what—we're dealing with here."

After holding his head in his hands for a few heartbeats, he looked up at me. "You told me about the Vanguard before. About what happens when someone from one...species, commits a crime against another. Something about a weregild?" He cleared his throat. "I might need to know more about that now."

I shared a wary look with Liam before I could stop myself. Andy caught it immediately. "What?"

I forced my face into the witchy mask I used any time I had to share unpleasant information. "A weregild is a deal two cultures make when one has made a transgression against the other and they need to establish a course of justice that suits both cultures. Usually when someone breaks a law that exists in one culture, but not the other, or when the punishment in one culture for that specific crime is radically different than in the other culture. It's meant to keep one group from calling out a member of another group for some obscure law and then punishing them with death or slavery or some such outrageous punishment. It doesn't apply if the crime is the same in both cultures, and both cultures have the same punishment."

Andy stared hard into my eyes, but I must have been more closed off than I'd meant to be. He looked to Liam.

"In your case," Liam said calmly, "murder is a crime in both human and kelpie society. And both kelpies and humans have the death penalty for murder."

"So why is the Vanguard involved?" Andy asked. "Why wouldn't Siobhan just kill me if she's so sure I did it?"

"Most humans are ignorant of the Otherworld, so you get a sort of 'diplomatic immunity,'" I explained.

"For example, if a human shoots a wolf near their farm, the Vanguard doesn't expect you to know that it could have been a werewolf," Liam added.

I winced. That did tend to be the most common one. Fortunately, most farmers didn't use silver bullets. "Right. So, the Vanguard represents humans because most humans don't know about the Otherworld and therefore don't have a representative to negotiate for them. Siobhan is asking the Vanguard to waive your 'diplomatic immunity' so she can formally charge you and mete out punishment. But first she has to make a solid case that you're guilty."

All emotion drained from Andy's face. "So you're telling me if they find me guilty, then they'll hand me over to Siobhan to execute me."

"They won't find you guilty." I shot to my feet, suddenly ready to get out of this room, off this boat. My magic writhed inside me, needing an outlet, needing to *do* something. "We need to get out there and talk to these witnesses that Siobhan is so eager to shove in your face."

Andy rose with me, then stopped himself and sat back down. "They aren't going to let me out there until they've finished processing the scene." He retrieved his new notebook and pen. "I'll stay in here and write down what I can remember. Maybe it'll jog something loose."

"Good idea," Liam said, nodding his approval.

"Right." I twisted the zipper on my waist pouch. "So right now, our main priority is to find out, one," I started ticking points off on my fingers, "is there anyone here with the ability to manipulate Andy's memory? Or, barring that, did someone specifically cause his concussion?"

"That would be difficult," Liam said doubtfully. "Head injuries are notoriously difficult to predict. And I seriously doubt they could have foreseen memory loss."

"Just covering all the bases at this point," I reminded him. I held up a second finger. "Two, we need to find out what happened to the kid Raichel tried to drag off. If she had a victim, then it's a moot point whether or not Andy shot her, because there are exemptions for acting in defense of a minor. The previous shooting helps us there, because it shows Andy believed his actions would be justified under Otherworld law."

"I'll be able to tell if someone was here earlier but isn't here now," Liam added. He snorted. "Trust me, there's no mistaking the smell of a teenager."

"I'd prefer to talk to the kid first. He's the one most likely to give us the part of the story that we need."

"Agreed."

I started to say something to Andy, though I wasn't sure exactly what. Hang tight? Don't worry? Be right back? It ended up not mattering, because Andy was already lost to his notebook, pen scribbling furiously as he tried to get all his thoughts out.

When we made our way back out into the open air, Siobhan was standing on the deck in the same spot as before. She and Rowyn stood on one side of the boat, with Evelyn standing nearer to the door, her blue face serene as if lost in thought. Or prayer.

"Did he confess?" Siobhan asked innocently.

"Where's the kid?" I asked. "The one Raichel was trying to drag off against his will."

Siobhan's smile widened. "Inside the bar. I thought it best if I remained out here. I wouldn't want to be accused of intimidating him."

There was still something in her voice I didn't like. She was far too happy, far too confident. And it didn't feel like bluster.

I let it go for now, but it nagged at me as I stepped off the boat and onto the pier. I didn't realize we had an unwanted guest until I heard too many footsteps behind me. It might have been my imagination, but even in human form, the footsteps sounded like hoof beats.

I turned. Liam was already facing the boat. Or, more specifically, the large male kelpie who'd just followed us off the boat.

Rowyn raised himself to his full height. "What? Did you think we'd let you go in there and speak to witnesses without supervision?"

"I will make certain everything remains aboveboard," Evelyn said calmly. "I—"

"If you'll forgive me for saying so," Rowyn interrupted, "the last time one of my kind was shot and killed by that man, the Vanguard did nothing."

"I'm sorry for your loss," Evelyn said gently. "But under the law, Agent Bradford did nothing wrong."

Rowyn stamped his foot, hard enough I was surprised the battered wood held. "Under fey law, Bradan did nothing wrong. And yet his *murderer* walks free."

Peasblossom tugged on the lock of my hair in her fist. "You

torture kids for fun. If you're expecting pity, you've got a long wait."

"You'll judge us, then?" Rowyn demanded. "Humans can torture animals all they like for their own amusement, fighting rings, rodeos, zoos, and that's fine, but—"

"Humans aren't animals," I interrupted coldly.

Rowyn clenched his hands into fists. "They are to us."

"This isn't the time or the place for this fight." Liam pointed at Rowyn. "You can come in and watch, but stay out of the way when we're talking to someone. If I think you're trying to intimidate a witness—"

"You'll what?" Rowyn raised his hands, palms up. "Doesn't seem like a werewolf is in any position to throw stones. Should I remind you how many people your kind have eaten?"

Liam took another step toward the kelpie, his aura flaring outward like heat escaping an open oven door. "Maybe," he said in a low voice, "I should remind you of where horses and wolves fall in the food chain. Respectively."

At first, I thought Rowyn would pounce. The kelpie was looking for a fight, that much was obvious. And kelpies were no pushovers. There was a reason "horsepower" was a unit of measurement for energy and strength. On land, Liam would likely win, not because he was a werewolf, but because he was an alpha, and that meant experience not just physical strength.

But if Rowyn could get Liam in the water, there was no question about who would win, and who would drown.

Over Rowyn's shoulder, I saw Siobhan take a step forward. "Rowyn."

The larger male kelpie turned.

Siobhan nodded toward the boat. "Stay here and guard the accused. I'll go with Mother Renard."

I held a witchy look on my face, refusing to give Siobhan any reaction to the sudden change in plan. If she wanted to tag along, fine. I'd need to interview her anyway.

"I'll wait here as well, then" Evelyn said smoothly. "I trust your own presence will be enough to reassure you that Mother Renard has conducted her inquiries with the thoroughness and discipline of a professional."

"A professional fixer, maybe," Rowyn muttered.

"Thank you, Evelyn," I said, meeting the *deva*-blooded woman's eyes. "It will put my mind at ease to know there will be someone on this boat capable of keeping a clear head."

"Well, it certainly won't be your partner," Siobhan needled.

I turned my back on her again, trusting Liam to keep an eye on the kelpie. Not that I expected trouble. Siobhan seemed very confident in the case against Andy, and I didn't think she'd do anything to mess that up. Not yet.

We made our way down the pier toward the back door of the bar. It wasn't until I got closer that I realized the lone customer at one of the small outdoor tables was eyeing me.

"Hello," I said, approaching him. "I'm Mother Renard and this is Detective Sergeant Liam Osbourne."

The Otherworld gentleman rose with an easy smile, his teeth bright against his smooth brown skin. "I am Hachim." He gestured to Siobhan's boat. "You are here about Agent Bradford?"

"Yes. And I was hoping I could ask you a few questions?"

Hachim sighed and rubbed a hand over his face. "Yes, a very unpleasant situation, isn't it?"

"What are you?" Peasblossom asked suddenly.

Normally, I'd have chastised her for being rude, but under the circumstances, the question was necessary. And Hachim didn't seem offended.

"I am a *redjal el marja*."

A *redjal el marja* was a Moroccan river spirit. Friendly enough as long as you respected their waters.

No mental manipulation ability.

I pushed away a stab of disappointment. "Hachim, would you mind if I asked you a few questions? It won't take long."

"Of course, I am happy to help. But I'm afraid I will be little use, as I did not arrive at the scene in time to witness anything helpful."

"That's all right. Just tell me what you saw," I prompted.

The door opened and a man stepped outside, shoulders hunched against the cold as he fished a pack of cigarettes out of his pocket. He nodded to us before taking a few steps onto the pier and lighting up. Hachim watched him with suspicious eyes.

"I was here," he said, gesturing at the chair he'd been sitting in when we approached. "I ran around the building when I heard the gunshot, but by the time I arrived, Palgun had already knocked Andy to the ground."

"Did anyone else see what happened?"

"There was one person. A short man sitting in his car at the back of the lot," he said, gesturing with one hand toward the east. "He got out of his car as I came around the building and he looked white as a ghost."

"That would be Deacon," Siobhan offered. "He belongs to me."

"He's your witness," I guessed. That would certainly explain why she was so pleased. "I assume when you say he 'belongs' to you..."

"He is my property," Siobhan confirmed. "And he's *well over* eighteen."

"So he'll say what you told him to say."

"He's not the only witness," Siobhan said smugly. "You'll need to talk to Mickey V too. He's the one Bradford claims he was 'protecting.'" She gestured toward the bar with her head. "He's inside if you want to speak with him."

Mickey V must be the kid that Raichel was trying to drag off. Yes, we'd definitely need to talk to him. I started for the bar, but Liam spoke first.

"Andy said the kelpies brought kids around here a lot," Liam said. "Can you tell us anything about that? Did you know any of them?"

Hachim jabbed a finger at Liam. "The homeless kids. No, I didn't know them. But there's a church a few blocks from here that runs a soup kitchen. I bet that's where they're finding them."

"Kids experiencing homelessness," I said automatically. "Not homeless kids." I met his eyes. "Just trust me. It matters to them."

"I believe you." Hachim nodded. "But as I said, I didn't know any—" Suddenly he stopped, his eyes narrowing at something behind us near the water. "Excuse me."

I turned as he stood and strode to the pier where a man was exhaling a puff of smoke as he turned back toward the bar. I thought he was human until I caught Liam scenting the air. He looked at me. "Kobold. Must be wearing glamour."

We both watched the man's eyes widen as Hachim bore down on him, one hand striking out with a flat palm. The smoker shot off the edge of the pier and into the river with a splash.

"Hachim!" I gasped. "What are you—"

"Pick up your cigarette butt." Hachim pointed at something in the water near the flailing man. "It's just there. Go ahead. Grab it."

I couldn't see into the water from this angle, but the man must have done as he was told. A second later, Hachim lifted his hand in the air, palm up. A surge of water shoved the sputtering man high enough for the *redjal el marja* to snag the front of his shirt and haul him onto the pier. Hachim kept a tight grip on the man's clothes, forcing him to look him in the eye.

"Eat it," he ordered.

The man spit out a mouthful of water, gaping with his mouth opening and closing like a fish. "What?"

"Eat. It." Hachim gestured to the cigarette butt. "Now."

The man shook his head. The river spirit started to heave him back into the water. He yelped and shoved the soggy roll into his mouth, forcing himself to swallow. He gagged, but one look from Hachim gave him the willpower to keep it down.

Hachim released his clothes and patted him on the back, making a wet, slapping sound against his soaked shirt. "Now. Wouldn't it have been easier if you'd disposed of your garbage in a proper receptacle instead of flicking it into my river?"

The man nodded miserably, clearly willing to do or say anything to get away. Hachim nodded. "Go on then." The man took a shaky step and made another gagging sound. Hachim narrowed his eyes again. "If you're going to throw up, you'd better make a run for the trashcan. You don't want to throw up in my river."

"Do you think he does that a lot?" Peasblossom asked.

Siobhan shrugged. "Hachim takes pollution very seriously."

Beside us, the unfortunate smoker barely made it to the trashcan before vomiting up the cigarette butt and a good bellyful of brown river water.

Hachim returned to us, waving his hands to dry them off. "Forgive the interruption. I put up signs." He gestured at a homemade sign that very clearly said *Do not throw trash in the river.* "Sadly, there are still those who would rather throw their refuse into my river than carry it the extra ten steps to the trashcan."

He waved a hand. "As I was saying, I don't know the names of any of the kids who've been here, but I can say that none were here tonight. I've been out here all night, I would have seen them. And Valter does not allow underage humans in his bar."

He paused, then added, "Ms. Renard, I do hope that you find some evidence to shine a better light on tonight's events. I do not believe Agent Bradford is a bad man and he's certainly never struck me as a cold-blooded killer." He made a fist. "He has always seemed more of a righteous man. Then again, there is often a fine line between righteousness and murder. A matter of perspective, one might say."

I could feel Siobhan's eyes drilling into me, and I kept my spine straight, refusing to give her the satisfaction. "Andy said he was defending a kid. And we know there was at least one kid here tonight. Mickey V."

Hachim's brow furrowed just as the door to the bar opened again, making me turn my attention to the new arrival.

At first, I thought it was a teenager. He was shorter than me, and I'd have been surprised if he was more than five feet tall. The light green dress shirt under his leather jacket was a little big on him, big enough to fit a slender energy drink in the pocket, ostensibly as a backup to the open energy drink in his hand. When he raised his hand to take a drink, I saw a watch on his wrist. It had the chunky look of a timepiece that could take a beating, something an athlete would wear.

He took a few steps toward Siobhan, but then the kelpie held up a hand, gestured to me. It wasn't until the he turned to face me that I realized he wasn't a kid at all.

His grey hair was mussed, and he had blue eyes so pale they were almost grey. His face was lined with decades of smiles, tanned from a lot of time in the sun. He was fifty years old if he was a day.

"Mother Renard," Siobhan drawled, "meet Mickey V."

CHAPTER 4

"You're Mickey V?"

Siobhan's obvious enjoyment of my shock gave me the strength to keep my voice steady and wrench my facial features into polite inquiry. Even so, it wasn't easy to block out the semi-hysterical voice in my head babbling *"Well hello, I see that you are in fact a grown man who could not possibly be mistaken for a teenager by anyone who got a good look at your face. And doesn't that just blow Andy's case for defense of a minor straight out of the water?"*

Mickey V gave me a small smile that was gone almost as soon as it arrived. I got the impression he smiled a lot, as people did when they were genuinely content with life. But it would be hard for anyone to smile so soon after standing right beside a murder victim.

He took a swig of his energy drink and approached me with the bouncy gait of someone jogging to catch up to a friend, or possibly someone who'd had springs installed in the soles of his shoes.

I wondered how many energy drinks he'd had tonight.

"That's me. What can I do for you?"

"I'm Mother Renard and I'm here about the murder."

Immediately his face fell. "Yeah. It's awful. Poor Raichel." He hesitated, glancing back at Siobhan before looking at me and Liam. "Are you from the Vanguard too?"

"I'm working on behalf of the Vanguard, but actually I'm a private investigator."

"A private investigator named 'Mother Renard?'"

I tilted my head. Interesting that he was obviously familiar with the Otherworld, but he didn't know the title for a witch. "You can call me Shade. This is Detective Sergeant Liam Osbourne."

Mickey nodded to Liam. "Nice to meet you."

"Can you tell me what happened tonight?" I asked. "Starting with when you got here?"

"There's not a lot to tell." He finished off his energy drink and threw it in the trash can by the door—earning a satisfied nod from Hachim—then shoved his hands into his pockets. "It was strange. This whole night was strange."

"How do you mean?" Liam asked.

Again, he looked at Siobhan.

"Tell them the truth," she encouraged, giving me a deliberate look. "We all want the truth."

"Well, for starters, usually Siobhan picks me up at a restaurant on the other side of town. But tonight she called me last minute and said she was running late, and I should meet her here."

"Did you go inside?" I asked.

"No, she was crystal clear that I was to wait outside. Said I shouldn't even look inside the bar."

I turned to Siobhan. "And why would you give him those instructions? Maybe so Andy wouldn't get a good look at his face? Couldn't spot that he wasn't a kid?"

"Or maybe," Siobhan drawled, "I didn't want him drawing

the attention of anyone in the bar. You never know what kind of trouble you'll find in a place like this."

Mickey snagged his other energy drink. His hands were shaking, and I didn't think it was just the caffeine. I scowled at the waterhorse. "Do you have to be here? Can't you just send Evelyn—"

Siobhan held up a hand. "Relax. I trust Mickey to be honest, despite any tricks you might attempt." She pushed off the railing and headed for the door. "I'll wait inside."

Mickey watched her go, seeming to breathe easier when the door closed behind her.

"You said the whole night was strange. What else happened?" I asked.

"Raichel showed up instead of Siobhan." He leaned closer, lowering his voice. "Only she didn't look like herself, she appeared to be Siobhan."

"She was wearing a glamour?" Peasblossom asked.

Mickey jumped, his eyes widening slightly as the pixie poked her head out from under my hair. "Um...yeah. I guess that's what you call it."

"Did you know it was Raichel right away, or did you find out after she was shot?"

Mickey shifted uncomfortably and cracked open the energy drink, releasing a puff of candy-flavored mist. "Mind tricks don't work on me. Including glamour."

I raised my eyebrows. Mickey felt human, looked and acted human. But I hadn't actually asked.

He watched my face, and seemed to guess my question. "I'm human," he said. "But I've been around people who aren't. Long enough to know it's good to have a little...protection."

"What kind of protection?" Liam asked.

Mickey swayed as if resisting the urge to take a step back. "It would defeat the point of having it if I made it easy to take away."

Easy to take away. So it was something he was wearing? I pushed my magic outward, letting it brush over Mickey's body. It was a spell I used all the time, and it was second nature now, just a flex of my will. If my third eye wasn't damaged, I'd see the spell like a net of silver light, and wherever it went, I'd see colored sparks to show me if there was active magic in its path. Without my third eye, there were no colors, but I could still feel the energy of a spell. Enough to know the watch Mickey was wearing had an enchantment on it. I guessed that was what let him see through illusions.

I thought of Siobhan, her parting words.

"I trust Mickey to be honest despite any tricks you might attempt."

"Did anyone else know about your ability to see through glamour?" I asked.

Mickey frowned. "Siobhan knows. She's introduced me to a few new racers that wore glamour, and she knows I saw through it. I don't think anyone else knew, but I can't say for sure."

"Did you know Raichel?" Liam asked.

"Of course I knew her. I've been riding at Turning Tides since the beginning, I was one of the first jockeys they hired."

"Turning Tides?" Liam repeated.

"It's the racetrack out on the lake. The racers are all waterhorses, kelpies, *each uisges, neugles, backahasts*, and such. Siobhan runs it, and Raichel is her assistant." He stopped, winced. "Raichel *was* her assistant."

Kelpies, *each uisges, neugles, backahasts*. None of them had the ability to alter someone's memories. For the most part, there was very little difference between them, other than minor personality quirks—*each uisges* were the most bloodthirsty—and some differences in how they tricked their prey—kelpies favored silver bridles that tempted people to attempt to take them, and *neugles* disguised themselves as logs in the water, waiting for the unsuspecting swimmer.

I stared at him, trying to process what he'd just said. "A racetrack. On the water."

Mickey grinned, and the smile made his blue eyes light up. "Yeah. It's incredible. Unlike anything I've ever done before in my life. If you've never been, you should go."

"Why does a waterhorse need a jockey?" Peasblossom demanded. "They know where they're going. They aren't *that* dumb."

Mickey leaned closer, obviously excited to talk more about his passion. For a moment, he seemed to forget the night's grisly events. "Think of a jockey like a third base coach. A baseball player can't watch the whole field, they can't follow the ball and watch the body language of the basemen and the catcher at the same time. They rely on the coach to watch all that, they focus only on their breathing, their body, getting ready to run when the coach gives them the signal. And that's what I do."

He started dancing from foot to foot, his eyes glazing over as if imagining himself riding in a race even as we spoke. "When I'm riding in one of these races, I pay attention to the details like what horses are creeping up on us, who's in the lead, who looks like they're getting ready for a break out. I watch out for anyone who looks like they might try something dirty, anyone who's tensing for a big push. I watch all of that, so whoever I'm riding just has to concentrate on the water, on the path ahead. They think of nothing but *running* and they trust me to guide them away from threats, to tell them when it's time to speed up, or time to hold back to wait for our chance."

His breathing came heavier than before, his pulse pounding under the pale skin at his throat. "Racing isn't just about running as fast as you can. It's an *art*. And there's nothing like running on the water."

"And you never worry that your mount is going to get overexcited and eat you?" Peasblossom demanded.

Mickey blinked. "I wouldn't dangle myself in front of them, especially right after a race when their adrenaline is high. But they enjoy a race as much as I do, so I don't think they'd hurt me."

"You're that good that you think they'd rather leave you alone than see you replaced with a new jockey?" Liam asked.

Mickey lifted his chin. "I'm not that easy to replace. I've won my last five races."

"So you're saying you're too good to eat?" Peasblossom said, letting her doubt show in her voice.

"I'm good enough to earn personal congratulations and patronage from Anton Winters, so, yeah, I think I'm too good to eat."

I froze.

Anton Winters was involved in Siobhan's business?

Ice crackled down my spine, and I took a moment to center myself before speaking, wanting to make sure that my voice was steady. "What does Anton Winters have to do with the races?"

"He's Turning Tides biggest sponsor." Mickey frowned. "You didn't know that?"

"I thought you said Siobhan ran the racetrack?" I said.

"Turning Tides was Siobhan's idea, but Mr. Winters is the one who funded the start-up."

I looked down at Mickey's watch. "That's a nice watch. Where did you get it?"

Mickey put a hand over the time piece, the gesture defensive, as if hiding it from me. "Anton Winters."

Well, that explained that. Anton Winters was protecting Mickey—his investment. And didn't that just make this entire case a little more frightening?

I took all that in, then tried to steer the conversation back to tonight. "So you were expecting Siobhan, but Raichel showed up disguised as her. Andy said you looked like you didn't want to go with her. If you knew Raichel, then why struggle?"

"I wouldn't say 'struggled,'" Mickey hedged. "Siobhan told me she was coming herself, and like I said, she was very specific about her instructions. If she'd wanted me to go with Raichel, she'd have said so."

He shifted uncomfortably on his feet. "I've been around the Otherworld enough to know strange things happen, and people aren't always what they seem. I wasn't going to risk not being here when Siobhan showed up. Especially since I was just late to the track two weeks ago. I missed my first race." He rolled his shoulders. "Mr. Winters doesn't seem like the sort of man you disappoint more than once. Not that he was mean about it, or anything," he added quickly. "He's not as scary as some people make him out to be."

"Are you afraid of Siobhan?" Liam asked.

Mickey leaned back. This time, I caught it. A slight deepening of the lines around his eyes and mouth.

"You don't like her," Liam said.

Mickey crossed his arms. "I owe Siobhan a lot, and I'm grateful she gave me a chance at all of this. That said, I'm not saying I agree with every decision she's made regarding Turning Tides."

"Why not?" I asked.

"Because she was getting greedy. Racing has to be pure. It has to be about skill, otherwise it's just a way to separate a fool from his money. But Siobhan was starting to care more about money and winning then she did about the race itself, and that's the death knell of any racetrack."

"Sounds like you would prefer it if someone else took over," I pointed out.

Mickey shrugged. "Sure. But not so much that I'd risk trying to kill Siobhan, if that's what you're getting at."

The thought had crossed my mind. Mickey was human. Unlike fey he could lie as much as he wanted. And he might be willing to risk the consequences of murdering someone he thought was hurting the business he loved—especially if he thought the vampire's favor would protect him.

"I'm not accusing you," I assured him.

He waved a hand. "It's fine. I don't blame you, and I don't have anything to hide."

"You said Siobhan was supposed to pick you up tonight. What for?" I asked.

"I was supposed to ride for a potential investor tonight," he said. "Rowyn was going to take me out to the racetrack so we could give them an idea of what went on, schmooze a little. But then Siobhan called me and switched the meeting place. And instead of her showing up here to escort me onto the usual boat with Rowyn like she told me, Raichel showed up. And she kept trying to get me to leave, but Siobhan was crystal clear that I had to wait for her. So I held back."

After a beat he hastened to add, "I'm not worried Siobhan would hurt me, mind you. But you can never really be too careful with tempers, especially among the horses." He glanced from me to Liam. "I'm not trying to be racist. It's just something I've noticed. Especially the *each uisge*. So I was trying to resist, without being insulting."

Now he glanced back toward the boat. "Then that cop guy came rushing out." His brow knit. "He gave me the weirdest look. I tried to tell him everything was fine. But then all the emotion sort of drained from his face. And he just...shot her." He shook his head. "Then a blond guy came out of the bar and tackled him, and I ran to the boat at the pier. I figured Siobhan's orders to stay put didn't apply under those circumstances, so I ran around back for Rowyn."

Liam prompted, "Did Rowyn run out to help restrain Agent Bradford?"

"I don't know. He had me get on the boat, but I don't know where he went after that. He could have run around to the front, I guess. Later he helped bring Agent Bradford onto the boat and Siobhan told me to wait in the bar for the Vanguard."

"Why aren't you wearing your silks?" I asked suddenly. "You said you were heading for a meeting with a potential investor. Seems like you might want to give them the full treatment. So why the street clothes?"

Mickey shook his head. "I don't put my silks on until just before the race. You never know what can happen on the way to the track, and you don't want to show up to a race looking like you crawled to get there."

I chewed my lip in frustration. This was not going well. If Mickey was telling the truth, then Andy had gotten a good look at his face before he shot Raichel. "Did you see any kids around the parking lot? Maybe the parking lot next door?"

"No."

"Were you wearing a glamour?" Peasblossom asked.

"No." Mickey winced. "I'm sorry. I know your friend has a thing about the kelpies, and I get that they can seem really scary. But I wasn't in any danger. And I did tell him that."

"Mickey, was there anyone else in the parking lot when Andy came out? Anyone else who might have seen what happened?" Liam asked.

Mickey nodded. "Deacon was in his car at the back of the lot. He'll have seen everything."

I gave Mickey a small smile, trying to look as if I were encouraged by the information he'd given me. "Thank you. I might have to talk to you again later, if that's all right?"

Mickey looked as if he knew damn well that if I wanted to talk to him again later, he'd have little choice in the matter. When I took out a notebook and pencil, he dictated his cell phone number. Then he nodded to me and headed back to the bar, draining his second energy drink first and tossing the can into the trash before going inside.

"Who do you want to talk to next?" Liam asked. "Deacon?"

I shook my head. "No. I have a few questions first. For Siobhan."

CHAPTER 5

THE REEK of the bar swamped me as soon as I stepped inside, infusing my clothes with the scents of rotting wood, alcohol, unwashed bodies, and a general fishy scent that lived up to the bar's name. It was bad enough to make me wrinkle my nose, and I could only imagine how much worse it was for Liam.

"Mother Renard! It's good to see you again."

The heavily accented Slavic voice boomed around me as soon as the bar door closed behind my group. I looked up in time to see Oksana push away from the bar and stride over to greet me.

Even without the shouting, Oksana was hard to miss. The female Vanguard member was a strix, a humanoid creature with enormous feathery wings and long sloping ears not dissimilar to a bat's. Her skin and wings were a blue so dark it looked black in the bar's shadowy interior, and the shock of white hair on her head matched her milky eyes. Her pale lavender tunic was barely thick enough not to call sheer. She didn't wear shoes, so it was easy to see that she had the same sharp claws on her feet that she had on the tips of her fingers.

She didn't try to shake my hand, which I appreciated since

claws like hers could be tricky. She nodded to Liam. "Detective Sergeant Osbourne, I had hoped you would come along as well." The lines around the corners of her mouth tilted downward. "I am afraid it does not look good for our friend."

Normally it would have unnerved me a little to be around someone who was this boisterous at a murder scene, but for some reason, it just seemed to fit the strix.

"So Agent Bradford is a friend of yours, too?" Siobhan said. She pushed off the wall she'd been leaning on near the patio door, probably eavesdropping on my conversation with Mickey. "How convenient."

Oksana flicked her gaze to the kelpie. "Do you have something to say to me, my equine friend? You wish to slander my honor? To suggest that I am not *fair*?"

"I'm suggesting that you were there the night her FBI partner killed Bradan. No one seems to think that makes him a murderer."

"I see." Oksana tilted her head, the birdlike gesture looking natural against the backdrop of her large wings. She raised them, making her seem to tower over the kelpie.

"Tell me, Siobhan. How many humans have you eaten this year?" She lifted a clawed finger. "I will know if you lie to me."

The kelpie leader didn't have an answer for that one. The Vanguard wouldn't go after a kelpie for one missing human. They were unlikely to ever notice a single human went missing. But if it were confessed—brought before them out of sheer chance—Oksana could bring her in for it. When she didn't respond, Oksana grinned, baring her teeth.

"Is it possible that you are nervous? It's difficult to prey on the weak when the weak have found themselves such a...*persistent* guardian. Is it not?"

"He killed Raichel for no reason," Siobhan seethed. "*She* didn't eat anyone."

"First of all," I said, "Andy believed Raichel was you. And you've tried to kill him before. Second, we don't know that Andy killed Raichel. Not yet."

Siobhan paused. Suddenly, the anger melted from her face, replaced by an ugly smirk. "Then I'd better let you get back to your investigation. This will be a more satisfying conversation when you realize the truth."

"That's fine, let's start with you then."

Her eyebrows shot up. "Me?"

"Why was Raichel disguised to look like you? And," I added, "let's skip the part where you dance around the question and lie without lying. I'm going to be speaking with Anton Winters about all this. Wouldn't it be easier if you give me the answers now? So you're not answering the same questions for him later?"

"I was held up. I thought if I met Mickey here, I'd make it in time, but then it became obvious I wouldn't. Raichel was nearby on a separate errand, so I told her to swing by for Mickey."

"Why?" I pressed.

She let out a huff of breath, annoyance pulling the skin around her mouth tight. "It looks bad for me to miss a meeting with an investor. I sent Raichel as me, so no one would realize I didn't make it."

"You really expect us to believe that?" Peasblossom demanded.

"I don't care if you believe it or not," Siobhan retorted. "This isn't anything new. I've had Raichel go to meetings in my place before pretending to be me."

"Why?" Liam asked.

"Various reasons. None of which are any of your business." She shrugged. "If you don't believe me, ask around. Jane can confirm it." Siobhan gestured to a short woman at one of the tables. "Another of my assistants, a wererat. She was with me at my meeting tonight. In case you need to confirm my alibi," she added.

There was a light in Siobhan's eyes that rubbed me the wrong way. As if there were a joke I hadn't gotten yet. It was the same look she'd had right before I found out Mickey was a fifty-year-old man, not a teenager.

She was trying to psych me out, but she'd have to do better than that. This had been one hell of a year for me, and right now, Siobhan wasn't even on the list of top ten for people who freaked me out.

To be fair, it was a long list.

Siobhan retreated to the back of the room. A kelpie's hearing wasn't as good as a werewolf's—not by a long shot. But the room wasn't large, so she didn't need to be close to eavesdrop.

"I need to talk to someone named Deacon," I told Oksana.

She nodded and gestured to a corner table. "That is him. The one with the tattoos."

I followed her gesture and raised my eyebrows. Tattoos indeed.

Deacon was not a large man. Even sitting down, I could see he was no taller than Mickey V. He had a mop of curly brown hair and the smooth, olive-toned skin that spoke of Greek origin. But even Deacon could never have been mistaken for a kid. Not with those knowing eyes, and muscular arms covered in tattoos exposed by rolling the sleeves of his sweater to his elbows.

The thorn vine design spread across his muscled chest into the deep V of his collar and down the lengths of both arms, spotted here and there with roses in different stages of bloom. There was languid sexuality in the way he moved, and I'd have bet his entire body bore the same markings. Like most tattoos, they probably held a deeply personal meaning for him, commemorative or something more abstract.

It took me a second to realize I was staring. And another

second after that to realize Deacon had noticed. His hazel eyes held amusement without mockery and a small smile played over his soft, supple lips as he watched me. He seemed pleased I found him worth staring at. Then his eyes flicked to the front door. Toward the crime scene. And the smile died.

"Satyr-blood," Liam murmured. "Faint, but it's there."

"So you're saying he smells like goat?" Peasblossom asked.

I made my way to the table without waiting to see if Liam would answer her. Deacon rose as I approached, a gentlemanly gesture that was rare nowadays, but had been the norm in the world I came from.

"Good evening." His voice was deep, almost musical.

I matched his formality. "Well met, Deacon. I'm Mother Renard and this is Detective Sergeant Liam Osbourne. We'd like to ask you some questions about what happened tonight."

"Of course." He gestured at the chairs. "Please, have a seat."

"Thank you." Liam pulled out a chair for me and I sat down.

The alpha didn't sit, choosing to stand beside my chair instead. He kept his body turned toward Siobhan even as he scanned the room. Looking for threats.

"I'm sorry to say that I don't think you'll be pleased with what I have to say. It's my understanding that Agent Bradford is a friend of yours?"

I must have looked surprised, because he winced. "Siobhan talks about you. And Agent Bradford. A lot."

"What does she say?" I leaned forward, then forced myself to sit back and not crowd him.

"Mostly she just talks about some auction she thinks you cheated her brother out of. She says Bradford killed Bradan and stole what was his. And you and the Vanguard helped him get away with it."

"Did she ever talk about getting even?" I pressed.

"She's never discussed specifics in front of me, but I'd be surprised if she wasn't looking for an opportunity."

"An opportunity like tonight?"

Deacon's gaze flicked to the door again and lingered for a moment before returning to my face. "Perhaps."

I folded my hands on the table. "Tell me what happened tonight."

Deacon wrapped his hand around the squat glass of bourbon on the table in front of him, fingers caressing the glass before he swirled the liquid inside. "I drove Mickey here to meet Siobhan so they could go to a meeting at Turning Tides." He paused. "Do you know about Turning Tides?"

"It's a racetrack Siobhan started," I said, nodding. "Go on."

"Siobhan told me to wait in the car until she got there. Mickey can't sit still long, so he got out to pace around out front. I'm not a fan of cold weather, so I stayed in the car with the engine running and the heat on. A little after seven, a van pulled up and Siobhan got out."

"You saw Siobhan," I clarified.

"Yes, but it was odd. Siobhan never drives a van. She never drives at all, she prefers to be chauffeured around now that she's leader of the team. Normally, that's my job, but tonight it would have been Jane, since they were coming straight from a business meeting. But Jane was nowhere to be seen. It seemed strange, so I stayed in the car to see what was going on."

A frown furrowed the skin between his brows. "It looked like she was having an argument with Mickey. Which also didn't seem right, because Mickey never argued with Siobhan. Not that he didn't want to," he clarified. "Mickey had *plenty* to say about her. But to her face, he was always the spirit of good faith."

"Did you hear what they said?" Liam asked.

"No. But it seemed to annoy Siobhan, because suddenly she

grabbed him. He leaned away like he was trying to make her let go."

"Was either Siobhan or Mickey holding any sort of weapon?" I asked.

"Not at that point." He met my eyes. "That's when your friend came rushing out. The FBI agent. He spotted Siobhan and Mickey by the van and I heard him shout 'Stop!' and he bolted right for them. Siobhan dragged Mickey back a step, then they were behind the van, out of my sight so I could only see them through the windows. Agent Bradford followed, then a second later, I heard a gunshot."

Deacon pointed to a man in the opposite corner of the bar. "Then that guy ran out and tackled the agent. I got out to take a closer look. It wasn't until I saw the body that I realized it wasn't Siobhan. It was Raichel." After a sip of bourbon he added bitterly, "Pity, that. Raichel was a typical kelpie, but although I wouldn't call her a good person she was still a sight better than Siobhan."

It was almost exactly the same story Mickey V had given us.

"Did you see anyone else in the area when Raichel was shot?" I asked. "Any kids? Was Mickey wearing a glamour, something that made him look younger than he should have?"

The satyr-blooded man shook his head. "I'm sorry. Mickey looked every bit his age the entire time."

I studied him closely. "Did Siobhan tell you what to say?"

"No, in fact she's been uncharacteristically absent from this evening's events, in more ways than one." His gaze traveled to Oksana. "She doesn't want to give the Vanguard any reason to think she's manipulating the investigation. She wants Agent Bradford to be found guilty—beyond a shadow of a doubt." Deacon leaned forward, lowering his voice. "Believe me when I say, I take no pleasure in any of this. If I had any information that would help your friend, I would give it to you. In a heartbeat."

"You don't like her." I didn't phrase it as a question.

"No," he answered, his voice low and hard.

His quick and emphatic answer gave me hope. "How did you come to work for her?"

"I'm not her employee," Deacon corrected me, closing his hand into a fist. "I'm her property. She won me in a race."

"She races too?" Liam asked.

"She didn't run the race." He sighed, then waved a hand. "Do you know anything about how Turning Tides works?"

"I only just learned of its existence a little while ago," I admitted. "All I know is that it was Siobhan's idea, and Anton Winters gave her the money to start it."

"Turning Tides is a racetrack exclusively, as you would imagine, for waterhorses. The races are run mostly by kelpies, *backahasts*, *neugles*, and *each uisges*, but anyone with a horse form can enter. The jockeys can be human or Other. Besides that, it's run like any other racetrack. And like any other racetrack, there are private events. Some with very high stakes."

Deacon's face darkened. "In one of those races, the horse owners wagered their jockeys. My mistress lost. Siobhan won." He leaned forward, his eyes flashing with sudden anger. "She doesn't even *want* me, for company or as a rider. I'm a feather in her cap, something to rub in my mistress' face, to remind people she won. Mistress Julia *loved* me. She appreciated my passion."

"You mean sex?" Peasblossom asked.

I gave her a withering look, but Deacon didn't look offended or surprised by her sudden intrusion.

"Not just sex, little one," he said honestly. "*Intimacy.*" He touched one of the roses on his arm. "Love is a magnificent thing. Not just true love, or love that lasts a lifetime, but even the small encounters between two people are beautiful. Worth remembering as moments they touched our hearts. Julia understood. She's a woman of science, but she had an appreciation for that which cannot be measured as well."

His voice softened. "I had thought she could be the one. She may still be, if Siobhan would release me."

"If she loved you, why did she gamble with you?" Peasblossom asked.

Again, it was a rude question. But this time, a fair one.

Deacon shook his head. "It was a trick. A manipulation on Siobhan's part."

"To get you?" I asked.

"No. It was a power play, no more. A way to show up my mistress. There are those who would like to see her embarrassed. Who would like to see her leave America." He smiled, and it was a genuine expression of affection. "It won't work. My Julia knows her mind. And her heart." He shrugged. "If anything, Siobhan's possession of me has done little more than convince my mistress to stay."

"If you tell me the truth," I said, pressing my hands against the table's scarred wooden surface, "I will do everything within my power to help you get back to her. Back to Julia."

That was a tricky thing to say. I hadn't exactly given my word, not formally, so technically I didn't think Flint would object. If Deacon demanded a formal oath, then I'd have to call the *leannan sidhe*.

I really hoped he didn't insist.

"You don't mean that." Deacon stared down into his bourbon, swirling the liquid with small, melancholy motions.

"Yes, I do," I insisted. "I will try to—"

"No, that's not what I meant." He shoved a hand through his curls. "You don't mean if I tell you the truth. You mean if I tell you the truth you want to hear. If I tell you the FBI agent is innocent. And believe me, nothing would give me greater pleasure in this moment. But I can't. I saw him shoot Raichel. In cold blood. I'm sorry."

My words caught on the lump in my throat. I fought to gather my thoughts, focusing on my breathing. Beside me, Liam's hand settled on shoulder, his aura pulsing against me in a warm rush. It was soothing, and I found my next breath came easier.

"You can understand why this whole situation seems...off," Liam said. "I'm not sure if you're familiar with Agent Bradford's history?"

Deacon snorted. "Oh, I'm familiar. Everyone knows Agent Bradford's history with the kelpies. Siobhan isn't subtle. In anything."

I sat up straighter. "So you see why this looks an awful lot like a set up? Siobhan arranges for Raichel to pick up Mickey right outside the door at a place she knows Andy's watching."

"A place he comes specifically because kelpies are hanging around with teenage humans and he's worried there's going to be trouble," Liam added.

"And if that was her plan, then it worked," Deacon said sadly. "But the fact remains, your friend killed Raichel. And he didn't do it to save anyone's life. Not a life that was in immediate danger. You might be able to argue that Siobhan was taunting him, but to argue incitement, you'd need to prove that she had solid reason to believe Agent Bradford would kill Raichel. And based on his history, I would not have thought he'd go through with it—not when he saw, plainly, that Mickey was no child. I'm sorry. I really am."

I stood from the table, suddenly needing some space between me and the satyr-blood's sympathy. "I was told Siobhan's other assistant is here. Jane?"

Deacon nodded to a table less than ten feet away. "That's her. The one in the suit."

"Thank you for your time."

"If you need to speak with me again, let me know." His smile turned bitter. "Siobhan will have to make me available if you ask."

I fought the urge to look at Siobhan as he mentioned her name. I could feel her eyes on me as I made my way over to the table where Jane was sitting. The wererat was a small woman, my height but thinner. She had short brown hair cut close to her head, and dark brown eyes that flicked back and forth across the small computer screen in front of her. The computer would have fit in my trench coat pocket, it was so compact, and I marveled at how the wererat was able to type so quickly on it.

She froze when my shadow fell over her. Then she took a deep breath, and looked up. Not at me. At Liam.

Ah. Predator. Prey. I should have had Liam hang back until I could make introductions.

Liam seemed to sense her unease. "Are you Jane?" he asked, keeping his voice in that higher, polite register people used when they answered the phone and didn't know who was calling.

"Yes. And you must be Detective Sergeant Liam Osbourne." She nodded toward Deacon. "I heard the introductions." She swiveled her gaze to me. "And you're Mother Renard."

She said "Mother Renard" with the formal awe other people might reserve for "the Queen."

Or possibly she was just very nervous.

"I need to ask you some questions about what happened tonight," I said. "Is that all right?"

"I'll help in any way I can."

I folded myself into the seat next to her. "Tell me about tonight. You were with Siobhan, and her plans changed at the last minute?"

"That's right. We were meeting with a gentleman about

adding more boats to the racetrack. Siobhan wants to expand."

"More boats?" Peasblossom asked.

Jane tapped the tiny keyboard with quick, sure movements. She pulled up an image of six boats in two lines, with an oval between them. Every ship in both lines was connected to its neighbors by a walkway, and another walkway connected the two ships at either end, so they surrounded the oval in the center. "Right now, we have six ships. Each of them has two stories. The lower decks are public, anyone can wander in and out of them, but the upper floors are private and can be rented by an individual or a group. We've been getting larger crowds lately, and Siobhan feels it's time to expand, add another ship to each side."

She called up another image, and this time there were eight ships surrounding the oval. "Of course she wants to make the track larger as well, so it still fits tightly within the boundaries."

"Not hard to do, since it's apparently just a matter of moving buoys as opposed to laying down new track," Liam observed.

Jane shot a furtive glance at Siobhan, a flash of annoyance there and gone on her face before I could even be certain I'd seen it. "Yes, that was Siobhan's thought. But she doesn't realize that it's not just about having space to run. There are a lot of creatures in that lake. And when you've got a group of horses running along the water for several races at least three nights a week, that draws some attention. Raichel had to negotiate with the mermaids for underwater security to make sure nothing tried to eat the waterhorses mid-race. And that's not just guarding the perimeter, they need to be spread out all over the track underneath the runners and the ships to make sure nothing comes from below."

I shivered at the thought. I knew what sort of creatures lived in Lake Erie. It said a lot that kelpies were actually on the less scary end of the scale.

She waved a hand in the air. "And don't even get me started on the ghost ships. Raichel kept a detailed calendar of the ghost ship sightings, so at least we could predict some of them. But there's always an outlier, some dead captain who hasn't realized he's dead and wants to argue about why duty demands he sail straight through to the shore." She pressed her fingertips to her temples. "And now it's my job."

I paused, considering Jane's face. She looked stressed, but she didn't look particularly sad.

She caught me staring and frowned. "What?"

"You don't seem very affected by Raichel's death. Beyond the anxiety over taking on her workload."

"Which you seem to be getting down to with impressive efficiency," Liam added.

Jane shrugged. "I liked Raichel more than Siobhan," she said, keeping her voice low lest she be overheard. "But it's the difference between working with someone who tolerates your presence, and someone who goes out of their way to make your life hell. Raichel wasn't my friend, and I certainly didn't trust her. But she was more reasonable than Siobhan. More... predictable." She rubbed a hand over her face. "Predictability is something I appreciate in a predator."

"How long have you worked for Siobhan?"

Jane leaned back in her seat. "I was at Fortuna's Stables when Siobhan's predecessor Gloria was in charge. Then when Fortuna's Stables went under, and Siobhan had the idea for Turning Tides, I was part of her team to get the whole process started, just under Raichel." She looked like she wanted to say more, but swallowed it back.

I knew that look. "Let me guess. Siobhan was the idea person, but actually figuring out how to make it work, making her idea a reality, fell to you and Raichel."

Jane shot furtive glances around the room, deliberately

avoiding the team leader. "Yes. Siobhan is clever, I'll give her that. The on the water racetrack was a brilliant idea, and it really helped her in terms of earning the loyalty of the team. Things were rocky for a while after Gloria died and the centaurs started taking over."

"Rocky in what way?" I asked.

"Well, Gloria was more of a people person than Siobhan. She had a sort of natural air of leadership, and people responded to that. She managed to hold her own against the centaurs, even though they had more of a land presence, and Stavros obviously favored them. But after she died, and Siobhan took over, the centaurs took advantage of Siobhan being new and somewhat inexperienced with the ins and outs of the racetrack. They started edging the waterhorses out of races, giving more spots to centaurs."

She leaned back in her seat. "But when Fortuna's Stables went under, Siobhan really came through. She had the idea for Turning Tides, and she managed to sell Anton Winters on the concept. And of course, the centaurs can't run on the water, so they were very neatly cut out."

"So the team loves her for getting them a better spot in the hierarchy," Liam mused.

"Loves might be a strong word," Jane muttered. "But, yes, they appreciate what she's done."

"So you and Siobhan were meeting with someone about adding new boats. And the plan was for Siobhan to pick up Mickey when the meeting was over," I pressed. "But then the meeting ran over. First Siobhan changed the meeting place, then she sent Raichel."

Jane nodded. "Initially Siobhan thought she'd still be able to make it, but she needed Mickey closer to reduce travel time. The kelpies have a boat at Something Fishy on Thursdays, so that seemed like the best choice. But then the meeting ran even longer, and she wasn't going to make it again, so she sent Raichel."

"And is it true that she often sent Raichel to impersonate her?" I asked.

"Yes. Siobhan hated being made to look foolish, but not so much so that she was willing to put in the effort to understand the details. She'd send Raichel to any meeting that involved spreadsheets. Disguised as Siobhan, of course, so no one knew she didn't have the mind for business that she claimed to have."

She tapped one finger on the table. "But this was a meeting with a potential investor. Those were her favorite meetings, the ones that let her talk about how great she is, and how lucrative her idea turned out to be. She wouldn't have missed this one intentionally."

"Who was the meeting with?" I asked.

"Mr. Chatterjee. He's a *naga* who invests in local businesses. I can give you his contact information, if you like?"

She tapped more keys on the computer and pulled up an electronic contact card. Liam looked over her shoulder and dialed the number on his cell phone before stepping away. I left him to confirm Siobhan's alibi and turned back to Jane.

The wererat was studying my face, and the pity in her eyes drove a spike of fear into my gut. "Siobhan wanted Raichel out of the way and that FBI agent too, and she got them both in one stroke. I just... I wish I could help you."

"Then help me," I urged her. "Tell me something I can use. I know this was a setup. It's an *obvious* setup. But I need help to prove it."

"It may have been a setup," Jane admitted. "In fact, I'm sure it was. But it's a setup that relied on your friend killing someone, not to save someone's life, but because he wanted them dead." She put a hand on mine, the sympathy on her face twisting the hard knot in my stomach. "And he did."

CHAPTER 6

"MR. CHATTERJEE CONFIRMS that Siobhan didn't leave his office until seven-thirty," Liam said, sliding his cell phone into his shirt pocket. He nodded to the bar. "Talk to the bartender next?"

Jane's words echoed in my ears, so loud I almost missed what Liam said. I could feel Siobhan's gaze boring into the space between my shoulder blades, like a physical weight. It made me itch, and it took more effort than I wanted to admit not to do something rash.

Like blast her through the wall.

"Shade?"

I shook my head, trying to force a smile for Liam. "Sorry, I was thinking." I looked ahead at the bar, eyeing the stools that looked like they should have gone to the scrapheap years ago.

Liam approached the bar ahead of me, nostrils flaring as he looked up and down at the line of barstools. "This is where he was sitting." He put his hand on the bar closest to the back door.

I stood next to the seat with its broken faux-leather and splintered wood, gazing out the rear door. Through the window, I could see the pier, and the edge of Siobhan's boat. "That window was filthy the last time we were here." I glanced at the front door, noticing that despite the fact it was essentially the dilapidated building's kickstand, it too was surprisingly clean.

Peasblossom tugged on my earlobe to keep her balance. "Andy cleaned the windows, didn't he?"

"It makes sense, if he wanted to keep an eye on things," Liam said.

"And no one thought that was weird?" Peasblossom threw up her arms. "Him coming in here to clean the doors?"

"This place probably has a high tolerance for weird," I muttered.

The bartender openly stared at us as he dried off a beer mug with a blessedly almost-white towel. He had a barrel chest so wide around I was surprised he could bring his arms together enough to dry the glass.

"You must be Mother Renard."

"You heard the introductions too?" I asked.

He shook his head. "Siobhan said you'd be stopping by. I'm Valter, and I own this bar. You have questions, I assume? Questions about why your friend decided to use *my bar* as his hunting ground?"

I let the hunting ground comment slide. "I do have some questions, yes. Let's start with how well would you say you know Agent Bradford? I understand he came here every week."

"I'm not surprised he killed Raichel, if that's what you're asking." Valter braced his hands on the edge of the bar. "I told him he should have stopped coming here. That obsession he has with the kelpies was never healthy. It was only a matter of time."

"Obsession?" Liam asked.

"Obsession, yeah. Been comin' here every Thursday night. Always staring at the kelpies—glaring at them, really. Especially if they had guests."

"You mean kids," I said, my voice cold. "When they had kids on their boats. Kids that didn't belong at a bar in the first place."

The veins on Valter's beefy arms bulged as he leaned forward. "I told him, as long as they're on the boats and not in the bar, I can't do anything about that. And as far as I could see, the kelpies never laid an aggressive hand on them." He shook his head. "Everyone's heard about his history with the kelpies. I knew it was going to be trouble some day. And I was right."

"You don't seem to like him very much," I observed, keeping my voice cool but still professional.

He paused, then sighed. "Look, the truth is, I don't think Bradford's a bad guy. He always pays his tab, and he always orders something, even though he never actually drinks it. Damn kelpies usually don't even order, just take up space along the pier. But that doesn't mean I'm not pissed he decided to shoot someone on my front doorstep." He gestured outside at the floodlights. "This is not good for business."

"What about the other patrons?" Liam asked. "Anyone have a grudge?"

Valter snorted. "Besides the kelpies? No, not really. But no one here likes him. He stalks around here like he's better than everyone else. And he definitely expected the worst from the kelpies."

"And you're telling me the kelpies never egged him on?" I demanded. "Never goaded him?"

"Siobhan never even looked at him," Valter said flatly.

"Agent Bradford said he ran outside because he believed Siobhan was trying to kidnap a kid," I said. "Did you see a kid anywhere near here tonight?"

"No." He grabbed the towel and picked up another glass from beside the sink.

"Did you ever see the jockey, Mickey V, turn this way? Did you ever see his face, or notice Andy looking in his direction when he was facing him?"

"I never met Mickey before tonight. And I didn't see any kids wandering around outside. But then, I have a bar to run, so I don't tend to notice people until they want to buy something. Speaking of which..."

He gestured behind me. As I turned, I almost hit a man with my elbow. "Oh! I'm sorry, I didn't see you there."

The man looked at me with big frog-like eyes, a grin spreading over his thin lips. At least, I thought he was grinning. It was hard to tell through the blond beard with the greenish tint.

"Does he have scales?" Peasblossom hissed.

"I think they're tattoos," I murmured.

"Not tattoos," the man said, his words trailed by a wet sound between a wheeze and a gurgle. "Those are real."

He dropped his glamour on the last word. His skin grew paler and took on the same green tint reflected in his beard. The scales I'd mistaken for tattoos gleamed with a metallic iridescence—where they weren't coated with slimy algae. He looked like he should have smelled awful, but on my next breath I caught a hint of rosemary. That jogged my memory, and I knew what he was. A *bolotnik*. A swamp spirit.

Mostly harmless. No magical ability that could affect someone's memory.

"I'm sorry, I didn't get your name?" I asked.

"Maks." He lifted his empty beer glass at Valter and the barman grunted and reached to take it for a refill. When he handed it back, Maks happily took a deep swig, losing almost as much to his beard as he managed to get down his throat.

"Do you know Agent Bradford?" I asked him.

"I would have, if he'd had the decency to join me for a drink." He shuffled back a few steps until his rear end hit one of the tables, then he grabbed a chair. "I invited him plenty of times, but he could never be bothered. Not one to enjoy a drop, that one." He settled into his seat, letting his beer glass down hard on the table and wiping his mouth on his forearm.

"He doesn't drink," I agreed.

Maks shook his head. "Would have done him some good if he had. Or if not drink, then some other outlet. A man can't live by duty alone."

"Duty?" Liam asked.

The *bolotnik* sighed. "He made no secret of it. He was sure the kelpies were up to no good, and he was determined to catch them in the act."

"And did he?" I asked. "Catch them in the act?"

"You're talking about the murder tonight. I was inside the whole time, so I couldn't tell you." He snorted. "What I can tell you is that man of yours has demons he isn't ready to face. Combine that with no drinking, no smoking... Hell, I hope he has a lover. Though the evidence suggests not!"

He slapped his knee and let out a guffaw that filled the air between us with another burst of rosemary. Liam's aura flared behind me, singeing my back. I looked over my shoulder at him, but his face didn't give anything away.

"The witch is not sleeping with the FBI man," a new voice announced. "Her lover is much more sensual. Sex on two legs, if you know what I mean."

I narrowed my eyes as a man swaggered over to the *bolotnik's* table. His large belly protruded over the waistband of his pants, his too-tight T-shirt giving up on covering his girth an inch too soon, revealing a strip of brown skin. His puffy cheeks were flushed and his gait wobbled as if he'd been drinking for some time.

"Refer to my sex life again," I said in a low voice, "and I will hex you so that every sip of alcohol turns to pure water on your tongue."

The man's mouth fell open, and he swayed back as if I'd

struck him. "No call for...for that." He scowled. "You're just cranky. I was here when you and your handsome...friend, saved him the first time." He continued, a slight slur in his words. "But you won't save him this time."

"You've had one too many again, Gesupo!" Maks slapped him on the back, sending the rotund man into the table so quickly he almost keeled over.

Gesupo struggled to straighten up, swaying back and forth before finding some semblance of equilibrium. "FBI shot that kelpie like a crippled racehorse. Palgun saw him!" He threw out an arm to gesture at a man sitting at a table in the corner and almost fell over. "Ask him! Your FBI man is kelpie food."

"Did you see it happen?" Liam asked.

Gesupo shook his head. "No, I was having a drink in the corner. But I was here the last time Bradford had a go at the kelpies. The night you were here." He pointed at me, but his finger wavered as if he saw two of me and wanted to make sure he included us both. "He'd have killed one that night too. If you and pretty boy hadn't come along to pull him out of the water."

"Neither of you seem very upset about the fact that there's a dead woman outside that door," I said coolly.

Maks looked offended. "Didn't know her, did we? We get the gossip, but the high and mighty at the precious Turning Tides don't slum it around here, do they?"

I wasn't wasting my time with belligerent patrons who had nothing to tell, so I nodded to Maks, then headed for the table in the corner. Three different witnesses had named Palgun as the one to tackle Andy. If there'd been anyone else outside when it happened, he'd be the one to ask.

Palgun watched me approach with a less than friendly look in his watery grey eyes. He sat up straighter, casually tossing his head to send his long, flowing blond hair over his shoulder.

"Hi. My name is Mother Renard. I'm told you were the one who tackled Agent Bradford earlier."

"After he murdered Raichel, yes."

Liam stepped up behind me, his aura a few degrees cooler now. "You're Palgun?"

The aloof blond man raised his eyes to Liam. "Yes. And if you're here for help clearing Bradford's name, then I'm sorry to disappoint you."

"You saw him shoot her?" Liam asked.

"As good as. I ran out the door right after. Caught Bradford standing over Raichel's body. Like the witch said, I'm the one that tackled him."

My stomach lurched. "You saw him with the gun in his hand?"

Palgun frowned. "No. It was on the ground at his feet. He must have dropped it when he heard me hit the door."

"But you don't know that," Peasblossom pressed, flying into the air between us, looking down on Palgun with all the superiority of her tiny species.

"I know he didn't hit his head hard enough to forget anything," Palgun said. "Head wounds bleed something awful, even when it's barely a scratch. He's faking it."

"And you would know that, would you?" I forced myself to stop, find my center. The last thing I needed right now was to come off as a hotheaded witch. Hotheaded witches made people nervous, not chatty. "I'd appreciate it if you just stuck to the facts. When you ran out, did you see anyone else? Anyone at all in the parking lot?"

"I saw Bradford standing over Raichel's dead body. The jockey was already running away, around the building. He's the one that called for Rowyn." He met my eyes. "He went to the kelpies for protection against your partner. Not the other way around. Does that sound like your friend is innocent?"

"It sounds like you've already made up your mind," I said.

Palgun sighed. His let his shoulders slump and tucked his long hair behind one ear. "Listen, I don't mean to be cruel. But trying to spare your feelings will only hurt you more in the long run. I'm a *kul*, Mother Renard. I know when misfortune is coming. It's coming for your friend now. If I were you, I'd get out of the way."

Kuls were Siberian water spirits. Not malicious, per se, but rather portents of misfortune. Similar to a banshee.

No magic that would allow for mental manipulation.

Dammit.

I looked away from Palgun and scanned the bar. There was no one else here. Oksana stood near the bar, surveying the room, watching to make sure no one was congregating out of the normal routine. Evelyn had fallen back beside the strix after we'd spoken with Deacon, and Siobhan leaned against the back wall.

Jane was busy typing on her tiny computer, buried in all the work Siobhan had neither the brains nor the inclination to do herself. Mickey was sitting at the bar on the stool closest to the front door, one leg bouncing with the energy I'd expect from someone on his fifth energy drink. His eyes darted around the room, as if he couldn't believe he'd finally been let inside and was just waiting for someone to notice him. And Deacon just sat in the corner, watching me with an expression far too close to pity for my liking.

Liam walked to the front door and opened it to speak to someone outside. I started toward him, but he'd accepted a slip of paper from the person and closed the door before I reached him. He shook his head at me. "Vincent says he won't have the ballistics report and other results for us until tomorrow."

"There has to be something he can tell us now," I insisted. I pointed at the slip of paper. "What's that?"

"Vincent got the serial number off the gun used. I'm going to run it, see if I can trace the owner."

"The serial number was filed off?" I perked up at that. "What else did he say?"

Liam's face remained carefully blank. "He said he has nothing to tell us right now."

The brief flare of hope died down as I realized an illegal weapon could just as easily be more damning evidence against Andy. He was an FBI agent. He'd know where to get an illegal gun.

"You mean Vincent has nothing *good* to tell us. And he doesn't want to speak with me until he has something that isn't more evidence against Andy."

"We won't know until tomorrow," Liam asserted.

I nodded and turned toward the back door. I felt rather than saw Siobhan fall into step behind us, trailing in our wake as we headed back to her boat.

"Mother Renard, I do hope you got the information you needed?" she chirped as she passed me by to all but hop onto the deck.

I stared her down as I boarded the boat again, walking right up to her until a slight arm extension would have let me shove her overboard.

"I want Agent Bradford—"

"Out on bail?" Siobhan smiled. "Of course. I'm not heartless. You can have a little more time with him. One last investigation, as it were."

That had been too easy. If Siobhan really believed Andy tried to kill her, she should have some fear of his release. Especially if he felt he had nothing to lose. It wasn't as if he hadn't proven he was a match for a kelpie. I opened my mouth, but she kept talking.

"On one condition, of course. Just in case you—or Agent

Bradford—decide to run when you see how completely hopeless your case is." She took a swaying step forward, invading my personal space and bringing the scent of the lake with her. "If Agent Bradford is released to your custody, you must give your word that *you* will serve his sentence yourself if he escapes. To be clear, that means if he escapes before he's turned over, *or* after." She leaned forward, lowering her voice. "I'll give you a moment to call your Master and make sure that's okay."

Well, that explained part of it. Siobhan was getting greedy, trying to get a two-for-one. And if she was a real gambler—and it seemed she was—if she did end up claiming me, who's to say she wouldn't try to bargain with my freedom to get a favor from someone else? Flint, or maybe Liam? *Opportunistic and a sadist.*

Liam's aura kicked up another few degrees, snapping against my skin like embers thrown off a bonfire. The heat felt good out here in the cold air with the wind rolling off the water to steal whatever warmth I might have produced on my own. I didn't have to look at his face to know what he thought of me putting myself up as collateral. But to his credit, he didn't try to stop me.

Smart man.

Flint didn't answer my first call. Or the second. My pulse sped up a little faster with each failed attempt, and by the time I dialed his number a sixth time, I was ready to chuck my phone overboard and try calling him in a less mundane fashion. Something that would require bloodletting.

Thank the Goddess he answered.

"What's wrong?"

I swallowed a sigh of relief as Flint's voice came over the line, sharpened by the fact he'd no doubt noticed the five missed calls before this one. "I need permission to sign a contract," I blurted out.

"What contract?" Wariness crept into his voice. I heard the clink of a bottle being set down.

"Andy's been arrested for killing a kelpie. I want to bail him out, but to do that I need to agree to serve the sentence myself if he runs."

"What sentence?"

I looked at Siobhan. "Put a number on it."

"A human lifetime at Andy's age would be fifty years."

"Fifty years service to Siobhan," I told Flint. I held my breath.

"Siobhan. The sister of Bradan. The kelpie Agent Bradford killed."

I closed my eyes. "Yes."

Flint was silent for a long minute. "You are never boring, Shade. I can honestly say you are never boring."

"Just give me an answer, I don't have a lot of time."

There was a too-long pause, and another clink of glass before he answered. "I'll allow you to sign the contract under two conditions."

I gritted my teeth. "Which are?"

"You owe me one more month on our contract."

Peasblossom hissed, but I held up a hand. "Fine. And?"

"If you fail to clear him and he does not submit himself to serve his sentence, forcing you to take his place, you will serve the same sentence with me when your time with Siobhan is done."

I really wished I'd been sitting down. "Fifty years. With you."

"I think it's very fair. Considering you're asking me to interrupt our contract so you can save Agent Bradford's life."

I had a lot of words for what he wanted, but fair wasn't one of them. Unfortunately, I didn't have the leverage to argue. "Fine."

Peasblossom let out a squeak of outrage. The nauseated

feeling in my stomach grew worse, but I didn't have a choice. I tried to shake it off. This would all be moot once I proved Andy was innocent. Another month wouldn't kill me. "Fine."

"Then you can agree to Siobhan's terms."

I ended the call before I could change my mind. Technically, I was supposed to wait for Flint to end the call, but I didn't think he'd make a big deal out of it. Not when he'd just gotten so much out of our short exchange.

I ignored the smug look on Siobhan's face and went down to retrieve Andy.

He didn't look up right away when I entered. The notebook he held looked half full, and his eyes flitted back and forth over what he'd written. It felt good to see him this way, his analytical mind taking over, focusing on the details. I cleared my throat.

He tore his attention from his notes to face me. "Did you find out what happened?"

I gestured for him to follow me out of the boat. "I arranged your bail. Come with me, we'll talk in the truck."

He must have wanted to leave more than he wanted answers, and I couldn't blame him for that. I waited until we stepped off the pier before I began filling him in on what we'd learned. I tried to sound as positive as I could, but it was hard to make the facts sound less damning than they were. There was no getting around the fact that two different witnesses had seen Andy leave the bar, get a good look at Mickey's face, and then shoot "Siobhan," anyway. Combined with the fact that more than one patron considered Andy's behavior to be stalking, it didn't look good.

Which is why it seemed strange that Andy's mood seemed to improve as we walked.

"Kylie and Vincent won't have forensic results for us until tomorrow," I finished. "So far, I haven't seen anyone with the power to manipulate your memory. But Vincent's results will be more accurate, and he'll be able to tell me if someone was there tonight but managed to leave before we got here, or if someone had a potion or an artifact that could have done the job."

Andy wasn't looking at me, and he was only half-listening. I frowned as he walked past Liam's truck, heading for a tree at the border of the bar's property.

Liam followed him, then halted and wrinkled his nose. "What smells like ammonia?"

"It didn't smell like that when I put it here." Andy reached up to a bundle of leaves lodged in the V of a lower branch. It wasn't until he moved it that I realized what it was.

"A camera?" I stared at Andy. "You had a camera here?"

Andy nodded, turning the device over in his hands. It was small and compact, and I never would have seen it if he hadn't reached for it first.

My mouth fell open as the full realization of what this meant hit me. "You have the shooting on video."

Andy nodded again. "I should. I didn't want to say anything where others might overhear, just in case..."

Liam made a face as he looked at the camera. "Someone wiped it down with ammonia. If it wasn't you, then someone else knew about it."

Andy flicked open the camera. I waited, but he didn't move, didn't speak.

Finally, Peasblossom launched herself off my shoulder to fly into the air for a better look. "It's empty," she moaned. "The SD card is gone."

I stared at Andy.

A smile twitched at the corner of his mouth. "Someone stole the SD card."

Suddenly, I found myself starting to smile too.

"Why are you smiling?" Peasblossom demanded. "That's a bad thing isn't it?"

"Not necessarily," Liam said. I could tell by the tone of his voice he was thinking the same thing I was. "If the video on that SD card would have showed the same thing the witnesses claim they saw, then there'd be no reason to take it."

"Which means, whoever took it was afraid it would prove the witnesses were wrong. Or lying." I couldn't help looking back at Something Fishy, toward where Siobhan still stood on her shiny boat, thinking she'd won. I smiled. "It's not over yet."

CHAPTER 7

THE MORNING after Andy's arrest I woke up late for me, at nine a.m. I'd been sleeping later ever since the psychic attack on my third eye. Healing that kind of injury takes a toll, and even though I *could* stick to my usual schedule—up with the sun—forcing my body to rise before it was ready would only make my third eye heal slower. The only problem with sleeping late is that I started my day feeling hours behind schedule.

I sensed Peasblossom frowning at me as I pulled on a clean pair of leggings and long-sleeved back knit shirt. "I still think we should have tracked down that SD card last night," she groused. "It's all we need to prove Andy's innocence."

"And like I told you last night, there was nothing we could do." I snagged my waist pouch off the bedside table and strapped it on. "We had to let Vincent and Kylie examine the camera and search us, otherwise Siobhan could have claimed we stole the SD card because it proved Andy was guilty. And Liam tried to track who might have retrieved it, but the ammonia they used to wipe down the camera hid whatever scent trail there might have been."

"It was funny watching him try to follow the scent trail of ammonia." Peasblossom snickered.

"Don't laugh, ammonia is a terrible smell for anyone. I can't imagine what it was like for Liam." I headed out of the bedroom for the kitchen. "Whoever took that SD card left in a car. The trail didn't leave the parking lot."

"So how are we going to find it?"

"We might not. If whatever's on that card would clear Andy, then whoever took it probably destroyed it. But even if we don't find it, the fact that it's missing means there's something someone doesn't want us to know. And hopefully, after we talk to Kylie and Vincent, we'll know what that something is."

I could feel Peasblossom staring at me as I passed the fridge.

"I don't want a hard boiled egg."

I set up the Keurig for my first cup of coffee, putting my Batman mug under the drip even though I'd just be dumping it into a travel mug anyway. "You don't have to eat it. But you should have some milk with your honey. You need protein."

"Honey has protein."

"No, it doesn't."

"It has vitamins."

"No."

"It has—"

"Sugar, Peasblossom. Honey has sugar. And antioxidants."

"Well, there you have it. What more do I need?"

I let my forehead fall against the refrigerator door, enjoying the cool surface against my skin before taking a deep breath and heaving it open to retrieve the milk. "You're having milk with your honey. We need to be better about eating, especially when we're on a case. Once we pick Andy up, we're going to be really busy, so we might not have time to eat for awhile. I don't want you hyped up on sugar and then crashing when it counts."

"I do not crash," Peasblossom said sullenly. "My wings are fine now."

That wasn't what I'd meant, but for the life of me, I couldn't be sure if Peasblossom knew that. I shook my head and retrieved two hard-boiled eggs from the bowl I kept on the top shelf. Liam was right, I did tend to neglect my dietary needs when I was busy, and that wasn't good for anyone. Having hard boiled eggs on hand was a quick way to make sure I didn't cheat with magic food.

Though Peasblossom was clearly already sick of them.

"All right, so Kylie told Liam they should have results for us this morning," I said, cracking one of the eggs. "Liam's picking us up, then we'll swing by for Andy, and we're off to Kylie's for the autopsy results."

"It would have been easier if Andy had just stayed here," the pixie pointed out, wrinkling her nose as I took a bite of my egg. "Then we wouldn't have to make the trip to his house. Kylie's house is far enough."

"Peasblossom, have a heart. The man is under enough stress right now, he deserves to sleep in his own bed."

At the sound of a knock at the door I shoved the rest of my hardboiled egg into my mouth. I snagged the other egg to eat on the way, then dumped my coffee into a travel mug and hurried to let Liam in.

He smiled when he noticed my breakfast on the go. "You remembered to eat."

I chased the last bite of egg with a swallow of coffee, relieved that the amount of milk I'd dumped into it had cooled it enough to drink quickly. "Did you?" I teased.

He grinned as he reached around me to grab my red trench coat. "Two pounds of bacon, six eggs, and four pieces of toast."

I let him help me into my coat. "Show off."

Liam chuckled and we made our way out of my apartment

building to his truck. The sun was bright this morning, and I squinted as the beams stabbed me in the eye through the glass of the front doors.

"Is Scath coming with us today?" Liam asked.

"Yes. She took Majesty outside to..." I stopped, unsure how to put it.

"To set him off so he doesn't sneeze magic later," Peasblossom supplied.

The flare in Liam's aura told me he was remembering the last time Majesty had flexed his magic. A rather unfortunate experience that had involved slowing Liam in time—right after he'd been shot. It occurred to me now that he might not want Majesty along this time. And if that were the case, we'd need to have the awkward conversation about how part of the kitten's magic seemed to be showing up when I least expected him.

Fortunately, Scath chose that moment to trot up to us wearing her service dog disguise. Without the glamour, Scath was an enormous beast with the body of a panther, and the ears of a lynx. Her body wasn't so much black fur as shadow, or maybe just a moving hole in the universe.

I didn't stare too hard at her without the glamour. That way madness lies. Typical of the Unseelie Court.

Majesty peeked out of the pouch slung around Scath's body, and I caught a glimpse of blue eyes in a white-dusted face on what was otherwise a grey cat with black stripes. On his good days, I could almost appreciate him for the adorable kitten he was, all but forgetting about his chaos magic and the turmoil it caused me.

I'd already caught Scath up on what was going on last night after I got back to the apartment. She didn't like to take human form very often, and she really didn't like to talk if it wasn't absolutely necessary, but she'd resumed human form long enough to share her thoughts on kelpies. Apparently, there was a sort of don't-ask-don't-tell policy among the Otherworld when it came to creatures that ate humans.

According to Scath, there were those among the Otherworld who looked at creatures that preyed on humans—such as kelpies—much the way humans looked at deer hunters who kept the herd numbers down.

I hadn't asked Scath if she had ever eaten a kelpie. I wasn't sure I wanted to know.

"Do you think Oksana was right about why the kelpies really hate Andy?" I asked Liam.

"You mean that they hate him because he's not going to look the other way when they eat humans?"

"As opposed to wanting revenge for Bradan's death, yes."

"It makes sense to me. I don't know a lot about kelpies, but based on my limited experience, they aren't really herd animals."

"Which is why you call a group of waterhorses a 'team' not a 'herd,'" Peasblossom added.

"Right," Liam agreed. "They're loners that only get together as often as they do now because some of them have decided they want a presence on land. The days of lurking around the lakes for fun and food are done, and some of them want the power that only comes from participating in society outside the water." He tilted his head. "I've only had two cases involving a waterhorse, and both of them were in the past two years." He glanced at me. "Why do you ask?"

I leaned back in my seat. "Having to explain justice in the Otherworld to Andy has made me think about the ins and outs more. I mean, I knew that too many Otherworlders were getting away with preying on humans. That's why I became a private investigator, to take the cases that were too small or obscure for the Vanguard to bother with."

"And isn't Andy helping you with that? Isn't that why the two of you teamed up, so you could help him identify cases that had an Otherworld component?"

"Yes. But now I'm wondering if it was a mistake to involve him in a justice system that..." I trailed off, unsure how to finish.

Liam raised his eyebrows. "I see. You mean, a justice system that generally ends with the criminal facing punishment within their own closed community, or with—"

"Being killed," Peasblossom finished.

"And it's the second part that's the problem. For humans, punishment for a crime usually means jail. But the Otherworld just doesn't do that, not often. When a werewolf commits a crime, you rehabilitate them within the pack. For the *sidhe*, they get sanctioned—or executed—at court. For those who don't have a strong community justice system, the criminal is more often than not killed by the victim or the victim's family."

"And you think Andy is being seduced by that idea," Liam said slowly.

"I think Andy is a smart man who does his research. You heard the people at the bar. Andy's been watching the kelpies. He's meticulous, and he's smart. If he started looking—*really* looking—how long do you think it would take him to compile a list of missing persons last seen near water?"

"As a police officer, I've had to watch some bad people walk away because I couldn't get the proof to convince a court of law," Liam said quietly. "I won't deny that the thought of meting out justice vigilante-style is tempting. But crossing that line... It doesn't lead anywhere good."

"The question is," I said half to myself, "how close has Andy come to crossing it?"

Liam tapped one finger against the steering wheel. "I ran the serial number for the gun. It's unregistered."

"So it could be Andy's or it could be someone else's," I murmured. "Not good news, not bad news."

No one said much the rest of the way to Andy's. I wasn't sure how interested Scath was in the conversation, but she obviously wasn't interested enough to take her human form and weigh in. Finally, we arrived at his house, and I got out to fetch him.

There was no answer when I knocked on the door. I frowned and knocked again. Still no answer. I tried the knob, but it was locked.

"No answer?" Liam asked, getting out of the truck.

I rose on tiptoe to look through one of three diamond-shaped windows in the door. I didn't see anyone, but there were no signs of a struggle either, no overturned furniture or broken windows. "I don't see him."

I held a hand out toward the doorknob. Normally, using a lockpicking spell on the door to a personal home was risky. A threshold held a type of magic all its own, and its response to an invasion could be unpredictable. But I'd been here before, used this spell here before. I was reasonably certain the threshold wouldn't attack me.

Reasonably.

"*Recludo,*" I whispered.

To my relief, the lock clicked. I turned the knob, and the door opened easily, so I stepped inside, Liam following behind me.

Liam's nostrils flared. "No one else has been here recently. But neither has Andy. His scent is faint, as if he hasn't been here for a long time."

"You mean not since last night?"

Liam shook his head. "I could be more accurate in wolf form, but even now, I can tell it's been weeks. I can almost smell the wood of the furniture and the dust more than him."

"But we dropped him off here last night."

"But we didn't watch him go inside. Based on what I'm smelling, it seems like he must have left right after we did."

"Check upstairs," Peasblossom urged.

I was already headed for the stairs. "Wait here," I said over my shoulder to Liam.

I found the door to Andy's parents' room locked, but it didn't take me more than a second to open it. I pushed the door open and stepped inside. "Mr. and Mrs. Bradford?"

Two ghosts appeared to my left, tickling my peripheral vision as they materialized. I recognized the woman with the short white hair and the cotton blouse with blue flowers on it. I also recognized the concern in her eyes as she rushed toward me.

"Shade," Andy's mother said. "Oh, thank goodness you're here! Where is Andrew?"

"I was going to ask you the same question. Did he come home last night?"

"No." She wrung her hands in front of her, her features pinched tight with worry. "I heard him at the door, and I heard a car pull away. But he didn't come inside. And when I went downstairs to look, he was standing at the end of the driveway. A taxi picked him up eventually."

A knot of dread hardened in the pit of my stomach. "When was the last time you saw him? Inside, I mean?"

The second ghost stepped forward, a man wearing a grey suit and starched white shirt. Andy's father. "Not since August." His lips pressed into a thin line. "Is Andrew all right?"

Blood and bone. I stared at them, and I knew my attempt to hide my concern failed when his mother reached for her husband, one hand pressing against his chest until he took her hand in his and squeezed it.

"What's wrong with Andrew? What's happened?" Her expression grew pained. "It's us, isn't it? He's not comfortable with us being here like this." She gestured at their ghostly forms.

I shook my head. "It's not you. I don't think it's you." I backed toward the door. I hated to leave them like this, to leave without giving them any answers. But I didn't have any answers to give. And I had nothing to say that would be of any comfort. "I'm going to go find him right now. I'll come back, and I'll bring him with me."

Mrs. Bradford let her husband gather her to his chest. He nodded at me, and there was more emotion in that one gesture than I think he'd wanted to show.

I retreated down the stairs and gestured for Liam to follow me out before I locked the door behind me. "Andy's parents said he hasn't been home since August."

It was hard to get the words out past the lump in my throat.

Liam froze. "His parents? Aren't they—"

"Ghosts. Long story." I hurried back to the truck and climbed inside, already groping for my cell phone in the side pocket of my pouch. I dialed Andy's number with shaking hands. It went straight to voicemail. Four more attempts got the same result. "He's not answering. His phone is off."

Liam started the truck and backed out of the driveway. "We'll check his office. If he's not sleeping here, he has to be sleeping somewhere."

I dialed Bryan's number. Bryan Foundling worked security at the FBI building where Andy worked. He'd been the one to introduce us, and I trusted him enough to ask him questions that might arouse suspicion in his other coworkers. Maybe Andy had gone in to work?

"Mother Renard," Bryan said in lieu of hello. "It's good to hear from you. How've you been?"

"Keeping busy," I said honestly. "Bryan, have you see Andy around lately? Did he come in today?"

Uncomfortable silence filled the air. Then Bryan cleared his throat. "He didn't mention his...vacation?"

"I thought he used up all his vacation days this spring?"

Bryan cleared his throat again. I heard him murmur under his breath to someone, as if excusing himself. After a minute, he came back. "Mother Renard, Andy was 'encouraged' to take a vacation a month ago. If you know what I mean?"

"You mean he was unofficially suspended." I took a slow, deep breath. "Why?"

"He struck a suspect in custody," Bryan said quietly. "Lost his temper and just... Well, he hit the guy pretty hard. Another agent was watching the interrogation, and he broke it up quick, but..." He sighed. "If he didn't have the clean record he does, it would have been a lot worse."

I looked at Liam. He didn't take his eyes off the road, but I could tell by the set of his jaw that he'd heard everything.

"Thanks for telling me, Bryan," I said, keeping my voice as light as I could manage. "I'll talk to him."

"Please do." Bryan let out a deep breath. "Shade, Andy's been under a lot of stress, and I get that. But if he doesn't get a handle on it soon, I'm not sure he's going to be able to come back."

"I'll talk to him," I said again. "I'll call you back later, Bryan."

I hung up before he could say anything else.

"You don't think he ran, do you?" Peasblossom asked carefully. "Because if he did—"

"I don't think he ran," I said quickly. "But I do think he's in trouble. I think he's been in trouble for a while, and for some reason, he hasn't told me about it."

"He didn't know the terms of his bail," Peasblossom pointed out. "He would never have run if he knew what it meant for you. But he didn't know, so maybe..."

Scath's head shot up at the mention of 'terms.' Suddenly there was a giant feline head between the two front seats, her service dog glamour abandoned, and her murky green eyes bored into mine.

"I didn't mention it because it's not a big deal," I said calmly.

"I made a deal with Siobhan that if Andy doesn't show up to take his punishment when the case is over...I'll take his place."

A sound crawled out of Scath's throat, one of those blood-curdling sounds all cats seemed capable of. I rubbed my arms to get rid of the goosebumps and scowled. "He's not running. He wouldn't run."

Scath snarled and retreated to the backseat, but she didn't lie down again. Tension rolled off of her in waves, and she stared out the window as if she might spot Andy running away.

When we pulled up to Andy's office the run down old building didn't look any more welcoming now than it had the first time. If anything, the broken steps and boarded up windows of the single story structure looked even more desolate now that I thought Andy might be living here. Sleeping here. *Blood and bone*, this wasn't a safe place to work, let alone sleep. What had he been thinking?

"Let me go in first," Liam said. "It'll be easier to pick up the scents of the place if I'm around fewer people."

I paused with my hand on the truck door. "All right. Let me know when I can come in."

Scath leaned forward, her green eyes following Liam's progress as he let himself in to the building. After a moment's hesitation, she butted my shoulder with her head.

"Is that an offer of comfort?" I said weakly.

She snorted. Then she bumped my shoulder again before resting the full weight of her giant skull on my arm.

"Thanks," I whispered.

I could tell it wouldn't be good news the second Liam walked out of the building. He gestured for me to come inside. I climbed out of the truck with Peasblossom burrowing under my coat on my shoulder. Scath prowled behind me like a shadow down the short hallway to the door to Andy's office.

"He's been sleeping here," Liam said grimly. "But he hasn't been here today. And there's more."

He opened the office door. The wall across from the threshold was covered in pictures and index cards, with brightly colored Post-its here and there with notes and speculations. I'd seen these before. They were part of Andy's investigation into Flint, his attempt to help me understand exactly what my *sidhe* master was up to.

Liam tapped me on the shoulder, then pointed to a grouping of photos on the opposite wall. I turned—and froze.

Kelpies. Not just kelpies, but other waterhorses. *Each uisges, nuckelavees, backahasts.* The differences were subtle, but Andy had clearly labeled each of them. And he was only wrong about one. The pictures depicted some of the beasts in their equine forms. He'd caught them at the edge of the water. One of them had apparently just leapt out of a boat. One stood on a dock I didn't recognize. There were pictures of humans too, but I could tell even from the photographs that they were waterhorses. They had that green or blue tint to their skin, and their pupils were too large, their eyes too glossy. The ones that were smiling showed large, flat teeth.

Some of the pictures had index cards next to them. The index cards referenced file numbers. I looked at the table in the center of the room, and spotted the files in question. Liam had already opened one, and he stood staring down at the file's contents with his mouth set in a hard line.

"You were right," he said, his voice low. "What you said before about Andy being capable of tracking them down, finding out if they killed someone. He's got a decent case against at least one of them. College boy went missing. Police found his blood on the side of a boat, thought there must have been an accident out on the water. But they found horse hair at the scene that the investigator put down to some sort of paintbrushes."

I traced a hand over the file. "We need to find him. If I can get something he's touched recently, I might be able to do a tracking spell. Do you have a map?"

"In the glove box. I'll grab it, hold on."

Liam retrieved the map while I continued studying the files. Andy was thorough. Every bit as good as I'd believed he was when I asked him to help me figure out what Flint was up to. But why hadn't he asked for my help with these missing persons cases? Because I was too busy doing Flint's bidding?

Or because he planned to get justice for these victims his own way?

I pushed all that aside as Liam spread the map across the table over top of a scattering of file folders and more photographs. With Bizbee's help, I was set up for the spell in no time.

I was just about to light the first candle when my cell phone rang.

Scath huffed a sharp breath on the match I held just in time. The sudden trembling in my fingers nearly set the whole table of papers on fire. I fumbled with my cell phone, putting it to my ear before taking the time to check the number.

"Hello?"

"Mother Renard. Is Agent Bradford with you?"

The severe tone in Oksana's heavily accented voice sent a chill through my blood. I stepped away from the table, grateful I hadn't cast my spell yet. "No, I don't know where he is. I was supposed to pick him up this morning, but I seem to have missed him."

"Mother Renard, you must be truthful," Oksana warned. "This is important. I have been tasked with tracking down Agent Bradford, and it is better that I am the one to find him. Believe me. If you know where he is, if you have any idea, then you must tell me now."

I believed her. "What happened?" At her hesitation I prompted, "Please, Oksana. I need to know."

Oksana sighed. "I'm sorry, Mother Renard. You know I like Agent Bradford."

"What. Happened?"

"There's been another murder. Deacon is dead."

CHAPTER 8

I PUT a hand over my mouth for a second, willing myself not to be sick. "I'll find him. Oksana, you know he didn't kill Deacon."

"Deacon was shot," the strix said grimly. "It is Agent Bradford's signature weapon. And you have admitted he was not with you. Why is he not with you?"

"Because he's an innocent man who deserved to sleep in his own bed without someone watching his every move. Didn't Vincent or Kylie tell you about the camera?"

"The camera with the missing SD card that only Agent Bradford knew about?"

I gritted my teeth. "The SD card was gone. Andy didn't have a chance to take it. He was tackled right after the shooting, and dragged to the kelpies' boat right after that."

Oksana drew a breath, but I kept talking.

"As to the shooting, anyone who's even heard of this case would know Andy's been involved in at least two shootings. And they'd know by now that we found the camera without the SD card. And they'd draw the same conclusion we did, that there's something on that recording the real killer doesn't want us to see. Maybe Deacon knew what was on the SD card. Maybe they're watching Andy's house and they know he was alone, so they decided to frame him."

"You do not yet know the details of this murder," Oksana said, her voice colder than it had been a second ago. "And I have no time for your conjecture. I must find Agent Bradford before the others do. If you have any idea where to look, tell me now."

"I'll find him. We'll come in and get this all cleared up." I hesitated. "Where was Deacon killed?"

Voices called out in the background, and the strix put her clawed hand over the phone to make her reply. Then she demanded of me, "You did not know where Deacon was, then? You swear this to me, you did not know?"

"I didn't know. I still don't, you have my word. Where was he killed?"

Oksana let out a harsh breath. "Deacon was on a houseboat at the home of Marilyn the *leannan sidhe*. The place where Agent Bradford shot Siobhan's brother."

Liam's arm came around me, and it was that alone that kept me on my feet. The world tilted, and I dropped my phone. Liam caught it with his free hand, passed it back to me. Peasblossom put both hands on the back of my neck, pulsing energy against me, using our empathic bond to send calming vibrations into my mind. Even Scath came forward, pressing her huge furry head against my hip.

Marilyn's. Deacon had been at Marilyn's.

Morgan stayed at Marilyn's.

Morgan was the one who kept pointing Andy at the kelpies as if he were her own personal handgun.

"Mother Renard, they will not let you on the scene," Oksana was warning me.

"I'll see you soon," I mumbled. "I'll find Andy."

"Shade, what do you want to do?" Liam' voice was as calm as ever as I ended the call, but his aura writhed against me. He'd heard everything. He knew how bad it looked.

"We need to find Andy," I said, my voice strained. "Now."

"We will. We'll find him."

I braced my hands on the edge of the table and closed my eyes. My heart still pounded, my breathing coming too fast. I took a deep breath in for the count of seven, then let it out for the count of eight. I repeated it a few more times.

"She has to calm down," I heard Peasblossom whisper. "Tracking spells aren't her specialty."

My head dipped. My familiar was right. Under perfect circumstances, with the blood of the person I wanted to find, willingness on their part to be found, and a clear, calm mind, I'd have a decent chance. But I didn't have blood, at best I had the pen he'd been using or some hairs from where he slept, and items from his parents' house wouldn't help me either after his long absence. And if Andy wanted to be found, he'd answer his phone.

I could fight for the calm and clarity, but the other two were beyond me.

I tried anyway. I lit the candles, I concentrated on my breathing. And I dangled the crystal on the end of the string, swirling it in a tiny circle.

I don't know how long I tried. I stared at the piece of crystal as if I could force it to move with my mind, force it to tell me where Andy was. I probably could move it with my mind, but that wouldn't help.

Liam's hands closed over my shoulders. He didn't pull me away, didn't make me stop. He just stood there. Anchoring me. I dropped the crystal.

"I texted Blake," he said quietly. "He's calling the cab

companies to find out who picked Andy up. We'll find out where he went, and I will personally track him down." He leaned forward, putting his mouth closer to my ear so I could feel his breath on my neck. "I will find him."

"I know you will." I cleared my throat, concentrating on the heavy weight of Liam's hands before he withdrew. "We should go to the crime scene. Kylie and Vincent will be there, and we were supposed to meet them anyway."

"Makes sense to me."

He didn't point out that Oksana had said I wouldn't be allowed at the crime scene, even though I knew he'd overheard. It didn't matter. I needed to talk to Vincent and Kylie.

And I was most certainly going to talk to Morgan.

We all climbed into the truck, and I got my cell phone out and pulled up the map function. I'd programmed Marilyn's address into my phone the night her protégé Simon was cursed. I hadn't been able to help him yet, but I was working on it. I wouldn't forget. I laid the phone on my lap, leaving it to the electronic voice to give Liam directions so I could lay my head back and stare out the window.

"A second murder means new evidence," I said finally. "It's a fresh chance to prove Andy didn't do it. The real killer might have made a mistake this time."

"Why would anyone want to kill Deacon?" Peasblossom asked, flopping down on my shoulder, her wings slowly fanning the air. "He said Andy killed Raichel. Isn't that what Siobhan would have wanted?"

"The obvious reason would be Deacon changed his mind," I said slowly. "Maybe he was lying before, and for some reason he decided to come clean." I squeezed my eyes shut. "I knew there was something off. Something he was holding back. I should have pushed it last night."

"If he had something else to say that would have cleared Andy, he wasn't going to tell you with Siobhan standing there," Liam argued.

"Well he can't tell me anything now, can he?" I took another deep breath in for seven seconds, then exhaled for eight. "I'm sorry."

"Don't be, you're fine." Liam tilted his head. "If Deacon overheard that the SD card was missing, that could have changed his mind. Maybe he was worried about what would happen when we found it. The Vanguard might have a reputation for not going after the little things, but I can tell you that they do not consider lying to the Vanguard a 'little thing.'"

"So Deacon decides to change his story, and someone shoots him." I nodded. "That could be why the kelpies took him to Marilyn's. I always wondered if Marilyn offered them any compensation for what happened to Bradan."

"You think she'd kill Deacon for them?" Liam asked.

Peasblossom grunted. "It wouldn't be a big deal to someone like Marilyn. Deacon is property. And even if Siobhan didn't explicitly tell her to kill him—maybe she just hinted it'd be convenient—the punishment for killing him would be next to nothing. A half-satyr's life just isn't worth much to them, even if he wasn't property."

"So then the question would be, what change would Deacon have made to his story?" Liam asked.

I twisted in my seat. "What if Deacon killed her?"

"You think he could have shot her?"

I tried to keep up with the new direction my thoughts had taken. "Think about it. Deacon couldn't see through the glamour. He thought it was Siobhan. He sees Andy run out, gun drawn. He says he stayed in the car, but what if he didn't? What if he got out and ran up to Andy?"

"Andy doesn't shoot," Liam said slowly. "Deacon takes his

gun and shoots Raichel, thinking she's Siobhan." He frowned. "You think he could have gotten Andy's gun away from him?"

"We don't know what happened to Andy," I pointed out. "What caused the blackout. If it happened before Deacon took the gun..."

"But Mickey saw it," Peasblossom argued. "Why would he say Andy did it?"

"All right, how about this." I held up a hand. "Deacon thinks Raichel is Siobhan. He sees her manhandling Mickey, and he thinks this is his chance to get rid of his unwanted mistress? Anton Winters favors Mickey, so Deacon thinks he can convince the vampire that he killed Siobhan because she was hurting his prized jockey."

"But Siobhan is the one running the business he has a financial stake in," Liam countered.

"But according to our witness statements, Siobhan wasn't a good businesswoman," I argued. "She was an ideas person, and that's it. Raichel or even Jane herself could have kept the place going."

"That's a stretch," Liam said doubtfully. "There's just as much chance the vampire would be furious that Deacon killed the person leading a lucrative business he has an interest in."

"Which is why they blamed Andy," I reasoned. "Deacon realizes he shot Raichel. Siobhan shows up, and he claims he killed Raichel because he thought she was trying to drag Mickey off and make him miss the investor meeting to discredit Siobhan. He suggests blaming Andy, she loves the idea."

"It's just as likely Siobhan is the one who suggested blaming Andy in the first place," Peasblossom pointed out.

"And Mickey goes along with it regardless of who suggests it, because he doesn't want to risk the whole mess interfering with the running of Turning Tides," I finished.

"That would explain why Deacon's dead now," Liam

admitted. "If Siobhan figured out that he was actually trying to kill her, then she'd want him dead before he could try again. And she'd definitely want him dead before anyone could figure out it was him, not Andy, that shot her."

"We still need to find out how Andy's memory loss plays into all this," I said, biting the inside of my cheek in frustration. "I didn't see anyone at the bar with a natural talent for manipulating memory."

"Palgun seems to have acted alone and seems pretty confident his takedown of Andy didn't result in a severe head injury," Liam agreed, "so if his injury didn't affect his memory, what did?"

"We'll know more after we talk to Vincent," I said. "If Andy's condition was worse than Palgun thought, or there was someone —or something—there that could affect Andy's memory, he'll know."

By the time we arrived at Marilyn's, I was so desperate for answers I was ready to jump out of the truck and run up the driveway. I forced myself to sit still, staring down at the notes I'd scribbled as Liam pulled up the drive. There was no guard in the small building outside the gate, and the gate was open.

Liam parked at the top of the drive close to the house, and I led the way to the lake. It was a distressingly familiar path to me now, and I'd never made this trip without finding something extremely unpleasant at the end.

Marilyn had a large property, and it took some time to cross her expansive green lawn to the rocky hill that separated the main property from the beach. My heart sank as I saw Marilyn and Morgan standing on the pier. *Leannan sidhe.* Why did this case have to involve the *leannan sidhe*?

Suddenly, a figure separated from Marilyn and Morgan, revealing herself as she took three quick steps down the pier toward me. Siobhan's black denim jeans contrasted with the pale green of her skin. Her eyes burned as she swung her arm up to point at me.

"You! Get away from here! Were you a part of this? Did you help him find Deacon?" Her features twisted as she looked from me to Liam. "Deacon should have been safe here. He should have been safe from *all of you!*"

Marilyn took a step with Siobhan. She was beautiful as always, with her blonde hair piled on top of her head in a complicated style that involved braids and waves, and at least thirty pearls. When my attention shifted to the fey woman standing beside her, my magic pulsed, the desire to call a spell and blast Morgan into the next county all but overwhelming.

"What are you doing here, Mother Renard?" Marilyn asked.

"I'm working as an agent of the Vanguard as Agent Bradford's legal defense," I said, not taking my eyes off Morgan. "I have every right to be here."

"*She* did this!" Siobhan hissed. "She's so desperate to save the human that she killed my Deacon!" Her lip curled in a sneer. "It won't save him. Mickey V saw Bradford shoot poor Raichel too. Let's see you kill him. See what Winters will do to you then."

"I had nothing to do with this." I lifted my chin. "And neither did Andy."

"Then where is he?" Siobhan demanded. "Why isn't he with you?"

"I have no intention of bringing him to a crime scene where he might contaminate the forensics in a way that would let you put him here at the time of the murder," I said coldly.

"And where were you, Mother Renard?" Siobhan pressed. "Last night, after you left the bar. Where were you?"

I gritted my teeth. "I was home. Sleeping."

"And I was with her!" Peasblossom added.

I took a step forward, and Siobhan planted herself in front of me. "Where do you think you're going?"

"I was supposed to meet with Kylie and Vincent now to talk about last night's findings," I said calmly. "I'm going to speak with them."

"They're busy," Siobhan snapped. "They have *another* scene to process now that your trigger-happy friend has got a taste for murder."

"You may as well wait to hear the evidence of both scenes," Marilyn spoke up. She moved closer, not putting herself between me and Siobhan, but making sure she was in the kelpie's peripheral vision. A reminder of whose property we were on. "They will finish soon, I'm sure. And until then, you're welcome to wait at the house."

"I'll wait here, thank you," Siobhan said flatly.

She pivoted on her heel and marched to the end of the pier to glare at Vincent and Kylie where they worked on the scene. Marilyn gave her a withering look, but didn't say anything.

Again, my attention shifted to Morgan. She stood there on the pier with a look of uncertainty, wringing her gloved hands in front of her, the soft grey leather silent in the way only very expensive leather could be. Her skin was still blue from her unfortunate encounter with Majesty, and a thick, ugly scar stood out on her left cheek. My stomach turned as I remembered how she'd gotten that mark. How she'd carved it into her own flesh under Marilyn's influence. Punishment for what she'd done to Simon.

Something seemed different about her. Something more than just the doubt that looked so out of place in her expression. It took me a second to realize what it was.

She wasn't transfixed by Scath.

For the first time since I'd been bringing Scath around,

Morgan wasn't looking at the feline *sidhe* with that pale expression of horror usually reserved for victims confronting criminals who've wronged them. Or vice versa. So what had happened to distract her from her obsession?

"Marilyn, why was Deacon in your boathouse?" I asked.

"Siobhan asked if he could stay here. She seemed to feel he was in some danger after being witness to a murder. A murder committed by Agent Bradford?" Her voice lilted at the end, making it a question.

"He's innocent, and I'm trying to prove it. I would appreciate it if you would answer some questions."

"You're attempting to prove him innocent of the original murder, or this one?" Marilyn asked.

"Both." I took a deep breath, trying to keep my temper under control. It wasn't easy. Not with Morgan standing there. Maybe it was just me, but she looked guilty.

"Have they found any evidence to even suggest Agent Bradford was here?" Liam asked. "Surely you would have known if he was on your property?"

Morgan winced. "Actually, he was here. And I'm afraid that's my fault."

I stared at her, a thousand words fighting to be the first out of my mouth. "What?"

Marilyn's eyes brightened with interest as she looked between Morgan and me.

"I called Andy." Morgan bit her lip. "I invited him here."

I lost my voice for a second. I hated hearing Andy's name on her lips. She had no right to call him by his first name, let alone sound so familiar. Not when so much of this was her fault.

Even more than I'd suspected five minutes ago.

"Why did you invite him?" Liam asked.

Morgan smoothed her gloved hands down her skirt. "When

Siobhan brought Deacon here, I found out about what happened at the bar. I'll admit I felt some...responsibility."

Peasblossom crossed her arms. "I would certainly hope so."

Morgan didn't look at the pixie. "I asked Andy to come here. I told him I might have a way to help."

"How?" I asked, not bothering to hide my incredulity.

Morgan spread her hands in front of her. "I thought perhaps Deacon would speak more freely here, without Siobhan present to intimidate him. Surely that occurred to you?"

I narrowed my eyes. "Yes. But I certainly wouldn't have done it *here*. And I certainly wouldn't have left him alone near Deacon, without a witness, so that someone could frame him for a *second* murder."

Morgan stiffened. "I'm so sorry I spilled my wine and had to change. I didn't see a problem with leaving Andy alone, since I don't believe he's guilty." She cleared her throat. "And I realize I should not have encouraged Andy the way I did. With the kelpies. Part of this whole mess feels like my fault, and I wanted to help."

"You can't possibly expect me to believe that!" I sucked in a breath as I forced my voice back down to a normal conversation level. "You lured him here, where the witness was. It didn't make sense for him to come here. He *shouldn't* have come here."

"I can't win with you, Shade," Morgan said, the first hint of anger warming her voice. "But maybe Andy has a higher opinion of my motives."

"And look where it got him," I growled.

Morgan crossed her arms. "He came over, and we shared a meal. I offered to take him down to the boat where Deacon was staying. Then I spilled wine on my dress, so I had to excuse myself to change." Her gaze flitted between me and Liam. "Andy told me to take my time. When I returned, we finished eating, and he left."

I caught Liam looking at me out of the corner of his eye, and for some reason it rubbed me the wrong way.

"Did he have a gun on him when he came here?" I said, forcing the words out before I could reconsider.

Morgan flinched. "He did. But I made him leave it in the car," she added quickly. "Anyone could have taken it."

"Is there anyone else on the property that's familiar with guns?" Liam asked. "Anyone who'd be comfortable using one?"

I gritted my teeth. He was using a weird voice. Overly cautious. As if he were worried about my reaction to his questions. I lifted my chin and looked Morgan in the eye, waiting for her answer even as my heart pounded. Chances of someone else familiar with firearms here were slim. Not many *sidhe* took the pains Flint did to carry a weapon with a minimum of iron.

Morgan hesitated, then looked to Marilyn. Seeking permission.

I turned my attention to the blonde *sidhe* who owned the property, and by all available evidence, held some sort of control over Morgan. Marilyn paused, clearly debating whether or not to let her answer.

"How's Simon?" I kept my voice low, not rude but with an edge that suggested I could become so very quickly if circumstances warranted it.

If I hadn't been watching her face so carefully, I'd have missed it. The slight tightening of the skin around Marilyn's eyes.

"He's doing well with his therapy," she said finally. She clasped her hands in front of her. "You may as well come up to the house. There is one guest here who's familiar with those wretched weapons."

"Who is it?" I asked.

Marilyn turned and started back toward her manor. "Raphael has been my guest for a couple of months now."

Raphael.

Liam turned to me, sensing the rigidity in my body language. "Who's Raphael?"

Peasblossom shot into the air, her wings buzzing furiously behind her. "Someone who tried to kill my witch!"

CHAPTER 9

"He tried to kill you?"

Liam's aura flared, searing the side of my body closest to him and making me take a step away. He noticed my reaction, and I felt him wrestle it back under control, returning to a low humming heat that wasn't altogether unpleasant on a cold October afternoon.

"Not exactly." I flexed my fingers, trying to get rid of the need to throw a spell. First the second murder, then seeing Siobhan, then Morgan. Finding out Raphael was here as well wasn't doing anything for my nerves. Or my temper.

I was starting to understand why Mother Hazel had held off on training me in magic for so long. Why she'd stressed so many other skills before that one, weighted them more heavily. My magic wanted to be used, and there were far more situations that would be made worse by magic, than those that would be made better.

Like this one.

Raphael's voice echoed in my memory, full of fury as he charged the stage after Marilyn ended my auction and handed me over to Flint.

"You'll pay for your crimes!"

I still had no idea what crimes he was referring to. I'd never met Raphael before that night. Not that I remembered, anyway.

"He tried to attack me after the auction, but Scath intervened." Saying her name made me look down. Scath stood on all fours beside me, her green eyes locked on Morgan, seemingly oblivious to the conversation going on over her head.

This time when I looked at the blue-skinned *sidhe,* Morgan was very obviously trying not to look at Scath. There was enough tension singing through her spine that I swore I could hear it vibrating like a tuning fork. And she curled her hands into fists so tight, if she hadn't been wearing gloves she'd have drawn blood.

Marilyn noticed all of that, and seemed to be considering the implications. It wasn't until then that I realized Marilyn didn't look at Scath the same way Morgan did.

"Peasblossom?" I asked after she'd settled herself behind my neck, speaking low enough not to be overheard. "When this is over, remind me to make a list of everyone who reacts oddly to Scath."

The pixie's wings stilled, then continued fanning from her spot under my hair. I felt her nod.

On the way to the main house, I filled Liam in on the basics of my previous experience with Raphael. Including the *leannan sidhe's* gift. Every *leannan sidhe* had an emotional specialty on top of their natural ability to boost the abilities of others through "inspiration." For Raphael, it was pure adrenaline, the excitement that usually drove people to engage in questionable hobbies, like bungee-jumping and running with the bulls.

Liam tensed when I mentioned that part of Raphael's gift. Though he recovered quickly I noticed the hesitation in his step, and the reason dawned on me.

Raphael's gift could have disastrous implications for a werewolf.

It was too late to turn back now. Marilyn led us in the front door, through the cavernous foyer to the same sitting room where I'd been just a few short months ago. The room where I'd greeted the suspects in the last case Flint had assigned me. The one that had ended with him fleeing to Europe. And then to Andy investigating him.

To finding out about Anton Winters' five million dollar donation to the Buy Shade fund.

"Morgan, wait here with our guests while I invite the others to join us."

Marilyn's voice tore me out of my reverie. I saw Morgan shift her attention from Scath long enough to give our blonde host a nod.

As soon as Marilyn left, I whirled to face Morgan. "When was Andy here?"

Morgan walked over to a gilded cart with glass shelves full of hand-crafted bottles of what I assumed was expensive liquor and wine. She grabbed a tumbler and poured a reddish brown liquid into it. "He arrived a little after one o'clock. Maybe one-thirty." She glanced up at me. "Unsurprisingly, he wasn't sleeping when I called."

"And how long did he stay?"

"He left a little before three." Morgan put her hand on her glass, but hesitated. "He really didn't tell you he was coming here?"

She didn't look at me when she asked the question, which was fortunate, since I was pretty sure the look on my face was murderous enough to void a hospitality agreement. "What did you and Andy talk about? Specifically?"

"Why don't you ask him?"

"I will as soon as I meet up with him later," I said lightly. "But for now, it'll be easier if you tell me."

Morgan took a sip of her drink, obviously buying a second to compose herself. "I'm sorry, Mother Renard. I'm not comfortable sharing Andy's personal business without his permission."

"You called him," I said tightly. "It wasn't his personal business, it was yours."

"It started that way, yes."

The urge to lash out was strong. There was no smugness in her voice, but it was the lack of smugness that felt like mockery. As if she knew just how much her calm got under my skin.

"He's about to be charged with a second murder," I ground out. "A murder he wouldn't be on the hook for at all had he not been here. I need to know why he was here and what he talked to you about."

"Then I suggest you ask him."

I bit back the string of swear words that sprang to my mind. "Morgan, if I can't prove Andy's innocent, Siobhan will kill him. And it will be on your head."

Morgan winced. For the first time, I noticed her hand was trembling. "I won't tell you what we talked about," she said quietly, "but I will tell you that now that I understand his reasons for certain behaviors. And if I told you what we'd talked about, you would wish you had never asked."

"You're wrong. You keeping secrets about Andy will not do me any favors."

Morgan pressed her lips together, then took one of my hands in her free hand. "Let me rephrase that. It's better if you can honestly say you didn't know."

That got my attention.

I stared at Morgan as she released my hand and stepped back. I didn't know what to say to that. I shared a look with

Liam. His blue eyes looked darker than they had before. As if there were new shadows there. Doubt maybe. Or sadness.

Part of me worried he was starting to believe Andy was guilty.

"Maybe you should text Andy and tell him about the deal," Peasblossom whispered.

"What deal?" Morgan asked quickly.

Scath growled and padded a step closer to Morgan. The *sidhe* jerked back. This time she did spill her drink. Her pupils swallowed the rest of her eyes until they were a solid black. The air filled with the musty scent of feathers, and for a moment, I swore I could hear wings rustling.

"Don't threaten me," Morgan seethed. "I am not easily fooled. And I will not hesitate."

Scath bared her teeth, her green eyes glowing brighter.

"What is this bad blood between you and Scath?" I demanded. "How do you know her, or about her? Or does she know something you've done?"

Morgan didn't answer. And she didn't look away from Scath. The sound of wings got louder. In the distance, I heard the croak of a raven.

"Am I missing out on the fun?"

Raphael's voice didn't have the same smooth, silky tone of Flint's. It wasn't seductive or alluring. Instead, Raphael's tone made my heart skip a beat, gave me a sudden rush. As if I were standing in the open doorway of a plane about to leap out, with nothing but silk and string to save me from a violent death.

The *leannan sidhe* strode into the room with the swagger of someone who most definitely had a weapon somewhere on his person. He looked exactly as I remembered him. Tall and lean, but with enough muscle in his upper body that I knew his plum dress shirt had been tailored to fit him. His long dark hair faded to blond four inches from the ends. His grey eyes brightened when he looked at me, and I wondered if he was wearing kohl, or if his lashes were really that thick.

"Mother Renard, we meet again. How are you enjoying life with your master?"

I forced myself to smile. "Flint's been enjoying an extended vacation in Europe, and I find his absence most satisfying, thank you." His change in demeanor nagged at me, and I tilted my head. "Are we to be friends, then? This is quite a change, given how the last time we met you seemed sure I deserved to be punished."

Raphael shrugged. "I'm thinking along very different lines now. Perhaps my initial anger was...misdirected." His eyes glittered with flecks of silver as he stepped closer, almost but not quite invading my personal space. He smelled of leather and metal and mead. Bottled Valhalla. "Flint is a fool. If I had purchased you, I would not have left you." He took another step, leaned closer until I could feel his breath on my face. "And you would not have let me if I tried."

My heart gave a sudden, painful beat, thundering against the wall of my chest so hard it took my breath away. Adrenaline scalded my veins. I didn't know if Raphael was flexing his power over me, or if his advance was merely the last straw on the pile of stress that had been building since I'd found out about Andy's arrest.

It didn't help that I had Liam on the other side, his energy boiling the air around me and letting me know exactly what his thoughts were on Raphael's comments. I clenched my teeth and backed away from both of them, fighting to clear my head.

"Raphael," Morgan warned. "Mother Renard is Marilyn's guest."

"I'm offering her no harm," Raphael murmured. "Quite the opposite."

Liam rolled his shoulders, tendons cracking and popping.

Raphael's eyes darted to the werewolf. I didn't like the considering look he gave the alpha.

"As it happens, I'd be only too happy to part with your company. After you answer a few questions."

"Questions? About what?"

"Morgan tells me you're comfortable with firearms," I said. "Do you own a gun?"

Raphael arched an eyebrow. "I own a lot of guns. As well as a variety of other weapons. There's a reason so many call my house Valhalla."

"Lots of dead people?" Peasblossom muttered.

I rubbed the bridge of my nose. "Raphael, you are so cliché, it hurts. It really does."

The skin between Raphael's brows creased, his amusement fading away. I cut him off before he could retort.

"Where were you when Deacon was shot?" I asked.

"What time was he shot?"

I didn't know the time for sure, because I hadn't talked to Kylie yet. But Siobhan had asked me where I was last night after I left Something Fishy, so that seemed like a safe bet. I started to say around one a.m., then reconsidered. It would be just like a *sidhe* to use something as simple as a too-specific time to lie. "Where were you between midnight and when they discovered the body?"

"I was here. Sleeping." He shifted, and somehow he managed to give the impression he'd gotten closer without actually moving farther into my space. "Alone. And isn't that a pity?"

"So you have no alibi?" I pressed.

"I don't need one. I have no reason to kill Siobhan's toy."

He seemed to be speaking the truth, but if he didn't benefit personally from Deacon's death he still could have acted on someone else's behalf.

"Nor do I have any reason to frame your FBI partner. He isn't the one who robbed me the night of the auction. If I were going to frame someone, or kill someone, it would be your master. Flint Valencia." He lowered his voice. "You'd like that, wouldn't you? If I killed him for you?"

I didn't rise to the bait. "Who else was here when Deacon was shot?"

"I was here, of course," Morgan said. "As were Simon and Marilyn. And Raphael and his sister, Luna, are Marilyn's guests. They were both here as well."

"I'm surprised Raphael is here at all," I said slowly. "If I remember correctly, he wasn't happy with Marilyn on his last visit."

Raphael sighed. "I was...frustrated that Marilyn ended the bidding so prematurely. Flint did not deserve you." He dragged his gaze up and down my body, but the heat in his eyes didn't feel sexual. He didn't look at me like Flint did. Or Liam. He looked at me as if I were a Christmas present in glittery wrapping paper and a tight, complicated ribbon that would need a sharp blade to remove.

"Raphael is here because Luna is here," Morgan said. "Marilyn asked Luna to come because Simon needed help sleeping."

"She's really been helping Simon?" I asked.

Movement near the doorway caught my eye. I jerked around to face the woman walking toward me. I would have guessed she was Raphael's sister. She was his twin, the feminine version of the warrior *sidhe*, with the same pale grey eyes, and long dark hair with the blonde ends tickling her lower back. She was softer than Raphael, but not by much. She had enough muscle to make it clear she worked to maintain her physique instead of relying on genetics to keep her strong and slim. Like her brother, she either used a liberal amount of kohl for her eyes, or just had enviably thick lashes.

There was a hypnotic sway to her walk that matched the steady gaze she swept over the room. Then her eyes settled on me.

"You sound as if you think I'd harm the boy. And we haven't even been properly introduced yet. I'm Luna." When she came closer, I could tell that, also like her brother, she smelled of mead and metal and leather. She glanced from me to Liam, then arched one questioning eyebrow.

"Luna," Morgan said. "This is Mother Renard and her associate Ms. Scath. And this is Detective Sergeant Liam Osbourne." She paused, as if she'd only just remembered something. "And he's also the alpha of the Rocky River pack."

Raphael's head lifted, his eyes locking onto the other man with renewed interest. Liam stood still, his expression set in that unreadable cop face that was so similar to Andy's. Which was impressive considering I could tell from the amount of heat rolling off him that he was definitely not calm.

Suddenly I was not at all sure that it was safe to be in the room with these particular guests without the hostess present. "Where's Marilyn?"

"She'll be along in a moment." Luna advanced, her eyes sharp. "You seem nervous. Do you not trust us?"

"I'm having a trying day," I said, trying to keep my voice from betraying how close to the edge I was.

"I can see that." Luna closed in like a snake making a lazy serpentine pattern in deep sand. "I can help you. If you'll let me?"

Her power reached me before she did. The muscles in my shoulders gave up their tension as if warm oil had been poured over my body, seeping into my skin, soothing and relaxing every muscle as it passed. I hadn't realized how tense I was, from my eyebrows to the soles of my feet. I took a deeper breath than I'd believed myself capable of. It felt *good*.

My thoughts floated on a warm bath. I nearly swayed on my feet, but I didn't care. My forehead touched something warm, and even my third eye gave up its tension and pain. I took another deep breath and sank further into that warm, fuzzy feeling.

"Shade?"

Liam's voice. There was concern in it. And a warning. I tried to frown, but couldn't flex the muscles necessary to do so. Goddess, had I ever been this relaxed?

My familiar's emotions pulsed against me, tiny panicky beats. But even that couldn't make it through. It was like being underwater and hearing someone splashing at the surface. Audible, but far away. Irrelevant. I felt amazing.

And I didn't *want* to give it up.

Peasblossom stabbed me. I felt the needle slide into my skin, a prick that should have hurt a lot more than it did. I smiled. Actually, it didn't hurt at all. No more than acupuncture.

"Whatever you're doing," Liam growled, "stop it now."

His voice vibrated against my skin, making me realize I was leaning on him. My cheek pressed against his chest, my body nestled under his arm. In fact, he was the only thing holding me up. That was nice of him.

"I'm helping," Luna said mildly. "She is very stressed. She needs to relax."

"You heard him, Luna," Raphael spoke up. "He wants the witch to wake up. And I can certainly help with that."

I was half asleep now. I knew because it felt like the room was bobbing up and down, and I was only vaguely aware of what was being said. Luna's ability was relaxation. Forced relaxation, so strong I was willing to bet she'd slowed my heart rate. Could probably slow it even more if she chose. I wondered if she could kill me that way.

"Shall I wake her up?"

Raphael didn't wait for an answer.

His power crashed down on me. The warm bubble of relaxation popped, and reality smashed into my body with all the gentility of a runaway freight train. I gasped, wincing as my entire body spasmed in time with my pounding heart. *Blood and bone*, I could barely breathe, as if each beat of my heart was a physical blow to my chest.

It wasn't until the roar that I realized we had bigger problems than my heart rate.

I knew that roar.

Blessed Goddess, Raphael hadn't just aimed his power at me. He'd hit Liam too.

Another roar. This one feline. My blood ran cold.

And Scath.

No.

Liam roared again, the sound more animal than man, at the same time that Scath let out another feline scream that curled my nerve endings. I straightened up so fast that the rush of blood made me pitch backward in a loss of balance.

Liam's eyes shone like melted pools of gold, his body contorting, already beginning to change.

Green eyes burned bright as Scath crouched, ready to strike.

Liam fought it, twisting away from the *sidhe*, teeth gritted. But Scath's mouth was open, sharp teeth glistening. She fixed her gaze on Raphael.

"Don't bite him!" Peasblossom screamed.

Majesty meowed.

And all Hell broke loose in a blinding explosion of light and color.

CHAPTER 10

IT TAKES a special kind of adrenaline rush to energize every cell of your being to where as soon as your body hits the floor, you spring up like a cat that just fell in the bathtub to find it wasn't empty. I was back on my feet before I realized I'd fallen. Everything hurt, as if the force of the blood pumping through my veins had bruised me from the inside out. I couldn't hear my own thoughts over my thundering pulse, but that was fine.

There was no time to think.

Majesty's light display had only half-blinded me. I'd been too loopy when he went off, upright but with my eyes still half-closed from when I'd lolled against the thick warm wall of Liam's chest. I'd only caught the end, so my vision was grey and a little fuzzy, but sufficient.

"Shade, stop Scath! Don't let her bite!" Peasblossom wailed.

I whirled around. Raphael stood five feet away, his feet braced shoulder width apart, his hands held out to his sides as if he were willing the very ground beneath him to rise at his command. His grey eyes shone like polished hematite. But I could tell by his stare and the way he tilted his head, listening for clues to what was going on, that he hadn't been so lucky in regards to Majesty's light show.

He was fighting blind.

That didn't stop him from pumping his adrenaline rush around the room. Liam was mid-shift, his clothes tearing as his body flexed and grew to a shape they weren't meant to contain, his jeans holding on for dear life. His face protruded outward in a snout that could hold all the teeth of this new form. Unlike Raphael, Liam didn't need his eyes to fight. His sense of smell was plenty. His head swung toward the *leannan sidhe*, lips pulled back in a snarl.

Peasblossom's warning echoed in my head, and I spied Scath ten feet away from me, gathering her strength, body tightening as she shifted her weight to her back legs, ready to leap at Raphael.

I dove for her just as her body began its upward movement, wrapping my arms around her neck and my legs around her body. I held on for dear life as if this were, in fact, my first rodeo. Scath snarled and whipped her body in a circle. Tears burned my eyes as my body continued to produce more adrenaline than was good for my heart. It was too much, and if I didn't do something with it soon, I was going to throw up from the sheer intensity of it.

I buried my head in the thick fur at her neck, straining to maintain my hold as the feline *sidhe* went mad with fury. Something heavy fell on me—some*one*. Their weight was too much, and my hold on Scath's neck broke as I was pushed to the ground beneath a black dress.

"Morgan!" I snarled. "Get off of me!"

"I fell!" Morgan yelped. "What in the mother of crows is going on? Raphael, *stop this!*"

"Everyone *calm down!*" Marilyn hollered. "This is *unacceptable!*"

"Marilyn!" Luna cried. "I can't see! What's going on, what did that beast do to us?"

If I'd had the time, I'd have sent a spell at Raphael's other half just to shut her up. I felt something tiny hit my shoulder.

Peasblossom.

The pixie had fallen out of the air and struck my shoulder on her way down. Every nerve in my body seized at once. My imagination supplied image after image of her being trampled in the free for all, and suddenly my world narrowed down to saving my familiar. I bracketed my hands and knees on the floor, forming a shelter with my body as I searched for her, blinking furiously to clear my vision to catch that flash of pink.

"Peasblossom!"

Scath roared and leapt away from me, free to escape now that my attention was elsewhere. My peripheral vision told me she was heading for Raphael again, charging at the large *sidhe* still standing with his arms out, his blind grey eyes unmoving as he listened and waited.

"Scath, no!" Peasblossom shouted. "Liam, *stop her!*"

I followed the sound of her voice and spotted her beside my right knee, her wings so close to my body I was afraid I'd already knelt on the delicate limbs. I eased back then scooped her up, careful not to squeeze her wings. I lifted her to my shoulder.

Liam's next roar made me spin around on my knees. My eyes bulged.

The alpha had gotten between Scath and Raphael. The feline *sidhe's* jaws were closed around Liam's forearm, teeth buried in his flesh, blood running past her lips. Liam roared again, the pain in the sound twisting my nerve endings into knots. Scath released him and reared back, her head low as she backed away.

I didn't believe she'd meant to bite Liam. Only Raphael. But it was hard to ignore the way she licked her lips, her green eyes looking brighter than before.

My heart skipped another beat, my blood flooded with a new rush of adrenaline that had nothing to do with Raphael's power.

"You hurt him," Raphael snarled. "You have violated the sanctity of Marilyn's home!"

Raphael drew a dagger from a concealed sheath. I caught the glint of the blade as he turned to face Scath. He blinked, then his gaze locked onto the huge black cat. Scath screamed at him. Blood glistened on the fur of her muzzle.

Magic crackled in my hands, begging to be released as I stood to face Raphael. "Don't. You. *Dare.*"

The retort died on his lips as a feminine voice behind us swelled into song.

The melody was soothing and pleasant. Unlike Luna's power, the heated oil that poured over you and washed away your will to fight, your will to *move*, this song just took the edges off. My heartbeat slowly returned to normal, my breathing evening a little more with each note instead of all at once. My shoulders dropped and my magic shifted from a painful sizzling electricity to a warm buzz not unlike Liam's aura when he was calm.

Liam.

I tore my attention from the song, not bothering to look for the source of the voice. Liam knelt on the floor, back in human form. His jeans still clung to his lower body, but his shirt was more decoration than anything at this point. His chest rose and fell with labored breaths, and sweat dripped from his forehead. His face was too pale, his blue eyes too bright.

"Liam?" I knelt beside him and he didn't move as I swept his hair back from his face. "Are you all right? Say something."

"Heck of a...bite." He winced and curled in on himself.

My heart stopped. "Peasblossom!"

The pixie dropped onto Liam's shoulder and pressed her hands against him. I did the same, calling a healing spell. Energy flowed from my hands, surging over his body in a race to his injured arm. As soon as our magic touched his wound, I could sense something in the bloody teeth marks sucking it down, drinking it like a marathon runner at the halfway point. His breathing evened out, but the blood continued to drip down his arm, the wounds still open.

I pulled my hands back, a deep cold settling into my stomach. I turned and looked for Scath.

When the *sidhe's* eyes met mine I saw a flicker of emotion. Shame? Shock? Anger? Before I could decide, before I could be sure, Scath whirled around and bolted out of the room. As I stared after her, I noticed Morgan withdrawn against the wall. Her wide eyes met mine.

"I told you to be careful," she whispered.

"When?" I asked, my voice high and shaky. "What are you talking about?"

Morgan stared at Liam. "She bit him. It was only a matter of time."

"What are you talking about?" I demanded again.

"I can't tell you," Morgan said miserably.

I stood, stepping toward her with my fists clenched at my sides. "You—"

"Mother Renard, is everything all right?" asked a voice in a heavy Dacian accent.

I whirled around, expecting to see Borgia, the opera singer whose impressive soothing powers I'd witnessed at a show a few months ago. Daughter of a siren mother and *leannan sidhe* father.

Marilyn gestured at a phone sitting on an end table near one of the chairs. "Borgia's not here, Mother Renard. I called her."

"Your phone is connected to your sound system?" I asked, looking around for the speakers that would have been necessary to project the singer's voice.

"It's part of Simon's therapy. Borgia helps to calm him when Luna is not here."

"Mother Renard," came Borgia's voice again, "is everything all right?"

"No. No, everything is not all right." I glared at Raphael and Luna, then turned my focus to Marilyn. "We were attacked by Marilyn's *guests*."

"We were trying to help," Luna protested.

Raphael nodded. "Luna was only trying to offer you the peace you so obviously needed. And then the detective seemed to be alarmed by your relaxed state, so I offered to wake you up a little." He glared in the direction Scath had vanished. "The only one to cause harm was the cat."

"You are treading a very fine line," Marilyn said coldly. "Your behavior has led to violence within my home. Be grateful Borgia was available to stop this insanity. I promise you, you would not have liked my solution."

While our hostess bid polite farewell to the half-siren, Liam lurched to his feet. I grabbed his arm to help steady him as he listed to the side. His jeans slid down, baring the muscled ridges of his left hip. I waved a hand over him, using my Cinderella spells to mend his clothes in the way I'd hoped my healing spell would do for his injuries. He tried to reassure me with a smile, but failed. His skin was too warm and clammy under my hands. Feverish.

"Liam, we need to get you home." I unzipped my pouch. "Bizbee, I need some bandages. And—"

A first aid kit popped out of the pouch, hefted up amid a flurry of cursing in Gaelic. I took the kit and fished out antibiotic cream and some bandages.

Liam started to protest, then stopped. "I'll help you finish here." His voice came out a hoarse rasp, and he cleared his throat. "Then I'll need to rest."

"You could rest here, alpha," Marilyn offered. "Not as a favor. As an apology. You've come to harm in my home. I would make things right."

"I appreciate the offer. But I'll heal faster with my pack."

"Of course." Marilyn turned to Raphael and Luna. Her blue eyes glittered, and not with pleasure. "Both of you, get out. We *will* discuss this later."

The twins didn't move. Like a matching teapot and sugar bowl, they remained side by side. Their grey eyes glowed, and each of them held the same coiled tension. As if they were debating their options.

"Morgan," Marilyn said serenely, "take off your gloves."

Morgan stiffened, but did as she was told.

Raphael and Luna both glanced down at her hands. The thick, ugly scars over her palms.

"Tell the siblings why you scarred your hands. And your lovely face."

Morgan looked at the twins. When she spoke, her voice was detached. As if she had to mentally distance herself from the memory in order to say it out loud. "I disobeyed Marilyn."

The twins shared a look. Then, as one, they turned and left.

Marilyn let out a disappointed sigh. "You would think being over seven hundred years old would bring a certain amount of maturity. But, alas, it is not so."

I stared at Marilyn. "They're older than you?"

Marilyn gave me an amused smile. "Yes."

I filed that note away as I finished bandaging Liam's arm. That would explain why she hadn't been confident her own power could stop both of them amidst the chaos. She wouldn't want to risk failing in front of witnesses and in her own home.

Marilyn wielded enormous personal power and influence, but age mattered greatly when it came to the *sidhe*.

I didn't understand why the twins had risked Marilyn's ire to cause all that chaos. But one thing was certain. I definitely needed to learn more about them.

And Morgan.

And, apparently, Scath.

"Morgan, that will be all. You can go."

Morgan pulled her gloves back on and left, but she gave me one last pained look before she did. Frustration made my skin taut, made me itch with the desire to chase her down, force her to explain what she'd meant when she'd told me to be careful. To make her tell me why she'd manipulated Andy the way she did. Liam hissed as I wrapped the bandage around his arm. Later. I would find Morgan later.

I gentled my grip on Liam as I continued to bandage the bite. It was still bleeding, and that was a bad sign. Hopefully it would stop by the time I got him to New Moon. I finished the bandage and pulled him toward the door.

"I need to get him home. But I'll need to speak with Morgan again soon."

Marilyn frowned. "I suppose."

Liam put an arm around me as we left the manor. I tried not to think about how badly he must be hurt if he was leaning on me. Or how weak his aura felt. It was hard not to notice the absence of the usual warmth as we made our way to his truck in the bracing autumn air. The coroner's van was still in the driveway, reminding me I'd need to chase down Kylie and Vincent when they were finished with the new scene.

Liam stopped me as I started to open the passenger door, pressing his keys into my hand.

I stared at him. "How hurt are you?"

"I'm fine. But I feel weak. It's best if you drive, no point in taking unnecessary risks."

Peasblossom reclined against Liam's neck and tugged his shirt up like a blanket to ward off the chill. A pulse of energy flowed through our link. She was still trying to stabilize Liam, doing her best to help him until his own healing kicked in.

I got into the driver's side and started the engine, then leaned over to turn on the seat warmer on Liam's side and flick on the truck's heat.

Liam fell asleep on the way to New Moon. Normally, sleep was good for healing, and I'd have said rest was exactly what he needed. But the fact that whatever Scath had done had taken so much out of him terrified me.

By the time we reached New Moon, my nerves were shot. I pulled up to the front doors, then threw the truck into park and left it running while I bolted inside like a maniac.

Sam was working the front desk again, and they shot to attention when I burst through the doors. They dropped something that looked like a pair of ropes tied in an intricate knot to the floor.

"Liam needs help," I blurted out, pointing behind me to the truck.

And just like that, I got to see a pack in action. Sam grabbed a walkie talkie from their belt, barked an order for a medical team to meet them out front. They came to the front door, but didn't abandon their post, instead looking right at me.

"What happened?"

"He was bit by a *sidhe* with unknown abilities." I hesitated. "It was Scath, and it was an accident. He's weak, and he's not healing right. I'm not sure exactly what's wrong, but he wanted to come here."

Sam nodded, and the medical team they'd called brushed past both of us to the truck. I stood helpless as they opened the passenger door and helped Liam out. Their leader let them take most of his weight as they carried him inside. He gave me a half-smile as he passed. Probably to reassure me. It might have worked.

If I didn't notice the blood soaking through his shirt sleeve.

"Stop!" I cried.

The two medics paused, but both of them gave me a less than friendly look. I shook off the uneasy feeling that I deserved it and concentrated on calling my magic. I sent a wave of power over Liam, power that would have been silver if my third eye hadn't been blind. I stepped forward, holding my hands out, trying to concentrate on what it felt like. Maybe...

There. I couldn't see the energy, couldn't identify the spell, but I could feel it sucking at me, drinking the detection magic.

"What's wrong?" Liam's voice was still a low rasp, and his eyelids drooped a little more with each passing minute.

"There's some sort of energy leeching away your strength. I think it's what's keeping you from healing."

I put my hands on his arm, called my magic again. I closed my eyes, centered myself. *"Dispello."*

Liam sucked in a sharp breath, then sagged in the medics' arms. The one on the right shot me a glare that drove me back a step. "What did you do to him?" he demanded, pulling his patient away from me.

Sam took a step closer, muscles tensed. Ready to grab me.

"I banished the magic that was hurting him." I kept my hands up, avoiding sudden movements. "I need to check him again. It's a simple detection spell. Please, Sam?"

After a beat Sam nodded.

This time, when I used my detection spell, the wound was just a wound. Nothing reached out for my magic to drink it down. My shoulders slumped and I nodded. "It's fine. The hindering magic is gone. He should heal now."

Liam took a bracing breath and struggled to stand. "If that's all it was, I can come with you."

The medics went rigid, sharing a look that said they were giving serious consideration to restraining their alpha for his own good.

"No, you need to rest," I told Liam. "I stopped it from getting worse, but you still need to recover from what you already lost. Your pack can help you in ways I can't."

I was afraid he'd argue with me. But he must have felt as bad as he looked, because he just nodded. The medics carried him away quickly, as if worried he'd change his mind.

Sam watched me with a considering look on their face.

"Keep me updated?" I asked.

Again, they just nodded.

I gestured outside at Liam's truck. "Keys are in the ignition."

"I'll send someone out." They turned away without another word.

If Sam realized that leaving Liam's truck here meant I didn't have a ride, they didn't show it. I wasn't in the mood to ask for favors, and I definitely wasn't in the mood to stand around and wait for Sam to start asking difficult questions. I wanted to talk to Scath before I discussed the incident in further detail with anyone else.

I called for a taxi, then waited by the road. Out here under the gloomy grey sky, it was hard to keep unwanted thoughts at bay. Calling Andy's cell phone over and over didn't help either. Not when it kept going straight to voicemail.

I debated trying to get hold of Silence, but quickly dismissed the idea. If Andy's phone was off, there was nothing the technomancer could do.

My legs shook when I got out of the cab and headed into my apartment building. I opened the door and stepped inside. The apartment was starting to smell less like Flint, and more like me.

Overcooked potion, coffee, and drying herbs that would be overcooked potions eventually. It should have made me feel better, but somehow I felt worse.

I didn't want this place to smell like me. This wasn't home.

"He'll be okay, Shade," Peasblossom whispered.

"Andy or Liam?" I asked bitterly.

"Both. We'll figure this out."

I rubbed my hands over my face. "I need to talk to Kylie and Vincent. I want some sort of physical evidence before I talk to Morgan again." I dropped my hands and turned to face Peasblossom where she perched on my shoulder.

"You think she's involved in framing Andy."

I braced my hands on the counter and closed my eyes. "She encouraged him to attack the kelpies. She suggested the auction that was supposed to end with her purchasing a year of service from me. She obviously knows something about Scath that she's not telling me. And last night she deliberately lured Andy to Marilyn's, knowing Deacon was there, knowing he was a witness. It's not a coincidence. But I don't know enough about Morgan to even begin to figure out what motivation she could possibly have for any of it."

"Allow me to help you with that," said a male voice.

I turned and bit back a curse as Flint Valencia stepped out of my bedroom. His hazel eyes glittered with an emotion I couldn't quite place.

"We need to talk about Morgan."

CHAPTER 11

"I THOUGHT YOU WERE IN EUROPE."

Flint tilted his head, his gaze flicking over my hands gripping the kitchen counter behind me. It was only a little after two o' clock, but I'd already had a long day, and the last thing I needed right now was another *sidhe*.

"I was. But after your phone call, it was clear to me that I was needed here."

"I'm fine, actually."

His hazel eyes narrowed, and he circled the kitchen island till he stood close enough that his cologne tickled my nose, its scent soft and understated in the way only the really expensive colognes could be. And underneath it was the scent of Flint himself that called to mind clean bedsheets and bare skin. He was dressed in a black Henley that was open at the neck and blue jeans that clung in all the right places. As usual, he looked like he could have stepped off a movie set.

"You're fine. Really." He nodded toward Peasblossom. "The little one said 'he'll be okay.' And then you asked if she meant Andy or Liam. I'm aware of Andy's situation, but tell me..." He leaned closer. "What's happened to the alpha?"

I opened my mouth and he held up a finger in warning. "Don't insult me by dancing around the question. And don't lie to me."

Anger pulled my spine upright. I shoved myself away from the counter and jerked open the fridge to grab a can of Coke. "There's been another murder. Deacon, one of the witnesses to the first murder—and a possible suspect—is dead. Apparently, Siobhan took him to the houseboat at Marilyn's to keep him out of the way, but someone found him and shot him."

"He was shot." Flint's stress on the last word made his insinuation clear.

I closed the fridge door harder than necessary. "Yes."

Flint rested one denim-clad hip against the kitchen island. "Agent Bradford shot him."

"We don't know who shot him," Peasblossom protested. "We're *investigating*."

Flint didn't take his eyes off me. "You said you think Morgan's involved. Explain."

I cracked open the can of soda, half-expecting it to explode because that was just the way this day was going. "Apparently, when Siobhan brought Deacon to the houseboat, she shared the details of Raichel's murder with Morgan. I don't know if she and Morgan have a pre-existing relationship, or if that's just the sort of thing that passes for small talk. Or if Siobhan didn't talk, someone did, but the point is Morgan definitely knew Andy stood accused of Raichel's murder."

"Raichel being the kelpie that was shot at Something Fishy, go on."

"According to Morgan, after she heard about the murder, she decided she would 'help' Andy. She invited him up to Marilyn's so he could talk to Deacon without Siobhan hovering."

"And she's a fool if she thinks anyone will believe that," Peasblossom muttered.

"You say Deacon was a witness and a possible suspect?"

There was no point in holding back, since our contract gave him the power to demand answers from me on any topic he chose —unless a different contract said otherwise. So I told him everything I'd learned thus far. How Andy had made a habit of going to Something Fishy, how the kelpies taunted him by bringing teenagers around. When I explained about the jockey, Flint's jaw tightened. I wasn't the only one who found that suspicious.

"I was supposed to meet with Kylie and Vincent today," I finished. "But now I'm waiting for them to process a second crime scene."

"And Agent Bradford was at Marilyn's when Deacon was shot."

"Yes. Because of Morgan." I took a gulp of soda, wincing as the carbonation burned my nose. "According to her, Andy had a gun on him when he showed up. She made him leave it in the car while they had a late meal."

"If she was with him, wouldn't that make her his alibi? I assume she's not admitting compliance?"

"She claims that she spilled wine on her dress and excused herself to change, leaving Andy alone."

Flint's expression clearly said what he thought of that coincidence. "And what does Agent Bradford have to say about it?"

I squeezed my can of soda, not meeting Flint's eyes. "I don't know. His phone is off, and no one's seen him since last night."

Flint considered that for a long moment. "I assume Vincent and Kylie confiscated the gun that was found at the scene of the first murder?"

"Yes."

"So Agent Bradford had another gun?"

I frowned. That hadn't struck me as strange before. But now

that he mentioned it... "Are you suggesting an unregistered gun was planted on Andy, or that there was a second unregistered gun at one or both of the murders?"

Flint arched an eyebrow. "No. I'm wondering if you think it's odd that your friend had not one, but two unregistered weapons. If it were anyone else, wouldn't you start to think that many unregistered guns suggest criminal intent?"

"Not necessarily, if the person with the weapons was a human dealing with Otherworld threats," I contended. "Andy's been involved in several of my cases, he needs some form of self-defense. His official weapon is a matter of record, he has to account for every bullet. How's he supposed to explain a bullet that went into a goblin, or a kelpie? He can arm himself under Ohio's concealed handgun license law, but with any registered gun he would still risk facing questions he can't answer from local law enforcement."

"I suppose," Flint said slowly.

"Wait a minute," I said, pointing a finger at him. "Didn't you bug his SUV? When we tracked him to Something Fishy the first time?"

"Ah, yes. Well, it seems our Agent Bradford is a difficult man to fool more than once. He found the tracker—I assume after he had time to wonder how we found him that night. It's proven... challenging, to replace it."

"Blood and bone," I muttered. "The one time your stalker ways might have proven useful."

Flint let that one go. "You still haven't addressed my original question. How does Osbourne fit into all of this?"

I took a longer gulp of soda, considering my words carefully. "Liam came with me to Marilyn's after we heard about the second murder. I asked Marilyn if there was anyone on the property who had experience with firearms." I met Flint's eyes.

"She confirmed there was. Apparently, Raphael has been her guest for a few weeks now."

"Raphael?" Flint's voice dropped, turning the name into a growl.

Oh, yeah, he remembered him. "Yes. What do you know about him?"

"I know he's old. And he and his sister Luna had a special relationship with the Unseelie Queen for a long time."

"Special relationship?" I echoed.

Flint waved a hand. "Raphael's gift is to rev people up, speed their heart, flood them with adrenaline. His sister, Luna, can do the opposite."

"I've felt what they both can do." I tried to shake off the memory of that warm, oily sensation, the feeling of my muscles going liquid, leaving me helpless. "They're quite the pair."

"Yes, they are, and you need to stay away from them. When they work in tandem, their powers are deadly. And that's if you're lucky."

"What's that supposed to mean?"

Flint shook his head. "Tell me about Osbourne first."

Damn. "Liam was there when I tried to question Raphael. During the conversation, his sister joined. One minute she's telling me I need to relax and calm down. The next I'm half-asleep on Liam's shoulder, weak as a kitten, and having trouble stringing two words together, let alone a complete thought."

"I'd imagine the detective had some thoughts about that?" Flint deadpanned.

I wasn't sure if he was referring to me laying on Liam, or my incapacitation, so I didn't comment. "Liam told her to knock it off, and her brother took that as an invitation to 'wake me up,' and—"

"And Raphael flooded the room with adrenaline," Flint guessed. He paused, tilted his head. "So Osbourne lost control?"

"No. He shifted, but he didn't lose control." I hesitated. "But Scath did. She attacked Raphael. Liam got between them, and she bit him instead."

Flint frowned. "And?"

"And, he was hurt, so I took him to New Moon."

"Because of one bite?"

I fought the urge to fidget, hiding my anxiety behind another long drink of soda. "One bite, yes."

"Shade." His voice held a warning now.

I shrugged. "My third eye is still out of commission, so I couldn't examine the wound very closely. But there was some sort of magic in it that was draining Liam's strength. I dispelled it, and he'll be fine."

Flint seemed to mull that over. "Why are you anxious to talk to Morgan when it sounds like Raphael and Luna stirred up the trouble, possibly to derail your line of questioning?"

"I didn't sense Raphael was lying when he said he had no personal reason to kill Deacon, though I suppose someone could have put him up to it. Morgan, on the other hand, has been rallying Andy against the kelpies since they met. And she lured him to Marilyn's the night Deacon was shot. I just don't know what her angle is." I paused. "You said you could help. With Morgan. What did you mean?"

"You told me once that you'd found out Morgan was at Nightcap asking about you and Scath," Flint reminded me. "And then there was the...situation with my mother's artifacts, and the resulting change in Simon. Morgan seems intent on investigating you, and a *sidhe* doesn't haunt oracles for no reason. And since you belong to me now, I thought it would behoove me to find out why Morgan is so interested in you."

It was on the tip of my tongue to remind him that our relationship was temporary, but I held it back. This was one of the few times that relationship would work for me.

"With that in mind, while I was in Europe, I asked around about our friend."

"Spit it out, what did you find out?" Peasblossom prodded.

"Morgan's mother was half-*leannan sidhe*. But her grandmother was a *fury*. Word around the court is both Morgan and her mother favored Morgan's grandmother."

Dread curled at the base of my spine. *Furies* were spirits of vengeance, female creatures born from drops of blood that fell from a murder victim. There were different types, but they all shared a thirst for punishment, a deep desire to seek justice for the wronged. It was said that the *furies* were the ones who pursued oathbreakers in the old days.

"Why is she at Marilyn's?"

"Details about that are very difficult to come by. Though I did find out that Morgan's mother chose to fade just under a century ago."

Morgan's mother had faded. The *sidhe* version of suicide, when they simply gave up on life. Faded away to rejoin the cosmic web. It was a very rare occurrence, one mourned by *sidhe* society as a whole when it happened.

"Morgan took it very hard, and she...burned some bridges socially. Among them, her family's position in the Queen's good graces. Marilyn was the only one who would take her in after that. And, as you know, without the protection of a house, a *sidhe* can find the world very unfriendly indeed."

"What about the rest of her house?" I asked. "Surely they wouldn't have turned their back on her?"

"Well, now that's where it gets interesting. According to my sources, Morgan's house was heavily influenced by her heritage. The Queen herself staffed most of her enforcer positions— guards, bodyguards, torturers, etc.—from Morgan's house. She also employed them to punish oathbreakers in very public, very ostentatious social events. Most of the court was terrified of them."

He rubbed a hand over his jaw, his eyes losing focus. "Then something dreadful happened. Something no one would talk about, not even hint at. Morgan's house disbanded." He shook himself, then his eyes locked onto mine with an intensity that almost made me step back. "Morgan's mother wasn't the only member of that house that chose to fade. At least seven members are dead."

"That's horrible," I said.

Flint arched an eyebrow. "You'll forgive me if I'm somewhat surprised to hear you express such concern. I've always gotten the impression you think a good *sidhe* is a dead *sidhe*."

"Suicide is never something to be glib or happy about. And given how rare it is, there must be a dramatic reason. What could have made her house disband?"

Flint pointed at me. "I told you, no one will talk about it. No. One. Or perhaps what I should say is no one *can* talk about it. I was my most charming self, and I couldn't get anyone to speak a word."

His most charming self. So he'd used magic, along with every dirty trick in the book. Yes, very charming.

I stared into space, letting my mind replay what Morgan had said. "Morgan's always hinting that there's something I need to know, but she can't tell me. I thought maybe she was under some sort of contract, but if it's more than just her, that's not a contract."

"It's a *geas*," Flint said grimly.

"A *geas*?" Peasblossom scoffed. "No one does those anymore. They're too hard to hold. And to lay a *geas* on not just one person, but an entire house? The amount of power that sort of thing takes is just short of a familial curse."

"It's not just one house," I corrected her. "If it is a *geas* that prevents people from speaking about whatever happened to disband Morgan's house, then it's true the amount of power necessary would be...well, I can't think of any one person who could do it."

"Whatever happened was a long time ago," Flint declared. "Centuries. Centuries ago, a *geas* would not have been so uncommon. And there are many who have lost power as the world has become more industrialized, more metal and technology, less faith, fewer offerings."

"All right, then centuries ago, who could have done it?"

Flint rubbed his neck. "Either Queen could have done it. They have not only their own power, but the power of their entire court."

My stomach lurched, threatening to send the Coke back up my throat. "Are you saying...that you think the Unseelie Queen laid a *geas* on her people not to speak of what happened to Morgan's house?" I didn't add that Morgan's reaction to Scath hinted at a connection. And Majesty had been sent by the Unseelie Queen. And Scath certainly seemed defensive of Majesty...

"Where is Scath?" Flint asked.

The hairs on the back of my neck rose, and I couldn't resist the urge to look behind me. It was silly, but I truly expected Scath to appear there. She did it often enough. She'd told me once she could always find me.

That sounded more sinister now.

I shook my head. "Wait a minute. How is any of this related to Andy? How does any of it explain why Morgan keeps interfering with him?"

Flint leaned forward, bracing his arms on the bar. "Think about it. Morgan is part *fury*. Her house was full of punishers, people who sought vengeance or justice. When did Morgan become interested in Agent Bradford?"

"The night of the auction."

"Specifically...?"

I shared a look with Peasblossom. "After he confronted the kelpies."

"So Morgan saw a human man confront a group of monsters preying on a screaming teenage human." Flint tilted his head, considering. "She saw him kill Bradan and walk away. If I remember correctly, Agent Bradford never backed down, never stopped arguing that he was on the right side of the law."

"You think Morgan sees Andy as a kindred spirit?" I asked.

"One of the people I talked to in Europe said that when Morgan's house was in power, they actively pursued new members. Apparently, they had a particular fondness for lawmen whose pursuit of justice didn't always fit within the lines."

I shook my head. "No."

"From what I've gathered, Agent Bradford would have been very appealing to them," Flint pressed.

"No, you're wrong."

Flint retreated to the table beside the couch and picked something up. When he came back, he tossed the file on the kitchen island. The label bore Andy's name, neatly printed in small black letters. The same file he'd tried to give me before.

"I'm not reading that. It's personal, and if Andy wants me to know—"

Flint ignored my protest and flipped open the file. Before I could turn away, he slapped a hand down on the first photograph and slid it to the side, fanning out the stack of photos.

So many photos.

"Oh, Andy..." I took a step closer. I couldn't help it.

The boy in the pictures was young. Some of them showed him as a teenager, which was the only reason I knew the pictures of the four-year-old were him too. The teenager was the missing link. The skinnier, harder Andy. The one with brown eyes that stabbed at me from the photo, his chin thrust out with defiance that dared me to judge him for the mug shot. The accompanying report for assault and battery.

An expression that dared me to pity him for the earlier pictures.

"You need to see this," Flint said gently. "You need to understand."

"I saw the scars on his back." I lowered myself into one of the kitchen chairs as if I were made of glass and would shatter if I sat too quickly. I lifted one of the photos, and choked on a small sob. "I didn't want to press him about it."

Flint didn't comment. He just stood there as I went through the pictures. Read the arrest reports for Andy's biological parents, and finally for Andy himself. I'd seen anger before. I'd seen people overwhelmed by it, people—human and Other—who'd lost themselves to that fury, did things that none of us wanted to believe anyone was capable of, let alone ourselves. It never got easier. Seeing the consequences of that rage.

"He tried to protect his little brother." I held one particularly heart-breaking photograph. Another boy who resembled Andy so closely they might have been twins.

"He tried."

I put the pictures and reports back into the folder, one by one. It gave me time to think, time to tuck my emotions back into a little box in my mind where I could save them to go through later.

"I don't understand what any of this has to do with the case."

"You and I both know that's not true. Agent Bradford stands accused of murder. This," he put one hand flat on the file, "is as relevant as a match at an arson scene."

"No," I ground out. "This," I pressed a finger on top of the file, "is as relevant as a bloodline. This can tell you where he came from, but it can't tell you where he's going. This," I jabbed the file again, narrowly missing poking Flint's hand, "tells me how far he came. How hard he fought—how strong he is. If anything, the fact that he became an FBI agent—one with an *exemplary* record—after all of this, tells me he's not a murderer."

"Well, what it should tell you is that Agent Bradford is an ideal candidate for someone recruiting vigilantes," Flint said, a hint of exasperation in his tone. "This kind of pain and anger doesn't just go away, Shade. You know that. It needs an outlet."

"And it has an outlet," I argued. "Andy is a cop. He channels all of this into finding criminals and making sure they're punished—the right way."

"And when he encounters a particularly monstrous criminal that the law can't or won't punish?" Flint countered. "What then? And let me remind you," he said, seeming to sense my coming objection, "that I'm one of the criminals Agent Bradford tried to punish. He knew I was guilty of murder, he had me in a cell, and then he had to watch me walk right out again. He was there. I saw his face. Just like I saw his face after I bought you at auction. And I can promise you, Shade, it was not lost on him that if he'd succeeded in keeping me in jail, then I never would have been at the auction that night."

I refocused my attention on my soda. I needed time to think about all this. I needed to think without him looming over me, watching me.

Flint settled into a chair beside me. "My understanding is that Morgan's house was so dedicated to finding the best members, the ones most closely aligned with their values, that they recruited from all species. Including humans. And they were known to share power with them."

"Share power?"

Flint nodded. "They had artifacts they would give to those

they felt could handle them. And in some cases, they even went so far as to use artifacts to add new recruits to their own bloodlines. Formally and magically."

"They used artifacts like your mother's."

Flint looked away. "Yes."

I stared at the file. For a long time, I couldn't look away.

"It's not just a physical pain, when your own parent attacks you," Flint said quietly. "It's the rejection. The betrayal. It's watching someone who's supposed to love and protect you above all else in the world turn against you. Seeing them use your suffering to improve their lot in life. That kind of pain is bottomless. It lights a fire inside you. And that flame attracts monsters."

He put a hand on my shoulder. "Andy's father—the one who took him in—did everything he could for him. By all accounts, he was a very good man. But the line between justice and vengeance is so thin. It's easy to step over it and not even notice until it's too late to go back."

I shoved the file away. "It is *never* too late to go back."

"The kelpies were practically designed to be Agent Bradford's nemeses," Flint said. "They prey on the young and the isolated. They're unapologetically sadistic, taking the time to terrify their victims before they kill them. And what's more, he was able to kill one of them to save a child, and he walked away a free man. A man still on the right side of the law—in his eyes. You have to see how easy it would be for Morgan to encourage that. To guide him to a place where there were more kelpies, where they found their victims."

I held up a hand. "So you think Morgan recruited Andy the way she would have recruited someone to her house centuries ago. This was some sort of test, to see if Andy continued pursuing justice against the kelpies."

"I think Morgan misses what she used to be, the way so

many who've lost power do," Flint said. "And more than that, Morgan's house wasn't just about power. They *believed* in what they were doing. They pursued criminals and oathbreakers because that's who they were. That was their purpose."

"But according to the witnesses, Andy didn't shoot Raichel because she was hurting anyone. He thought she was trying to kidnap a kid, but it turned out it wasn't a kid. It was a fifty-year-old jockey. Mickey was very clear, Andy saw he was a grown man, heard him say he was fine, and he killed Raichel anyway. Which does not sound like justice."

"Then maybe you're right, and Siobhan set the whole thing up," Flint suggested. "Morgan could have sent Andy there with the intention of policing the kelpies, but that doesn't mean Siobhan couldn't have noticed his presence and built her plan around it."

I frowned. "So, assuming Siobhan did set Andy up...Morgan, with her desire for proper justice, wouldn't like that."

"She certainly would not."

Peasblossom landed between us. "So if Morgan is mad that Siobhan set Andy up, why set him up again by luring him to the scene of Deacon's murder? And why punish Deacon for Siobhan's scheme?"

"If Deacon helped to frame him, then in Morgan's eyes, he'd deserve to die too," Flint said slowly.

"And now Andy's missing, and if she was the last person he saw..."

"Maybe Morgan is hiding him," Flint finished.

CHAPTER 12

MY PHONE WENT off with a text message alert when we were halfway to Marilyn's. I shifted in the bucket seat of Flint's tiny sports car, digging in the side pocket of my waist pouch to get my phone. My heart pounded, and I said a short prayer that it was Andy, calling me to tell me where he was.

"Is it him?" Flint asked.

My shoulders slumped. "No."

"That's Kylie's number," Peasblossom said, pointing at the screen from her perch on my shoulder.

"Thank the Goddess." I swiped my finger across the screen to answer. "Kylie?"

"We just finished processing the second scene," the half-ghoul said, skipping the pleasantries. "I'm still going to need some time for the full autopsy, but it seems pretty cut and dried so far. I'm sorry we couldn't meet earlier, but if you have time now, we're ready."

Her voice was professional and just this side of curt. The stab of disappointment in my gut forced me to acknowledge that part of me had been holding out hope that she would call to say they'd found exculpatory evidence. Maybe they'd found someone else's fingerprints on the gun, or evidence of a spell to make Andy black out.

"We're packing up, but we'll be back at the lab by—"

"Actually, Kylie," I interrupted, "are you still at Marilyn's?"

"Yes. Why?"

"Could you just stay there? Flint and I are on our way. We need to talk to Morgan again."

"Did Vincent already call you?" Kylie asked, a hint of surprise in her voice.

"No. Why?"

After a pause Kylie said, "Wait till you get here, then I'll explain what we've found."

I nodded, realized she couldn't see me, and answered, "Okay." Now it was my turn to hesitate. "Is it good news?"

"It's not as bad as it could be," Kylie hedged. "You said Flint is coming with you?"

"Yes." I didn't look at Flint. He probably couldn't hear Kylie, but if he got the notion we were talking about him, he could make me tell him anything that was said.

"Where's Liam?"

I leaned back against the headrest and closed my eyes. "That's a long story. We'll talk later?"

"All right. How far out are you?"

"Ten minutes, maybe?"

"I'll find Vincent and we'll get everything ready for you." She hung up without waiting for a response.

I slid my phone back into the pocket of my waist pouch, staring out the windshield at the grey sky. It was three o' clock now, but the sun was so muted by the clouds, it could have been later.

Not as bad as it could be, what did she mean by that? Any evidence that pointed to someone other than Andy would be good.

Flint didn't ask me any questions. I gathered he'd figured out what was going on easily enough from my side of the conversation. And the nice part about him driving was that he didn't need directions. The magic that turned uninvited humans away from Marilyn's property wouldn't do any good against him.

When we reached our destination I spotted Kylie and Vincent's van in front of the main house. Vincent waited in the driver's seat, and he looked over as Flint drove up the driveway. He seemed to steel himself before climbing out, as if bracing to deliver unpleasant information.

Or maybe I was just paranoid.

The familiar sight of his unkempt hair and tweed wardrobe was less comforting than usual as I drew closer. He groped to button his dark brown overcoat that draped him like a blanket over a pale blue dress shirt that probably never saw a hanger. Vincent greeted me with a smile that didn't reach his eyes. "Mother Renard, I'm sorry I was unable to meet with you earlier as we'd planned."

"I certainly understand why the delay was necessary," I said, trying to keep my voice light. "Hopefully it's been productive?"

"Straight to business." Vincent nodded and gestured at the back of the van. "This way."

Kylie leaned against the van's rear bumper. The cold was less of a concern for her, being half-ghoul. Technically, she wasn't dead, but she was closer to it than most. The same necromantic energy that made her crave rotting flesh also helped her thrive in colder climates. She raised white-gloved hands to open the van's rear doors.

"We haven't gone back to the lab yet, so the body is still here," Kylie said, pulling the doors open. She nodded to the stretcher inside and the black body bag that held Deacon. "I've completed my initial review of the body, but the more detailed autopsy will have to wait. Though, as I said, it all seems pretty cut and dried. He was shot in the stomach and bled out."

"No traces of magic, or anything like that?" I asked.

Vincent climbed inside the van. The stretcher took up most of the right side, but there was a narrow desk to the left and a small stool. He sat down and opened a file. "Perhaps we'll start with the first crime scene, then move on?" he suggested. "Everything in order?"

I frowned, but nodded. "Okay."

Vincent cleared his throat. "Right. So, there were ten people present at Something Fishy when the shooting occurred, most of them water spirits or creatures of some kind. Names and species are as follows: Hachim, *redjal el marja;* Maks, *bolotnik;* Valter, *nakki;* Palgun, *kul;* Gesupo, *matabiri;* Mickey V, human; Raichel, kelpie; Andy, human; Rowyn, kelpie; Deacon, satyr-blood. None of the aforementioned have any magical ability that would allow them to change or influence Agent Bradford's memory."

I ran through the list in my head, double-checking. *Redjal el marja*, that was a Moroccan water spirit in charge of protecting the purity of whatever river they'd chosen as their own. Hachim certainly was protective. *Bolotniks* were swamp spirits, no magic, just aquatic creatures that were peaceful enough if you left them alone. *Kuls* were Siberian water spirits who foretold misfortune, oft predicting drownings and terrible fates at sea. And the *matabiri* were spoken of in Papua New Guinea. They, like the *bolotnik*, were harmless swamp spirits who didn't bother anyone who didn't trespass in their homes.

The *nakki* though...

"*Nakkis* are shapeshifters," I spoke up. "Yes?"

"They are," Vincent agreed. "But they have no innate magic."

"Not necessarily. I've heard rumors that some *nakkis* can enchant with their songs. I seem to remember one woman who was lured to her death in a lake following what her friend said was the most beautiful song she'd ever heard."

Vincent shook his head. "It is more likely that the *nakki* from that story was not a pureblood. There are many, many creatures who live near the water and use the power of enchanted song to lure in their victims. Most likely, the creature in your story had ancestry that included *rusalka*, or siren."

He seemed to sense my next question before I could ask it.

"Valter has no such enchantment in his lineage. He is a shapeshifter, but that is all."

"So Andy's memory loss had to be caused by his head injury," I said.

Kylie shifted on her feet. "I examined Andy's head wound when I arrived, before Vincent healed him. Unfortunately, it's not possible to determine the veracity of his memory loss from a physical examination alone. There's just no way to predict how someone's brain will react to a concussion, there's too much variety. But based on what I saw, I can say it's possible he doesn't remember what happened."

Vincent rubbed the patch on his left elbow. "I examined Agent Bradford for any spells that may have contributed to memory loss, including a tox screen for potions, but I didn't find any. Of course, magic can be dispelled, so even if someone had enchanted him, or perhaps even enchanted something outside the bar that would affect him, they could have removed it later. In which case, the only way to be absolutely certain that his memories were manipulated by magic would be to take him to a specialist. And there are those at the Vanguard that could perform such an examination..."

"But?" I prompted.

He cleared his throat again. "But Agent Bradford was not... amenable to that idea."

"He wouldn't let you call someone in to look at his memories?" I asked.

"I don't blame him," Flint said. "I wouldn't want a stranger poking around in my head at the best of times. And it's plain to see why Agent Bradford might have more reason than most not to trust an Otherworlder to that extent."

My brain flashed back to Andy's file. I shoved those mental images away before I could drown in them all over again. Yes, I could understand his trust issues. Why he wouldn't want anyone, especially someone he didn't know, seeing those memories.

"But it could clear him," Peasblossom argued.

Flint looked at me. "Perhaps he has faith you'll prove he's innocent. He might agree to let them look inside his head later, but for now, it would seem he truly believes it won't be necessary."

It was the same impression I'd had earlier when Andy so obviously relaxed when I arrived. Back then, I'd thought the trust was subconscious, an instinct. But if Flint was right, then Andy's faith in me was greater than I'd thought. I threw back my shoulders. I would not let him down.

Vincent continued. "I found no magic artifacts at the scene. The bar is the favorite dive of several Otherworlders, but none of them demonstrated the inclination to collect artifacts or items of power. I tested all food and drink, and none of it showed evidence of being anything other than mundane. Unless you count the bottles of whiskey Valter dug out of a bog that are now strong enough to make a troll cry." He shivered. "I smelled one of them. Not a mistake I'd make twice."

He stopped suddenly, holding up a finger. "Before I forget." He dug into his pocket and produced a small amber orb. "Speaking of artifacts, Evelyn asked me to give this to you."

"Shiny. What is it?" Peasblossom asked.

"A one-use spell. She said it brings clarity of mind. You throw it on the ground in front of someone who's..." He trailed off, trying to think of the right words. "Someone who's not thinking clearly," he finished finally. "The activation word is *Tranquillitas.*"

I took the orb, studying it for a second before putting it into my waist pouch. "I'll thank her when I see her." I peered at the file. "What about prints on the gun?"

Vincent studied the open file with the intensity of someone who wanted to avoid eye contact. "Agent Bradford's prints were the only ones on the weapon. I was able to confirm that the gun found at the scene is definitely the one that shot and killed Raichel."

"Did you confirm with Andy that it was his gun?" I asked.

"Agent Bradford confirmed that the gun was the same make and model as one he'd brought with him to the bar. But he was unable to swear it was his gun exactly because the serial numbers had been filed off. I was able to use a simple spell to repair them." He cleared his throat. "The gun was used in a robbery two years ago. The thief was arrested weeks later, but the gun was never recovered. It would seem it made it to the black market."

"So, not Andy's gun," I clarified.

Kylie stepped forward. "It wasn't his legal FBI-assigned weapon, but he admitted he purchased a gun from a street dealer. And given his prints were on the gun, it does seem likely that the murder weapon is the same gun he purchased."

She didn't come right out and say how bad it looked that Andy had an illegal weapon, but I could see it in the grim set of her mouth.

I fought to keep my voice calm. "He's dealing with creatures of the Otherworld. He's an officer of the law, he can't have bullets being traced back to him when he can't tell the truth about why he fired the gun—and at what."

Kylie didn't look convinced, but I moved on. "What about gunpowder residue?"

"I tested the hands of everyone present, of course," Vincent assured me. "Unfortunately, that test also proved positive only for Agent Bradford. I'm sorry, Shade."

"That doesn't prove he fired the killing shot," I argued, trying to keep the desperation out of my voice. "Spells could clean gunpowder. And couldn't that residue have come from earlier, like being at the firing range, or from someone putting the gun into his hands after the fact?"

"No one there had the magic necessary to clean gunpowder," Vincent said calmly.

"A shapeshifter wouldn't need it," I pointed out. "And anyone could have worn gloves."

"True." Vincent took a deep breath. "But in the end, Agent Bradford is the only one with the means, motive, and opportunity. He is well-acquainted with firearms and his prints are on the gun that killed Raichel. His feelings about kelpies are also well-documented, and multiple testimonies including his own confirm it could have looked to him as though a kelpie was trying to kidnap a young human. And of course, he was armed and outside with Raichel at the time of the shooting."

"We tried, Shade," Kylie said quietly. "I searched the body for any signs that she could have been shot from a different weapon or from farther away. Raichel only had the one entry and exit wound, close range. It was center mass, just like FBI agents are trained to shoot. I looked for some sign that Mickey may have been fighting her off, so Andy might have had good reason to believe he was saving him." She shrugged helplessly. "There was nothing, no defensive wounds."

"And I searched every inch of the scene," Vincent added. "I used every test I could think of to find some trace of magic or a spell that could have been used to make Andy see something that wasn't there, or conceal something—or someone—present. There were no echoes of glamour, no magical artifacts. I checked every bottle of alcohol, every food item. I searched every inch of the parking lot, every inch of the bar. I analyzed every speck of evidence my spell revealed. I found nothing."

My throat constricted, strangling my voice. "Not all magic would leave a trace."

"Of course, you're right. There's always a chance whatever was used left no trail. And as I said before, magic can be dispelled." He tried to sound hopeful, but failed. And I noticed he struggled to look me in the eye.

He thinks Andy did it.

"Tell her about the second crime scene," Kylie prompted.

Vincent brightened. "Yes, the second scene. A little more hope to be had there—though not much," he warned.

"Just tell me what you found, I won't get my hopes up," I lied.

"Yes." Vincent closed the first folder and shoved it away before flipping open the second. "So first of all, the gun that killed Deacon was also unregistered. Also formerly used in a crime only to disappear before trial. So it's reasonable to assume it was purchased on the black market."

"You think Andy purchased not one gun illegally, but two?" I demanded.

"I can't say that for certain, that's beyond what forensics can tell us," Vincent said carefully. "But I can tell you his prints were the only ones on the second gun."

"He—"

"However," Vincent said, raising his voice, "the prints on the trigger were smudged. And I did find something else on the gun. A small speck of leather caught in the trigger."

He pulled out a photograph and held it out to me. It was a tiny fleck of grey leather.

"I think we can assume based on its location that this piece of leather came from a glove. If so, it comes from the outer layer, so no DNA. However, it is very fine leather. Even from this single flake, I can tell you it was expensive. Too much so, I dare say, for someone on a federal salary."

"The killer left the gun at the scene?" Flint asked.

Vincent frowned. Again, he and Kylie shared a look.

"What?" I demanded.

"We found the gun in Andy's SUV." Vincent furrowed his brow. "I'm sorry, I thought Oksana would have told you. She found Agent Bradford's vehicle."

"Where?" I asked. "Did she find Andy?"

"No. His SUV was found abandoned in a parking lot between Detroit Avenue and West 29th Street."

"There was no sign of foul play," Kylie rushed to add. "No blood, nothing like that." She looked at Vincent and jerked her head toward me. "But we did find something encouraging."

"What?" I resisted an unkind urge to strangle Vincent. That would only make him go slower.

"There is evidence that a female *sidhe* was in the SUV," Vincent said.

"Who?" Peasblossom's wings buzzed furiously next to my ear.

Vincent glanced toward the house. "Morgan."

Flint grabbed for my arm, but he was too slow. I'd already hurled myself in the direction of the manor, my magic scalding my hands as I clenched them into fists at my sides.

"Shade, don't do anything stupid," Flint warned.

I raised my fist to pound on the door, but stopped myself. I couldn't go inside like this. Flint was right, I had to calm down. I didn't want to give Luna an excuse to "help me relax" again.

My cell phone chimed with a text message before I could calm down enough to knock without punching a hole through the door. I almost didn't check it. Nothing was more important to me right now than finding Morgan. Finding her and getting the answers I needed. No more hints, no more teasing.

Then my phone started to ring. I didn't even realize Peasblossom had flown down to jab at the buttons until I heard her gasp.

"It's Andy! He has a different phone."

The door swung open. Morgan stood tall as though facing a firing squad. "Mother Renard. I've been expecting you."

I stared at her even as I reached for my phone. I pointed at her, signaling her to wait as I raised the phone to my ear.

"Hello?" I asked, not saying Andy's name. No reason to let Morgan know.

"Shade. I need your help. I'm going to text you an address. Can you meet me?"

I stepped back, still staring at Morgan. Andy needed help. The second call like this in less than twenty-four hours. A thousand questions vied for dominance to be the first on my lips. I couldn't ask them, not yet. Not until I was away from this woman. "I'm on my way."

Andy ended the call. His abrupt disconnect left me with even more questions. Was he alone? In trouble? Hurt?

"Who was that?" Morgan asked.

I shook my head, pointed at her again. "I'll be back."

The fury-blooded fey studied me, reading in my expression everything I hadn't said. Finally, she nodded. "I'll be waiting."

CHAPTER 13

"I DON'T TRUST THAT TIMING," Flint muttered. "What are the chances that Bradford would call right as we were about to corner Morgan?"

"Just say what you want to say," I said, not hiding my irritation. I stuffed the file folder Vincent had given me into my pouch. I'd look at the rest of it later, when I could concentrate.

"You know what I'm saying."

I did. He was suggesting that Morgan and Andy were in contact. I wrapped my fingers around the door handle and stared out the window at the derelict neighborhood Andy was apparently hiding in.

The housing collapse of 2008-2009 wasn't over for everyone. In some Cleveland neighborhoods, a combination of poor tax collection and a failure of banks to either transfer the house title into their name after an eviction, or inform the evicted that their name was still on the title led to the creation of what people referred to as "zombie homes." Abandoned properties falling beyond disrepair, into that sad place where a building had nothing left in its future but to wait around for someone to care enough to demolish it. I'd seen properties like this before.

I'd never expected to find Andy in one.

"You think they're working together." I turned in my seat to glare at Flint. "To what end?"

"You know—"

"I'm not talking about your theory that Morgan is molding Andy into a crusader against the kelpies," I interrupted. "I mean to what end do you think Andy called me for help now? Why ask to meet me here, now, after I was about to talk to Morgan?"

Flint looked like he wanted to say something, but held back.

"You know he wouldn't hurt me," I pressed. "This isn't a trap. You think he did it to keep me away from Morgan?"

"I think we all choose our friends. And as much as you might want to, you cannot choose Agent Bradford's for him. No matter how much you hate his choices."

I narrowed my eyes. "Andy is too smart to trust Morgan."

Flint was saved from having to respond when we arrived at our destination, and he pulled into the broken driveway.

I got out of the car and stood on the sidewalk, staring up at a house that had once been home to a family with small kids. At least if the abandoned, rusted tricycle half-buried in the yard was anything to go by. Now the muted sunlight revealed ivy taking over the pale blue siding, swallowing the columns of the wraparound front porch, and erupting from loose roof shingles. The steps leading up the front porch were barely more than large splinters, and crossing the porch to the front door would require a leap of faith. Or wings.

"You go inside first, I'll be right behind you," Flint said.

"Coward," Peasblossom muttered. She flew ahead of me, a soft pink light emanating from her skin. "You should let me go in and bring him out. Safer that way."

"No." I lurched forward and began picking a path to the door. "I want to see him."

"You'll see him when I bring him out."

"I'm going in, and we'll leave together."

"Then I'll just stand by and wait until someone needs stabilized," Peasblossom huffed. "Shouldn't take too long." She hesitated, then asked, "Any word from Scath?"

I didn't take my eyes off the porch, gingerly stepping over any board that looked too rotted to hold the weight of a healthy witch. "I tried to call her cell phone, but there was no answer. I sent her a text to let her know what's happening. Your guess is as good as mine whether she'll show up."

"She'll be here," Peasblossom said fiercely. "You told her you found Andy. She'll be here. She knows how important he is to you."

"But does she care?"

Peasblossom's wings stuttered to a stop and she dipped in the air before catching herself. "You don't think she cares?"

The piece of wood I was on groaned under my foot, and I quickly sidestepped. "She bolted from Marilyn's without waiting to make sure Raphael and Luna were done making trouble. Why? She wasn't injured. Where did she go?" I shook my head. "She had to have known what she did to Liam. She had to know I'd have questions, that I'd need information to help him. But she left anyway. Without a word."

I grasped the handle to the front door and turned it. The sunlight wasn't bright enough to pierce the shadows inside the house, especially with the windows overgrown with sagging ivy. I held up a hand. *"Lumen."*

Three balls of yellow light floated before me, letting me see the path forward. To my right, two orbs of green light stared at me from the shadows.

I jumped, my heart spasming in my chest so hard I clapped a hand over it. I landed on a spot to the left of the door, and the wood gave a muffled crack under my feet. I let out a squeak of dismay, trying to call my magic even as I threw my body to the side to avoid falling through the floor.

My hands touched a large, furred body. Scath. I grappled to hold onto her as she leaned away from the weak boards, saving me from seeing what the basement looked like.

Pulse pounding, I sat on the floor to regain my breath, leaning against her for support. I wanted to say something, but I didn't know where to start. Where the bloody hell were you? Thanks?

"Andy's here somewhere," I said instead.

Scath waited silently for me to regain my footing, making sure I was on solid ground before she swiveled her head toward the front door.

"Your feline friend is back," Flint observed from the doorway.

"Andy?" I called out. "Are you here?"

Scath paced ahead of me, searching out secure places for me to put my feet. Not only was the floor a series of potential land mines, there was debris everywhere. Newspapers and plastic bags, random tools and empty cans. I followed Scath, ears straining for any response from Andy.

"Don't fly too far ahead of me," I warned Peasblossom. "The ceiling is falling apart too, I don't want you getting crushed by a piece of plaster."

A low growl rumbled from Scath's throat, cutting off Peasblossom's indignant reply. I looked down at her and found her staring up at the ceiling. "What is it?"

Scath raised her head. Inside the house, the main floor was gutted. There were missing sections of plaster in the ceiling, but it was difficult to tell if any of them had gone clear through to the next floor because it was so dark. I squinted, but didn't see what had caught Scath's attention. I raised my hand, sending the yellow balls of light from my spell higher.

Flint picked his way over the floor to stand beside me. "What's going on?"

The gunshot made me jump.

Beside me, Flint grunted and fell backward. The wood gave way beneath him with a sickening crack. There was no giant hole that opened up that he fell through. Rather, it happened piece by piece, with one section being punched out by his arm as he tried to catch himself, then that rupture weakening the boards beneath him so they folded when his body made contact. It happened in seconds. He was there, then he was gone.

"Andy?!" Peasblossom cried.

I jerked my head up to find her hovering by the ceiling, pointing to a hole I hadn't seen before.

Scath bolted, heading for the dilapidated stairs and flowing up without a sound as if she were made of shadow.

"Peasblossom, check on Flint!" I shouted.

The pixie dropped from the ceiling like a falling star, winking through the hole in the floor to find the injured *leannan sidhe.*

Without Scath's preternatural grace, I couldn't run to the stairs like I wanted to. I had to weave my way over the debris, feel out for weak spots that might have been made even weaker by the new Flint-sized hole.

Another gunshot rang out.

"*Blood and bone,*" I snarled. I braced myself and broke into a run, trying to stay close to the edge of the stairs where the floor should be more secure, holding on to the railing in case I fell. I said a prayer to the Goddess to guide me, focused the orbs of light I'd conjured on the floor so they lit my path like theater running lights.

I reached the second landing with my heart pounding, my breaths ragged. The wall to my right was mostly solid with a few patches missing from the rose-colored wallpaper. To my left, a railing protected the stairs, but the walls that had once formed what looked like two bedrooms were mostly gone. The second floor was open, with the exception of a bedroom at the end of the hall on the left whose open door blocked the view beyond it.

"Hello, Mother Renard."

Raphael's voice flowed over my senses like heated whiskey. My pulse throbbed, making me swallow hard as my body remembered that voice, remembered what I'd felt the last time I heard it. I didn't know if Raphael was flexing his power again, or if the memory was still so fresh in my mind that he could awaken it with just his voice.

There was no time to fight it, so I didn't. Instead, I used that rush of adrenaline, poured it into my magic. I hurled my arm outward, sending more lights skittering into the shadows to illuminate the *sidhe's* face. His grey eyes glittered with malice and he held an upraised gun, but that wasn't what threatened to stop my heart in my chest.

Andy lay on the ground at Raphael's feet. His suit jacket was gone, his white shirt so bright it practically glowed in the dark. I took an unsteady step forward, straining to see some sign of movement, some rise and fall of his chest.

"He's alive, don't look so worried. I took the liberty of disarming Agent Bradford after he shot your master. You're welcome."

Scath snarled and drew nearer. I hadn't even noticed her when I came up the stairs, too distracted by Raphael. But now I could see she was limping. Her front left leg wouldn't hold her weight, and I soon saw the glistening patch of blood on her shoulder.

"You shot her?"

"I just told you Agent Bradford shot your master. Why would you assume I shot your pet and not him?"

I couldn't look away from Andy, but I didn't need to read

Raphael's face to know he was mocking me. "Why did you shoot her?"

The *leannan sidhe* shrugged. "She arrived rather suddenly. I'd only just disarmed your FBI agent, and I was...tense. Anyway, you can hardly blame me for being proactive in my defense after what she did to your werewolf lover."

I was getting really tired of the comments on my sex life, but I wasn't going to let him distract me from the matter at hand. "Why are you here?" I asked bluntly.

"I'm here to catch a murderer." Raphael nudged Andy with the toe of his boot. "And I did."

"Andy isn't a murderer." I closed my hand into a fist, feeling the pulse of the ring on my finger as defensive magic crawled over my skin. It wouldn't stop a bullet, but it would help against most other attacks.

"He killed Raichel and Deacon, that's apparent to at least one of us. And now he's killed Flint. Your master, whatever his lesser qualities, was still one of my kin. I had every right to intervene."

"Did Andy shoot Flint?" I asked, challenging him with my glare. "Or did you?"

"Andy shot Flint," Raphael said. "On my oath."

"And was he under your influence when he did it?" I demanded. "Did you pump him full of adrenaline the way you did to us back at Marilyn's?"

"No." Raphael snorted. "Come now, Shade, you're being deliberately dense, aren't you? Think about it. Why do you think Morgan invited Agent Bradford to see her?"

I stilled. I knew why *I* thought she'd done it. But suddenly I was very interested to know what he thought. "What are you suggesting?"

Raphael narrowed his eyes. "Either you're being coy, or you aren't as clever as everyone seems to think you are."

"Either you're being coy, or you have no idea why Morgan invited Andy to see her," I shot back.

Raphael grinned, a sudden baring of too-white teeth. "Touché. Tell me, what do you know about Morgan?"

"I know that she's part *fury*. I know she used to belong to a house of punishers." I stared into Raphael's eyes, searching for some hint to his thoughts. "I'll admit, I wondered if her interest in Andy was a holdout from her days at court. Maybe she's feeling the urge to recruit, the way her house did before it fell."

Raphael shifted his weight. "You know more than I thought, and less than you should."

"Enlighten me." I took a careful step closer to Andy.

"Don't come any closer, or I'll kill him here and now," Raphael said coldly. "We aren't done talking."

Anger surged through me, sharpening my voice. I faced the *leannan sidhe* with clenched fists, letting him see just how far he was pushing me by refusing to let me near my partner. "What do you want, Raphael?"

"What do I want?"

"You'd obviously prefer to talk about Morgan and what sway she has over Andy, but right now, none of that matters to me."

"Liar."

I pinned him with my gaze. "Right now, I care about getting Andy out of this house. Making sure he's not hurt. That is my goal. My only goal for the moment." I lowered my voice. "And the only thing standing between me and that goal...is you."

Raphael's eyes brightened, and his chest rose and fell a little faster with each breath. "Oh. Are you...threatening me?"

"I'm helping you to understand the precarious situation you've found yourself in," I said. "You're outnumbered. And if you're half as clever as you clearly think you are, then you'll realize you have nothing to gain by dangling this threat to Andy's life in front of me."

"What would you do if I killed him?" Raphael raised the gun, idly pointing it at Andy's chest. "If I shot him, right now. What would you do?"

"You know what I would do."

Raphael shook his head, slowly. "Tell me. Or I'll find out for myself."

Scath stood beside me. Her leg continued to bleed, as it would until I could bandage it. Andy's bullets would have a high enough iron content that she wouldn't heal as fast as she should. She could still fight, albeit slower, but I wasn't sure even she could make it to Andy before Raphael shot him.

"I would do my very best to make sure you never left this house alive," I whispered.

"How would you kill me?" Raphael pressed.

He was staring at me again. Staring at me the way he had back at Marilyn's, as if he were studying me, weighing an option I hadn't been aware of yet. He had the look of a man trying to figure something out. Someone who'd been presented with a new possibility, and couldn't decide if it scared or excited him.

I lifted my chin. "Slowly."

A grin spread over Raphael's face, wide enough that I saw one tooth on the left side of his mouth was crooked. His eyes glowed faintly in the light from my spell, bright silver like liquid mercury.

"I'll make you a deal, Shade," he said, his voice hypnotic. "I'll let you take your partner out of here. Heal him, put him to bed. I'll even join your futile quest to prove his innocence, offer whatever assistance, whatever information I can." He leaned forward. "If you'll agree to a new contract."

My temper reached a low boil, my magic simmering hot and ready inside me. "What contract?"

"Flint is dead. You're free of him. Which makes you free to engage in other partnerships. Sign a contract with me. One year, same as Flint. The contract I should have had in April. Do it, and I'll let your friend go. You'll have your chance to save him." He shrugged. "I'll even allow for a delayed start to our new contract. It won't go into effect until Andy begins serving his own sentence."

His gun remained steady, and there was no doubt in my mind that Raphael would do it. He'd kill Andy here and now. Without a second thought.

"Why do you want that contract so badly?" I stalled, trying to give my brain time to think, give Scath time to heal, give Peasblossom time to return to me. If Andy's shot had been true, the bullet would have killed Flint instantly, just as if he were human. Peasblossom would go invisible, come back to me. She could be here now...

Raphael tilted the gun down, pulled the trigger.

The shot was so much louder than I expected. Not just because we were indoors and only an idiot fired a gun indoors, but because I saw Andy's body jerk. A groan escaped his lips and he shifted, his leg curling toward his body. He hissed out a breath. Then another.

Raphael had shot him in the thigh.

"Your word," Raphael said, his voice low but still completely calm. "Your word you'll sign my contract. Same one you had with Flint, but with my name in place of that oversexed magic whore."

Another shot rang out. Raphael bellowed in pain, releasing the gun as he clutched his hand against his chest, leaving a smear of blood. His mouth twisted into a snarl as his gaze locked onto something over my shoulder.

"I'm afraid Shade's contract is not quite over yet," Flint said from behind me.

CHAPTER 14

FLINT'S VOICE had never been a pleasant sound for me, but in this moment, I could almost appreciate it. If only for the shock that fell over Raphael's face when his rival came up the stairs behind me. Flint looked suspiciously healthy for a *sidhe* who'd just been shot in the chest. Shot in the heart, if the hole in his shirt was any indication.

"You're wearing a bulletproof vest?" I sputtered. "That's what you were doing at the car after I left."

"I've invested in all sorts of new toys since we began our relationship," Flint murmured. "Though I'll admit, I thought it would be a little longer before your FBI friend got up the guts to shoot me. But staring down the barrel of one's own death does put things in perspective." He stepped closer to me, but didn't take his eyes off Raphael. "I knew Andy cared about you. Even when you didn't believe it yourself. Of course he'd try to kill me with the time he has left."

Raphael reached down and grabbed Andy by the back of his shirt. The thin white fabric ripped, but enough of the material held for him to haul Andy against his chest, using him as a human shield. Andy dragged in a sharp breath before shouting in pain as he tried to get his feet under him and put weight on his injured leg.

"Stop it!" I shouted. "Let him *go!*"

"He'll feel better if I don't." Raphael tucked his face close to Andy's ear, keeping Flint from getting a clear shot at his head. "Give him a second and he'll feel *much* better."

Andy's head lolled forward, and his chest rapidly rose and fell with heaving breaths as Raphael's influence spilled over him. I could see him gritting his teeth, sweat forming at his temples. My own body responded in sympathy, my pulse skipping a beat. I remembered that overwhelming sense of power. The feeling of invulnerability, the need to *act*, pain and injury be damned.

I was too caught up in the memory to notice at first that the bleeding in Andy's leg was slowing down. Or that he was resting his full weight on it without any apparent pain. I didn't see how tight his torn shirt was becoming against his skin, more than could be explained by Raphael's rough handling. It wasn't until Andy straightened, his head towering above Raphael's that I realized he'd changed.

Realized he was much *bigger.*

Flint cursed behind me.

My mouth fell open. Andy was seven feet tall if he was an inch. His body swelled outward, giving him the thick arms, barrel chest, and massive thighs that even five years of steroids and daily trips to the gym with a professional Hollywood trainer couldn't have offered. The scars on his arms, the ones that had left his skin looking like melted wax, were no longer smooth and pale. They *bled.* Rivulets of crimson washed down his skin as if whatever power had possessed him was making his body relive every injury he'd ever received. The tatters of his shirt hung from his body, the blood making them look more like torn strips of flesh. When Andy opened his eyes, they were no longer a soft brown.

They were black.

Solid black.

"What did you do to him?"

I meant to scream the words, but they came out a whisper. I was choking on my own magic, my anger so hot, so heavy in my head that I thought a sharp exhale from my lips might be enough to slay Raphael. I raised a hand, ready to blast the *leannan sidhe* out of the house. Out of my city.

"Raphael didn't do that," Flint said grimly.

Someone knocked me to the ground.

The world tilted madly, my head spinning with vertigo as my attacker carried me to the floor. My elbows struck the hardwood with enough force to jolt my entire body, rattling my bones. Cold hands clutched my face, long fingers curling around my jaw, seizing me with such ferocity that I couldn't have formed the words for another question—let alone a spell—if I tried. I took a short, surprised breath and was greeted by the scent of leather and metal.

Luna.

I gritted my teeth, raised my hands to pry her grip from my face. The collision had knocked the wind out of me, and I was too slow. Luna's power hit me like a cotton-wrapped sledgehammer. Relaxation forced its way into my muscles, stealing the tension and leaving me a heap of boneless flesh on the ground. My head fell to the side, giving me a view of Andy as the transformation finished, left him sucking in ragged breaths, his dark eyes scanning the room with the shrewd stare of a hungry predator.

A flash of pink near his hip caught my eye.

Peasblossom.

An idea struck me like a bolt of lightning. Maybe it was all

Peasblossom. Maybe she'd healed Andy, then used her glamour to change his appearance. She was bluffing, trying to make Raphael back off.

Smart pixie.

Another gunshot went off, too close for comfort. The weight on top of me tumbled to the side, a booted heel kicking me hard in the thigh as Luna fought to regain her legs underneath her. She giggled—*giggled*—and I heard metal striking metal. I couldn't turn my head to look, could barely focus my eyes. Flint grunted, followed by another sound of metal on metal.

Raphael's voice drew my attention away from Flint and Luna fighting behind me. The *leannan sidhe* was studying Andy with rapt attention, his eyes flicking from his bloody back and arms to the crown of his head, now so much closer to the ceiling.

"Well, aren't you full of surprises." Malicious delight dripped from every word, like a child who'd stolen someone else's Christmas present and opened it to find the very toy he'd wanted all along. "What are you, my boy?"

A black shadow streaked across the room and bowled into Raphael, driving him into the opposite wall. I couldn't follow the movement, but I heard the unmistakable snarl of a large cat, the sound of claws digging ragged furrows in the wood floor.

"Don't bite him!" Peasblossom shrieked.

Another snarl, followed by a hiss from Raphael. I tried to get an arm under myself, to rise and see what was happening. But my body still wouldn't listen, my muscles too warm, too liquid to get the necessary tension. I let out a moan of frustration, loud enough that I almost missed the tiny mewl of a kitten.

Peasblossom's next cry was "Look out!"

Scath's body hurtled through my line of sight. She crashed into Andy, hard, and then both of them were flying into the empty room on the left as if a hurricane had sprung out of nowhere and tossed them like so much debris. The crack of splintering wood and patter of crumbling plaster followed soon after.

"Shade, are you okay?" Peasblossom landed on my waist pouch and tugged at the zipper, fighting to get it open.

"Can't move," I whispered, my voice thick and sluggish.

"Hang on," she grunted. "I'll be right back. Bizbee! I need a sleeping potion!"

"Sleeping...potion?" I furrowed my brow in confusion, that one flex of muscle giving me hope that Luna's power was wearing off.

Peasblossom clutched the tiny bottle to her chest, then flew off in the direction of the room where Andy and Scath had disappeared.

"We aren't finished yet."

Raphael's taunt snared my attention and I watched with growing alarm as he prowled past me toward the room Andy and Scath got tossed into. "Agent Bradford, are you ready for another push?"

He didn't wait for a response. This time, his power wasn't focused only on one person. It flooded the second floor, sinking into my body like branding irons. My muscles stiffened, and *finally* I could push off the ground, force myself to my feet. I spared a quick glance behind me to check on Flint facing off with Luna.

His gun was gone, and a short blade lay a few feet away—Luna's, I guessed. Flint's shirt was torn, and his eyes had brightened from hazel to the polished tiger's eye that meant his power was active. Luna looked invigorated, but it was hard to tell if she was turned on by Flint's magic, or if she was just enjoying the fight. Blood dripped from the corner of her mouth, and she reached out her tongue to lick it away.

A loud roar from inside the other room sent my heart into overdrive, increasing the waves of adrenaline from Raphael's power until I was sure my heart would explode. I clutched my chest, fighting for calm, the control to take an even breath. Raphael still stood in the hall, his arms out wide as if making himself a target.

Scath didn't disappoint.

For the second time in less than a minute, Scath heaved herself straight at him, teeth bared, green eyes blazing. Her paws struck first, her injured leg scrabbling weakly against his chest while the other dug curved black claws into the muscle of his shoulder. Raphael hissed, but didn't lower his arms or try to defend himself.

"Scath, no!" Peasblossom shot into view.

I raised a hand, pointing at Raphael, a spell already spiraling up inside me.

From somewhere to my right, hidden in the shadows, Majesty meowed.

The floor exploded beneath Scath. The claws of her good legs scrabbled for purchase, tried to hold onto Raphael, the floor, anything to stop her downward fall. But the upward shower of splinters ripped through her hide, embedding themselves in fur and flesh, and she twisted in pain. She crashed down to the next floor below with a high-pitched screech of rage. Raphael plummeted with her, shouting in surprise as her claws in his chest tore his wounds wider, sending a rush of blood down his body.

Peasblossom sailed through the hole after them, the sleeping potion still clutched to her chest.

I didn't have time to worry about the chaos that had just vanished. I could still see Andy in my mind's eye, see his injured leg where Raphael had shot him.

"Andy!" I cried out. "Andy, where—"

Another roar. A male voice, so deep it made my body vibrate.

A huge hand gripped the edge of the doorway, and Andy dragged himself into the hall.

For a second, I couldn't breathe. Peasblossom was with Scath, down on the first floor. What I saw now, what Andy looked like now, had nothing to do with her pixie glamour or other magics. Or my magic.

Andy was still enormous. Still a hulking beast of a man. His clothes were little more than decoration at this point, bloody rags hanging haphazardly on a body several sizes too large. The veins in his neck bulged with the heavy beat of his heart, and the corner of his mouth was torn, revealing too much of his too long teeth. One eye was sunken in, bruised and bloodied, enough that I half feared to see an empty socket staring back at me. Black eyes fixed on me, but only for a heartbeat. Then they flicked up, locked onto someone behind me.

Flint.

"Andy, stop."

He didn't listen. I had the sickening sense of seeing my friend move in slow motion. I had all the time in the world to see his muscles bunch, see him take that first step toward Flint with murder in his black eyes.

My magic was so close to the surface, so ready, that I barely had to think the spell I needed and it was there. I gathered energy in my mouth, spit it out as Andy charged for the *leannan sidhe* behind me. Panic made me faster, and my spell flew at Andy, striking his legs and torso. Blue, sticky strands exploded like a net, tangling around him so he stumbled into a heap on the floor. He screamed, a sound of such rage that it raised the hairs on the back of my neck.

Suddenly Raphael was cresting the top of the stairs, halting as he took in the scene before him.

Flint held Luna with her back to him, her hair wrapped

around one of his fists, his other hand holding her arm twisted behind her back. Blood coated half her face from a cut above her eye, and though she was still grinning, a wheeze in her breath said she might have internal bleeding as well. He dragged her farther away from her twin, so we all stood in a triangle formation with Andy just behind me, closer to the far wall than the stairs.

My bulked up partner fought to get to his feet again, but the sticky blue cords lashed too tight around his ankles and he fell, striking the ground with his shoulder. He grunted and immediately struggled to get back to one knee.

"How long will that spell hold him?" Flint demanded, grunting as Luna thrashed in his grip.

I didn't know. I didn't know, and I didn't care, not right now, not yet. A thought was trying to make itself known, screaming at me from the corner of my mind. Raphael wasn't moving. He wasn't trying to attack me, or Andy, or Flint. He wasn't even trying to help his sister. He just stood there, and I could feel him still filling the air with his magic, pumping everyone up with a fight or flight instinct—emphasis on the former. *Why?* I wanted to shout at him. What could he possibly expect to gain?

I fought to make all the pieces fit, but I couldn't. I couldn't *think*, not with his damn power coursing through me like this. I could throw a spell, try to take him out. But he was fast. And he was far enough away—still close enough to the stairs to escape —that I might not hit him in time. He stared at my mouth, body tense. Ready to run if he saw me start a spell.

Andy made a satisfied sound deep in his throat. I realized another of the sticky bands had snapped, and he had one arm free. He looked at Flint, and there was nothing left of my friend in those black eyes. Nothing I recognized.

I couldn't help him as long as Raphael was keeping his blood heated, keeping him on that razor's edge where fury and violence felt normal, and the idea of calming down was no more than a pipe dream.

"Bring her to me," I ordered Flint, gesturing at Luna. "Bring her to me, and hold her still."

Flint didn't question me. He kept his eyes on Andy, but he dragged the struggling *sidhe* closer.

"A hostage, Shade?" Raphael chastised. "Really?"

I ignored him. Luna lifted her chin, gave me a smile that showed teeth stained pink with her own blood. I smiled back.

And seized her throat with both hands.

Luna's eyes flew wide. Her pulse throbbed against my grip, caught like a wild animal in a steel trap. Her free hand stopped groping behind her for a grip on Flint that would make him release her and started to claw at my hands.

Too bad there was nothing she could do with one hand that would make me let go. Flint wrenched the arm behind her back up higher. She would have cried out in pain. She tried to. But she couldn't draw air past my grip on her throat.

My magic writhed inside me, howling to be released. The rush of blood in my ears was almost enough to block out the sounds of Andy snarling and writhing on the floor, punctuated by the snap of more sticky blue restraints. I tightened my hands around Luna, staring into her eyes.

The spell opened up. I wasn't looking at Luna's eyes anymore, I was looking *inside* her. Feeling my power flow into her body, into her blood. My ears popped, and then the magic pushed further, reaching past Luna, tracing that invisible cord that connected one blood relative to the other.

I felt Raphael's throat under my fingertips.

I didn't need to hear his choke of surprise from the top of the stairs to know it was working. It was real as if I'd crossed the room on the material plane and grabbed him with both hands.

Blood is a tie that binds.

I squeezed harder.

Luna's face flushed red. Flint grunted as he fought to hold onto her, keep her from twisting out of my grasp. I held her until her nails stopped scrabbling at me, until her eyes drifted closed. She went limp, sagging in Flint's arms.

I didn't let go.

A tiny part of my brain registered Flint's expression as he watched me cling to the unconscious *leannan sidhe*. I beheld his satisfaction, his quiet triumph.

Another band of blue broke with an ominous twang, and Andy braced both legs under him. Only his left arm was still pinned now.

I shoved that thought out of my mind, holding on to Luna's throat. Raphael choked, tried to speak, maybe a threat, or a plea. I met his silvery eyes. His face had turned dark red, and his body swayed with the lack of oxygen. He gawked at me as if he'd seen a ghost. Then his eyes fluttered closed. His body pitched forward, and he fell down the stairs in a series of sharp bangs, dull thuds, and splintering wood.

I held on a few seconds longer, just to make sure. Then I released Luna.

Forcing someone unconscious isn't like the movies. They don't go down for the count only to wake up an hour later, disoriented, but fine. In real life, you have a choice between a few seconds, maybe a minute of unconsciousness—or death. I couldn't kill either of them this way, *sidhe* were hardier than that. But it had bought me the time I needed. I grabbed Luna's arm and pulled. Flint let me take her, watching with unabashed interest as I dragged her to the stairs and shoved her down. She tumbled tail over tea kettle to land on her brother, and I followed as quickly as I could.

"Bizbee, two sets of iron cuffs please."

The grig's antennae popped out of the pouch, but not his

face. There was the clink of metal then two pairs of handcuffs flew out of the pouch.

I cuffed the twins together, hands behind their backs. The iron would leave burns on their skin, but I wasn't inclined to feel any sympathy. The iron would keep them from rolling their power over the room, and it would make it much harder to run away.

I made my way back up the stairs, where Flint waited with a smile on his lips. I gestured toward the fallen twins. "Watch them."

"With pleasure." Flint retrieved his gun from the floor before sauntering downstairs. He gazed down at the siblings as if mentally planning what order he'd shoot them in.

I didn't care. For now, I had bigger problems.

Or rather, one *much bigger* problem.

"Andy," I whispered.

He didn't turn my way. Or rather, he didn't cease watching the stairway where Flint had disappeared.

"Talk to me." I knelt on the floor beside him, reaching into the pocket of my trench coat to pull out the orb Evelyn had given me. Andy's eyes darted to the small amber-hued bubble, and finally he stopped squirming to free his arm. I held my breath.

"Tranquillitas."

I threw the bauble to the floor between us.

My third eye couldn't show the energy of the spell, but I could see it working just watching Andy. He went still, almost seeming to choke on his next mighty prolonged inhalation that swelled his chest so he seemed to be getting even bigger. Then the breath left him in a loud whoosh.

When he exhaled, it was as if whatever magic had wrought his transformation went with it. His black eyes paled to brown irises and red-streaked white scleras. The muscles that had made him look so inflated, so unreal, coiled back into the gym-toned body of a middle-aged FBI agent who knew physical fitness could save his life.

I reached out slowly toward the wound in his thigh, calling the orbs of yellow light from before to hover over the bullet hole. Blood seeped from the entry point, slow and sluggish as if he'd already started to heal. He made no move to stop me, so I laid my fingers over his skin where the tear in his pants had left it bare.

Healing had been one of the few magics Mother Hazel considered worth teaching early in my education—after I'd learned how to treat injuries and sickness without it. That knowledge made my healing spells stronger than those of most practitioners—outside those who dedicated themselves to the art. I felt for the bullet and used my magic to seal the flesh behind it, pushing it out as I repaired broken tissue, muscle, and blood vessels.

It felt like a small eternity, and I felt exhausted by the time I was done. Unfortunately, even though neither the bullet wound nor the phantom injuries on his arms and back bled anymore, he'd still lost a lot of blood. Andy's shirt was still red, still wet. It clung to him, filled the air with the scent of copper. I gagged at the smell and the realization that at one time, Andy had suffered each of those injuries for real. This was the second time he'd bled from those wounds. And it never should have happened the first time.

I flung a hand at him, cleaning his clothes and mending them with a flex of magic that didn't lessen the buzz under my skin in the slightest. It wasn't my imagination that Andy's breathing evened out as his white shirt and dark trousers returned to their pristine state.

"Shade."

His voice sounded broken. As if that one word had escaped

by accident. I reached for his hand, giving him time to pull away if he wanted to. He let me hold his hand in mine, and I felt the gummy remnants of my spell clinging to his fingers.

"I'm here. Talk to me."

Andy closed his eyes. His fingers curled around mine, as if afraid I'd let go. "Do you remember Lorelei?"

I stared at him. Of course I remembered her. It was really hard to forget a demon at the best of times. It was even harder when they nearly got you killed. "Yes."

Andy kept his eyes closed. "When you came to get me that night on Siobhan's boat after I was shot, Lorelei was with you. There was a fight, and Lorelei almost died."

"Yes," I said, more slowly this time. I didn't want to rush him, not when he clearly had something important to tell me. Not when it was so hard for him. "I remember. You saved her."

"I gave her CPR."

"Right." I frowned. There was some connection eluding me, swimming in my adrenaline-infused brain.

"I think..." He stopped, took a deep breath before opening his eyes. "I think that's when she did it. That's when it started."

"That's when she did wh—"

I broke off.

Andy met my eyes, and with awful clarity, I knew.

"Demonic influence. What did you call it?" he asked quietly.

It took me two tries to get the word out. "Corruption."

CHAPTER 15

MY HEAD FELT TOO LIGHT, as if it would float away and leave me there. Staring at Andy, I realized just how blind I'd been. In a mad rush of images, my mind played back his behavior changes of the past months, the quick temper, the uncharacteristic mood swings and outbursts.

"Shade?"

Andy's voice sounded too far away, considering he was kneeling beside me. He took both my hands, held them until I managed to look at him. My vision blurred with tears.

"You didn't tell me," I said dully.

Andy let go of my hands to reach down and snap the last of the blue threads that held him, then sat with his legs crossed, getting comfortable. I had the stray thought that Evelyn's spell was impressive if it had calmed him this quickly, let him think so clearly. I should ask her for one for myself.

"I didn't realize it at first. I've always been...angry. As long as I can remember." He paused, his brows furrowing slightly. "But not now."

"It's Evelyn's spell," I said, my voice more of a croak than actual words. I cleared my throat. "It's a spell for mental clarity. Sort of like an hour's worth of meditation all at once."

"How long does it last?"

I shook my head. "Not long. I'm not familiar with this spell specifically, but magic isn't meant for long term mental control."

Andy studied my face. I tried to summon a witchy look, or a poker face, anything that would hide my thoughts. Would hide the images that had leapt to my mind when he talked about being angry for as long as he could remember.

I knew I'd failed when Andy tensed. Then he forced himself to relax again. "You've read my file."

"Today," I admitted. "I didn't want to, but—"

"It's fine. I should have told you about it before." He folded his hands together, squeezing until his knuckles turned white. "I don't need your pity."

"I don't pity you. I'm *angry* for you. Angry about what happened to you. What was done to you by people who—"

"It doesn't matter what happened, or who did it. All that matters is what it left behind."

He scrubbed a hand over his face, his fingertips lingering over his eye. The one that had been so damaged in his other form. I knew he was remembering that injury, remembering the day it happened. And suddenly I couldn't breathe through my fury.

How dare Lorelei make him relive that.

"Has this happened before?" I gestured to his body, indicating the physical change.

He fingered the sleeve of his shirt, tugged at the cuff to straighten it. "No. I could feel...something. Something's been growing inside me, and I can feel it when I get angry. It's harder to calm down, harder to think. The things I usually rely on to clear my head just don't work like they used to."

"The suit," I guessed.

"The suit, deep breaths, meditation. None of it makes a difference anymore."

"Have you ever had therapy?"

"Of course. Court-appointed at first. Then because my mom asked me to. My real mom, not the one who gave birth to me. And they tried to help, but there just wasn't anything they could do. Some things—some people—can't be fixed." He stopped, and furrowed his brows. "Or that's what I felt before. What I felt when I came here. But...I don't feel that way now." He tilted his head. "Evelyn's spell?"

I nodded slowly, my eyebrows rising. "I think so." I looked down at the broken pieces of the orb. "That spell is much stronger than I thought if it's letting you think through years of conditioning." I put my hand on his. "You're not broken. You see that now, right?"

"I don't feel that way now, but I remember how I felt before. I didn't just decide to give up, Shade. I fought it. I still fight it every day. I never stopped trying to move past it, and I never gave in to the anger. But it's getting harder, not easier. And now, with the corruption..." He looked into my eyes, and there was a plea in his own that broke my heart. "Is there any way to make this spell permanent?"

"No. And the more you use it, the less effective it will be." I hated to say it, but I didn't want to get his hopes up. There were no shortcuts in magic. Everything came with a price.

Andy nodded as if he'd expected that. "It's been building for a long time. The anger. Faster since Mom and Dad died. Being in their house, around their things helped. Then I broke all her figurines. I don't even remember doing it. I was going over a file, and there was a kid... Next thing I know, I'm sitting in the middle of the floor, and my mom's things are shattered all around me. And when you told me they were still there, their ghosts...and I realized she'd seen what I did. Seen what I am."

His voice grew quieter with every word, more and more hoarse until the last syllable was just an exhale of breath. "I feel stupid now, but at the time, I just needed to run. I needed to hide from them, keep them from seeing..." He clenched his jaw. "I didn't even know *that* was coming."

He didn't need to tell me what "that" was. I could still see his corrupted form in my mind's eye. His transformation had shocked me, I couldn't imagine how his parents would have reacted.

"I saw myself turn into that monster," Andy said finally. "When I looked into the oracle's eyes. Do you remember that?"

My breath caught as the memory came back to me. We'd gone to see Andrea the oracle, the one who'd led us to the case with the missing kids. Andy had looked into her reflective silver eyes, and fallen into a vision that had to be waited out, couldn't be stopped. I recalled their conversation from that day with painful clarity.

"What I saw. It's a possibility, not a certainty."

It was the first time I'd ever seen him fidget.

"There are many choices between now and what you saw. Any one of them could lead to a different path."

"Can you tell me how to avoid it?" he'd asked.

"I could tell you how to avoid what you saw," Andrea had said calmly. *"But it would do you no good. Just as the many choices between now and then could lead to a different path, so too could many paths lead you to the same choice. A frightening vision is more frightening out of context. It might well be that when the time comes, you will feel differently."* She'd paused before adding, *"If what you saw comes to pass, remember this. You cannot lose a true friend. You can only hide from them."*

Andy had been angry then, angry and uncomfortable. *"That doesn't make any sense."*

I'd heard Andrea's sigh, and then her final words. *"It will."*

"You can't lose a true friend," I repeated now. "You can only hide from them."

"And I did. Hide from you, I mean." Andy rubbed his hands over his face. "And my parents. When you told me their spirits had lingered, I couldn't stay. I didn't want them to see me like this."

"And now?" I asked. "How do you feel now?"

"I think I never needed to hide from them," Andy said quietly. "I think they know where I came from. They saw me struggle. They were the ones that helped me then, and I feel ashamed that I didn't trust them to stay with me now."

He shook his head. "But that's just Evelyn's magic talking. I love my parents. I didn't want to leave, I knew they'd worry. But the thought of staying, of letting them see me overwhelmed by these emotions, these urges...I couldn't stomach it."

I took a deep breath. "Tell me about going to see Morgan. What did she say to you?"

"After you and Liam dropped me off at home last night, I called a taxi to take me back to my office. That's where I've been sleeping. I was only there for about an hour, going over some files, when I got a call from Morgan. She said she'd heard about what happened, and she wanted me to meet with her. She believed she could help me."

"But why go?" I asked, unable to keep the hint of desperation out of my voice. "Why would you trust her?"

"There's just something about her that..." He trailed off, gathered his thoughts. "I think she understands."

"Understands what?"

"Understands what it's like to know someone's going to do something horrible, and to have the rules of society force you to let it happen, before they'll let you do anything about it." Tension wove through his shoulders, making him hunch over. "I talked to her about the kelpies. She told me that there are those in the Otherworld who think the kelpies are more monstrous than humanoid, and they want to put them in the same category as chupacabras and wendigos. Because—"

"Because there's no penalty for killing a chupacabra or a wendigo," I finished. "They're predators who can't control the urge to kill, opportunistic carnivores that threaten the Otherworld with exposure."

"Right. Morgan said that it's only been recently that waterhorses have made an effort to have more of a presence in the human world. They get jobs, join society. Make a coordinated effort to keep their people from eating humans. Morgan said they're lobbying for representation at the Vanguard."

"She's right." I twisted my hands in my lap. "But it's an uphill battle. Most waterhorses don't see eating a human any differently than humans see eating cows. And they aren't shy about saying so."

"But the Vanguard doesn't do anything about it."

I sighed. "The Vanguard treats kelpies killing humans the way they treat vampires killing humans. If it happens on rare occasions, no one does anything. It's part of the food chain, and for the most part, vampire society as a whole fights to keep its members from killing humans. The Vanguard only intervenes if they kill too many people and risk exposing the Otherworld, or if they give up the pretense of discouraging that kind of murder and just let their people run free killing as they will."

Andy shifted in place, hunching even more. "I think Evelyn's spell is wearing off."

"It's okay, we'll—"

"No, I mean I need to get this out fast." Andy took a deep breath. "If the police were allowed to go after people they knew were going to commit a crime, instead of waiting until after they committed it, my brother would still be alive. And knowing that is a big part of what makes me so angry all the time."

His voice heated. The anger was definitely coming back.

"But I know you can't punish someone before they do something. That's where the line is. My dad spent a lot of time helping me understand that line. He knew as well as I did that I couldn't trust my judgment. I was too angry, too emotional. Everything felt too personal. And if I couldn't trust my judgment, then I needed to know where that line was, in detail. The letter of the law."

He sucked in another long breath. "Morgan gave me permission to doubt that. Fighting the anger, keeping it locked inside, following the letter of the law... It's hard. It's so hard, and it never gets easier. I do it because I know it's the right thing to do, because I trust my dad, and he said it was the right thing to do. And he's a good man, and I want to be a good man, so I trusted him. But Morgan... She made it sound like there was another option. Not a *bad* option, just...different."

He kept going, talking faster so I couldn't interrupt.

"And I'd just learned about the Otherworld, and part of me thought, maybe my idea of justice had a place there. I got angry with the Vanguard for not stepping in for those kids. And for not doing something about the kelpies, when I could tell you after watching them for just a month that they spend most of their time waiting until they can get away with another murder. But then I thought, if justice is different here, maybe *I* can be different. Maybe I don't have to fight so hard. I'm not human anymore. Maybe my concept of justice and right and wrong don't have to stay the same either."

My thoughts must have showed on my face. Andy looked away, dragged in a deep breath that sounded like it hurt.

"It was already so hard," he said quietly. "And then when I realized how much harder it was getting... The blackouts... That feeling of…something growing." He looked at me then, his eyes begging me to understand. "I could barely fight it as it was. But now that I'm…" He choked, then forced himself to keep going. "Now that I'm corrupted, what chance do I have?"

"There's always a choice," Flint said.

I whirled to find the *leannan sidhe* standing at the top of the stairway. He was studying Andy as if he were a brand new species.

The effect on Andy was instantaneous. He shot to his feet, hands fisted at his sides. I stood too, putting myself between the two men.

"Go away!" I glared at Flint. "You aren't helping. Go watch the twins."

"I can see them just fine from here," Flint said placidly. "And I doubt they'll want to be shot again when that iron on their wrists would make healing so much more difficult."

He met Andy's eyes. "Morgan encouraged you to kill me. Didn't she?"

"I didn't need encouragement." Andy's voice grew deeper with each word. "If I'm going to be killed for Raichel's murder, taking you out before I go sounds like a fantastic idea."

"Yes, I thought it might." Still unruffled, Flint paused, considering. "Now that you've joined the Otherworld in your own way, this might be a good time for a piece of advice. You feel more powerful now than you were before, but don't let that fool you. Compared to those of us born with our gifts, you are a child just taking his first steps. Power without control is nothing."

Andy grunted, then bowed his head. Panic spiked inside me and I put a hand on his shoulder. "Andy, don't. Evelyn's spell is wearing off, and I don't know if I can help you come back from the edge after the beating your willpower took from Raphael's influence."

"Perhaps you should let him go off," Flint suggested. "This

might be a lesson better learned now than later. Face me." Andy lifted his head to glare at him, their gazes locking. "If you think you can kill me, try now. Fail now."

"Flint, stop it," I ground out, my temper heating my voice. I put a restraining hand on Andy's chest and he looked down at me. "We need to talk about your corruption. The more you use whatever gifts it's giving you, the more influence it will have over you. Resist the urge."

"Don't give him advice he can't follow," Flint said sharply. "You're not doing him any favors. He's a human who's chosen to play in the business of Otherworlders, those gifts might be his only chance of survival—*if* he can be smart about how he uses them." The *leannan sidhe* leaned forward. "You can't cure him of this. Corruption isn't possession, there's no way to push that power out of him. It's who he is now. He needs to learn to control it, not to repress it."

"He can decide for himself." I lowered my hands to my sides and tried to project calm, but keeping the edge from my voice proved harder. "It's not your choice to make, so back off."

Flint shook his head. "It doesn't surprise me that you both only see the downside here. But I'm telling you, mourn the death of the straight-laced FBI agent if you have to, but when you're done, please consider that this may, in fact, be the best thing that could have happened to him."

"How can you say that?" I demanded.

Flint looked past me, at my partner. "Your anger made you scary and dangerous to humans." He leaned even closer. "But now you're part of the Otherworld. And you don't scare me."

"Andy, you and I will talk about this later, we will figure this out." I put myself more firmly in front of him, trying to crowd out the sight of Flint behind me. "I need to talk to you now, while you're thinking clearly, before the spell wears off. Do you remember anything else about the night of Raichel's murder?"

Andy dragged his gaze away from Flint, focusing on me with visible effort. "I still have a blank spot in my memory between yelling at Siobhan to get away from the kid, and waking up on her boat." He pressed his lips together. "At first, I thought I'd done it," he said, his voice so low I strained to catch it. "I've had a few blackouts in the last few months. Like when I destroyed my mother's figurines. It happens sometimes if the anger gets to be too much, my brain just...shuts down."

He trailed off, then searched my eyes. "But someone stole that SD card, the one that would have shown the murder. And that has to mean something. If I killed Raichel, and that recording proved it, then why take it? The only people who'd steal proof of my guilt to protect me, are you and..." He stopped. "Well, just you."

There was something soft in his voice when he said 'just you,' and it took all my self control not to hug him.

"Wait a minute," I said suddenly. "Did you ever have a blackout at Something Fishy before?"

Andy frowned. "Once. It was on one of my first trips there, and I was sitting outside with Hachim. I overheard Siobhan asking one of the teens when her birthday was. She made some comment about celebrating her becoming an adult. I remember standing up, then the next thing I knew, I was in the river. Hachim was helping me out, smacking my back, saying I slipped."

"He knocked you into the water to snap you out of it," I guessed.

Andy shrugged. "He never said. But, yeah, that was what I figured."

"Who saw that happen?" Flint asked.

I bit down on the urge to tell him to shut up.

"Siobhan was there with Deacon, and a kelpie named

Cassidy. I think she's Rowyn's girlfriend. Rowyn showed up later. But that was after I came to, in the river."

"So any of them could have seen your rage blackout." I narrowed my eyes. "And they were spying on you, so it's possible they witnessed it happen again. And as I recall, they were spying on you while we worked Lorelei's case, so it's entirely possible they could have put two and two together."

"You think they might have figured out what was happening to him and used it against him," Flint said. "Pushed him knowing he'd black out?"

"Deacon couldn't see through Raichel's glamour," I said slowly. "He thought the real Siobhan was there that night. And everyone knows how much you hate her."

"You think the satyr-blood set him up?" Flint asked.

"If Deacon knew about your blackouts, he could have been waiting for the chance to take advantage. Siobhan was taunting you all the time, she was bound to push you too far. He could have seen you come out of the bar, seen you losing control, and seized the opportunity."

"So he sees Bradford come out, jumps out of his car, shoots 'Siobhan,' and then what?" Flint looked hard at Andy. "How would he know you wouldn't kill him?"

"I have a hard time believing that there are circumstances where I would feel anger toward someone who'd just shot Siobhan," Andy said wryly. "And I'm pretty certain that anyone at the bar would know that."

"He'd need to count on Mickey not to turn him in."

"Mickey didn't like Siobhan either," I said. "He thought she was ruining the track. I think if he saw Deacon kill her, as long as there was someone else to take over the business, he'd have just kept his mouth shut for the sake of disrupting the races as little as possible."

"If Deacon did shoot Raichel, and Siobhan figured that out,

then that would explain why he needed to die," I pointed out. "I can see her taking advantage of the situation to let Andy take the fall, but I don't see her letting Deacon get away with an assassination attempt."

Flint arched an eyebrow. "You think Siobhan had Deacon killed? The evidence pointed to Morgan. What would her motivation be for helping Siobhan?"

"If Siobhan found out that Morgan is the one who sent Andy to Something Fishy in the first place, then it's very possible that she hinted to Morgan that if she didn't kill Deacon, Siobhan would make it known that she was also complicit in Raichel's death," Flint said. "If she sent Andy there, knowing he has a penchant for killing kelpies..."

"No, there's no way Morgan would ever be punished for something like that," I said flatly. "No *sidhe* is going to care about a dead kelpie, and no kelpie is going to go up against the *sidhe*."

"Normally, no," Flint agreed. "But if Siobhan had a powerful business partner..."

I froze. "Anton Winters. You think Siobhan hinted that he might see the attempted assassination as an attack on one of his business interests."

"It's what I would have done." Flint shrugged.

I clenched my teeth. "I need to speak with her again. And Mickey V."

"Might I suggest you go to Turning Tides first?" Flint glanced down the stairs to where the twins were still tied up. "You know nothing about the racetrack, or about Deacon's former mistress, or indeed, any of the gossip a regular at the track would be privy to."

"It would be good to know if Morgan was ever at the track," Andy agreed grudgingly. "Though I doubt it."

"I'd also like to find out if anyone aside from her assistant

Jane knew about Siobhan's tendency to let Raichel impersonate her at important meetings," I added.

Flint nodded. "I would suggest learning as much as you can there, and then speaking to Morgan and Mickey when you're better prepared to call them on any lies or omissions."

I nodded and stood, mentally feeling for Peasblossom through our empathic link. A pulse of calm came from my familiar, letting me know she was fine. "Let's scoop up Majesty, fish Peasblossom and Scath out of the hole, and head to Turning Tides."

Andy didn't stand with me. "I can't go."

I wanted to argue, but he shook his head. "I can't be surrounded by kelpies," he said quietly.

I almost kicked myself. Of course he couldn't go to the track. That was asking for trouble. But then again, leaving him alone hadn't gone so well last time...

Andy seemed to read my mind. "I'm going to call Evelyn. She told me I could call her if...if I needed help."

"She knew about..." I stopped. Of course she knew. "She didn't just come to heal you. She came along because she knew you were corrupted. But how..." My mouth fell open. "Vincent knew. He scanned you when he got there to heal you. He requested her, didn't he?"

"I asked them not to tell you. I'm sorry, I just..." He shook his head. "It was bad enough for them to know, but I wasn't ready for you to find out."

"It's not easy to show our dark sides to the people we care about," I said, trying not to let the words sound as numb as I felt. "I understand. We'll call Evelyn and Oksana. You need witnesses with you so no one else can frame you."

I tried to inject some levity into my tone. "Well, it looks like I'm off to see a man about a horse. Or vice versa."

CHAPTER 16

"So we're not going to talk about the corruption at all?" Flint asked when we stopped at a red light.

I stared down at the notebook in my hands, tapping my pen on the plastic spiral around the top. "I don't intend to discuss it with you at all. Assuming you give me a choice and don't force me to talk about it."

"Which I could."

"Yes, you could."

It was just after six o' clock, and it was already dark. Well, as dark as a city like Cleveland ever got with all the artificial lights illuminating the streets and buildings. I twisted around in my seat to look into the back.

Scath lay on the rear seat. Her eyes and mouth were closed, and without those green eyes, or shining white teeth, there was nothing to break up the solid shadow that was her body. In fact, I could almost convince myself she wasn't there at all, that the blob of darker shadow was just my mind playing tricks.

If it weren't for the bag slung around her body with the slight bulge of a sleeping kitten inside.

Peasblossom shifted on my shoulder where she'd tucked

herself inside my shirt collar to keep warm. She patted my shoulder, and I felt a pulse of reassurance through our link. Back at the house, I'd come down the stairs to find Scath asleep in the basement after her tumble through multiple floors, with Peasblossom sitting on top of her. The pixie had been stroking her fur, murmuring under her breath in Gaelic. I hadn't asked any questions about why she'd put Scath to sleep, or why she'd been so determined not to let Scath bite Raphael. I'd ask those questions later, without Flint around.

"Bradford will be a lot harder to kill now," Flint said finally.

"But not impossible. And given his current situation, I'd like to focus on the immediate future instead of talking hypotheticals about what you think is best for my partner."

"Fine." He glanced at my notebook. "What are you writing?"

"I'm organizing my thoughts." I leaned back in my seat. "Right now, Deacon is our best suspect. He had means, motive, and opportunity."

"When you say means, are you suggesting that he brought his own gun and then put Andy's prints on it when he was unconscious? Or do you think he took Andy's gun from him?"

"More likely he had his own gun. Andy was always armed when he went there, Deacon could have got the same type, then filed the serial number off. Andy bought the gun without a serial number, so he has no way of knowing if that gun was his."

"Shooting someone isn't as easy as most people think," Flint cautioned. "Do we know if Deacon had any experience with firearms?"

"We can ask his mistress when we get there."

Flint nodded. "What else?"

I studied my notes. "I need to know what the agreement Siobhan had with Deacon's mistress specified would happen if she died. Would he return to Julia, or could Siobhan basically will him as property to someone else after her death? And I need to know who would take over at the racetrack. Whoever it is might have an interest in encouraging Deacon. Or killing Siobhan themselves."

The Whiskey Island Marina was probably beautiful during the day. Rows and rows of boats bobbing serenely in the protected shelter of Lake Erie's West Basin. It may even have been beautiful at night under different circumstances. But right now, with my partner corrupted, Liam injured, and me off to face down a racetrack full of kelpies, I just couldn't see the marina as anything but a gateway to misery. I barely resisted the urge to throw a rock into the water. Just in case.

"I don't suppose you know someone with a boat?" Flint asked as he parked the car.

"Sort of." I glanced down at my cell phone, re-reading the text message from Vera. It had been a bold move, but I'd figured since the case I was investigating involved one of Anton Winter's business interests, he might be willing to help out. Or, rather, his wife might. Vera was much more approachable than her husband. She'd been the one to invite me to the opera on my last case, so I'd hoped she might help me again. And I'd been right.

As I'd expected, the Winters had a boat in the marina that they used specifically for travel back and forth to the racetrack. And Vera had been only too happy to point me toward it.

Per the instructions on Vera's text, I marched to the end of the pier, far enough that I could see a boat meandering closer to the edge of the basin that protected the small marina from the more enthusiastic waves of Lake Erie. I'd expected something grand, mostly because Anton could afford for everything in his afterlife to be grand. But the boat heading for me with the fuzzy lights glowing merrily in the darkness didn't look like a rich man's property.

"Do you hear that?" Peasblossom lifted off my shoulder, flying a few cautious inches over my head.

I listened. Gradually, I became aware of a song. An old man's voice carried over the water, and I caught the distinct lilting notes of 'too-ra-laddie, too-ra-lee.'

"Is he singing 'The Liar' ditty?" I asked.

"He is," Flint said dryly. "And he's singing it the way it's meant to be sung."

"Drunk," Peasblossom said happily.

I stared at the boat as it circled the edge of the marina and headed for the pier. "Vera sent a drunk Irish folksinger to pick us up?"

"There's nothin' wrong with my hearing, lass, and you'd do well to mind your manners if you intend to get on the boat I call my own."

The boat came close enough for Flint to catch hold of the rope the captain pitched over the side—though I didn't like his chances of grabbing it without preternatural agility. The drink might not have hurt the captain's hearing, but it had done a number on his aim.

Now that he was near enough to make out, I could see that the captain was a man of small stature, with bright silver hair under a black bowler cap, and a suit that would have done just fine for church on Sunday. Despite his admonition about my manners, his eyes were bright with merriment, and he gave me a big smile. "Michaleen Thornton. At your service, ma'am."

For a moment I thought I was hearing an echo, the song he'd been singing still reverberating in my ears. Then I realized someone *was* still singing. I stared at the captain as Flint hauled the boat alongside the dock. As the boat turned, the lights from the marina struck a tiny figure lying on the brim of Michaleen's hat.

It was a sea fairy. A very drunk, pale green sea fairy, saved from falling off the hat only by the stiff edge of the brim, and probably the grace of the Goddess herself. The fairy was continuing on where Michaleen had left off.

"Search until you tire, you won't find a bigger liar," he sang, his voice meandering through the notes as if he'd been marinated in something stronger than him.

Scath tilted her head, her ears perking up as she listened to the song. She snorted, and it sounded amused.

The Irishman followed the direction of my gaze. "You like my hat?" Michaleen asked, reaching up to tap the brim. "A finer tribute to the art of haberdashery, I dare you to find."

"She's lookin' at me, ye lout," the sea fairy grumbled, struggling to push himself into a sitting position. He groped at his head as if looking for a hat. Finding none, he squinted at me, Peasblossom, and Flint in turn. "I'm...I'm Hiccup. And I'll have another if you're pourin'."

I wanted to laugh, but held it in. Michaleen gestured for me to come aboard, so I climbed over the side with as much dignity as I could, then headed for the bow away from the captain and his wee friend. Flint walked with me, so close I could feel the warmth from his body fighting back the cold night air. If he'd been Liam, I would have leaned closer to take advantage of shared heat. But I'd rather push him overboard than share anything with the *leannan sidhe*.

Scath squeezed between me and Flint. I got the impression it was her way of trying to make up for our earlier conflict by acting as a physical block between me and the *sidhe*. And I appreciated it.

Lake Erie was fifty-seven miles wide from the southern shore that held Cleveland in Ohio to the northern shore that bordered Ontario in Canada. There was plenty of lake to lose an entire nation, so it didn't surprise me that Siobhan had managed to stash an entire racetrack on the water's surface. Back in the day when humans sailed by stars, they might have stumbled upon it, but now that they used modern technology—which even the youngest of fey could wreak delighted havoc on—hiding from them was...well, child's play.

My first sighting of the racetrack was churning water. White froth kicked into the air, catching the light from the huge spotlights set on top of the boats so it looked like glittering silver fog. I held my breath, leaning out farther over the rail. I had to squint, but I could see the horses in that silvery haze. Beautiful white steeds, which could have sprang straight from the pages of a fairy tale about brave knights, charged along beside equine monsters with blazing red eyes. Blue horses with seaweed for manes flowed like the wind beside them, along with black beauties that loped across the water in leaps and bounds like obsidian skipping stones.

Buoys marked the track, a huge oval encircled by six elegant boats. I could just make out the square, glass-exterior of the ships, with blobs of color inside that I assumed were spectators.

"First time here?" Michaleen guessed.

He offered me a squat glass with rich brown liquid inside, but I held up a hand to refuse. "It's my first time, yes."

"A sight to see, isn't it? Do you see those platforms at either end of the track?"

I followed his gesture to see what looked like a floating dock with several small shelters on it sitting on either end of the track between the last boats. "Yes."

"When the race is over, they'll move those to the center to form a courtyard. That's where the mermaids groom the horses before and after the races."

"They stay in equine form the entire time, then?" I asked.

Michaleen drained the glass in his hand and leaned down to grab the bottle off the deck. "Only for an hour before and after each race. The spectators like to see them as they mean to race, so they can get a feel for what they're betting on. When that hour is up, they can meet the racers in their human form, if it pleases them."

"It certainly pleases some of them," Hiccup agreed. "Those that can afford a bedroom or who don't mind—"

"Not in front of the lady!" Michaleen chastised him. He lifted the glass over his head.

Hiccup grabbed the edge and hauled himself up. "She's no lady. She's a witch." He heaved himself over the edge and promptly fell headfirst into the glass, landing with a splash in the whiskey.

Michaleen scowled and fished the sea fairy out of his drink. "Have some manners!"

Peasblossom stayed on my shoulder, holding on to my hair. All the moisture in the air made her wings heavy. It wasn't a good idea for her to fly, not when the race was kicking up enough water to cause waves to rock our boat. "Do you come to the races often?" she asked Michaleen.

"I do. Mr. Winters likes a commentary when he comes to watch, and I know more about these horses than some of their owners do."

"What do you think of Siobhan?" I asked.

Michaleen snorted. "That lass is going to get into trouble one of these days. Sure I keep tellin' her, you can't run a racetrack like you run a casino. She wants to be the next Stavros, and that's going to make her more enemies than friends."

My voice sharpened. "You knew Stavros?"

He nodded. "I used to watch the races down at Fortuna's. Talked to the man himself more than once. Arrogant, he was, but clever like a fox. But even he knew better than to treat the racetrack like the casino."

"What do you mean?" Flint asked.

I'd heard all this before from Mickey V, but I didn't stop

Michaleen from answering. It was always good to confirm information with a secondary source.

"The casino has a 'house.' Everyone who comes in to bet is betting against the house. And the house always wins. Everyone knows that, but they risk it anyway for the chance to be rich without workin' for it."

He pointed at Flint with the hand holding his whiskey. "A racetrack isn't like that. The owner of the track is just the middle man, the one who provides the land and the organization to have the race. It's the owners who put up the horses, who put up the money by buying a spot. And of course the bettin' public's money is the bulk of it. But Siobhan keeps a private stable of three horses at a time, and they run in all races. If one of her horses wins, that's between ten and ninety percent of the purse that stays with the track. Money she didn't put in."

He shook his head. "Nope, not a popular decision, that. Though of course it's made the track very profitable, since she pours all the money back into it." He sighed. "Gloria would turn over in her watery grave."

"Gloria who oversaw the races at Fortuna's Stables?"

Michaleen nodded. "She was a grand leader for the herd before Siobhan took over."

The race ended then. A few minutes later, I noticed the buoys moving toward the main ships that housed the racetrack's viewing rooms.

"Mermaids," Peasblossom whispered.

I followed where she was pointing and caught a brief glimpse of the track's lights playing over scales as the mermaid pulling the buoy swam away from us.

A woman's voice spoke from directly below me. "Michaleen, you've missed the race."

I leaned over the balcony as the captain tipped his hat to the speaker, drawing a squeak of protest from the sea fairy as he rolled with the movement.

The mermaid's dark hair flowed down her back to writhe in the water around her, the silken locks only a few shades darker than her skin. She gazed up at me with sharp eyes, her attention flicking from me to the captain.

"I was called upon to fill another duty tonight, Aerwyna, but I'll be here next week, you mark my words."

"Excuse me, Aerwyna," I broke in, "But my name is Mother Renard and I would like to get to the bottom of what happened to Deacon the jockey. Could you tell me where I might find his former mistress, Julia?"

"She's here," Aerwyna said. "Though I would warn you, she's in a foul mood. It might be best to wait until she's had time to process Deacon's death."

"You know about Deacon's death?" Peasblossom asked.

Aerwyna snorted. "Everyone knows the details by now. The racing world is full of gossips and word travels fast over the water."

"Deacon's death is precisely what I wanted to talk to her about."

"Have you...met Julia before?" the mermaid asked.

"No. But it's urgent I speak with her, so if you could—"

"All right, all right." Aerwyna shook her head. "Is it the legs that makes you hurry all the time? It must be the legs... You'll find Julia in the southwest ship." She pointed to the ship in question. "Go through the door on the side facing the courtyard. Ask anyone inside, they'll point you toward her quarters."

"Thank you."

"Don't thank me," Aerwyna said grimly.

Michaleen was already having another drink, but to his credit, it didn't seem to have any effect on his steering. I stared at the sprawling sea-haven of Turning Tides.

The ships were only two stories, but somehow they still gave the impression of skyscrapers. They just had that metal and glass look to them, that sophisticated simplicity that screamed wealth. Walkways connected each ship, pristine constructions of fiberglass and polished metal. They looked slippery, but I didn't see anyone falling on their backsides, so maybe not.

Michaleen stopped at the corner beside one of the large ships. Once again, he left it to Flint to jump onto the walkway with the rope and haul it close enough for me to disembark as well.

"Don't bother tying it off," the captain told him. "Just pitch the rope back onto the boat. I'll sail out a ways to make room for the others comin' for the later races. You come back here when you're ready to head on, and I'll spot ye."

It said something about the state of my nerves that I didn't question the alertness of a sea captain in his cups. I followed Aerwyna's directions and found myself standing outside a glass door, looking in at what looked like an aristocratic dinner party —circa the early 1900s. It was hard not to notice that the people inside were nearly all women. Most of them wore funnel-shaped, ankle-length wool skirts, and their upper bodies were draped in tasteful jewelry and snug in pouter-pigeon bodices. For a moment, I felt myself transported back in time.

I'd worn dresses and baubles like that once.

"So they're older than they look," Peasblossom observed, taking in the women's style.

"But not fey." I nodded toward them. "Most of them look like they're in their late thirties, early forties."

"What kind of Otherworlder do you think they are?" Flint asked.

"I don't care." I opened the door and stepped inside. Immediately all movement stopped. One of the women closest to the door—a woman with dark brown hair pinned in a no-

nonsense fashion beneath a flat-topped straw hat, stepped forward to greet me.

"Hello. My name is Emily Hodges. How can I help you?"

I forced myself to stand still and observe the social niceties. "My name is Mother Renard. This is Peasblossom, this is Flint Valencia, and this is Scath. I'm here to speak with Julia. Could you tell me where I might find her?"

Emily studied Flint, and I didn't know if it was because he was a man, or if she was just taking a moment to appreciate his appearance. If I had to guess, I'd say it was the former. "If I might ask, what do you want to speak with her about?" she said finally, turning back to me.

"It's about Deacon. I'm trying to find out who killed him, and I need her help."

Emily's eyes sharpened. I remembered what Aerwyna had said about Julia still processing his death. "For whom are you performing this investigation?"

"Myself," I answered immediately. "A friend of mine is being blamed for it, but he didn't do it. I want to find and punish the person who's truly responsible."

"How do you know your friend didn't do it?" she asked warily.

If I wanted to meet Julia, I clearly needed to pass Emily's test first. She didn't know Andy, and would have very little reason to take my word for it that he wouldn't have murdered Deacon. Just as there was no reason that I knew of that she'd take my word for Morgan's culpability.

I looked around the room again. This time, I noticed something else. Not only was the room full of mostly women, but almost all of them had a book. Either in their laps, or close by. I could only make out the titles of two books. The blonde woman in the grey dress was reading *String Theory and M-Theory*. And the redhead in the green was reading *Spinoza* on *Philosophy, Religion, and Politics: The Theologico-Political Treatise.*

An academic bunch.

I turned back to Emily. "Forensic experts found a small speck of fine leather caught on the gun's trigger. Expensive leather, beyond what my friend could afford. The one person on the property known for wearing such gloves also happens to be a woman that I believe has been responsible for an attempted murder in the last twenty-four hours. But, of course, early in the investigation, I can't say with a certainty that anyone is guilty or not guilty. I need more information. And I'm very much hoping Julia can provide it."

Emily considered me for another moment. Then she nodded. "Follow me."

As pleased as I was that she had agreed to take me to Julia, a tiny voice in my head screamed that I shouldn't be walking deeper into a ship, amidst people whose powers I did not know, to meet a woman to discuss her dead lover. Scath pressed against my side as we walked, hard enough to let me know she was there but without setting me off balance. I looked down at her and she held my gaze.

I relaxed. As I passed another brunette, this one wearing a lovely peach-colored dress and matching cameo jewelry, I paused and looked down at the book across her lap. The title read *Advances in Culture Theory from Psychological Anthropology.*

She looked up at me when I stopped, and I nodded at her book. "No spoilers, but the chapter on dual inheritance is fantastic."

She blinked at me and I smiled before following Emily up the stairs. I was still mindful of the risks, but when we reached Julia's door and Emily gestured her permission, I didn't hesitate.

I opened the door to a small vintage décor study. The room smelled of antique furniture, ancient books, and a faint hint of

French perfume. The aroma engulfed my senses, and again I felt as if I'd been transported back in time.

Way back.

If I closed my eyes, I could almost imagine I'd see my sister when I opened them...

A heavy Chippendale desk stood against the far left wall, and a chaise couch against the right. Beside it was a squat table whose flame mahogany matched the desk, piled with gilt lettered books and legal pads. A tall woman attired like the others, with long blonde curls so rich and gold that I doubted it ever saw the sun, sat reading on the lounge with her legs gracefully folded beside her. Her blue eyes left the text to peer at me from a face that held a classic, porcelain beauty with just enough lines around her eyes and mouth to suggest she'd passed her fortieth birthday.

"May I help you?" She offered me a pleasant smile.

Suddenly, I knew what she was.

What they all were.

My heart stuttered.

Vampires.

CHAPTER 17

"BREATHE, DEAR," Julia said. "Remember to breathe."

I hadn't realized I'd stopped. As soon as she said that, the breath rushed back into my lungs in an audible gasp.

The vampiress across the room watched me with unabashed interest, so it seemed only fair that I could do the same.

She wore a pale blue blouse buttoned all the way up to the base of the high collar that hid her throat and tickled the top of her neck with delicate ruffles. Sapphires sparkled in her matching antique silver earrings and rings. Her pleated skirt was a darker shade of blue and high-waisted. In her curled up position on the couch, the long skirt rode up just enough to give me a glimpse of knee high soft black leather boots intricately laced with silk ribbon. A pair of soft leather gloves that matched the boots lay on the table next to her. Not grey leather like the piece caught on the trigger of the gun that killed Deacon, I noted automatically, but the same high quality.

Of all the things I'd expected from Deacon's former mistress, being a vampiress hadn't been one of them.

She lowered her book, and I noticed the title printed on the front cover. "You're studying autopsy pathology?"

"I am." This time her smile didn't reveal any fang. It made me think my earlier glimpse of her elongated canines had been deliberate. A way to let me know what she was.

"Allow me to properly introduce myself. I'm Dr. Julia Ouellet." She laid the book on the cushion beside her as she slid her legs off the couch and planted her booted feet on the floor. "And you are...?"

"Mother Renard." Using my title was the equivalent of her flashing her fangs. This immediate and easy sharing, without all the back and forth that usually came when members of the Otherworld tried to feel one another out without being rude—or particularly honest—was a breath of fresh air.

I shrugged my shoulder, prompting the pixie to reveal herself. Another show of good faith. "This is my familiar, Peasblossom."

Peasblossom marched out from under my hair, her chin held high, her wings raised to show off their glittering perfection. "Hello, Dr. Julia," she said, inclining her head ever so slightly.

"You have a pixie for a familiar." Julia smiled. "It speaks well of you that one of the wee ones would be so inclined to serve you."

Peasblossom preened under the compliment.

"And this is Scath, my bodyguard," I added, nodding at her.

The vampiress slid her attention to the feline *sidhe*, but only for a moment. The quick dismissal caught me off guard. I wasn't sure if she'd assumed Scath was merely a beast, a brute force used only for self-defense, or if she were hiding a different reaction. Or maybe I was just so used to people having a dramatic reaction to the *sidhe* that Julia's nonchalance surprised me.

"And you?" she asked Flint.

"Flint Valencia."

Julia tilted her head. "Peasblossom is Mother Renard's familiar. Scath is her bodyguard. What is your role?"

A shrewd question. I didn't know if Julia knew about my contract with Flint or not—though it wouldn't surprise me, since Siobhan knew and Aerwyna had commented on how fast gossip traveled here.

Flint considered Julia for a moment, probably weighing whether or not to dance around the question.

"I think you'll find I value honesty," Julia said softly. "Let's begin as we mean to go on, shall we?"

Flint inclined his head. "I'm her master."

Julia's expression shut down, no longer the open book of before. "Oh?"

It shouldn't have bothered me as much as it did that he'd thrown that bit of information in, but I'd had a truly horrendous day, and it wasn't over yet. "Don't let it speak well of the *sidhe* that he owns a witch," I said stiffly. "He did nothing to earn it. It was a simple—and temporary—financial transaction that was necessary at the time to keep bad things from happening to good children."

"I would like to hear more of that story. But perhaps at another time. You must have a reason for seeking me out?"

Now that she said that, it occurred to me to find it odd that no one had told her why I was here. Or indeed, even announced me.

Julia seemed to read my mind. "I make it a point to surround myself only with those I trust. Had you not had a good reason for seeing me without an appointment, you never would have been shown to my study." She glanced at Flint. "On that note, I'm afraid I'll have to ask that you wait outside, Mr. Valencia. I would prefer to speak with Mother Renard without her master present."

I didn't know what I would have done if Flint had refused to leave. Or refused to let me talk to Julia alone. Thankfully, he seemed content with the knowledge that he could make me tell him anything we discussed later anyway. And since Scath's presence made his need to stay for protection purposes redundant, he merely offered a slight bow, then left as requested.

Julia smiled. "Much better. I find conversations flow so much smoother when there are no men present. Now, what has brought you to see me?"

I clamped down on the urge to get right down to business. I wanted answers, desperately, but Deacon had spoken fondly of Julia. Her absence of mourning garb didn't prove she didn't return his affection, and I needed to treat this moment with the dignity and compassion that discussing a deceased loved one deserved.

I gestured to the couch. "May I sit down?"

"Please." She moved her book to the coffee table beside her gloves before patting the cushion.

I took a seat facing the vampire. "I'd like to start by saying how sorry I am for your loss. I only met Deacon yesterday, and didn't have the chance to get to know him well, but he spoke very fondly of you. I could tell he missed you very much."

"And I him. Thank you for your kind words." She cast her gaze across the room to a small table that held a single picture frame. "Deacon was such a sweet man. He had a poetic soul and a true gift for helping people find their passion, find what inspired them. He was so easy to talk to."

Anger pinched her features. "I never should have let that woman take him. If I'd had a little more time, I could have proved she cheated. I would have had him back."

"If you'll forgive me for asking, why did you wager with his life to begin with?" I asked. "Deacon said Siobhan won him in a race?"

"Siobhan," she ground out. "It was all her doing. It was never supposed to happen that way. Deacon was never meant to be held up as a prize to be won."

"Tell me what happened," I encouraged her.

Tension squeezed her shoulders together, and she smoothed a lock of curly blonde hair behind her ear, visibly fighting to retain her composure. "Siobhan has always been a showwoman. She enjoys pomp and circumstance, she loves attention and high stakes, and she revels in having power over others. It makes her vivacious and charismatic, a natural marketer perfect for an industry as adrenaline-infused as racing. One day last month she announced a very exclusive race, only three horses running. It was advertised as a contest between the best of the best, with several qualifying races leading up to it."

"Mickey V said Siobhan runs the racetrack like a casino, with some horses serving as the 'house,'" I put in. "Was one of the horses in this exclusive race Siobhan's?"

"Yes," Julia said bitterly. "And of course her horse did not have to run the qualifying races. Cassidy was new to the track, a complete unknown. It was part of the draw. The two winners of the qualifying races would go against a 'mystery' runner."

"You said Deacon was never meant to be the prize," Peasblossom spoke up. "So how did that come about?"

Julia rose from the couch fast, startling me. I saw her deliberately slow her movements so as not to do it again as she approached the table, skirts rustling softly, and lifted the small picture frame. "When she first announced the race, the prize was to be an artifact. Something of great power. Only at the last minute, the artifact was 'confiscated by the Vanguard.'"

"What artifact?" I asked.

Julia waved a hand. "Rasputin's cloak. But what the artifact was doesn't matter. The point is, the Vanguard very conveniently seized it the day before the race."

"It was that powerful that the Vanguard stepped in?" I couldn't help the surprise in my voice.

"No." Julia gave me a disapproving look as if I'd latched on to an inconsequential detail and was holding up the story. "Apparently, the true owner is still alive, and he requested that the item be returned to him."

"Rasputin?" Peasblossom squeaked. "He's alive?"

"No. The holy man is dead, but his royal charge still lives." She shrugged. "In a manner of speaking. Regardless, this man claimed ownership on the basis that Rasputin's cloak was his when he was alive."

I had a sneaking suspicion I knew who the owner was. There was only one man still living "in a manner of speaking" who could both claim ownership of Rasputin's cloak, and use the Vanguard as his own personal delivery service.

I was starting to get very uneasy about how many times Anton Winters seemed to pop up in this case.

"With the artifact out of play," the vampiress continued, "Siobhan had the 'sudden' idea to wager our jockeys in its place. It just so happened that everyone participating in the race— Siobhan, myself, and a sheik—owned our jockeys, and had the authority to put them up." Julia set the picture frame down with a sharp clatter of metal on wood. "I do not believe that was a coincidence."

"Deacon lost," I guessed.

Julia clasped her hands in front of her, then forced them down again. "She cheated. I don't know what she did to Deacon, but he was a disaster when that race started. Cold sweat dripping from his forehead, his skin flushed until he looked as if he'd been turned inside out. He was *terrified*."

"Maybe he was just nervous because he was risking his life in that race?" I asked. "Perhaps what you saw was the worry that he might lose you."

"That's what Siobhan claimed," Julia muttered. "But it's not true. I promised Deacon that if he lost, we would be together again. I promised I would find a way. He was calm when he left my bed before the race."

I rose from the couch and came closer to the table so I could see the photo better.

It wasn't a photograph of Deacon, as I'd first thought, it was a small painting. The artist had caught him looking up at someone out of the picture, but I saw the skirts brushing his arm where he sat on the floor. I guessed it was Julia.

"I felt him die," she whispered. "We were connected." She turned to catch my gaze. "Siobhan didn't care for him. I knew that. But she should have protected him. He was her *responsibility*." She cleared her throat, looking away as if to rein in her emotions. "If she didn't want him, I would have bought him back from her. I offered to buy him back."

I considered her for a long moment. I didn't know Julia very well, but I knew vampires. The younger ones might be prone to bloodlust and less likely to have impulse control, but not the older ones. If Julia agreed to allow Deacon to run in that race after Siobhan switched the terms, she must have had a reason. Either she didn't care for Deacon as much as she said she did, or she had thought of a way to benefit from his loss in the event he didn't win. Unfortunately, unraveling her motives would take time that I didn't have.

"It seems to me there were a lot of areas where Siobhan fell somewhat short of professional expectations," I said, gently steering the conversation back to the case. "Mickey V certainly seemed to think she wasn't the best person for the job. In all honesty, I'm surprised Anton Winters was so willing to bankroll this place with her in charge."

I name-dropped the vampire not just because he was relevant, but also because I wanted to see Julia's reaction.

The vampiress slid her gaze to meet mine. "You speak of Anton as if you know him."

There was no emotion in her stare, but there was something about the *lack* of emotion that made the hairs on the back of my neck stand straight up. I had the sinking feeling that I'd walked into a verbal trap.

"We've met." I didn't take a step back right away, didn't want to look like I was retreating. But I did call my magic, holding it ready in my palms. Just in case.

To my surprise Julia changed the subject. "Deacon told me about Raichel's murder. A human shot her. The same FBI agent they're accusing of shooting Deacon. You don't conduct yourself like a member of the Vanguard. How did you come to be working on this investigation?"

"I'm a private detective, but I've worked with the Vanguard before."

"And were they the ones who invited you to investigate this case?" she pressed. "Or is there something more personal at stake for you?"

I refocused my stare on the space between her eyes, avoided looking into them directly.

"Mother Renard, I don't intend to force answers from you. It is my belief that unlike men, women do not require such heavy-handed tactics. I'm asking you for information. Just. Asking. And I believe that you understand how important this matter is to me. And because of that, I have faith that you won't withhold information just for the sake of hoarding it—like some people I could mention."

She was referring to Anton Winters. My suspicion that she was leading the conversation increased.

She stepped away from me, allowing me more space. "I've laid my heart out for you, Mother Renard. I have more to tell you, but I need to know what this is about for you. I need to know how invested you are in finding out the truth."

I still didn't look her in the eye. But she sounded sincere. And when all was said and done, there was little harm in telling her why I'd taken on this case.

"The man charged with murdering Raichel isn't just an occasional investigative partner, he's my friend," I said finally. "But I believe he's innocent. Deacon was a witness, but I think Siobhan may have been controlling his testimony."

It was the best I could do to answer her question without coming out and accusing Deacon of the murder.

As it turned out, Julia could read between the lines.

"You think Deacon killed her."

I curled my hands into fists, concentrating on the feel of magic against my palms. "I don't know. Right now, I'm still gathering information, trying to learn more about the witnesses and the victim. Both victims. It's why I came to speak with you."

Julia's eyes didn't leave mine, despite my rigid dedication to staring at her forehead. "Tell me your theory."

There was no compulsion to her voice that I could feel. Peasblossom hugged my neck, her heartbeat a frantic pulse against my skin. I took a slow, deep breath. "Raichel was glamoured to look like Siobhan that night. Agent Andrew Bradford was at the bar, and he'd garnered quite a reputation for himself among the kelpies after he killed Siobhan's brother Bradan during an attempted kidnapping."

Julia nodded at my use of the word kidnapping. I guessed she was familiar with the story, and the disputed contract the kelpies had held with Grayson at the time.

"I think Deacon saw Andy run out of the bar with his gun drawn. When Andy didn't shoot right away, he could have grabbed his own gun, got out of the car, and shot her."

"While your friend stood there and watched?"

"My friend blacked out. Something he'd done before at the bar when his...emotions were high."

Julia considered that. "It seems like quite a risk. But then, Deacon could be very opportunistic. He has an artist's passion."

My heart skipped a beat. "Julia, did Deacon have any experience with firearms? Do you think he could have shot her?"

"I think Deacon could learn any skill he felt was worth his time to have," Julia said firmly. "Once he set his mind to something, he usually achieved it." A small smile ghosted over her lips, as if at a pleasant memory.

"If he'd killed Siobhan, would he have returned to you?" I asked. "Did her ownership end with her death?"

"It did." She smiled wide enough to flash a hint of her fangs. "It's a small detail that I insist be present in all my contracts. They end at death for either party. Deacon became mine again as soon as the life left his body."

"So you think my hypothesis is possible," I clarified.

"I don't have access to all the information about what happened that night," Julia said regretfully. "I know only what has made it through the gossip mill." Her expression soured. "And I have not spoken to Deacon since Siobhan took him from me. She forbid it. So I can't speak to what Deacon may have been planning, or whether he'd made any...preparations in anticipation of finding an opportunity to free himself." She paused, tilting her head. "However, with your help, I could speak to him tonight..."

"You're a necromancer?" Peasblossom squeaked. "I didn't think—"

"I am not a necromancer, brave one," Julia corrected her. "But Deacon was mine for a very long time before I lost him to that wretched woman. Our relationship wasn't just sex and blood. We were bonded. He was mine, in every way. Our bond was not so strong that his death hurt me physically, but the connection is there. I can still feel him, however faintly." She looked toward the door. "The bond will break with next sunrise. But for now, it remains."

I realized I was still holding my breath after the gasp I'd taken when Julia mentioned talking to Deacon. I forced myself to exhale, forced my shoulders to relax as I summoned a witchy look to hide the storm of emotion raging through me. "As much as I would like to hear the truth from Deacon's mouth, you'll understand why I'd be nervous that he'd be as likely to lie to save himself again. As he may have done before, to avoid Siobhan's wrath."

Julia shook her head. "If Deacon killed Raichel, then his death is payment for that crime. Especially if a kelpie was involved in his murder. Guilty or not, Deacon would be free to return home with me. I would have no reason to make him lie, and he would never lie if I asked him for the truth."

I shifted my weight from one foot to the other. "You can really raise him?"

Julia's eyes brightened. "It would take but a few drops of my blood, a small ceremony. In a matter of hours, you could look into Deacon's eyes, and get all the answers you need."

This was it. This was the break I needed. Unlike Mickey, Deacon had witnessed both murders, and had nothing to lose. And with his contract to Siobhan broken, she couldn't make him lie. I could find out the truth.

I had to swallow twice before I could speak. "Then we'll make that happen."

Julia brushed her hands down her skirts as if preparing to enter a business meeting. "There is one minor complication."

Warning bells went off in my brain. Her tone was too casual. Too deliberately light. I narrowed my eyes. "Complication?"

Julia trailed one short fingernail over the gilded edge of the frame holding Deacon's portrait.

"As I told you before, I'm not a necromancer. The only reason I would be able to raise Deacon is because a vampire has some control over those to whom they are bonded. Normally, one cannot turn a dead person into a vampire, but my bond with him makes that possible. I could strengthen that bond between us, shift it to the bond between a vampire and his sire…"

I blinked. "You want to raise him as a vampire."

"Yes. The process was already begun for all intents and purposes, it's merely a matter of finishing it." Julia cleared her throat. "However, because this is not my city, if I am to do such a thing, I will need permission."

Ice settled at the base of my spine. I knew who Julia was talking about. And suddenly parts of our conversation made a lot more sense.

"I need you to negotiate permission for me, Mother Renard. With Anton Winters."

CHAPTER 18

I FLEXED my fingers to stop my hands from curling into fists. If I made a fist, I might use it. She'd walked me right into this. Led me by my nose. And I'd *fallen* for it. "That's why you asked about my relationship with Anton Winters. You need me to ask him for you."

Still fingering Deacon's portrait, Julia turned to face me, her blue skirt wafting around her ankles. "I meant what I said, Mother Renard. I care for Deacon. I want him back. And I want to know who killed him. None of that has changed."

"But there's more, isn't there?" Peasblossom spoke up from her position on my shoulder. "You're still holding back."

"There is one more thing," she said lightly. "I am powerful in my own right, but the ritual required to raise Deacon is not easy. I may need a little...boost."

I took an involuntary step back. "You want to drink my blood?"

She chuckled as if she'd anticipated my reaction. "No, Mother Renard. I don't need your blood. I was speaking of something much less sanguine. Just a little help from your...master."

The warning bells in my head turned into warning air horns, deafening in their urgency. I took another step away from Julia, not because I was afraid of her, but because I was afraid if I stood too close, I might give in to the sudden urge to shake her.

"You knew all about me before I ever showed up here. You knew about Flint and what he could do. That he owns me. You knew I was trying to save Andy's life, and I needed to solve Deacon's murder to do it. You knew I'd worked for Anton Winters."

I shook my head. "You've been waiting for me, haven't you?" I laughed, a short, helpless sound, gesturing around the room. "You've sat here as if this were your own doctor's waiting room— and you brought a book!" I flung a hand at the text on the table. "Thought you'd get a little work done while you waited for the witch?"

"I always have a book," Julia said. "I strive for personal improvement in all the spare moments of my afterlife. As do all the people I invite to join my circle." She lifted her chin. "And, yes, I knew who you were. What you wanted. And none of that changes anything."

"Of course it does!" I pressed my boot against the floor, resisting the urge to stomp my foot. "How do I know this wasn't your plan all along? Maybe Deacon killed Siobhan, framed Andy, and arranged his own murder, knowing I'd take the case, knowing I'd come here, and knowing that in the end, he'd be raised as a vampire—free of Siobhan—and you'd have everything you wanted!"

"I won't waste my breath arguing with you," Julia said, exasperation seeping into her tone. "None of that matters. The facts remain the same. Your friend is accused of two murders. You need Deacon's unfettered testimony. And to get that, you need me. Because I promise you, Mother Renard, I am the only one who can raise him as a vampire. You might find a necromancer to raise him as a zombie, but we both know what happens when you raise a murder victim. Death is traumatic enough, but murder? Well, what is left of the mind after something like that isn't pretty. Unless you want to risk the possibility that you would raise him and he would immediately seek out and kill his murderer?"

I picked a point on her forehead and stared hard at it. "You would have been better off being up front with me. We could have come to this conclusion much faster."

I pivoted on my heel and marched out, refusing to look back. "Let's get this over with."

I hoped my abrupt agreement with the terms surprised her, but I doubted it. *Stupid witch. Foolish witch.* Dr. Julia Ouellet, indeed. She's a vampiress. Her kind plotted farther ahead than *sidhe*. They were infamous for it. The patience of the dead. And I'd never seen it coming.

I found Flint draped on a chair in the room just inside the glass door, surrounded by the four women who'd been in there when I first arrived. He was holding a cup of tea, chatting with a very tall brunette about the case pending before the Vanguard about whether leaving a cursed item to someone in your will constituted assault. He looked up when I approached, and read my expression with his customary ease.

"We're leaving now," I said shortly. "We need to see Anton Winters."

The woman beside him got to her feet, raising her brows at Julia as she came to stand beside me.

"Yes, I'm going to ask him to let her raise Deacon." I fisted my hands at my sides as I faced the *leannan sidhe*. "She needs your help."

Flint smiled easily enough as he looked at Dr. Ouellet. "If I might have a quick moment with Mother Renard?"

"Of course." Julia gestured to the southwest corner of the

room. "I have a boat outside waiting to return us to the mainland. If you'd join us when you're fin—"

"We have a ride," I cut in. My warm feelings for Julia had cooled significantly, and I saw no reason to pretend otherwise. It wouldn't fool her anyway.

Julia inclined her head. "Then I will meet you at the marina."

I watched her leave the ship, trailing her ladies in waiting like ducklings. Scath prowled after them, watching them through the glass as they paraded down the walkway toward the water.

"So... What happened?" Flint stepped in front of me, blocking my view.

I didn't look at him at first. I was impatient, and this was a conversation we could have just as easily on the boat. "I'll tell you when—"

His hands closed on my arms, tightening until I looked up at his face. "What. Happened?"

"Julia offered to raise Deacon as a vampire so he can tell the truth about both murders. To do that, she'll need Anton's permission as the master of this city to raise a vampire. And since Deacon died, in order for her bond to him to be strong enough to actually raise him, she'll need a boost from you."

Flint dug his fingers harder into my arms, not enough to bruise, but close. "She planned this."

"Looks like it."

"And you walked right into it."

"I wouldn't have done anything differently if I knew."

He dropped his hands, stared at me as he took a step back. "Is there anything you won't risk to save him? Anything you won't give up, any line you won't cross?"

"I don't have time for this." I tried to take a step past him.

Flint's hand swung up, seized my arm, and this time he

dragged me to him until our faces were inches apart. His hazel eyes shone with the light of his power, his irises transformed into bands of brown and gold.

"Answer the question. Is there anything you wouldn't do?"

I lifted my chin. "Nothing comes to mind."

My answer didn't seem to surprise him. I hadn't expected it to.

"Do you know how easy it is to manipulate someone in your position?" he asked intently. "You may as well paint a giant target on your back. Stand under a sign that says 'Will do anything for information that may lead to Andrew Bradford's release.' You've given me another month of control. And now you've agreed to intercede for another vampire to *Anton Winters*."

Nothing he said wasn't true. And he was right, I'd very likely regret some of these choices later. But for now, all I could think about was Siobhan laughing as she dragged Andy under the water. The horrors that waited for him if the kelpies won. "Let. Go."

"Did you know that how powerful a vampire is when it's raised depends largely on how powerful the sire is?" Flint released my arm, but he didn't move back. "How powerful she is *at the time?* If I inspire Julia and make her strong enough to do this, then Deacon will rise more powerful than your average vamp. Which will in turn, increase Julia's power—*permanently*."

"Can we finish this conversation on the way to the ship?" I prodded. "I don't know how long it will take to flag down Michaleen. And I assume you approve of my decision to turn down Julia's offer of a ride on her boat?"

Flint gaped at me, then swiveled to Peasblossom. "Talk some sense into your witch." He glanced down at Scath. "You call yourself her protector. You must see what she can't. Tell her."

"I'm not going to stand here talking about vampire politics. Every minute we waste here is another minute someone, somewhere could be plotting to make this entire investigation *more difficult.*"

Flint grabbed me yet again. This time when I faced him, he stared at me with the calm facade of a *sidhe* at court. "If you get permission from Winters, I will help. But when this case is over, there will be a change. You're too reckless when it comes to Agent Bradford. And if you can't control yourself, then I will."

I was too angry to be entirely sensible. And I was so very tired of people threatening me, and of hearing variations of this same speech from him.

"Do what you will, *Master.* But remember, extra month or not, our contract will end. I like who I am now. And if you try to force me to change, I will consider that a threat to me and everything I am. And if you think I'm reckless in my pursuit to save my friends, imagine what I'll be willing to do to save *myself.*"

He released me and I threw myself forward, out the door, and down the walkway to where I'd arranged to call for Michaleen.

Turning Tides wasn't as crowded as a mundane racetrack. Without hoards of humans crowding the place, it looked more like a fundraiser than anything else. Wealthy Otherworlders strode around, talking about the race, pointing to the courtyard platform that had been moved to the center of the main ships, connected to each one by a separate gangplank. I could make out some of the horses standing there, waiting for the next race, and I couldn't help searching for Siobhan in the crowd.

I spotted her standing near one of the horses. I assumed from the wreath of roses around its neck that it was the winner of the last race, so of course Siobhan would be standing there.

As if she could feel my stare, the kelpie turned. Her eyes met mine, widened briefly. She took a step toward me.

"Time to move," I muttered.

"It's a public place, we don't need her permission to be here!" Peasblossom protested, glaring in Siobhan's direction. "And we're leaving anyway, who cares if she tries to kick us out?"

"I'm not worried she'll kick us out, I'm worried she'll delay us. It'll take almost an hour to get back to shore, and I still have to get Anton's permission for Julia to raise Deacon."

Flint clenched his teeth, but kept quiet. Fortunately, Michaleen wasn't far off, and within ten minutes, we were all aboard and sailing back to Cleveland. I stared back at Turning Tides as we sailed, finding Siobhan in the crowd. One of the guests had cornered her, roping her into conversation. I breathed a little easier.

Flint came to stand beside me. This time, he didn't leave room for Scath between us. The freezing night air stole the warmth from my face, every breeze that came over the water like a breath of ice.

"Dr. Julia Ouellet is a very enterprising woman," he said casually.

"I don't—"

"I can make our long trip back to shore unpleasant for one of us if you force me to it, so do yourself a favor and listen."

I pressed my lips together, swallowing the rest of what I wanted to say.

"What do you know about vampire society?" Flint asked.

"I know it's changed a lot over the centuries. Back home, the only vampires I knew of were the royal family in Dacia. And of course there were rumors about the island of Paradise. Apparently full of vampires being punished for whatever it is vampires consider a crime."

Flint stared at me. "How old are you?"

"Older than you."

He raised his eyebrows at that, but didn't comment. "Do you know anything about modern vampire society?"

"Not much. I've never had reason to. Mother Hazel wasn't one to spend a lot of time on politics. She taught me to respect vampires the same way she taught me to respect anyone else."

Flint snorted. "Failed lesson, that one."

"I know that they keep their numbers under tight control. Vampires are territorial, and when a vampire accrues enough power, they take control of an area. Nowadays, that usually means a city. Any vampires that come into a city under another vampire's control either make their presence known and ask permission, or risk the vampire finding out on their own and taking steps to get rid of them. Those steps range from a notification to vacate, to just destroying them outright."

Peasblossom shivered and abandoned the lock of my hair she'd wrapped around herself in favor of snuggling underneath my coat.

Flint kept up his lecture. "And do you know how they increase their power?"

"By surviving long enough to grow stronger, and making more vampires."

"Right. The more vampires in a sire's line, the more power they have. But that has to be balanced, because the more power a sire has, the more powerful their new vampires will be."

"Which increases the chances that one of their children will stage a coup," I finished.

"Which is exactly why making a new vampire is serious business." Flint shook his head. "Winters will not approve of this. Even if you talk him into it, even if you're willing to bargain. He won't appreciate being put in this position, and he won't forget it was you who put him there."

I stared out at the water, sifting through everything Flint had said. "Did you get the impression Julia's people know Anton?"

"If she's in Cleveland, she knows Winters. She's too smart to come to a city this big without knowing exactly what she's getting into."

I listened to Hiccup sing "All for Me Grog" from where he was still halfway to passing out on the brim of Michaleen's bowler. Manipulative or not, I believed Julia cared for Deacon. Even if tonight had been rehearsed, Deacon's affection for his mistress had been true.

But Flint was right. I'd been too open. Too willing to treat Julia as an ally because I so desperately needed her to be my ally. If I was going to make this work, if I was going to make it to the end of this with no regrets, I needed a plan. A better plan.

I spent the entire voyage back to the mainland thinking about it, considering what I had for leverage, what I could expect to negotiate. I couldn't continue stumbling forward, agreeing to whatever someone asked of me in exchange for their help saving Andy. I needed to be taken seriously. To remind people who I was. The problem was, this case had brought too many surprises. Big surprises. And I'd been trapped on the defensive. I needed to find a position of strength. I needed to remind everyone who they were dealing with. What it meant to go after someone I cared for.

By the time Michaleen docked in the marina, I had a plan. I took a deep breath and held my head high, nodding to Michaleen and Hiccup as I took Flint's hand, allowed him to help me off the boat. When my foot hit the deck, I put some weight behind it. I let my steps echo on the weather-beaten wood, the sharp, rhythmic thuds of my flat boots helping me center myself, helping me calm my heartbeat. I walked with confidence, projected confidence.

"Mother Renard?"

I looked up to find Dr. Ouellet standing at the bow of her boat. It was larger than Michaleen's, but sleek, with long lines and a brilliant white paint job. The name on the side marked it as the *Lemniscate*. Lemniscate, the Greek word for "decorated with ribbons." Also used by some mathematicians to symbolize infinity.

Clever name for a boatload of educated female vampires.

"Are you coming with me?" I asked. "To see Anton?"

"No need," Dr. Ouellet said calmly.

I frowned. "What?"

Julia gestured beyond me. I turned. And froze.

A long black car sat parked at the edge of the marina parking lot, positioned so it was perpendicular to the long pier where Julia's boat was moored closest to the lot. As I watched, the door to the backseat opened, and a man unfolded himself from the dark interior.

Anton Winters.

"It's not a good sign he's here waiting," Peasblossom muttered from her spot inside my coat on my shoulder. "He *knows*."

Anton stepped aside, his pale blue eyes still boring into mine. It was becoming harder and harder to avoid those eyes for a safer spot, like his forehead, or his nose, so I tore my gaze from him to see who he was helping out of the car now.

A woman accepted his hand, taking a moment to smooth a hand down her black skirt. The white blouse she wore underneath her short suit jacket had an Old World quality to it, a little more lace at the neck than one usually saw nowadays. Her grey eyes were so pale, she almost looked blind as she turned to study the boat that held Dr. Ouellet and company. I recognized her. It was Illyana, Anton Winter's personal sorceress.

"Julia wouldn't have told him her purpose," Flint said under his breath. "There was a reason she wanted you to be the one to ask him."

"It's not rocket science," I said, matching his volume. "Vera allowed us the use of Michaleen's boat. He's their employee. Of course he would have informed them that I was talking to Julia. How many visiting sires by that name can there be in Cleveland?"

I walked down the pier, but instead of heading straight for Anton Winters, I went to Julia first. I stared hard at the spot directly between her blue eyes.

"If I do this," I said coldly, "you and Deacon will make yourselves available to me at any time I ask from now until sunrise. And you will answer any question I ask, truthfully, and completely."

Julia's eyebrows rose. "Any question relevant to your investigation."

"Any question *I* deem relevant to my investigation," I clarified. "No limitations."

The vampiress appraised me for a long moment. Weighing her options. I imagined it was more difficult for her to negotiate with Anton watching. It would be harder for her to sail away now, leave empty-handed.

Finally, she nodded. "Very well. I agree to your terms."

I didn't waste time reveling in my success. That had been the easy part.

I trudged over the pier and through the strip of grass that separated the wood from the asphalt parking lot of the marina's offices. The boat trip back to shore had drained most of the warmth from my body, and I hoped the stiffness of my movements would be blamed on that instead of nerves. Anton watched me approach, and his stare made my hackles rise.

"I need to speak with you," I started.

Anton held up a hand. "Mother Renard, I am aware of what you intend to ask me. And I don't think you fully appreciate the...measure of the woman you're so eager to make a deal with."

"Dr. Ouellet says she can raise Deacon," I said. "If she raises him as a vampire, there's a good chance she can bring him back with his mind intact. Isn't that part of the process? Restoration?"

"I'm aware what she has offered to do. As I'm sure she made you aware, she would need my permission to do it." He smoothed a hand down his jacket. "Mickey has told me about Agent Bradford's situation. I understand why you're trying to do this."

I could hear the 'no,' coming, like a child who's asked for dessert despite the full dinner plate lying untouched in front of them.

"This could be my only chance to prove beyond a doubt Andy is innocent," I said quietly.

"And as I said, I understand. I know why you think this will help him. But you must understand the ramifications of what she's suggested." His gaze cut back to the boats. "Dr. Ouellet is an ambitious woman. Every step she takes, particularly of this magnitude, is carefully considered and planned. She is not raising Deacon because she loves him. She would never do something like this on a mere emotional whim."

I didn't believe that, but this wasn't the time to argue the temerity of a woman's feelings for her lover. "You think she killed Raichel to frame Andy, knowing I would get involved? And then killed Deacon to force me to deal with her to prove Andy innocent of both murders?"

Anton's blue eyes narrowed. "I would not put it past her. But at the very least, she was quick to find a way to turn Deacon's death to her advantage. And of course, manipulating Agent Bradford's memory would be child's play for a vampiress of Dr. Ouellet's power."

I hid my thoughts behind a witchy look that would have made Mother Hazel proud. Anton could be right. Dr. Ouellet could manipulate Andy's memory, or even hypnotize him to kill

Raichel. It was more likely that Andy had blacked out again, that his corruption had overcome him when faced with his personal nightmare—a kelpie abducting a teenager. But I couldn't argue that possibility without telling Anton about Andy's corruption. And I wasn't willing to discuss that with the vampire.

"I get nothing out of this arrangement," Anton said bluntly. "Quite the contrary, you're asking me to hand power over to a woman who has proven to be most—" He cut himself off, visibly casting about for the right word.

I almost dropped the witchy look in sheer surprise to see the vampire floundering. If I didn't know better, I'd say he was biting back an insult, trying to find a more politically neutral way to express his feelings toward Dr. Ouellet.

"I once mediated a fight back in my village between Mrs. Crenshaw and Mrs. Rockford," I mused. "Apparently, Mrs. Rockford had made a hobby out of outbidding Mrs. Crenshaw in online auctions, swooping in at the last minute to snatch an item which Mrs. Crenshaw insisted her rival only wanted to keep her from having it."

Anton stared at me, waiting for me to make my point.

I gestured at his face. "Mrs. Crenshaw used to get the same expression when she talked about Mrs. Rockford as you get when you mention Dr. Ouellet."

Anton looked pained, but finally he inclined his head. "It's not a terrible analogy. Dr. Ouellet has made a rather bad habit of interfering in several of my business deals. She can be very...frustrating."

I frowned, glancing from him to Julia and back. "She's not getting off the boat. You told her she couldn't enter your territory, didn't you?"

"Yes. And that has not changed. She is not welcome here."

I started to open my mouth, ready to barrel forward, but I stopped myself. Flint was right. I was taking too many things for granted, speaking to him and to the vampires as if I had any sort of guarantee they wouldn't kill me. I needed to remember who I was talking to.

"Mr. Winters," I said, trying for a mild, respectful tone. "Please. Deacon is my best chance to clear my FBI partner, who proved himself most invaluable in my first case for you, among others. Whoever framed Andy has worked very hard to make sure the physical evidence is stacked against him. I need Deacon's testimony."

"I understand what is at stake for you, and for Agent Bradford. But you must understand what is at stake in the larger picture. Do not let Dr. Ouellet fool you. She is no more altruistic than I am." He shook his head slowly, without taking his eyes off me. "The answer is no."

CHAPTER 19

"MOTHER RENARD?"

Julia's voice pierced the roar of my pulse in my ears. I was studying Anton in a way I'd never allowed myself before. Looking for weaknesses.

Considering how I might force him to give me a different answer.

And things were really, really dire if I was considering trying to force Anton Winters to do anything.

I glanced over my shoulder, back at the vampiress. I guessed she'd read my body language, had deduced that the master vampire had refused his permission. Probably guessed I might be about to do something rash.

"You may consider telling Mr. Winters about the consequences if Agent Bradford were to be found guilty and escapes," Julia suggested, raising her voice to be heard from the boat but not shouting.

Anton went completely still. "Consequences?"

"How did she know about that?" Peasblossom demanded.

"I would imagine Siobhan has been talking about it at Turning Tides," I murmured. I didn't add that the truly interesting part was that *Anton* hadn't known. A breakdown in communication perhaps? A flaw in his spy network at the racetrack?

Perhaps Julia's doing?

I promised myself I'd look into these vampire politics more when this was all over.

"In order to get Andy out on bail, I had to agree to serve his sentence myself if he escaped. Whether he escaped before or after he was turned over to the kelpies."

Anton's eyes glowed red. One searing moment of pure crimson that should have burnt a hole straight through my body. "You agreed to that? Your life, your freedom, hinges on the honor of a corrupted man?"

Before I could react to his knowing about Andy's condition, movement drew my attention to a van pulling into the space beside Anton's limo.

Peasblossom pointed at the words "Cuyahoga County Coroner" on the side panel. "Who called Kylie?"

"I took the liberty of having Deacon's body brought here," Julia said casually. I looked back at her ship to find her leaning on the rail, the other members of her group lined up on either side of her. "In the interest of expedience," she added.

It wasn't until that moment that I truly understood what Flint had been trying to tell me. For the first time since I'd met him, really met him, I saw a hint of Anton Winters' temper. He looked down at me, crimson flakes glittering in his eyes, and I felt real fear. Real, immediate, *visceral* fear.

And in that moment, three things occurred to me at once.

One, in January Anton Winters had hired me to work a case despite the fact that a man in his position could have hired any number of more experienced, more powerful investigators.

Two, Anton Winters had loaned—or given—Flint five million dollars to buy one year of my life.

Three, Dr. Ouellet believed that Anton Winters could be convinced to agree to a ritual that would give her—his competition—significant power just by pointing out that if he refused, there was the possibility that the kelpies would own more of my life than he—or his proxy—did.

I'd known before that Anton had an interest in my life. That was clear from the five million dollar loan. But it wasn't until now that I realized he wasn't just interested—he was *invested*.

Blood and bone, I thought, heart pounding. *What have I done?*

Anton looked up at Dr. Ouellet, coiled tension in his posture. "We need to talk." He gestured behind him. "My car."

I held my breath, half-expecting Julia to argue, to negotiate a more neutral space. But she just bowed her head in acquiescence. I stared at them both as Anton led them to his limo, gesturing for Dr. Ouellet to get in first. The vampiress was smart enough not to look smug, and she kept her face carefully composed in a decent poker face.

Waiting for them to finish their meeting nearly killed me. I wanted to know what they were talking about. I knew they had to be negotiating, and, worse, I knew it had to involve me in some way. I should have been allowed to be present.

"Don't even think about it," Flint murmured.

I paused, realizing I'd actually taken a step toward the limo. I made myself stop, forced myself to wait. And if I made a small sound of relief an hour later when the door finally opened again, then who would judge me?

Anton helped Dr. Julia out of the car as if she were his date, and not someone he'd forbidden to so much as step foot on his territory not more than an hour ago. I could tell by the look on Julia's face that she was satisfied with the outcome of the negotiations, but Anton was harder to read. He approached the coroner's van, and I spotted Kylie. The half-ghoul looked up at

Anton Winters and he spoke to her too low for me to hear. Kylie nodded and moved to the back of the van.

Julia went with her.

Anton looked back at me and raised a hand, gesturing for me to come forward.

"Mother Renard," he said, "when you've concluded this investigation, please come by my office at your earliest after-dark convenience."

Torn between relief and a very strong sense of foreboding, I managed a weak smile. "Thank you. Tell Vera and Dimitri I said hello."

"I will be staying," he said placidly. "Dr. Ouellet may not perform her ceremony unless I'm present."

He walked away without another word, and Illyana trailed after him, watching everything with unabashed interest. It was the prerogative of a sorceress to be keen on observing any ceremony, and the more unfamiliar it was, the more valuable the experience. I daresay that few sorceresses would have ever seen a vampiress raise a satyr-blood with the help of a *leannan sidhe*. Even I would have been interested, if the entire situation wasn't such a bloody mess.

Kylie opened the back door of the van, then stepped back, making room for Julia. Dr. Ouellet waited with her hands clasped in front of her, the epitome of patience. She radiated confidence, but she made sure to keep me between her and Anton.

Julia gestured for Flint to enter the van with her. It was a tight squeeze for both of them to stand to one side of the stretcher with Flint positioned behind Julia so he could put his hands on her shoulders. The vampiress practically vibrated with excitement, a soft smile on her lips projecting her triumph loud enough that I could feel ire rolling off Anton Winters in waves.

For a moment, all I could think about was what that anger would mean for me. What it could possibly mean for Andy.

I shook myself out of those thoughts in time to see Flint take a deep breath, then tighten his hold on Julia. His hands massaged her shoulders, pressing into her muscles as if he were kneading his power into her body. I couldn't feel the energy, but I remembered what it felt like well enough.

Julia took a deep breath, centering herself amidst the rush of power. She drew something out of her pocket. It was a small satchel, and I would have bet my last healing potion that it contained some of Julia's grave dirt. She reached into her opposite pocket and retrieved a small candle that she placed near Deacon's head on the opposite side from where she stood.

A resurrection ritual of any flavor was nothing to rush through. I stood in the cold air as Julia cleansed herself and Deacon, waving her hands down their bodies, brushing aside lingering energies that might inhibit his return to the semi-living. Pressure built inside the van and rolled out over the observers as Julia concentrated on the bond between her and Deacon, strengthening it, focusing on it as if trying to make the dead man aware of that pull.

Scath pressed against my side, and I realized I'd started tapping my foot. I stopped and forced myself to calm down.

Finally—*finally*—Julia lit the candle, then raised her wrist to her mouth and used her own fang to open a vein. She pressed her bloody skin to Deacon's lips and murmured under her breath. The candle flared, then went out.

Deacon grabbed Julia's wrist.

The vampiress made a sound between a hiss and a gasp as Deacon latched on with his new fangs, drinking her blood with all the clumsy violence of the newly risen dead. He sucked and licked, digging his fingers deeper into her arm, anchoring it to his mouth. After a minute that probably felt much longer to the vampiress, she reached out with her free hand to touch his cheek.

"That's enough."

Deacon winced, but he removed his fangs from her flesh, turned her hand over to lay a delicate kiss on her knuckles. The sheet around his hips fell a little farther as he sat up, reaching for Julia to draw her into an embrace.

"Mistress. I've missed you so."

Julia pulled away, but took his hand in hers and held it against her chest. "And I you. But we will bask in our renewed acquaintance later. There is much to do, and I've promised Mother Renard a word first."

Deacon's gaze slid to me. It was a little unnerving, watching him stare at me when I could still see the dark bullet hole in his pale chest. His eyes were glazed over with a pink sheen.

Julia tugged at Deacon's hand even as she turned back to me. "We'll speak on my boat, if that's all right. I want to get Deacon inside, cleaned up and dressed."

I knit my brow, but Julia raised a hand to ward off an argument.

"Mother Renard, Deacon was murdered. He was cut open, autopsied."

Her words drew my attention to the Y incision on his chest. The wound stood out like black marker on his pale skin, the stitches seeming too jagged somehow. I shifted uneasily.

"Rising from the dead is traumatic no matter the circumstances," Julia reminded me. "I want him to feel as comfortable as possible, as quickly as possible. If you don't feel safe getting on the boat with me, that's fine. But then I would ask you to wait until I've had a chance to take care of him before we talk. I will be as efficient as possible."

Peasblossom was trembling now, and she tucked herself completely under my coat.

Julia tilted her head. "Your familiar is cold. It's warm on my boat. And I give you my word no harm will come to you on my ship. Contrary to what Mr. Winters would have you believe, I am not a danger to you or your companions." She arched an eyebrow at Anton Winters and lowered her voice. "Men are so paranoid around strong women. Don't you agree?"

I did, actually, but I didn't say so. I glanced at Scath. The feline *sidhe* didn't seem to have an opinion. Her attention was on the small kitten poking his head out of the satchel slung across her body. Majesty seemed to be recovering from his exertion with the *leannan sidhe* twins, but he still looked like he'd just been rescued from a storm drain. He let out a pathetic mewl, and Scath licked him across his tiny face.

Flint took a breath as if he'd weigh in, but I spoke first. "Fine."

Anton Winters watched me as I turned to head back toward the pier, and one look at those cold blue eyes made me hope my investigation would last until sunrise. I needed some time to figure out how I was going to appease the angry vampire.

And more time to ponder exactly what he wanted from me.

I walked past Kylie, and the half-ghoul bit her cheek, her gaze searching my face. The worry in her expression confused me, until I remembered Andy. If Vincent had known about the corruption and not told me, had Kylie known too?

I paused just long enough to look a little harder at her. Her neck muscles corded, as if fighting not to look away.

Yep. She'd known too.

I gritted my teeth and headed for Julia's boat with heavier footsteps than before.

"You're angry with the coroner's assistant."

Flint's voice didn't help my mood. "It's not important right now."

"Do you have a personal relationship with Ms. Rose?" Julia asked.

I glanced over my shoulder. She was following behind us, her arm around Deacon's shoulders. The new vampire had the sheet from the coroner's van wrapped around his waist and nothing else. I shivered in sympathy even though as a vampire, the cold would have no effect on him.

"If you'll forgive me for saying so, I'd rather not discuss my personal life with someone who's clearly already learned more than she let on." I kept my voice even, but Julia was a smart woman. She'd sense the anger.

"I don't blame you for being upset with me." I paused by the gangplank leading up to her boat, and she circled around me, still guiding Deacon. "But I do hope you'll give me a chance to explain once we're in a more comfortable setting."

I wanted to point out that the last thing I needed was another vampire weaving a verbal tapestry to get around actually sharing information, but I resisted.

Julia opened the door to the boat's cabin. A glorious burst of heat washed over me, and I patted Peasblossom where she burrowed into my shirt. She poked her head out and gave a happy sigh.

The same women I'd met at the racetrack were inside waiting for us, and Julia beamed at them as she towed Deacon further into the room. "Ladies, if you would take Deacon below and help him get cleaned up and dressed? Quick as you can, Mother Renard needs to speak with him." She glanced back at me. "Unless you're in enough of a hurry that you'd like to go with them?"

I almost said yes, but then held back. Julia had promised to answer any questions *I* deemed relevant to my investigation. "No, that's fine, I'll wait. I have some questions for you anyway."

Julia gave me a small smile. "Of course. What would you like to know?"

I waited for the women to take Deacon away before I spoke. However angry I might be, I wasn't cruel. As soon as they were gone, I faced Julia. "You let Siobhan win Deacon. You wanted her to take him."

"Sort of," Julia hedged, completely unsurprised by the accusation. "I had no intention of wagering with Deacon's life when we agreed to that race. But you're right, I could have withdrawn when Siobhan changed the wager."

"But you didn't," I said.

"No." She moved to a small cart that held a bottle of wine and several tall glasses, quirking a questioning eyebrow at me.

"I don't drink," I said coolly.

She poured herself a glass of white wine. "Siobhan wanted to take Deacon from me as a childish power play. I was willing to let her think she'd won."

"Leaves her cocky enough to make mistakes, plus it gives you a spy," I guessed.

"Precisely." She gestured to the stairs. "And though I appreciate your discretion, there's no need. Deacon knows why I let him go. Just as he knew I'd get him back."

"You said before that Siobhan wouldn't let you talk to Deacon. So how did you know so much about the night of the murder?"

"Deacon talked to Jane, and Jane talked to me." Julia made a tsking sound. "You'd be very surprised how often Siobhan completely underestimates someone she considers beneath her."

"So Deacon—through Jane—contacts you the night of the murder and tells you what happened. And you saw your chance." I stared at her, the wheels in my head spinning. It was a longshot but I asked anyway. "Did you kill Deacon?"

Julia traced the rim of her wineglass. "No. As I said, I can't set foot in Cleveland without risking political and possibly literal suicide. Besides, if I'd killed Deacon myself, it would have voided my contract with Siobhan and risked the chance she may have passed him on to someone like so much furniture after her death." She shrugged. "But I may have said a few things in passing to the people at the track that may or may not have gotten back to Siobhan."

I shook my head. "We're not talking in hypotheticals. I want straight answers from you. Did you arrange Deacon's murder?"

Julia arched an eyebrow, but then inclined her head in acknowledgment. "I hinted that Deacon was the one who tried to kill Siobhan. And then, when Siobhan was fully committed to seeing Agent Bradford pay for the crime, I had Jane tell Deacon to start acting guilty, pretending to be tormented by his conscience. His job was to make Siobhan believe that he was the one who'd shot Raichel, and he was working up the courage to confess that fact to you."

"But he already told Siobhan that Andy shot Raichel," I argued.

"Not exactly. It's common knowledge that Siobhan was taunting the FBI agent, trying to goad him into committing a crime against the kelpies that she could punish him for. When Raichel was murdered, I suspected that the circumstances were too good for Siobhan to pass up the chance to see Agent Bradford blamed. It makes sense that she wouldn't ask Deacon for the truth, she would hint to him what she wanted the truth to be and 'encourage' him to tell her what she wanted to hear. Which is exactly what she did."

Hope flared in my chest. "So Deacon didn't really see Andy shoot Raichel?"

"It's complicated," Deacon said.

I jerked my attention back to the stairs that led to the lower level. Deacon stood there, dressed in a soft pair of black linen pants and a royal blue shirt that brought out the color of his hazel eyes. He went to Julia's side and kissed her cheek before turning to face me.

"I lied to you before. When I said Siobhan didn't tell me what to say. Julia is right, Siobhan led me to say what she wanted to hear, no question about it."

His expression softened with sympathy. "But I did see Agent Bradford run out and aim his gun, exactly like I told you. Siobhan was coy, but she didn't need to be. What she wanted me to say I saw was the truth. But there was something else, something I wasn't allowed to tell you." He paused, looked back to his sire. "I can tell her?"

Julia nodded. "You are mine again. Siobhan's orders to you are no longer binding."

Deacon let out a relieved sigh that reminded me how recently he'd been alive. "Mother Renard, forgive me. I wanted to tell you before, but Siobhan forbid it."

"Tell me what?" I demanded, trying to keep my voice calm.

Deacon leaned forward. "A few days before the murder, Siobhan gave Mickey an unregistered gun. For protection. I swear he had it that night when I drove him to Something Fishy. But later, after Raichel was shot I drove him home...it was gone."

CHAPTER 20

"WHAT?" Peasblossom yelped.

Deacon licked his lips, then winced when he cut his tongue on one of his fangs. "Siobhan gave Mickey a gun. For protection, she said."

"What kind of gun was it?" Flint asked.

Deacon shook his head. "I don't know. Guns aren't a specialty of mine."

I unzipped my pouch. "Bizbee, could I have the file with the forensic photos from Raichel's murder?"

Bizbee's fuzzy antennae bobbed as he popped his head out of the pouch and hefted the requested file up with him. He moved with his customary speed, not pausing to look around more than was necessary. But when he turned to shove the file in my direction, he caught sight of Julia. He jumped, his beady black eyes growing wide. "Dr. Ouellet?"

"Bizbee?" Julia laughed. "Bizbee, is it really you?"

"Is it really me?" he scoffed. "And who else do ye think could organize a witch's odds and ends? The state of this place, if ye could have seen it!"

"How do you know each other?" Peasblossom asked warily.

"Bizbee worked with a wizard detective on the Toronto police force when I was coroner," Julia explained, her eyes bright with pleasure.

"And what are ye doin' now?" the grig asked, leaning on the edge of the pouch. "I—" He froze. He looked at Julia. *Really* looked at her.

"Bloody hell," he whispered. "You're dead."

Julia clasped her hands in front of her, her smile dimming. "I am."

"How? What happened, lass?"

Julia's gaze swung to me. "I'm afraid our reunion will have to wait. Mother Renard needs Deacon's help, and I'm sure she's in a hurry."

I was already flipping through the file, and when I found the picture of the gun that had killed Raichel, I held it up to Deacon. "Is this the weapon you saw Siobhan give to Mickey V?"

"Looks like it. But like I said, I don't know guns."

I shoved the picture back into the pouch, wincing an apology when Bizbee glared at me and snatched it out of my hand. "If Andy bought an unregistered gun to carry on his surveillance meetings at the bar, then Siobhan could have found out what kind of weapon he was carrying. She could have bought one that was the same make and model easily enough."

"So she buys an identical weapon and gives it to Mickey. Why?" Flint asked.

My brain spun with new ideas, new theories. "Waiting for an opportunity. She's been taunting Andy for months. Maybe she was getting impatient. She could have been waiting for a situation exactly like this one. A case of Andy confronting a kelpie, no one else around. Maybe she told Mickey to make sure any situation like that ended with lethal force."

"And he'd be there with a matching weapon to make sure Andy was blamed," Flint finished.

I looked back at Deacon. "You're certain it was Andy who fired, not Mickey? You said you only saw Mickey and Raichel through the window of the van. Couldn't Mickey have shot Raichel while her attention was on Andy?"

Deacon considered that. "It's possible. I couldn't see their hands. And everyone else's attention was on Agent Bradford. No one thought anything of it when Mickey bolted for the boat to get Rowyn."

"But we know Mickey saw through the glamour, so unless Siobhan ordered him to do it, did he have a motive to kill Raichel?" Flint pointed out. "Wasn't he one of the few to show sadness at her death?"

Perhaps it had been more than sadness—regret. I addressed Deacon again. "We need to talk to people who knew Mickey. Who did he talk to at Turning Tides? Besides Siobhan, I mean?"

"The horses," Deacon said immediately. "He spent all his time with them. Talking about their strengths, what it was like to run on the water. He tried to ride as many of them as he could. He said he needed to get a feel for how they moved, and what the water was like in different conditions."

"Then I need to talk to them."

"Easily arranged," Julia said. "You can ride to the track with us."

I nodded. "Deacon, what about your murder? Did you see who shot you? Was anyone around?"

Deacon shifted uneasily. He looked like he was trying very hard not to look at Julia.

I stared at the vampiress. "You knew all along, didn't you? You knew who shot him."

Julia put down her wine glass and folded her hands in front of herself. "Morgan shot him. And before you ask, she did it because I made it clear that once Deacon was dead, he would return to me. And that is something he and I both wanted very much."

"You told her to kill him." The words tasted strange somehow.

Deacon took one of Julia's hands in his, but his eyes never left me. "It was always going to be that way. It was the only way for me to come back."

"But there was no guarantee." I shook my head, trying to rid myself of the shock. "You needed Anton's permission, you needed Flint's—"

Realization struck me so hard and so fast, I'd taken a step forward before I realized it. Deacon read my expression and tensed, ready to throw himself in front of Julia if need be. He didn't, and I wasn't sure if that was an acknowledgment of my self-control, or if he knew Julia was not a woman who needed— or appreciated—being protected.

"That's why Morgan had to call Andy and get him to Marilyn's," I said, my voice strangled. "It had to be a frame-up for Andy...because you needed me to be desperate enough to help you. You knew I'd come to see you after Deacon was killed, and you needed me to be willing to do whatever it took."

Julia didn't say anything. She didn't have to.

But I wanted to hear it.

"Say it," I ground out. "Tell me you set me up."

"I did what I had to do to save my friend from Siobhan," Julia said softly. "I trust that sentiment sounds familiar?"

I jabbed a finger at her, fighting to make sure it was just a finger, not a spell. "No. No, it is not the same. I didn't hand Andy over to Siobhan as some sort of power play. You gave her Deacon. You used him, knowing it would come to this. And then you used Andy. And me."

Scath growled beside me, one of those eerie feline growls that send tendrils of ice up your spine. Julia didn't flinch.

"You're right. I used you, and your friend, and I'm sorry it was necessary. But I had nothing to do with Raichel's murder. I set Agent Bradford up for Deacon's murder because he was already on the hook, but I'm not the one who put him in jeopardy in the first place. I wouldn't have done that."

I inhaled for the count of seven, then exhaled for the count of eight. My magic still burned inside me, so I did it again. And again.

"Why would Morgan agree to do that?" Peasblossom asked. "Killing Deacon could have put her in a bad position with the Vanguard, not to mention Siobhan, and Marilyn! She killed him in the middle of an ongoing investigation. And she's too old to be that stupid."

"Obviously I couldn't spell everything out," Julia said calmly. "The rumors I started about the night of Raichel's murder weren't so specific that Siobhan would have been certain Deacon killed her. They would have worked just as well to convince her that Deacon had seen Mickey kill her. Regardless, Siobhan would have a reason to want him dead. And I'm sure Morgan could make Siobhan think it had been all her own idea in the first place. *Sidhe* are very talented at that sort of deception."

Pot, kettle. "You've wasted so much of my time," I said, pressing my fingers to my temples. "I don't think you understand the damage you've caused. How much your little power play has cost me." I thought of Raphael and Luna. They'd targeted Andy after seeing him with Morgan. And that fight with them, Raphael's influence, had driven Andy so much closer to the edge. And then pushed him over it. All because the vampiress arranged a murder to get her lover back.

"And now I'm saving you time by being honest," Julia soothed.

"And how has that helped me so far?" I demanded.

"Deacon's story is the same as it was before. And the second murder has nothing to do with the first. So what exactly have you offered me that could possibly compare to what I've given you?"

"Now you know Mickey carried an unregistered gun, from Siobhan," Julia reminded me. "Was he one of your prime suspects before?" She smoothed her hands down her dress. "Talk to the racers at the track. Mickey isn't a cold-blooded killer, that I know. If Mickey did agree to kill Raichel in the event Agent Bradford didn't, so the agent could still take the fall, that betrayal will have affected him. And the racers will know. I believe tonight he was set to ride Charlotte's Web."

I must have still looked angry, because she sighed. "I will be at the track for the night. I will make myself available should you require more information."

"Yes, you will," I agreed. "And in addition, you'll owe me three questions. I can ask whatever I want, whenever I want. And you must answer truthfully." I glanced toward the cabin of the boat, thinking of all the women inside—all the highly educated women who would be an asset to any investigation I might encounter.

Julia smiled as if guessing the direction my thoughts had taken. "Agreed."

That was two vampires who owed me three questions each.

Even Flint looked impressed.

When we finally docked, I said goodbye to Julia, and noted that she seemed happy to see me go. I headed toward the small courtyard that sat in the middle of the four ships. The horses were still there, but now they were in human form, marked as racers only by the fact they still lounged about in stalls marked with their names. The walls were lower than a real stall, giving the entire area the appearance of a parking lot full of parade floats more than anything else. It looked ridiculous to me, but then I supposed I wasn't the target audience.

I had just stepped onto the walkway that connected the southeast boat to the courtyard when something landed on my head. The sensation was very similar to Peasblossom when she got too tired to fly and didn't want to admit it. I held completely still until I heard a tiny voice.

"Thanks for the ride, M-Missss." Hiccup giggled. "I'd be most grateful if ye could allow me a wee rest before I'm off to find that drunken fool Michaleen. And in exchange for...for this kindness, I will...make introductions."

I almost turned down the offer, then thought better of it. Arguing with a sea fairy wouldn't get me anywhere, and his information could prove useful.

I hadn't gone three steps when I felt the familiar itch that meant someone was watching me. I turned, following the sensation. The stall on my right was constructed of unprocessed birch limbs. The leaves had been stripped, but the tree had been left largely intact, with the thick trunk pointing toward the opening of the "stall" and the tufts of thinner branches connecting at the back. The result looked similar to the spider webs one usually had to go to Australia to find.

Or one of my nightmares.

The racer sitting on a long bench inside the stall watched me with murky blue eyes that shifted like oil on water. Long brown hair fell down his bare back, and he peeked out at me from under a fallen lock. He wasn't naked, but he was close enough. I didn't know if his attire—or lack thereof—was a practical nod to his shapeshifting abilities, or if it was part of the show. Based on the number of attendees giving him appreciative glances as they sipped their cocktails, I'd have guessed the latter.

"Hello," I greeted him. "I'm Mother Renard. You were one of tonight's racers?"

"Aye." He held out a hand, and I noticed the extra skin that connected his fingers close to his palm. "I'm Charlotte's Web."

His voice made me want to clear my throat. It was too wet to be a rasp, but not quite enough for a gurgle—something nice and uncomfortable in between.

"Nice stage name," Peasblossom said.

I took his hand, trying not to wince at the stickiness of his palms. His skin felt as if it were coated in a thin layer of beautician's wax, and it took a lot of self-control not to use a spell to clean off my hand. "You're an *each uisge*."

He tilted his head, making the lock of hair slide farther over his face, casting more of it in shadow. "Aye."

"He's also a front runner," Hiccup offered, his words almost clear compared to the man in the stall.

"What's that?" Peasblossom asked.

I swallowed a groan. This was not the information I needed.

"A front runner," Hiccup slurred, "is what's known as a 'speed' horse. Our Charlotte here likes to get out of the gate quickly, stay in first place the whooooolllllle time." He hiccupped and almost slid off my head. I gritted my teeth as he renewed his grip on my hair to hold on.

"Y'need a hat," he grumbled. "No much for me t'perch on, is 'er?" He cleared his throat. "Anyway, he keeps his energy, y' see, holds it in, lettin' it out in spurts so his lead grows, and grows, and grows, and gr—"

"Thank you, Hiccup," I said loudly. "Mickey V was your rider tonight, Charlotte's Web?"

"He was."

Those strange eyes didn't move from my face. He looked expectant, as if he was waiting for me to ask a specific question.

"How did he seem?" I asked.

"How do you mean?"

"I mean, did he seem upset about anything? Nervous?"

He grinned, baring his teeth. "Mickey V doesn't get nervous. But if he did, it'd be hard to tell. Shakes like a leaf no matter what. It's all the energy drinks, if you ask me. The man is more caffeine than blood."

That lined up with what I'd observed myself. "Was he happy here, did he get along with everyone? Anyone have a problem with him?"

The *each uisge* shook his head slowly. "You're investigating Raichel's murder, and you're asking me about Mickey?"

"Who should I be asking about?"

Charlotte's eyes gleamed. "If I were you, I'd be asking about Raichel. And who might have wanted her dead."

"Someone wanted her dead?" Flint asked. "We've heard everyone respected Raichel."

"Not everyone."

"Siobhan," I guessed.

"Siobhan," the *each uisge* echoed. "Yes. She loved Raichel when she was making her look good, but Siobhan is arrogant, not stupid. I think she knew Raichel was about to give her a taste of her own medicine."

I leaned in. "What's that supposed to mean?"

"Rumor has it she'd recruited statisticians to study the racing odds and was passing out tip sheets on the side under Siobhan's nose. It's the same thing Siobhan used to do when Gloria was ruling the racetrack at Fortuna's. Drove Gloria mad. Now Siobhan's getting a taste."

"Excuse me," came a woman's voice from behind me.

I turned to find a woman in a large hat and a dress covered in black and white stripes that gave me an unsettling feeling of vertigo. She held a martini in her hand, and a bottle of baby oil in the other. "We're all supposed to get a chance to talk to all the racers. So if you don't mind?"

"Talk?" Flint murmured, eyeing the bottle of baby oil.

Charlotte chuckled, a deep sound that reverberated in his chest and held none of the rasp that his voice did. "You'll have to excuse me, Mother Renard. Unless you'd like to stick around..."

I gave him one of my darker witchy looks. "Thank you, but I should be going."

Charlotte shrugged, but the amusement never left his eyes. There was another racer in the next corner, so we headed in that direction.

This stall was constructed of blackened wood, and smelled like someone's house after a kitchen fire. The man sitting on the bench inside this area had skin as white as the inside of a clam shell, with blond hair and brown eyes that looked like a section of an old log, the edge of his iris slightly irregular. A *backahast*. He watched me approach like a child watching a waiter getting closer with a tray of desserts.

"Mother Renard," Hiccup announced, stirring as he found purchase on the center of my head again. "May I introduce Shadow of Death. Unlike dear Charlotte, Death is more of a stalker." He scooted forward and leaned down over my forehead, peering into my eye from less than an inch away. "That's not a legal term," he clarified, squinting as if trying to focus. "That's...a racing term. Death likes to stay off the pace, but he stays within striking distance of the frontrunner. He lets them tire themselves out then *wham!*"

This time, he did fall off. I caught him in my hand.

"Hiccup, you've had too much again," Death teased. Then his brown eyes locked onto me. "You're a witch, are you? Not many witches come to gamble. Boss never encouraged magic users, too likely to take an unfair advantage."

"The boss. Would that be Siobhan...or Raichel?"

"Someone's been talking out of turn." He looked over my shoulder. "It was Charlotte, wasn't it? Such a sucker for pillow talk." He leaned closer to me and sniffed the air over my skin. Then he drew a finger over my palm. "No baby oil?"

I jerked my hand away. "That's not what I'm here for."

"Don't mix business with pleasure?"

"I'm trying to find out who killed Raichel. Rumor has it she had an eye on Siobhan's position as leader."

"There are a lot of people around here who don't think Siobhan earned her position because she didn't win a challenge fight for it. But if you ask me, getting something by being clever counts just as much as brute force." He nodded toward Charlotte. "Take the sticky one for example. Always bursts straight out of the gate, runs hell-bent for leather for the finish. A waste of energy, a blatant reliance on physical strength. I beat him in two out of three races."

"Very admirable," I said politely. "You said Siobhan is clever. What about Mickey, is he clever?"

Death's grin widened. "He managed to make himself the vampire's favorite, didn't he?"

I really hoped that Death wasn't about to insinuate that Mickey V had been enlisted by Anton to take out threats to his new business venture. If the master vampire had told Mickey V to kill Raichel because she was upsetting Siobhan's apple cart, I was going to need a lie down. "And how did he do that?"

"By being insane. By being willing to ride any mount. Not just climb up, hold on, and get through it, but *really* ride. He spent hours with us, talking, coaxing rides. He'd go out on the lake in any weather, even during a storm." He chuckled. "The man has no fear. I might not eat him even if he didn't enjoy the protection of the vampire."

"Have you talked to Mickey V tonight?" I asked.

Death's mouth thinned into a hard line. "No. He rode Charlotte tonight."

"Can I assume this race was among that elusive third that you don't win against Charlotte's Web?" Flint asked.

"I think we're done here," Death said flatly.

"Wait." I held up a hand, fighting the urge to drive my elbow into Flint's midsection. "You said Mickey is insane. Did that insanity extend beyond the racetrack?"

"Yeah. Mickey would do anything for an adrenaline rush."

"Did you ever see him with a gun?" I asked.

Death went quiet, then he shook his head. "I'm done talking. If you'll excuse me, I have patrons to schmooze before I have dinner."

My temper flared. I planted my feet, ready to give him a reason to answer the question, but footsteps behind me made me turn.

Another racer approached. Like the other two, he was nearly naked, wearing something akin to a leather loin cloth slung around his hips almost as an afterthought. He had light brown hair and chocolate brown eyes. He was smaller than Charlotte's Web and Shadow of Death, but he was every bit as muscular.

"You're Mother Renard?" he asked cautiously.

"I am." I hesitated, unwilling to turn away from Death just yet. If he knew something, he needed to tell me. And I wasn't leaving until he did.

"I'm Puck. Puck's Folly. *Nuckelavee*." He gestured with his head. "Can we talk?"

I shook my head. "I'm not finished here."

"Oh, but I am." Death stood, and it wasn't until he stepped closer that I noted just how big he was. He must have been slouching in addition to sitting, because he was six-foot-five if he was an inch. And the closer he got, the more aware I was of the water lapping against the floating courtyard. The dark lake that was so close. So dangerously close...

Puck's nostrils quivered like a nervous stallion's. "You're

asking around about Raichel. Trying to prove that FBI agent isn't the one responsible for the murder." He leaned in, spoke with his mouth right next to my ear. "I believe he's innocent too."

I tensed, then studied his face over my shoulder. Trying to determine if he was telling the truth, or just saying what I wanted to hear to make me leave Shadow of Death. "You do?"

Puck gestured with his head. I hesitated, but only for a second. With one look down at Scath to make sure she was still with me, I followed Puck as he led me to a third stall. This one looked laughably like the set of an old cowboy movie— complete with a lasso hanging on a hitching post.

"It's too much of a coincidence," Puck said under his breath. "Raichel meets with Anton Winters last week, and now she's dead?" He shook his head. "Siobhan is behind this. I know it."

I tried to stay calm. *Don't get excited. Get more information. Get proof.* "Raichel met with Anton Winters?"

"She did. I doubt Siobhan was meant to know about it, but I guess someone told her. Given the timing of Raichel's death... well, Siobhan is lucky but not that lucky."

"You think she arranged for Raichel to be killed, or you think she killed her?"

I knew Siobhan hadn't done it herself. The forensics left no wiggle room for that. But I was interested to see if Puck tried to lie about it.

Puck's eyes darted around the deck. Charlotte was watching him with those oily blue eyes, and he quickly angled his back to the *each uisge.* "People have been getting more and more angry with Siobhan lately. Especially Mickey V. She cared too much about winning, about controlling everything. The racetrack was starting to get a reputation that the races weren't fair." He stamped his foot. "I *like* racing. I'm not going to lose this place too because Siobhan wants to feel powerful."

He tossed his head. "Not to mention we were heading for the

perfect storm, coup wise. Everyone's getting mad at Siobhan for being greedy. Even Anton noticed. He knew the only person holding this place together was Raichel. Then he met with her last week, right after Siobhan had that mistake with the jockey being late to the race. Everyone was whispering that Raichel was being groomed to take over."

"And you think Siobhan was worried enough that she'd arrange Raichel's murder?" I asked.

Puck leaned closer. "Little hard to ignore the possibility when that's how she came to power in the first place. Fool me once, and all that."

My mouth fell open. "What?"

Puck frowned. "No one told you that?"

"Told us what?" Flint said impatiently.

Puck looked back and forth between the two of us. "Siobhan's predecessor Gloria was murdered."

CHAPTER 21

THE WORLD TILTED AROUND ME, a momentary vertigo as my brain rearranged all the information I had so far to make room for this new bombshell. "Tell me what happened," I said, my voice hoarse.

Puck looked around again, as if nervous about being overheard. The floating courtyard was getting less crowded, making our whispering group more obvious. The *nuckelavee* gestured for us to follow him and headed for the ship opposite the one where I'd met Julia.

The interior of this ship didn't have the same Old World luxury as Julia's. Everything was modern, and the air smelled strongly of new leather and glass cleaner. There was another scent underneath it, but a too-deep breath tickled my nose with the chemical scent of the cleaner, so I opted for shallow breaths instead. Puck led us inside, just far enough from the windows so we wouldn't be too noticeable.

"Gloria's killer was also a human, oddly enough," he said, keeping his voice low. "A gambler back at Fortuna's. Gordon, I think his name was. He lost more than he won, but Gloria knew exactly how to handle him. He wasn't dangerous, and she knew it, so she found his tantrums amusing. He'd rant and rave, and she'd just sidle up to him, comp his drinks, let him tell her all about why his horse should have won. Half the time I think he just wanted someone to listen to him. I got the impression he'd lost his family to his gambling addiction."

"Was he ever violent with her?" Flint asked.

"Before the day he killed her, he never laid a hand on her. Then one day he lost *big*. I mean, he lost all the time, yeah, but he never had that much to bet. Then one day he comes in with this huge grin. Clapping everyone on the back, all joy and bluster. Word around the track was he'd gotten a tip of some kind. Something so good, so reliable, that he sold everything he owned. His house, his car, everything. Granted, neither were worth very much, but still." He stared at me, shaking his head as if he still couldn't believe it. "And he put it all on a horse under a *bug boy*."

Hiccup spoke up. "A bug boy is a jockey who 'asn't ridden a winner for a long, long, long, long, looonnnng time."

I'd forgotten the sea fairy was up there.

Puck snorted. "Not like him to make a mistake like that. But even weirder was the fact that he was convinced *Gloria* had given him the tip. He claimed she's the one who promised him it was a sure thing."

"Could she have?" I asked.

"No," he said emphatically. "Never. Gloria *never* gave out tips. Unlike Siobhan, who was always giving out unofficial tip sheets, making nice with the customers behind Gloria's back. I think Siobhan appreciates how obnoxious that was now, after Raichel did the same on her watch."

"What happened, exactly?" Flint asked. "The day Gloria was killed."

"After he lost, Gordon went out of his mind. As usual, Gloria was the one to try and handle him. She pulled him aside, out of sight of the public—which was standard operating procedure. Nothing puts a damper on a race like someone screaming about how he's lost everything. She took him up to the viewing booth where the announcer sits, kicked the announcer out. Sometimes that calmed Gordon down, getting to sit up there in the big boy seat. No one saw them for awhile. Then Siobhan went up to check on her and found her dead. Iron across the throat."

"Siobhan found her?" Peasblossom demanded.

"Just a little suspicious, isn't it?" Puck said dryly.

"Did no one think that maybe Siobhan did it?" Flint asked.

"Siobhan wasn't allowed in that room. There was a wizard on the forensics team, and he confirmed there was no trace of her at the scene, DNA or otherwise. She opened the door, saw what happened, and broke the news to the rest of the team. She claimed Gordon was gone when she got there."

"And you're sure Gordon was human?" I asked.

"Positive. He was human, and he had no idea what we were. Stavros made sure we all wore glamour so the humans didn't see what was really there." He laughed. "And he sold enchanted opera glasses to the Others so they could see the real thing if they wanted. Of course there's no need for that out here," he added. "Not like you can let humans watch us race on water."

"Then how did he know to use iron to kill Gloria?" Peasblossom asked.

"The iron was in the room—a weapon of convenience. I think it was a scythe."

"A scythe just sitting around in the announcer's booth?" I asked, doubtfully.

"An iron scythe left there specifically to make sure there was iron in the room," Puck corrected me. "There was silver there too, but since silver is expensive, that wasn't left out in the open. Those were just some precautions Stavros took to make sure no

Otherworlders tried to manipulate the announcer. Iron for the fey, silver for the shifters."

I took a deep breath, trying to stay calm. "Are you saying you think Siobhan set Gloria up? Worked Gordon into a froth so he'd go after her?"

"You said he was never violent before," Flint argued, "so why would Siobhan choose him for her dirty work?"

An idea occurred to me. "Wait. Was there any evidence of a *sidhe* in the room where Gloria was killed?"

Flint stiffened. "You think it was Raphael."

Puck waved both hands. "No, no, no. There were no *sidhe* in that room. That, I would remember. And to answer your other question, Gordon was never violent to Gloria, but he got into plenty of scrapes with other observers. I got the impression he knew better than to mess with Gloria since she had the authority to ban him if he went too far."

I shook my head. I wanted to believe all of this, but it didn't make sense. Yet. "What exactly makes you think Siobhan was involved? Do you have any proof?"

"What I know is that Siobhan has never been happy being just another part of the team. She always thought she was meant for bigger things. Gloria had to discipline her on more than one occasion for breaking the rules—like giving out tips. Siobhan didn't have what it took to beat Gloria outright, so she just weaseled around her, trying to find some weak spot."

Flint looked unconvinced. "How could she have known that she'd get to take over if Gloria was killed?"

"That I can't tell you. All I know is, shortly after Gloria punished Siobhan, a degenerate gambler blamed Gloria for a phony tip and killed her. The only person who benefited from that whole mess was Siobhan. Suddenly Fortuna's is shutting down, and Siobhan is buddy buddy with the vampire starting a new business as leader of the team." He shrugged. "Maybe you have a higher tolerance for coincidence than I do."

"Do you know where I can find this gambler that killed Gloria?" I asked.

"Not a clue. Never saw him after that." He paused. "Of course, if you believe Siobhan, she killed him."

"Siobhan killed Gordon?" I stared into Puck's eyes, searching for some sign he was toying with me. "She said that?"

Puck nodded. "She claimed she hunted him down and found him on one of those casino boats. Said she ate him."

"But you don't believe her," Flint pressed.

Puck shrugged. "Either she ate him, or claiming she did was a good way to convince the rest of the team not to go looking for him. Not that they needed much convincing. We aren't herd animals, not really. And even if we were all the same breed— which we aren't—we don't need a leader. Most of us are solitary creatures. We seek one another out when the urge to have children catches up with us, but other than that..."

He gestured at himself. "I'm a *nuckelavee*. Shadow of Death is a *backahast*. Charlotte's Web is an *each uisge*. Siobhan and Rowyn and Cassidy are kelpies, and so on. None of us particularly like each other. And the only reason we're a team at all is because we've chosen to have a life out of the water. That requires money. Earning money when you're Other requires self-control or a leader to organize you and give you a job among people like you."

"And you aren't known for self-control," Flint noted.

Puck shrugged. "We're water creatures. Not many of us are known for self-control. Even the mermaids can be a bit brash."

"You said Gordon was a frequent loser and Gloria would comp him drinks," I said. "Do you remember his last name? Is there any chance she kept some sort of record of him?"

"His last name was Larkin. I don't have his last address or

any contact information, but I'm sure she would have," Puck said immediately. "Gloria was almost as good with record-keeping as Raichel was." He hesitated. "But those records will be in Siobhan's office. Well, it was more like Raichel's office since she's the one that did all the work, but you know what I mean."

"Can you tell me where it is?" I asked.

Puck pointed up. "Second floor. This is Siobhan's boat."

I stiffened. "This is Siobhan's boat?" *How many did she have?*

Flint cursed under his breath, immediately looking out the glass walls of the boat, searching the thinning crowd for kelpies.

Puck watched him with unabashed amusement.

"I'm starting to see where you got your name." I took a step closer to the *nuckelavee*. He fell back, surprised by my sudden movement, and I moved with him, staying in his personal space.

"I don't like being toyed with on the best of days," I said, my voice low. "But you have picked a particularly bad day to test my patience."

"Did I?" Puck kissed the tip of my nose, a quick peck that could not have surprised me more if he'd quacked like a duck when he did it. His brown eyes shone with merriment. "Siobhan has been in a meeting with a temperamental sea nymph for the past half hour. I don't know how much longer she can stand to listen to her prattle on, but if you want to see those records, I'd suggest you stop wasting your precious time with me."

My temper flared, bringing my magic close to the surface. The twinkle in his eyes said he was enjoying this. How much of his "help" had been true, and how much had been a desire to draw me here, in this place, so Siobhan could catch me on her territory?

"Scath," I hissed. "Watch him."

"If he moves, eat him," Peasblossom added, multifaceted pink eyes glittering with malice.

Hiccup rolled over on my head, tangling himself in my hair. "Oof. That's harsh."

I left Puck's Folly in Scath's tender care and headed for the spiral staircase in the center of the room. The floor above still held the faint odor of new leather, but it was overwhelmed by the familiar scent of an office supply store. Printer ink and paper, and the faint metallic hint of paper clips. A computer sat at a huge desk against the wall to my right, and filing cabinets lined the wall to my left.

"How are you with a computer?" I asked Flint.

"Better than you."

It was a myth that magic naturally interfered with technology. Controlled magic was no different from controlled electricity, and the two got along just fine as long as the magic user—and the electrician—knew what they were doing. But I let the comment go and headed for the filing cabinets. I preferred paper anyway.

Flint sat at the desk and fixed his attention on the computer. With the sound of keys clacking in the background, I stared at the filing cabinets, reading the labels.

"Expenses." I opened that filing cabinet and thumbed through the files, looking for the year I needed.

Peasblossom launched herself off my shoulder. She landed on a filing cabinet at the end of the row and began tugging on the drawers one after the other.

I was still thumbing through files when Peasblossom shouted, "This one is locked!"

"Try that one," Flint said without looking away from the screen.

"You think?" I muttered. I closed the expenses drawer and went over to Peasblossom. The pixie was already sticking her sword into the lock, wiggling it around. She had it open before I got there, and I snagged the handle of the drawer and pulled it open.

Andy's name leapt out at me.

"*Blood and bone,*" I whispered.

Peasblossom peered over my shoulder. "'*Agent Bradford's Frequented Places,*' '*Agent Bradford's Allies,*' '*Agent Bradford's Assets.*' We already knew she'd been spying on him."

I grabbed one of the files and flipped it open. Surveillance photos. And judging from the daffodils in some of them, they dated back to spring.

"She started having Andy followed right after he killed Bradan," I whispered. "She's been in his house."

"Worse than that," Peasblossom said grimly. "Look. Those pictures are of his new office building."

I gripped the papers tighter. Did Siobhan know about Andy's investigation into Flint? How much did she know?

I searched through the photos, but didn't find any of the inside of Andy's new office. Hopefully she hadn't gained access yet. And Liam hadn't said he smelled any kelpies there when we investigated earlier.

I put the file back. As I did, I noticed another file in the very back of the drawer. I stared at the label, and my field of vision narrowed down to the words typed on that small tab. "'*Agent Bradford's Death.*'"

Peasblossom landed on my shoulder. Even Hiccup seemed to take interest, scooting forward on my head as I flipped the folder open. There was only one thing inside.

An SD card.

"Andy's missing SD card?" Peasblossom squeaked.

It took me two tries to find my voice. "We don't know that. Why would it be in a file labeled as his death?"

"Because hiding it will mean his death?" Hiccup offered.

Part of my brain noted that Hiccup sounded significantly less drunk now. But then he groaned and flopped over, so it could have been my imagination.

"Give me the card, I can see what's on it right now," Flint ordered.

I gave him the card. My heart pounded so hard I could barely hear my own thoughts, but that didn't matter anyway. Not with how chaotic my brain had suddenly become.

Flint slipped the SD card into the slot. The clicking of the mouse sounded too loud in the sudden silence. I gripped the back of Flint's chair, trying to restrain myself from reaching over to jab a button to make it go faster.

"These are all video files." Flint hovered his mouse over each of the files in turn. "Seven files."

"Just open the one with the date of the murder on it," I urged.

Sweat beaded on my forehead as Flint obliged. The image showed the front door of Something Fishy. It was night, but the bulb in the street lamp lit the scene perfectly. Like a spotlight. I held my breath as he clicked play.

From what I could see, the tape started to record right before sunset. I watched the sky darken, watched the patrons come and go. Flint fast forwarded the video feed, stopping when a familiar figure came into view.

"That's Mickey V!" Peasblossom hissed.

"And that," Flint said, pointing at the screen, "is a gun."

I leaned closer, my eyes glued to the screen. Mickey V stood outside the bar, just like he'd described. Only he hadn't mentioned the gun before. The weapon was a dark spot on his hip, barely visible where it was tucked into his waistband. I shook my head. I was ignorant when it came to firearms, but even I knew it was a bad idea to tuck a gun into your pants like that. Clearly I'd underestimated Mickey's desire to live dangerously.

A van pulled up. The camera was set at a different angle than Deacon's car had been parked, so the view of Raichel and Mickey was unimpeded by the van. I watched Raichel approach Mickey, gesture for him to come with her. Mickey took a step back, obviously noticing that Raichel was not Siobhan as she claimed to be. His hand drifted lower, reaching for his gun. He hesitated.

Raichel noticed the gun. She grabbed his arm, shouting at him as she dragged him closer to the van.

The front door flew open. Andy rushed out, gun in hand.

Mickey turned, his face showing surprise. He held up his hands.

His empty hands.

"Siobhan" raised her hands too.

I stared at the screen. I barely felt Peasblossom cuddle against me, barely noticed as Flint pushed his chair back and stood, resting one hand on my shoulder.

Andy stared in shock at Mickey V's face—saw the jockey in all his aged glory. A tremble ran through his body, and he hunched over as if someone had punched him in the stomach. Then he was baring his teeth, the muscles in his neck straining. I couldn't see his eyes, but I'd have bet my favorite coffee mug they'd gone black.

Andy looked from Mickey V to "Siobhan."

Then he raised his gun.

And shot her.

CHAPTER 22

MY CELL PHONE RANG.

I answered it without looking. Even after Flint closed the video and ejected the SD card, I just kept staring at the screen.

"Hello?"

"Hello, Mother Renard. Did you enjoy the video?"

Siobhan.

I sank to the floor, and only Flint's arms catching me saved my knees from slamming into the hardwood. Rage threatened to swallow me, the heat making my thoughts swim. Siobhan was talking again, but I could barely hear her. I looked around, trying to find her. Or the camera that she must be using to watch me.

"Look on the desk, Mother Renard."

I stood with help from Flint, searching the desk. It didn't take long to find the small web cam now that I was looking for it. There was no light to tell me if it was on, but Siobhan's chuckle was proof enough.

"That was incredibly satisfying," she said. "Watching your face. You are so delightfully expressive."

What could I say?

Siobhan laughed as if she knew exactly how I felt. And maybe she did. My magic swelled, and I knew with sudden clarity that I could blow up this entire room. Sink the boat. It would be less effort than holding it in. I could just...let go.

"Don't do it," Flint murmured into my ear. "Calm down. Do it for Andy."

The tremor running down my arms threatened to shake my entire body, but Flint held me closer, absorbing the vibration. He was right. I had to stay calm. For Andy.

"Remember, you might have talked the Vanguard into letting you handle this case personally," Siobhan continued, "but you'll still need to turn over your evidence to them at the end. Including the SD card. So no funny business. Oh, and of course I have a copy. Just in case." She laughed again. "I'll give you until sunrise to bring Agent Bradford to me. My other boat is still at Something Fishy. See you soon, Mother Renard."

She ended the call.

"Shade," Flint said, his voice soothing, "it's going to be all right."

I barely heard him over the chaos in my head. I had less than seven hours to sunrise.

I lurched forward, pulling away from Flint as I went. I stumbled to the filing cabinet, unzipping my pouch with one hand while I pulled out the drawer with all Andy's files with the other. I shoved them all into the pouch. Siobhan probably had backups, but I didn't care. I wanted to know what she knew. And I wasn't leaving any piece of Andy here. Not even a photo.

"Her web cam is still active and she can charge you with theft," Flint said carefully.

"It's not theft. I'm acting on behalf of the Vanguard, and I say this is evidence. She'll get it back eventually."

That was a lie, but this time Flint stayed silent.

When we made it down to the first floor, Puck took one look

at my face, and all traces of amusement vanished. He didn't try to run, but he did back away from his spot near the door, giving me a wide berth. I studied his face, his eyes, his body. Made it clear that I was committing his details to memory.

"I won't forget this." The witchy look slid over my face, without any effort on my part. A comfortable mask. "I *will* see you again."

"I look forward to it."

Tough words, but they lacked the bravado they needed to make them work. I stared at him a moment longer, then turned my back on him. "Scath, make sure Majesty lets off some steam before we leave."

I didn't wait. I left the boat, leaving Scath behind to snag a mewling Majesty out of the satchel. There was a feline squeak and then Puck shouted something that sounded like a curse but was too muffled for me to be sure. A truly horrible smell that reminded me of hot two-week old garbage rolled outward from the open doorway.

"Corr, what is that stench," Hiccup complained. His voice sounded like he was pinching his nose. "That's awful."

Scath caught up to us, and I flicked my hand behind me, using a spell to clean the smell off her fur. It took two shots of magic to make it go away, but that was fine. I was brimming with energy, and it was better I let some of it off before I got on a boat. And it pleased me a little to know it would be much harder for Puck to get that smell off of him.

"Hiccup, where's Michaleen?"

"Northwest corner."

The sea fairy's voice was completely sober now. It could have been my change in attitude that had sobered him up, but I was willing to bet the entire alcoholic routine had been a ruse. If Michaleen worked for Anton Winters, then Hiccup was probably on the payroll too. People already spoke far too freely in front of the wee ones, a drunk fairy probably overheard everything from secrets of the heart to bank passwords.

Tears blurred my vision as I made my way to Michaleen's ship. The little Irishman watched me approach and sighed. He held out the bottle in his hand, but I shook my head. I didn't drink, and this was definitely not the time to start.

I sat on the deck and leaned against the wall of the main cabin. It would have been warmer in the ship's cabin, but I wanted the frigid October air on my face, numbing my skin so it matched my insides.

Flint sat down beside me, his body pressed against mine. Sharing body heat again. The tears in my eyes hurt as the wind tried to turn them to ice. I didn't want Flint beside me. I wanted Liam. I wanted a *friend*.

Scath sat on my other side. After a second of hesitation, she lay across my lap, her heavy body a comforting furry blanket. I drew my hand down her back, noting that her fur was softer than I would have expected from an adult feline. She pressed her head against my stomach. Vibrations spread over my legs, and I realized she was purring. My tears fell faster.

Someone came out of the cabin behind me. I looked up, surprised to see Charlotte's Web. The *each uisge* tilted his head to the side. He studied Flint and Scath, then nodded and took a seat opposite me.

"Puck has a cruel sense of humor. It's a characteristic he shares with Siobhan."

"Why are you here?" I asked.

"It's part of the package for the more influential guests. The racers escort them back to the marina."

"Are there private rooms in the bottom of this boat too?" I muttered.

Charlotte put a hand on my knee. "Would you like me to take you to one?"

Flint stiffened beside me. I couldn't help but laugh, even if there wasn't any joy in the sound.

"Thank you for the offer, but no. You'll forgive me if I'm feeling a little distrustful of everyone equine right now."

He leaned back and relaxed his hands in his lap. "Seems to me you felt that way from the beginning. You were just willing to put it aside to get information."

I looked at Flint. He still held the SD card. "And now I have it."

The *each uisge* didn't say anything to that. We both stared at the SD card for a minute, then I shook my head, forced myself to look away.

"Deacon told me Mickey had a gun. I saw it on the video. But nowhere in Vincent's file does it say they found another gun. Do you know what happened to it?"

Charlotte considered that. "Rowyn has an iron burn on his lower back. Mild, so not pure iron, probably an alloy. Could be the shape of a gun."

"He probably took it off Mickey after Raichel was shot," Flint said. "They wouldn't have questioned him right away, and no one would think it was weird that Mickey ran to him after the shooting."

"Not that it matters now." I leaned my head back against the wall. "I'll bet that was a backup plan. Siobhan was hoping Andy would shoot Raichel, but if he didn't, then she had Mickey there to do it." I remembered the jockey's phone number in my waist pouch, but what was the use?

Flint looked at Charlotte. "Would Mickey have shot Raichel if Siobhan told him to?"

"There's not a lot Mickey wouldn't do to keep racing at Turning Tides. He'd have rather shot Siobhan, but if she made him believe she could cut into his racing time? He might be confident Winters wouldn't let her fire him, but there are all

sorts of ways she could make his life miserable." He considered it, then nodded slowly. "He would have shot anyone."

"But he didn't have to." I swallowed, trying to force the lump in my throat to go down. "Because Andy shot her."

No one had anything to say after that. Charlotte sat with us for a while—Goddess only knew why—then he went back inside the cabin. By the time we reached the marina, I couldn't feel my face at all. Peasblossom was tucked deep into one of my inner pockets, and even Flint shivered as we got off the boat. Michaleen and Hiccup waved at me, but the gestures were half-hearted.

"I need to talk to Anton Winters."

Flint froze with his hand on his driver's side door. "What?"

I opened my door and waited for Scath to climb in before collapsing into the bucket seat. "You heard me. Also, he invited me."

Flint got in the sports car, closing his door and trapping me in a small space with the scent of his cologne that seemed to have seeped into the fabric of the car itself. "I don't think that's the best idea at this precise moment."

I turned in my seat to face him fully. "This will end one of two ways. Either you'll take me to see Anton Winters now, help me see this case through to the end...or you'll forbid me to continue. You'll make me go back to Andy and tell him I failed him. And I'll sit with him until it's time to watch Siobhan drag him away."

My voice broke on the last word, but I forced myself to continue. "And after he's gone, I'll be left wondering if I could have done something more. Wondering if I'd have managed a miracle in the few hours I have left. And I'll know that the reason I have to live the rest of my life wondering that, is because you stopped me."

He opened his mouth, but I held up a hand. "You said you

would help me. This is about keeping your word. This is about what kind of man you are. And I promise you, I am paying very close attention."

Flint started the car. "I don't know how many times I can watch you do this to yourself."

I leaned back in my seat and stared out the windshield. "Yes, it must be very traumatic...for you."

Peasblossom squirmed out of my pocket and crawled up my shirt to press her face against my ear. "Are you sure this is a good idea?" Her voice was gentle, less than a whisper. But it hurt, nonetheless.

I didn't answer, because I was tired of the question. An hour ago, I'd had prospects. Mickey V had seemed a legitimate suspect. Siobhan had a history that made her role as puppet master even more likely. And now all of that was irrelevant. Because of one SD card.

So the SD card was my enemy now. And it was time to learn everything I could about it.

I stared out the window until I spotted the Winters Building. At least I didn't have to worry about getting a meeting. Anton had told me to come see him at my earliest convenience. That would save some time.

The warmth of the building's excellent heating system wrapped around me as the front doors closed. It would take more than that to warm me up, but at least I could feel my face again. The man at the desk pushed his glasses farther up his nose and gave me a pleasant smile. "How can I help you?"

"I'm here to see Anton Winters."

"Of course, Mother Renard." He stood and made his way through the area behind the desk and lifted a section of the circular counter top to meet us where we stood on the other side. "Follow me."

I'd been through this building before to meet Anton

Winters. More than once. And every time I was here, I rode up a different elevator to the floor where his office was located. When we reached the right floor, our guide gestured for us to go ahead. Flint and I stepped off the elevator with Scath at my side and found ourselves facing a familiar waiting room. I turned, but the elevator doors closed, taking our guide with it.

The waiting room was a near-perfect square, with stark white walls that provided a sharp contrast with the black leather chairs. But before Flint or I could even reach said chairs, the door across from us opened, revealing Anton Winters himself.

The vampire's gaze slid over me, an assessment that seemed more like a search for possible weapons than anything else. He did the same with Flint, then gestured for us to enter with a wave of long, pale fingers.

Anton silently crossed the room to sit behind his desk. The enormous piece of furniture offered a perfectly smooth black lacquer finish that reflected my face back at me as I took a seat across from the vampire. Flint remained standing behind me. It would have bothered me if Scath weren't there as well. Watching him.

Directly behind the desk, two thick bookcases edged a bar displaying golden liquor and crystal tumblers. The gauzy white curtains framing the two windows to my right were pulled back, and the heavy electric shade was open, revealing the night sky.

"I'm surprised to see you here so quickly," Anton said.

"You mean Michaleen and Hiccup didn't tell you I was coming?" I asked lightly.

He paused, studying me as if debating how much time to spend on this inconsequential detail. "You found the SD card," he said finally.

"Yes. And I'm ready to ask one of the three questions you owe me."

Anton arched an eyebrow. "Oh?"

I grabbed the card in question from my pocket and held it out. "After looking at the video on this SD card, and using every method of analysis at your disposal, can you tell me this video shows me the truth of what happened, with no attempt to use magic or technology to manipulate events to appear other than they are?"

I'd spent most of the boat ride thinking about how I would phrase my question. I still wasn't sure I'd got it right. And besides that, Anton and I both knew he could argue if he wanted to. He'd agreed to answer a question, not to perform any work that might be required by a question. For example, I couldn't ask him what it felt like after he killed Siobhan, using the question to necessitate that he kill her in order to answer.

But I'd clearly piqued his curiosity.

He accepted the SD card, and slid it into the computer on his desk. It said a lot about his faith in his security system that he wasn't worried I'd attempted to put a virus on his system, or some sort of spyware. But then again, if Dimitri was my son, I wouldn't worry about that either.

There was no sound on the video, but I could tell by the twitch of the vampire's eyes when it started to play.

And I saw when he witnessed the shooting.

He clicked a few keys, still studying the screen. Finally, he looked up at me.

"Mother Renard, my greatest fear is that someday I will lose my wife or my son. That an enemy will strike them down in retaliation for something I've done, and I will face a future without them."

I stared at him. Of all the reactions I'd expected, that had been nowhere on the list. "That's not an answer to my question."

"I will answer your question in a moment. Did you hear what I said?"

"Yes, but I don't understand why you're telling me that?"

"I'm telling you this because it is important for everyone to be honest about their greatest fear. You must know what it is. And you must accept that others will find out. You must be able to face that fear, without flinching. To do whatever you can to protect yourself, all the while understanding that there are things you can stop, and things you can't. But either way, you will need to continue on if the worst happens. You will have to find a way."

"Sage advice," I said, my voice little more than a rasp. "Now if you'll just answer the question?"

Dimitri's voice came over the speaker on the laptop. "I'm sorry, Shade. The video is genuine."

The sound of Anton's son over the speaker didn't surprise me. That was why I'd brought the SD card here in the first place. Anton owed me the question, but it was his son the techie spy that I'd believed had the true answer. And he qualified as a means at Anton's disposal.

The air in the room was suddenly too thick to breathe.

"The answer to your question, Mother Renard," Anton said quietly, "is yes. I can tell you, after using every method of analysis at my disposal, that this video shows the truth of what happened, with no attempt to use magic or technology to manipulate events to appear other than they are."

"You only took a minute. Less than." My voice didn't even sound like mine.

"I promise you, Shade, if there was anything to find, I'd know," Dimitri said sadly. "This is what I do. There is no one better."

Tears were streaming down my face again. "You have to help me save him."

Anton's eyebrows rose. "I'm sorry?"

I swiped at the tears. "You have to help me stop the Vanguard from turning Andy over to Siobhan. She'll kill him."

"That is not for me to decide." A hint of anger worked its way into his voice. "I am not your employee. And I'm beginning to think you need a reminder of that. Something that will stay with you."

My rage flowed upward, boiling away my tears. I stood, bracing my hands on the table, magic licking at the bare surface in tendrils of energy. "You owe me."

"Do I?"

I shook my head. "I don't know why you're so invested in my life, but you clearly have some stake in what happens to me."

His face shut down. No emotion, no hint of what he was thinking. "And what makes you think I'm invested in your life?"

I almost mentioned the five million dollar loan to Flint. But I bit it back at the last second. I didn't want either of them to know I knew about that. I was going to save Andy, and he was going to continue his investigation. Compromising it now was as good as admitting I'd failed him. Admitting I'd given up. And I most certainly had not given up.

I pressed my fingertips into the table, trying to block out the urge to use magic to get me what reason had not. "You made it very clear early tonight with Dr. Ouellet. You were willing to give her more than you wanted to, but only after you found out about Andy's bail terms. I mean something to you, or you need me for something. And I'm telling you right now, I will not let the kelpies have Andy. I will do whatever it takes to stop that from happening. *Whatever it takes.* So if you give a flying fig leaf what happens to me, you will help me save him."

Anton held very still, his eyes locked onto mine. "You're not thinking clearly," he warned.

"I am *crystal* clear. I will stop it from happening. One way or another."

"That's not what I mean." He rose to his feet, slowly pushing his chair away from the desk. "If you're right, and I am...invested in your fate. If I do indeed have concerns about what might happen to you if you go off alone to save Agent Bradford...*helping* you is not my only option." He stepped around the desk. "I could," he continued gently, "simply remove you from harm's way until the situation has resolved itself."

My breath caught. Fear gripped my stomach in its fist, and it took more effort than I wanted to admit not to double over. I couldn't outrun him. Even if I'd started while he was still sitting, he was far too fast. Escape wasn't an option.

I locked my gaze on Anton's forehead, right between his eyes. "You could keep me here," I agreed. "But how long are you willing to hold me?"

"I don't believe it will be long. Siobhan is not a patient woman. And now that there is video proof of Agent Bradford's crime, whatever time she's allowing you with him is a courtesy."

"She's torturing me," I corrected him. "She wants us both to suffer."

Anton inclined his head, acknowledging that I was right. "It won't be long," he repeated.

"Well, that depends on what harm you're protecting me from," I hedged. "Are you protecting me from confronting Siobhan now to stop her from hurting my friend? Or are you protecting me from confronting Siobhan later, after she's killed my friend?" I tilted my head. "Because if I haven't made myself clear, I believe Siobhan set Andy up. And I might not be able to hold her legally responsible for Raichel's murder, but I do believe with all my heart that it's her fault. And I'll make sure she pays for it somehow."

Anton's eyes flashed red. "You'll get yourself killed."

"Maybe."

"I overestimated you," Anton said tightly. "Perhaps it's time to reconsider...many things."

Scath growled, a rumbling in her chest that sent a shiver up my spine even though it wasn't aimed at me. Anton didn't look at her, but I could see the sudden tension in his neck. And his renewed determination to try and trick me into making eye contact.

I glared at his ear. "I'm not done with my investigation yet. It isn't over."

"And what is there left to do?" Anton demanded. "You've seen the murder with your own eyes."

"I have reason to believe Siobhan had Gloria killed in order to usurp her position as leader of the team."

"And what does that have to do with Agent Bradford's guilt?"

"Nothing. But Siobhan is the leader, and it's up to her how Andy will be sentenced. If I can find proof that she's responsible for Gloria's death, then she might see her way to a...lesser sentence."

Anton blinked. "You intend to blackmail her."

I switched my attention to his other ear. I didn't feel the need to lie, considering the fact that the case he'd hired me to work for him at the beginning of this year had involved having me locate his little black book of blackmail. "Yes."

Flint had stayed out of the entire exchange. I didn't look at him, mostly because I didn't want the two men to think I knew what was between them. So I dropped my gaze when Anton looked over my shoulder at the *leannan sidhe*.

"Fine," he said curtly. "I will allow you to leave under one condition."

I ground my teeth. "And that condition would be...?"

"Take the alpha with you. Detective Sergeant Osbourne."

The demand surprised me enough that I almost met his eyes. Almost. I stared at the bridge of his nose as I fought down the immediate protest that Liam was injured, and I couldn't drag him out of bed for this. I didn't want to tell the vampire about what Scath had done. Not when I still knew so little about it.

"Fine."

"And Mr. Valencia can remain here with me. I'd like to hear about the investigation thus far."

"More than fine," I agreed.

Anton eyed me for a minute longer. I had the irrational thought that he was reading my mind, that he knew I wanted to make a small detour before going to New Moon. I hid my nervousness behind a glare of frustrated impatience, tapping my foot for good measure. Anton quirked an eyebrow at that, then nodded.

"We will need to speak again," he said finally. "Tomorrow night. One way or another, you should be finished with this investigation by then."

CHAPTER 23

THERE WERE three reasons it annoyed me that Anton Winters insisted on having his lackey drop me off at New Moon. First of all, it seemed like a very blatant comment on how little Anton trusted me to do as I'd said I would and go straight to New Moon.

Second, being dropped off might give Liam's people the impression that I expected their injured alpha to drop everything to chauffeur me around, which I didn't want.

And third, there was a small part of me that worried one of the wolves would somehow identify the driver, or the car, as one of the vampire's. I really didn't need them making that sort of connection.

The autumn wind tried to knock me over as soon as I got out of the car. It felt like a reprimand, as if the weather itself was horrified that I was about to drag an injured man out of bed on the order of a vampire. I looked up at the building as if I could see inside to where Liam was resting, trying to sleep off whatever Scath had done to him.

"I'm sure he's fine, and he'll be happy to see us," Peasblossom said.

I hesitated, then looked down at Scath. "I think you should wait out here. Not hiding exactly, but maybe just being...subtle."

Scath sat down and stared at me. The bag slung around her body writhed for a few seconds before Majesty poked his head out and meowed.

"Maybe you could go into the forest and set him off?" I suggested.

Scath snorted. I heard judgment in that sound, but maybe that was just me being paranoid. In any case, she turned around and loped off toward the forest across the road. I let out a sigh of relief and headed for the front doors.

As I strode in Sam looked up from a length of rope they'd been tying into a complicated knot. I spotted a book propped open in front of them—a handbook of knots, if the picture I could see was any indication. They closed the book when they saw me looking and put down the length of rope, a wary expression on their face.

"Hi, Sam. Nice to see you again." I cleared my throat. "I was hoping I could see Liam? Check on how he's doing?"

"He's still resting. His injuries are...unusual." They leaned over the desk and looked down. "Where's Scath?"

"She's outside." I gripped the edge of the front desk. "Can you at least tell me if he's okay?"

Sam studied me, weighing my words, reading my body language. I had hope that they were about to cave and let me visit their alpha.

Then I heard footsteps behind me. Two guards approached, and neither of them looked happy to see me. My shoulders slumped. My escort out of the building had arrived.

"You have to know I would never hurt him," I said gently.

Sam never took their eyes off my face. "I'm not accusing you of anything. But Liam is our alpha, and he was hurt. Bad. By your friend, while with you. He's not awake yet, and we haven't heard his side of things. So you'll understand if we're erring on the side of caution. I'll have him call you when he wakes up. That's the best I can do." Sam's voice wasn't unkind, but neither did it suggest there was room to argue. They nodded to the guards, and the first one gestured toward the door.

"Wait."

A familiar gruff voice made me spin around. "Edwin."

I'd met Edwin for the first time when he was working—against his will—for a very bad wizard, Stavros Rosso. Edwin had been injured when a bomb made from silver shrapnel exploded and left him with bits of the shining metal embedded in his face. The circumstances around the bomb had driven Edwin away from his pack, and right into Stavros' waiting arms. The wizard had opted to leave the metal there, healing Edwin only enough to keep him alive and reliant on his magic for survival. It was only after we'd chased Stavros out of town that Edwin had allowed Liam to bring him to New Moon, where he'd finally gotten the medical help he needed.

I didn't know if Edwin didn't smile often because the scar tissue made it difficult, stretching the stiff skin from his left eye all the way down to his nose as it did, or if he just didn't feel like it. Either way, he always looked cross, and now was no exception.

Thankfully, he didn't seem to be cross with me.

"Liam said her name," he told Sam, skipping the social niceties. "In his sleep. I think we can interpret that to mean that he would want to speak with her as soon as possible."

"That's not how I'd interpret it," Sam said arching one eyebrow. "You're aware they're dating?"

The insinuation was clear, and I blinked at Sam in surprise. It was surreal to stand here listening to werewolves discuss my hypothetical sex life. More surreal given everything that had happened in the past twenty-four hours. If I weren't so stressed out, it might have been funny.

"Well, I'm telling you he would want to speak with her. Now."

"You don't have the authority to override me," Sam pointed out. "So she leaves."

Edwin looked from Sam to each of the guards. "Fine. So when Liam wakes up, and I tell him that Shade was here, asking to speak with him, whom shall I say kept her from waking him? Which of you will take responsibility for sending her away?"

I had never loved Edwin more than I did in that moment.

The guards suddenly looked very interested in Sam's haircut. The androgynous werewolf's gaze bounced around the group, and I could almost see the wheels turning in their head. It would have been one thing to tell Liam they'd turned me away. It would be another to say they'd turned me away after Edwin had argued that Liam had made his wishes to see me known.

"Fine. Take her to him, stay until you have an answer about whether he wants to see her."

One of the guards looked annoyed, as if he'd really wanted to throw me out. But the second guard just looked relieved that the decision was out of her hands.

Edwin nodded. "I'll take her up."

"They're going too," Sam said.

I didn't care who escorted me, as long as we could get a wiggle on. Siobhan had said sunrise, and I had no idea how long it would take me to find Gordon, let alone get the proof I needed to prove Siobhan had hired him to kill Gloria.

I didn't mention any of that to Sam.

Edwin led the way past the check-in point and headed for the stairs.

"Edwin, how is he?" I asked.

"He's sleeping." Edwin paused, then looked over his

shoulder as he climbed the stairs. "He's been sleeping since shortly after he got here. We haven't been able to wake him up, but his vitals are strong. What happened to him?"

My stomach churned with a sudden case of nerves. "He was injured in a fight with two *leannan sidhe*," I said carefully. "One of the *sidhe* started pumping up everyone's adrenaline, and all hell broke loose."

"And Scath bit him."

I held my breath. "Yes. But she didn't mean to hurt him. She was diving for Raphael, and Liam put himself between them."

"Well, we need him to wake up and say so. Otherwise you might find it easier to get in than to get out."

I forced myself to keep walking, not to react to the barely-veiled threat. Edwin was just doing his job, protecting his alpha. There was no reason to discuss the ugly possibility that we'd find out for sure what it took to keep a witch against her will.

With Andy's life on the line, I didn't like their chances.

Edwin stopped outside one of the rooms and knocked on the door. After a minute that felt like a small eternity, the door opened, and a woman peeked out. A short blonde woman, thick with muscle, wearing a green hoodie that made her blue eyes look teal. "Yes?"

I recognized her as Liam's sister, Brenna. She seemed to recognize me at the same time, and a smile spread over her lips. "Shade! You're here to see him. Hold on, just a minute."

She closed the door. Another minute-eternity later, she opened the door all the way and scowled. "I still can't wake him up."

"I'll try?" I said hopefully.

She threw an arm out, pointing at a door across the small living room. "He's in there, be my guest."

The two guards twitched forward as if they'd follow me in,

but Brenna blocked their path. "I think she can handle this on her own, don't you?"

I didn't wait around to hear the argument.

The bedroom was dark and quiet, a soothing mix of shadows. I could see well enough to walk around the lumps on the floor that I guessed were clothes, and I avoided one of the chairs that were set up on either side of the bed. The lump of covers rose and fell as Liam drew deep, even breaths.

I crept closer to the bed. "Liam?" I whispered.

Nothing.

"Why are you whispering when the entire point is to wake him up?" Peasblossom demanded—not in a whisper.

I leaned forward. Liam's head was on the pillow, his face smooth with sleep. His broad shoulders were bare, and despite the darkness, I could make out part of his chest, the tight muscles of his stomach. I had the sudden urge to put my hand over his heart, feel it beating for myself. I touched his shoulder. "Liam."

"Wait, I have an idea!" Peasblossom said excitedly.

I should have known what was coming. It was cold outside, so of course my familiar was wearing her little pink slippers Mother Hazel had given her. The fuzzy slippers.

The ones that crackled when she moved too fast.

I felt the building static as Peasblossom shuffled over the sheet around Liam's body. My eyes widened, but before I could tell her to stop, she was there at the edge of the sheet, one tiny pink finger reaching for Liam's bare skin.

Bzzt!

Peasblossom leapt into the air, anticipating the need to dodge Liam's flailing limbs. The electric shock was strong enough that I saw a flare of bluish-white light, and I winced in sympathy. But Liam didn't move.

Peasblossom scowled. "I can try again."

"No, don't—"

Liam grabbed my hand.

I let out a squeak of surprise as he rolled over, dragging me underneath him, and pinning me in place with the covers still wrapped around his body. His elbows and forearms dug into the mattress on either side of my shoulders as he bracketed my body with his. I found myself staring up into the gold eyes of his wolf, and for a second, I couldn't breathe.

His nostrils flared. I held perfectly still as he leaned down to inhale a deep breath over my body, close enough to stir the air near my skin. It was an intimate gesture, and a sudden rush of heat flowed down my body, bringing with it another realization.

Liam had removed more than his shirt before going to bed.

His nostrils flared again, and he made a sound low in his throat. His eyelids fluttered and he shook his head, as if trying to wake up. When he looked at me again, his eyes were still gold, still very lupine. He bent his head again, ran his lips over my throat. Adrenaline poured into my bloodstream, and I writhed beneath him.

I tried to take a deep breath to slow my pulse, but Liam's wolf chose that moment to lower his body against mine and draw his tongue over my neck in a warm, wet stripe.

"Wait!" I babbled. "Andy—"

A loud snarl made my heart skip a beat, and gold eyes flared in the darkness as Liam lifted his head, a sliver of moonlight catching his irises and turning them into twin suns.

Angry twin suns.

Probably never a good idea to yell out another man's name when you're lying in bed with the man you're dating. "Andy needs our help!" I clarified, my voice still higher than I'd have liked.

Liam shook his head, let out a huff. He blinked, and

suddenly I was staring into eyes the dark blue of his human self. He squinted down at me, confusion pulling his brows together.

"Shade?"

His voice was gruff with sleep, and perhaps other things. Even with the confusion on his face, there was no mistaking the heat in his eyes as he dragged his gaze from my head down to where his body kept me pinned to the mattress and back up. I watched the conflict play out over his features, watched him try to remember how we'd ended up like this. His nostrils flared again, and his gaze flicked to my neck. Where he'd licked me.

"Andy's corrupted!" I blurted out. "And I found the missing SD card. He did it. He shot Raichel."

Liam shook his head, still trying to wake up, to process. I could have done a better job explaining, but so much had happened. And I was running out of time.

And it was really hard to think with him lying on top of me.

"I'm sorry, Shade," he rasped finally.

I grabbed his arms. "It's not over. I need your help. I need to find a gambler that used to hang around Fortuna's. His name is Gordon Larkin. He killed Siobhan's predecessor, and I think she put him up to it. Or tricked him."

"How will that help—"

I shook my head and pushed against Liam's chest. He let me squirm out from under him, but I didn't miss the way he flexed his right hand as if fighting the urge to pull me back.

"Siobhan gave me until sunrise. I can't prove Andy's innocent, but maybe if I can prove she killed Gloria, I can use that to save his life."

"You're going to get Larkin's testimony to prove Siobhan conspired to kill Gloria, and threaten to tell the team if she doesn't commute Andy's sentence."

I started pacing and almost fell when a discarded T-shirt wrapped around my foot. I couldn't read Liam's tone. It wasn't until this moment that I realized he might not approve. He was a cop, a man who believed in justice, believed in the guilty being punished. Maybe he'd think Andy deserved to get what was coming to him if he was truly responsible.

"Shade, I can practically hear you thinking," he said at last. "I'm not going to stop you, if that's what you're worried about."

I bit the inside of my cheek. I felt guilty for even thinking it, but I had to ask. "You don't have a problem with me trying to save him from the consequences? Even though he did it?"

Liam sat up and stretched, tendons in his neck popping, the sound loud in the darkness. "What about the second murder? Deacon?"

I scowled. "That is a long story. The short version is Andy didn't do it."

"Well, that's something." He got up from the bed, the falling covers confirming my suspicion that he'd stripped completely before his nap. I should have looked away, but right now, I was at the end of my rope, and any distraction helped.

I thought I saw a hint of gold in his eyes as he noticed me looking at him, and I half-expected him to leap over the bed and give me the distraction that was starting to sound so good. But he forced himself to turn and snag his jeans from where he'd thrown them on a nearby chair.

"You said Andy's corrupted?"

"Yes. He's with Evelyn and Oksana right now. He didn't trust himself to go to the racetrack when I questioned the racers. I'd thought for a while it might be Mickey V who shot Raichel, but then I found the SD card."

Liam wasn't looking at me now. He grabbed a clean T-shirt out of the closet on the far wall. "So Andy is corrupted, and he really did shoot Raichel. You want to get leverage on Siobhan to make sure she doesn't execute him for it."

"Yes."

He pulled the shirt over his head, then turned to face me. "Can I ask you a question?"

I didn't want him to, but I nodded anyway.

"How do you feel about the thought that if he gets away with this, he might just keep killing kelpies?"

I curled my hands into fists, then forced myself to relax. "I talked to him, Liam. He's devastated by the corruption. Terrified. It's not who he wants to be."

"Didn't stop him from shooting Raichel."

"No, it didn't. But shooting Raichel made him face the severity of his situation. And after talking to him, I believe he's ready to ask for help."

I took a step closer to Liam, meeting his eyes, letting him see the sincerity in my face, hear it in my voice. "I won't just turn him loose and cross my fingers he doesn't keep killing people. And even if I were inclined to do that, he wouldn't let me. He wants help. He wants *hope*."

My voice dropped to a whisper, mostly to keep it from breaking when I continued. "I can't let him die feeling the way he does right now. Like he's become the monster he's fought so hard not to be. Lorelei took everything from him when she corrupted him. But I believe he has the strength and the willpower to live with that corruption. I believe he can learn to control it, the same way he's always controlled his temper. He just needs a different kind of help."

I took another step, close enough to Liam now that I could feel his aura humming against my skin. "He wants to redeem himself. Not for me, not for anyone else. For himself. I need to make sure he gets that chance."

Liam slid his arms around my waist and pulled me against him. He leaned down to touch his forehead to mine, then nuzzled the side of my face. It was a werewolf thing, I'd learned.

The nuzzling, scenting your partner, being scented in return. It felt good, and some of the tension eased from my shoulders.

"You're a good friend, Shade Renard," he murmured.

"Not if I fail him," I whispered back. "I hate to ask, I know you're hurt, and that's my fault too, and—"

"I'll be fine," Liam interrupted. "This is what pack does. We pull together when things get tough." He pressed a kiss to my forehead, then stepped back. "So tell me about this gambler we need to find."

CHAPTER 24

"I CAN'T BELIEVE FINDING him was that easy," Peasblossom said.

I stared out the window of Liam's truck, my hand already on the door handle as he made another turn. According to his GPS, we'd be at the casino in seven minutes. Seven minutes until I'd get the answers I needed. Until I *hoped* I'd get the answers I needed.

"Searching local casinos was a good idea," Liam said, glancing at me.

"It wasn't a stretch," I demurred. "A man whose gambling addiction is strong enough to make him bet everything on one race isn't going to walk away from it entirely, no matter what the risk. And since he lost everything, it made sense that he'd stay in familiar territory."

"And most people don't actually know how to go about getting a fake ID," Liam added. "I doubt he'd have tried traveling under his own name after killing Gloria."

"Right."

"Even for a gambler he took a big chance that the kelpies wouldn't spot him and eat him, hanging around the city," Peasblossom chimed in.

"The waterhorses don't venture this far inland very often," I said absent-mindedly. "And even if they did see him, the bartender Blake talked to said Gordon doesn't look much like his picture anymore. He's living on the street for the most part."

"And people don't look too hard at the homeless," Liam said grimly. "Just a sad fact of life."

"People experiencing homelessness," I said automatically. My hand went to my stomach, where my late dinner of steak and fries, eaten while waiting for Liam's pack to canvas the local casinos with Gordon's driver's license photo, weighed heavily.

"You okay?" Liam asked.

"I'm fine."

"You should be," Peasblossom scoffed. "At this point, worst case scenario is you go to Siobhan and tell her we have proof that she lied when she said she killed Gordon. We found him, so obviously he wasn't eaten."

"No," I corrected her. "Worst case scenario is that Siobhan decides to face an angry team instead of bargaining with me for Andy's life. She could just as well say she ate the wrong person —oops—and then lead the charge against Gordon now."

"Don't think about the worst case scenario right now. Let's wait and see what he says." Liam paused. "Unless that's not what's bothering you."

I couldn't help it. I glanced toward the back of the truck. Scath reclined in the open metal bed, seemingly unperturbed by the frigid air rushing around her.

Liam's pack had not been happy to see their alpha get in the same vehicle as the *sidhe* who'd attacked him—maliciously or not. When Liam had come out of the bedroom looking almost like his old self, the relief among his guards had been palpable. It had also turned quickly to shock and dismay when he'd informed them he'd be leaving with me.

And Scath.

I still thought that if Scath had attempted to get in the cab with Liam instead of riding in the truck bed, Sam would have gotten up the nerve to confront the alpha about what a bad idea it was to let a threat like that stand without investigation.

"I got in Scath's way," Liam said calmly. "I know she wasn't attacking me."

"Your pack doesn't feel that way," I mumbled. "Edwin is the one who convinced them to let me see you at all, and even he looked horrified when you said you were leaving with us. Accident or not, be honest—how long do you think it's going to take them to feel comfortable around Scath? And by association, me?"

"We'll have to talk about it," Liam admitted. "I don't want you to stress about it right now with everything else that's going on, but I will need to know the specifics of what Scath's bite did to me. That was no ordinary wound. If she's going to be around my pack—including me—then I have a responsibility to find out exactly what I'm dealing with."

I looked down at his arm and the fresh bandages I'd helped apply before we left. There was no blood, at least he'd healed that much. But there was still a wound, red and angry, like a bad burn.

"I don't know," I admitted quietly. "I don't know much about her at all." I stared out my window, thinking about Scath and how hard it was to get her to talk about herself. About how much those little tidbits I had learned should scare me.

So why didn't they? Why did I trust her? Why did I feel, deep down in my witchy gut, that Scath was no threat to me?

"If you think it would be easier for you to talk to her alone, that's fine. You talk to her, try to get her to open up. And when she's ready, we'll talk together."

I didn't ask what would happen if Scath refused. What would happen if she opted to stay in beast form as she so often did. I hadn't even known she had a human form for months after she started following me around. If she didn't want to talk, she wouldn't talk.

Liam didn't mention that possibility either.

I didn't think either of us wanted to think about it.

Liam's GPS announced our arrival in a smooth mechanical voice, blessedly breaking the uncomfortable silence.

"A step down from Fortuna's," Peasblossom observed.

I had to agree. Gordon Larkin's new casino of choice was a much smaller establishment than Fortuna's had been, the sort of place that springs to mind when one hears the phrase "hole in the wall." The sign over the front door declared "Easy Street" in neon letters that had probably started out as pink, but now looked like a bloody orange.

I got out and headed for the front door without waiting. Scath caught up to me easily, and I noticed that Liam gave her a little more space than before. An ounce of prevention, I supposed. We made our way inside, and I wrinkled my nose as the scent of sweat, spilled beer, and the metallic tang of coins surrounded me.

"There he is."

Liam followed my gesture as I nodded my head to the man sitting at a slot machine. His eyes glowed with the reflection from the brightly lit game, making them dance with unnatural colors. The resemblance to the photo on his driver's license was fading, but he still had the same brown hair lightened with plenty of grey, and the same scar near his right eye. His spine was bowed, but that wasn't unusual for someone who spent as much time in a casino as I guessed he did. At least, if that giant bowl of quarters on a stool next to him was any indication.

As he dipped his hand into the quarters, I noticed something amiss. Specifically, a finger. His pinkie on his left hand was gone.

"She claimed she hunted him down and found him on one of those casino boats. Said she ate him."

I stared at the missing digit. Siobhan had lied, but like most lies from the fey, she had made sure there was just enough truth to sound good. I'd have bet Peasblossom's favorite sword that Siobhan had eaten Gordon's finger. All for a bit of truth for a lie of omission.

I hadn't realized I'd come to a stop until Liam moved around me, heading for Gordon. Just then, the gambler slammed a fist down on the machine, swearing at what I guessed was not his first loss of the night. He turned his head, and a shock jolted through my system as I got a good look at his eyes.

His *solid black* eyes.

I hissed and reached out to snag Liam by his shirt and haul him back.

He gave me a questioning look.

"His eyes," I whispered. "Look at his eyes."

Liam looked again. Tension seized his body, and his aura flared. "He's corrupted."

Adrenaline poured through my system, so intense I flashed back to my fight with Raphael earlier. I blinked rapidly, trying to get rid of the ghostly image of those silver eyes boring in to mine, the rush of gooseflesh that rose on my body as it remembered the rush of pure excitement. I shoved those thoughts away, my mind spinning with the situation before me.

Gordon is corrupted.

Each word pulsed in flashing lights in my brain to match the sign outside. I closed my eyes, opted for a calming breath.

"Shade, he's corrupted just like Andy," Peasblossom hissed. "And Siobhan had kelpies outside the church—"

"We don't know there's a connection," I said, as much to myself as to her. My heart pounded despite my argument. "We can't know there's a connection between Siobhan and Lorelei, not yet."

Peasblossom narrowed her eyes. "You think it's a coincidence that corrupted men killed two of her enemies?"

I waved my hands in the air. "Okay, new plan."

I pulled Liam to the corner of the casino and explained my idea to our group. If it was going to work, we'd need help from New Moon again. It made my stomach roll to think of asking more of his pack so soon after the incident, but Liam didn't share my qualms. He made the necessary call, and I kept an eye on Gordon.

Corruption wasn't the same thing as being demonic. Even if Gordon had been mentored or taught himself by trial and error how to use whatever ability he'd inherited with the corruption, he'd be no match for me. Not if I was smart about it.

Flint hadn't been wrong when he'd told Andy that power was nothing without experience. Unkind, but not wrong.

Liam went outside to wait for his pack members to arrive so he could give them instructions. We both agreed that it would be better if he met them alone, and Scath and I waited inside. By the time he came back in to tell me everyone was ready, I was about to climb the walls. I wanted answers now and I was so close.

"They're in position," Liam reported. He glanced at Gordon still glued to the same slot machine. "How far away do you want me?"

"Far enough that he doesn't see you right away, close enough for crowd control," I said immediately. I clutched the supplies Bizbee had retrieved from my waist pouch for me to my chest. "Peasblossom, are you ready?"

"Ready." Her weight lifted off my shoulder and I had a glimpse of a small sack of salt strapped to her back, with a ripcord gripped in one of her tiny hands. Then she blinked out of sight.

"Didn't you need to cast a spell to make her invisible last time?" Liam asked.

"She grows in power with me," I said, my eyes on our target.

Liam seemed to get that now wasn't the time for questions about power or pixie invisibility. He'd remember to ask later, I had no doubt.

"If he's corrupted, then he'll have a gift of some kind," I reminded Liam. "Try to keep the other customers away from him." I looked down at Scath. "Remember what to do?"

Scath looked up at me, managing to convey impatience even through her German Shepherd service dog glamour.

We were as ready as we'd ever be.

I closed my hand into a fist, feeling my ring of shielding on my finger, allowing the dull hum to provide some comfort as I approached the corrupted gambler. Gordon didn't take his eyes off the machine, not even when I stood close enough to touch him. The sounds of the slot machines around me jangled against my nerves, and the flickering lights played havoc with my peripheral vision. I drew on my power, forced myself to concentrate.

"Gordon Larkin?" I asked.

He didn't look up. "You have the wrong guy."

I glanced down. Peasblossom had started the salt circle. Thank the Goddess the casino wasn't very busy. The circle had to be big, and I didn't need anyone breaking it by accident.

"I want to talk to you about Gloria."

"You have the wrong guy," he repeated. "And if you don't leave me alone, you're going to be sorry. People have a habit of getting very unlucky around me after they piss me off."

Tough words, but I noticed the way he fisted his hand in the bucket of quarters. Probably grabbing a handful to throw if the need arose.

"That'll be the demonic corruption then, will it?"

Shock slackened his features as he turned to me. Then a broad grin spread over his face. He released the quarters and turned more fully to face me. "I don't like you," he said, still smiling. "And I don't like your chances of catching me."

His hand shot forward, reaching for my face.

But it hit the barrier of the circle first.

Pain pinched his face and he drew his hand back, staring at me as if I'd played a dirty trick. "What the hell?"

"I'm guessing the demon that did this to you didn't explain what would happen if you kept using your 'gifts,' did she?" I asked. "You said people get unlucky around you?"

"They do," Gordon said, trying to sound sinister. It might have worked better if he could quit looking back at the slot machine as if it called to him. Or stopped rubbing his knuckles as if he'd bruised himself on the circle.

"I've heard you're pretty unlucky yourself. Makes me wonder how you got that big bucket of quarters?"

"Payment for not making people unlucky." He jutted out his chin. "I see someone having more than their fair share of luck, and I ask for a donation. If they don't give it to me their luck goes away. I mean, it *really* goes away. I don't usually have to ask a third time."

"That must not make you many friends."

"I don't need friends."

There. I heard it in his voice. The lie. Gordon had been a regular at the track, and those sorts of crowds tended to be close. Lots of familiar faces. Passing tips, commiserating when you lose. And of course, celebrating a win was more fun with friends. As with all corruptions, Gordon's gift had come at a price. He could extort the money he needed to feed his habit, but it had left him alone. Alone with his habit. The fate of an addict.

"I can help you," I told him. "Answer my questions. Help me and I'll help you."

"I don't want your help. Go away."

I shook my head. "I'm not going anywhere."

"Too bad." Again his hand shot out, aiming for my face. Again it struck the energy of the circle, but this time, he was ready for it. He strained to push his hand closer to me, but it wouldn't budge. Frustration dragged a growl from his throat, and he dropped his arm and turned, tried to run.

But he had no luck there either.

The circle held.

"This isn't necessary," he said at last, trying to put his grin back in place. "I'm sure we can come to an arrangement."

"We have an arrangement," I said simply. "You're going to answer my questions, or I'm going to take you home with me."

His eyebrows shot up, and he gave me a once over. "That doesn't sound so bad."

"And every day I'll try something new to cure you of your corruption. You can be my guinea pig."

"Torture by holy water?" Gordon shook his head. "It feels a little warm against my skin, but nothing horrible. Like bathwater, really."

"I'll try holy water, sure. But there are a lot of other holy items much stronger than that. Things that can reach deeper, seek out hints of evil."

"You don't strike me as the torturing kind." He paused. "What do you mean 'guinea pig,' lady?"

I let all the emotion drain from my face. All the worry, and pain. All the hope. I stared at Gordon and let him see how close to the precipice I stood. "My friend has been corrupted. And I'm afraid if I can't find a way to help him, he'll give up. I can't let that happen."

Gordon glanced nervously around. He believed me.

Good.

"Are you looking for help?" I tilted my head. "Here? Among the people you abuse until they give you money?" I gestured at the bucket of quarters. "Fresh haul? And who did that come from? Do you think they'll help you?"

"You can't do anything to me here," he hissed. "What are you going to do, knock me out? Drag me out kicking and screaming? And what will you do when you break this little circle?"

I sighed. "Just remember. There was an easier way."

I held the spell ready as I took a deep breath and reached my foot closer to the salt circle.

"Somnum."

In one quick movement, I broke the circle, simultaneously shoving the spell into the corrupted gambler. Gordon reached for me again, but he tried to reach under my arm as I flung the spell, and his new trajectory made him strike the bucket of quarters. Coins spilled onto the floor, providing a metallic blanket for Gordon to collapse on.

Scath stood by, ready to tackle Gordon if he moved or otherwise managed to shake off the sleep spell. It was hard to predict what gifts the corruption may have given him, and I wasn't taking any chances. I dropped beside him, pulling out my cell phone and pretending to call an ambulance.

Liam approached then as well, playing the part of another concerned citizen, and together we told anyone who came to close to stand back and give him some air.

No one questioned the staff of New Moon as they entered dressed as EMS workers. They had some practice at this deception, having used it many times to retrieve werewolves who lost control, or new wolves who hadn't had control to begin with. The presence of EMS workers made stories like "bad drugs" or "psychotic break" go down smoother with the human populace.

In less than five minutes, Gordon was strapped to a stretcher and the werewolves carried him out to the waiting ambulance with Liam and me at their heels to "explain what had happened."

Liam slammed the back doors to the EMS vehicle closed. I sat beside the stretcher and brought Gordon around with a sound slap to his face.

"What the—" His eyes flew wide and he sat up, feeling his body as if to check for injuries. "Where am I?"

"You are at a crossroads," I said grimly. "Now's the part where you tell me what I want to know. Speak quickly. I need to decide if I'm taking you with me when I leave."

Gordon stared at me, weighing his options. Finally, he let himself sag onto the stretcher and covered his face with his hands. "What do you want from me?"

"Who corrupted you?"

"I didn't get a name. She used to come into the casino. Didn't work there, though." He dropped his hands. "I thought she was a prostitute. Heard someone call her Trixie once, but I don't know if that was her name, or just a pet name. I had better things to do with my money than pay for sex, but she was easy on the eyes, so I didn't shoo her away."

He stared at the ceiling. "She was a tall woman. Thin, but she knew how to work with what she had. Used to curl her hair up into these little balls on either side of her head, stab them with chopsticks the way girls do. Not my thing, really, made her look too young."

I tamped down on a surge of excitement. Lorelei wore her hair like that. But a hairstyle wasn't going to be enough proof for the Vanguard. "She never gave you a name. You said you weren't interested in sex, so why did she keep hanging around you?"

"Must have been my personality." He snorted. "She liked to sit with me while I watched a race. Said she saw my passion for it." He rubbed his chin. "Now that I think about it, she was a help then. She really knew how to read people. Like she could see if a jockey was having a bad day. I won more on the days she stood with me, watching the jockeys before the race."

"She gave you tips?" Liam asked.

"Sort of. She told me who her favorites were. I noticed her favorites tended to do all right so I started letting her pick my winners. Then one day she stopped coming. I should have known something was up. She kissed me before she left, and it tasted like a goodbye." Gordon's face darkened. "After that, I started losing, bad."

"What happened the day you killed Gloria?" I asked.

Gordon squirmed. If I'd been in a more charitable mood, I might have thought he felt bad for what he'd done. "I'd lost more than I usually did. I was on edge, losing my temper, shouting at people. I might have thrown a few things... Gloria noticed. She asked me about it, and I told her about Trixie. How she'd been helping me, then she just disappeared."

He shook his head. "I hadn't realized how angry I was until then, but that day it all hit me. I started shouting about Trixie, how she'd ruined me, made me depend on her. I used to be good at picking winners. Really good!" He ran a hand through his hair. "Anyway, Gloria pulled me aside and calmed me down. She set me up with a free drink, gave me a ticket on the house."

"I understand she did that a lot," I said.

He shrugged. "I guess. Gloria was..." He swallowed hard. "She was good to me, I guess. Anyway, I should have known something was wrong. Later she came to me, told me she felt bad that I'd been victimized. Said Trixie wasn't who she seemed, wasn't a good person. She said I wasn't the only one Trixie had targeted. Gloria said she'd give me a tip, but only this once. Told me to make it count, and if she gave it to me, I had to swear never to ask for a tip from her again. And I was never to mention it to anyone at the track."

"The tip was bad," Liam guessed.

Gordon threw back his head and roared, with an inhuman echo to the sound that set Scath's fur standing up, and sent Peasblossom's wings whirring against my neck in a response I knew to be more fight than flight.

"I lost *everything*. I bet my *car* on that race, I bet my *house*. I lost it all on a tip that should have been *golden*."

"So you killed her for it." Peasblossom's tone was scathing.

Gordon looked around for her, but she hadn't dropped her invisibility. "I didn't mean to! I thought about it, I'll admit that, but I wasn't going to. But I was on my knees, still staring at the track, when one of the other employees came up to me, a girl from the stable. She picked me up and dusted me off. She said I should cheer up, it could be worse. Said someone had seen her boss, Gloria, giving some chump a bad tip. Said if Gloria had broken her own rules she must be really tired of seeing that loser around the track, must have wanted to be rid of him once and for all."

I pulled out a picture of Siobhan in human form. My hand shook slightly as I showed it to him. "Is this her?"

"She looked more human when I saw her." He squinted, studied the picture a few more seconds. Finally, he nodded. "But yeah, that's her. She's the one who let slip that Gloria set me up."

I looked at Liam, my pulse galloping. "I need to talk to Lorelei. Now."

CHAPTER 25

THIS TIME when I called Andy's cell phone, he answered on the first ring. It was a good thing too. That spark of hope I felt when he was so responsive is the only thing that kept me from despairing when he said "Hello" in the tone most people shouted "What do you want?"

"Are you okay?" I asked, keeping my voice composed.

"No," Andy said shortly. His next breath sounded like a meditation exercise. "We're at Goodfellows. I'm here with Evelyn and Oksana, and Evelyn's helping me stay calm, but Siobhan keeps sending kelpies in and it's just…"

He trailed off, but I understood. I clutched the phone tighter. "She's taunting you again, trying to keep you on edge." *Or send you into another episode.* "Don't fall for it."

I looked out at New Moon's parking lot, watching as Blake and Sonar took over custody of Gordon Larkin. They were going to hold him at New Moon while I made arrangements to confirm my suspicions.

I heard a mug sliding across a tabletop, as if Andy were trying to find something to do with his free hand. "Have you found out anything that might help our case?"

"Maybe," I said lightly. "But I need to talk to Evelyn."

"Sure," Andy said, suspicion clear in his voice.

There was a muffled sound as Andy passed the phone to the paladin, then Evelyn's voice. "Shade, it's good to hear from you. How are things progressing?"

Her words sounded sincere, but there was no mistaking the strain in her voice. I wondered just how restless Andy was getting.

"Could you get somewhere private where we can talk?" I asked. "Away from Andy, I mean?"

Evelyn put a hand over the phone. A minute later, she was back. "I'm on the other side of the room. What is it?"

"I need to talk to Lorelei."

Evelyn inhaled sharply. "Shade, I want to help, but that's... That's not a good idea. Laurie is trying to find her way back to God, and seeing you... I don't think she's ready to handle a reminder of what she did. Not yet."

"I need to talk to Lorelei, not Laurie. Please. It could be the difference between life and death."

"May I ask how?"

"It's a long story. Please, Evelyn. I wouldn't ask if it wasn't absolutely necessary."

The *deva* descendant hesitated. "Even if I agreed, I don't think it's a good idea for me to leave Agent Bradford right now. He's...struggling. I'm afraid Siobhan has been relentless."

"I'll stay with him," Liam said from the driver's seat.

"Is that Detective Sergeant Osbourne?" Evelyn asked.

"Yes. He said he'll sit with Andy while you take me to see Lorelei."

She considered that. "Being corrupted isn't the same thing as being a werewolf. What makes your alpha think he can...help him?"

"Both situations require similar techniques to control your

mood and your physical reactions," Liam pointed out. "And if worst comes to worst, I can stop him from hurting anyone."

I'd told Liam the details about Andy's corruption while we were waiting for his pack to canvas the local casinos. He knew about Andy's...altered state. But I didn't think it was bravado that made him think he could still take the FBI agent. Not only did Liam have the experience to give him an edge, he was also an alpha. His power was fed by his link to his pack.

I'd have bet on him too.

"All right," the Ministry agent agreed finally. "If you're sure it's *absolutely* necessary."

"It is, I swear it is. We'll be there soon."

I didn't want to give her time to change her mind, so we ended the call there, and Liam took us to Goodfellows. My mind raced ahead to the upcoming conversation with Lorelei. It said something about the severity of my concern for Andy that it was easier to think about a bargain with a demon than to let my mind wander to the kelpies that were tormenting my friend.

"I could have a word with a few of the kelpies?" Peasblossom offered pointedly.

"We can't let them distract us," I said. "That's what they want."

Telling Peasblossom not to go after any of the kelpies taunting Andy was easier said than done. I couldn't help looking in the windows of the cafe, searching for signs of the malicious equines. I couldn't attack any of them inside Goodfellows without risking the ire of the witch who ran the place and had declared it neutral ground. But if any of them wandered outside...

Thankfully, Evelyn was waiting outside the cafe door, negating any reason I might have had to go inside. She raised a hand as I approached.

"It might be better if you don't go in," she said. "Agent

Bradford is...stressed. He wants to come with you to see Lorelei and he was not pleased when I refused."

"Not pleased?" Peasblossom echoed.

"Angry," Evelyn admitted.

I stared at the doors. "How bad?"

"Oksana can handle him." She cleared her throat and looked at Liam. "Perhaps you could go in? Now?"

Liam took the hint. I felt the swell of his aura as he drew more power to him before heading inside. It took a lot of effort not to follow him in. Assess the situation for myself.

"You're right though," I said, forcing myself to face Evelyn. "Andy can't confront Lorelei right now. Not yet. If he thinks the kelpies' taunting is hard to take..."

"Then he's nowhere near ready for a demon." She gestured toward the parking lot. "On that note..."

I don't know why it surprised me that Evelyn had her own car. I supposed even paladins had to get around somehow. Her little four-door sedan smelled vaguely of incense and mint chewing gum. An odd combination, but not unpleasant.

She handed me a blindfold, and I raised my eyebrows.

"It's a precaution the Ministry of Deliverance must take," she said apologetically. "For your safety as well as those of my colleagues. Demons can be very tempting as well as deceitful."

I took the blindfold and put it on, more to hurry things along than because I agreed. The idea that I'd ever get the urge to visit a demon prison for funsies was ridiculous, but I'd wear whatever she wanted if it would get me to my witness faster.

Peasblossom groused when asked to get into my waist pouch, but it didn't take her long to remember that's where all the honey packets were.

"Thank you for doing this, Evelyn. I really appreciate it," I said honestly.

She started her car. "I want to help, and if this is how I can do that, then I'm happy to. Well, not happy. The Abyss really isn't a good place to visit for the un-condemned." She paused. "Where's Flint?"

I couldn't see anything past the blindfold, so I tilted my head in the direction of her voice. "I went to see Anton Winters earlier, and he asked Flint to stay. I thought it best not to intercede."

"You went to see Anton Winters?"

"It's a long story."

I felt bad for not sharing the details, but part of me was afraid if I told Evelyn about the SD card, then she might be less inclined to help me. I had no doubt she'd do whatever she could to help me prove Andy was innocent, but I had less confidence she'd approve of blackmail. And I wasn't sure how much Lorelei would be able to help me yet.

The drive felt like it took hours, but I knew it couldn't have been more than thirty minutes. I was guessing Evelyn was taking a few extra turns, just in case I was trying to remember the way. Which I wasn't. Even if I'd been so inclined, I didn't have the presence of mind. It took all my mental energy to stop thinking about Siobhan's glee at the prospect of taking possession of my friend.

Evelyn helped me out of the car and took me deep inside the Ministry of Deliverance headquarters building before removing my blindfold. A series of grey hallways met my eyes, the dull paint periodically broken up by surprisingly rich paintings depicting religious scenes. Angels and shining lights. Gargoyles and sprawling churches. Fierce warriors and blessed saints.

She led the way down the winding hallways until she came to a door with symbols carved around the frame. The runes glittered in the light, and I realized they'd been plated with gold. Evelyn placed her hand on the door, palm flat, murmuring a prayer in a language I wasn't familiar with. Then she touched several of the symbols in what I guessed was a specific order. The runes glowed at the brush of her fingertips, and soon the frame was so bright, I had to squint to look at it.

Then the light faded, and she grabbed the doorknob and twisted.

Cold air rushed out at me, almost making me stumble back a step before I caught myself. I leaned into the breeze, pushing my way into the room. It was bare except for a circle of stones around a pit. Evelyn approached, then nodded to the pit.

"That's the entrance. There are rungs on the wall of the pit, but it's not very far down if you'd rather jump."

"Why would she rather jump?" Peasblossom scoffed, poking her head out of the pouch. "She's not a graceful witch, you know."

The paladin gave her a small smile. "The entrance is spelled to discourage both coming and going. You'll feel enchantment spells blocking your way, a general itch at the back of your mind urging you to turn around. Keep pushing through. The same is true when you try to leave, the spells will discourage you from moving forward and try to make you go back, but I'll be here to make certain you can get out."

"This is the entrance to the Abyss, or to Lorelei's cell?" I asked.

"The Abyss. But the entrance is enchanted, so I can make sure you come out near Lorelei. I assume you don't want to be *inside* her prison?"

"No," I agreed.

Evelyn hesitated. "One more thing. The Abyss has an energy all its own. It's designed to make its inhabitants reflect on their sins, with an eye toward redemption. When you get inside, you'll hear whispers. Voices in your head that remind you of any choices you feel guilty about, any wrongs you've done to yourself or others. It can be overwhelming if you're not used to facing up to things you've done. Or if you feel particularly guilty about something."

"Fantastic," I said weakly.

A snort behind me made me turn, and I saw Scath staring at me. Slowly and deliberately, she sat down against the wall.

She wasn't coming with me.

"Peasblossom, maybe you should—"

"If you go, I go. End of story."

I knew better than to argue with her. Or maybe I just didn't want to go down there alone. Gordon's words rang in my ears. Proof or no proof, I felt it in my gut that Lorelei had been the one to corrupt him. But if it was going to make a difference to Andy, then I needed to prove it. I hadn't wanted to get my hopes up, so I hadn't even shared my suspicion with Liam. But if I was right, Lorelei was the key to everything.

I groped for the rungs, and when I found them, I threw one leg over the stones. My foot found purchase, and I started down.

Evelyn's warning was accurate. Every step filled me with the urge to reverse course, climb back up to Evelyn and abandon my attempt to enter the cells. I kept forgetting why I wanted to enter in the first place, why on earth would I be trying to get inside such a place?

I couldn't afford to waste time. I could see the floor below me, and true to Evelyn's word, it didn't look more than ten feet, so I let go of the handles and pushed off, dropping the rest of the way.

I landed hard, my legs sending the message to the rest of my body that jumping was a young witch's game, and any further attempts to forget that simple fact would result in broken bones and bed rest.

"Do my eyes deceive me? Or is that a fallen witch I see before me?"

Lorelei's husky voice seared every nerve ending and sent a

rush of heat to my face that should have resulted in blisters. I stood on black stones, surrounded by the smell of iron and burning embers. But there was no heat. Only a wet cold that clung to my skin, made the fire in my cheeks feel even hotter by comparison.

Evelyn had been right about the voices. But it wasn't bad, not really worse than my usual self-doubts. And even though I did feel guilt for some of the choices I'd made, I didn't shy away from thinking about them. So the voices, while present, weren't overwhelming. I pushed them away, gently, and turned until I spotted the cage I needed.

Lorelei didn't have the bedraggled look I'd imagined in my nightmares. Her pale brown hair didn't have the same shine as when she'd been free to shower whenever she liked, use whatever products she liked, but it wasn't knotted or shorn. The clothes on her body were simple robes, a dark crimson that I assumed had been chosen to please both the demon and her Italian paladin host.

"Lorelei." Saying her name was harder than I'd expected— harder because of the temptation to follow it up by flinging a nasty spell. Something that would show the *dybbuk* in no uncertain terms how I felt about what she'd done to my friend. Not that my magic could touch her down here. Not with the circle melted into the floor around Lorelei's prison.

No one built a circle like a paladin.

The demon made no effort to hide the burn of her red eyes as she curled her lip into a sneer. "And what is it you've come for, Mother Renard? Is there something I have left you'd like to take away?"

"You corrupted Andy."

The demon's eyebrows rose, then her lips spread into a broad grin. "Agent Bradford. I remember him, yes. *So* much anger." She licked her lips. "How many has he killed?"

"Can you undo what you did?" I already knew the answer, but the question escaped me before I could stop it. Even if corruption could be purged, it wouldn't be anything Lorelei could do. The disease can't cure itself.

Lorelei laughed, loud and long, and a bit more enthusiastically than seemed natural. I didn't doubt she found the question funny, but she was hamming it up for my benefit. Insult to injury.

She shook her head. "I didn't add anything to your partner that wasn't already there. I am but the rain and sun on a plant that your Goddess placed inside him." She shrugged. "All joking aside, you must have known how close to the edge he was? For pity's sake, the man made crinkling sounds when he walked, no one should use that much starch. I've seen knights in metal armor that had more give than his suit."

My hands curled reflexively into fists and I strove to relax them, and my breathing. To remember why I'd come and how little time there was to waste. "Earlier this year, a gambler at Fortuna's was corrupted."

"And you think that's unusual?" Lorelei asked, not bothering to hide her amusement.

"Was it you?" I asked bluntly.

Lorelei threw herself on the small fainting couch that served as her bed, draping her body over it as if she couldn't help but sexualize every movement, regardless of the situation. "You're boring me. I get enough reminders of my past exploits from the wretched voices this prison puts inside my head, I don't need them from you as well. So if that's all you want to talk about, you can leave now."

"I'll make it worth your while," I promised.

The red glow in her eyes brightened. "How?"

I stepped closer to the bars, careful not to let my foot enter the circle. "I talked to Evelyn. If you agree to tell me what I need to know, she'll let you have visitors."

I didn't add that Evelyn had taken some convincing, and I'd spent the entire long drive here fighting to get this concession.

"Visitors?" Lorelei snorted. "Who on earth would I possibly want to visit me? What conceivable joy could I get out of visits that took place in this cursed pit?" She laid her head back so it hung over the arm of the couch, almost upside-down as she let her eyes drift shut. "Go away, Mother Renard. You have nothing to offer me that's worth suffering through your company."

"Your Acolytes will be allowed to visit you," I said. "Jack, Stacey, Jerome, Grant, Nina, Kelly…"

Lorelei didn't open her eyes, but her stiff posture told me my temptation had found its mark. "Why would I want to see them?"

"Because you care about them." I leaned forward. "I saw the way you looked at them. The way you laughed with them. You treated them like a family. They saw you as family. They fought for you, even though they knew they had no chance."

"Fools," she whispered, but there was no venom in it. She raised her head, slowly, meeting my eyes. "How often can they visit me?"

"Once a week."

"That's not enough."

"Prove you can handle it, and I'll help you argue for more." I let my shoulders sag and shook my head. "I know it's not enough," I admitted quietly. "And in some ways it might be even harder, seeing them once a week instead of all the time, or not at all. But this was the best I could do with the time I had."

"What does that mean?" Lorelei demanded. "What limit is placed on your time?" She gestured at her cage. "I'm certainly not going anywhere."

I stared back, trying to keep the emotion from my face to hide my mistake.

It didn't work.

"You found out I corrupted Agent Bradford," Lorelei murmured. "How?"

If I refused to answer her questions, she'd shut down and refuse to talk to me at all. "He killed a kelpie."

Lorelei's eyes widened. "He killed a kelpie. And you said your time is limited. He's been convicted, hasn't he? Siobhan will have her revenge."

Now it was my turn to seize on a piece of information. "How did you know Siobhan was involved?"

The demon waved me off. "It wasn't difficult to guess. She's the one who wanted revenge last time, it stands to reason."

"It stands to reason that Andy would have killed Siobhan," I corrected her, trying to keep my voice steady despite my racing pulse. "But you assumed he killed a different kelpie, and Siobhan is still alive, and about to get revenge."

Lorelei huffed out a breath and crossed her arms. "How long will my weekly visitations last?"

"No less than one hour, no more than twenty-four," I said immediately. "Beyond that, the length of the visit will depend on your behavior and theirs."

Lorelei considered that. Finally, she nodded. "Fine. What do you want to know?"

"Why did you corrupt the gambler at Fortuna's?" I asked.

"I corrupted the gambler because Siobhan asked me to," Lorelei said, revealing the information with a vocal flourish. "She made it sound like a lot of fun. And she was right. It was delicious to watch his downfall."

I stepped forward, closing my hands around the bars. She could be lying, telling me what I wanted to hear. "His name?"

"Gordon Larkin."

A thrill ran through me. My hands trembled against the bars. "And why did you corrupt Andy?"

Lorelei hesitated, then shrugged. "When I thought I was going to be exorcised, I grew sentimental. I wanted one last bit of fun in the paladin's body. Laurie hated it when I corrupted people, so when Siobhan approached me and asked if I'd like to help her out again, I agreed." She wrapped her hands around the bars over top of mine. "The anger in him, Shade, you should *feel* it. It was a crime that he ever held back the way he did, and it was my pleasure to set him free."

She was taunting me, but it didn't matter. Not anymore. I turned to Peasblossom with a smile. It all made sense now. I knew what Siobhan had done. And how.

"Oh, you've set him free," I promised Lorelei. "Just not in the way you think."

I turned my back on her, speaking to my familiar as I headed for the exit. "Peasblossom, we need to call the Vanguard. Andy's innocent."

CHAPTER 26

THE LEADER of the Vanguard himself had picked up when I called. Mac Tyre was even older than I was, and the first member of the Vanguard, if rumors were to be believed. He had been the one to show up last April when the Vanguard had come to Marilyn's to settle the matter of an FBI agent—Andy—protesting the contractual enslavement of teenagers.

Now, as I stood outside the National Acme Building in the freezing October air at six a.m., I clung to the fact that as fearsome as his reputation was, there wasn't a soul on this plane who would call him unfair.

I rested a hand on my waist pouch, where I'd stored the two witness statements I'd just obtained with the two phone calls I'd made after hanging up with Mac Tyre. Julia had faxed me Deacon's statement at the Ministry's HQ before Evelyn had taken me home, and Anton had sent Mickey V's. I could add "receiving a fax from a vampire" to my list of weird accomplishments and cross it off. Twice.

Scath headbutted my hip to make sure I paid attention to the black SUV pulling up. Mac Tyre got out. "Mother Renard, a pleasure to see you again." He looked as severe as ever. Every article of his suit was as black as his hair, and his dark eyes were no different.

"If only we could stop meeting under such unpleasant circumstances," I said, reaching to take his offered hand.

The Vanguard elite had a square jaw covered with a neat black beard trimmed close to his face, and he reached up to scratch it now as he surveyed our surroundings. "You chose an interesting locale for this meeting. May I ask what it was about this place that made you choose it?"

I followed his gaze. The National Acme Building was abandoned, a sprawling factory filled with garbage by a less than scrupulous owner who'd taken over after the factory shut down. It looked better now, in the shadows of the pre-dawn than it did during the day, when there was sunlight to illuminate the shattered windows and rotting shingles. Even the graffiti couldn't brighten it up.

"Let's say that I have my doubts Siobhan can take it as well as she dishes it out."

Mac Tyre looked skeptical. "You expect her to be upset by the results of your inquiry."

"Oh, yes."

"I find that interesting. Especially considering the package she handed me before I left my office." He removed a small envelope from his pocket.

I could tell from the small indentations in the paper that it held an SD card. No doubt it was the copy Siobhan had referenced.

"I look forward to sharing my findings with everyone," I said.

And I meant every word.

The sound of feathered wings beating the air preceded a tall, dark figure landing not five feet away. Oksana beamed at me, her pale eyes looking brighter against the gloom around us. "The alpha has told me that you have good news," she said, folding her wings against her back before stepping closer. "They were right underneath me all the way here, they should be pulling in soon."

On cue, I heard the crunch of tires on gravel and looked up to see Liam's truck pulling in with Andy in the passenger seat. Liam guided his truck in a circle, coming to park behind me.

But they weren't the only ones.

A van followed close behind them with Rowyn at the wheel and Siobhan beside him. Their vehicle had been blue at one point, but now it was more panels of rust with blue patches here and there. It sat low enough to the ground that I guessed it either had a large number of passengers inside, or a few very large passengers.

Mostly likely equine passengers. Horses were heavy.

For a moment Rowyn seemed to be tailing Liam as if he intended to park right upside the truck and crowd Andy as much as possible. But then he kept going, circling around Liam and parking on the opposite side. When Siobhan opened her door the overhead light in the van case eerie shadows over her face. Her smile reached from ear to ear, and even though she had the flat teeth of an equine, there was something sharp in that smile. Something hungry.

"You're certain your investigation is complete?" Mac Tyre said in a low voice. "Once Agent Bradford leaves this place, I don't believe you'll get a chance for an appeal."

"He's not going anywhere with Siobhan," I answered. "And she's the one who will be begging for an appeal."

Mac Tyre's face didn't betray any emotion, but Oksana's wings ruffled, and she opened and closed her clawed hands with the anticipation of someone who expected to spill blood soon.

Siobhan climbed out of the van and was immediately flanked by Rowyn and three of her racers behind her. Puck's Folly winked at me, and it took a Herculean effort not to grab the nearest debris in the lot and chuck it at his head. Shadow of Death rolled his eyes, but his lips twitched as though amused by Puck's taunting. Charlotte's Web ignored both of them, staring at me as if he were certain I was about to do something interesting and was looking forward to the show.

"Send Bradford over," Siobhan called out. "Or will you make me take him?"

"I'd like to see her try," Peasblossom snarled from her warm spot inside the neck of my coat.

"Ignore her. She won't be smiling long." I raised my voice so Siobhan would hear me. "If you don't mind, I'd like to present my case first with regards to Raichel's murder." Thankfully word had already spread that Andy was off the hook for killing Deacon when he'd been Siobhan's property, so I only had one case to present. "I trust you're not in a hurry?"

It wasn't really a question. Siobhan couldn't take Andy until the Vanguard's arbiter for the proceedings bestowed formal permission. And I hadn't presented my case yet.

But Siobhan was nothing if not a showwoman, so she grinned and gave me a shallow bow. "I look forward to hearing it."

"Wonderful."

The sound of car doors opening and closing behind me made me glance back. Liam rounded the truck on the driver's side, meeting Andy in front before escorting him to my side.

"What's happening now?" Andy asked me.

His voice was tight, and his hand twitched toward his shoulder, as if resisting the urge to draw a gun he didn't have.

"This is Mac Tyre," I said, introducing the Vanguard elite. "He's the Archon of the Vanguard, basically their principal civil and judicial officer. He's the one I have to hand over my report to, the results of my investigation. He'll make the decision whether or not to convict you of the murder charge and hand you over to Siobhan—which will not happen," I added.

"Don't be cruel, Mother Renard," Siobhan chastised me. "It's too late to get his hopes up."

Andy took a step forward. I put out a hand to stop him, then hissed when my fingers landed on his stomach and I felt him burning up through the thin material of his shirt. I glanced at him and was relieved to find his eyes were still brown. He wasn't losing control yet.

"Some of us haven't been to bed yet, Mother Renard," Siobhan said impatiently. "If we could get on with it?"

Scath bared her teeth, letting out a low growl. Siobhan didn't step back, but she did shut her mouth. Small favors.

I looked to Mac Tyre. "I assume you've seen what's on that SD card?" I asked, pointing to the envelope in his hand.

"I have."

"I took a copy of it to Anton Winters. Do you know his son, Dimitri?"

Mac Tyre's face didn't change, but I thought I caught a muffled sigh. "I do, yes."

"Well, Dimitri confirmed for me that everything on that SD card is true."

Siobhan grinned, an expression that was mirrored by Rowyn and Puck's Folly. Shadow of Death looked satisfied, but in a more muted fashion. And Charlotte's Web just watched with the same considering look he'd worn since I'd met him.

I gestured at the kelpie leader. "Siobhan has claimed that Agent Andrew Bradford is a murderer. She claims he shot a kelpie named Raichel in cold blood. That he killed her because he thought he was shooting Siobhan herself, the kelpie who once kidnapped him. Who almost killed him. The kelpie who has sworn vengeance on him for the death of her brother Bradan."

I expected Siobhan to speak up. This would be the point where she would argue that Andy *had* murdered her brother, that Raichel wasn't the first of her kind he had slain.

But she didn't. She just stood there, smiling, shaking her head. Still so confident. She didn't need to plead a case for her brother. Not when she was so certain she had Andy for Raichel.

"But Andy isn't the murderer." I glared at his accuser. "Siobhan is."

Siobhan barked out a laugh. "Everyone knows I have an airtight alibi. So unless you're suggesting I hired Andy to kill Raichel, I'm afraid—"

"That's exactly what I'm suggesting." I held up a finger. "In a manner of speaking."

Siobhan's smile never slipped but I didn't miss the tension that crawled up her spine, the way she held her shoulders a little stiffer than before. None of the other waterhorses reacted.

Interesting.

"Five months ago," I continued, "the equines that make up the racing team were led by a *backahast* called Gloria. From what I understand, Gloria was a strong leader. She organized races at Fortuna's Stables, kept a good relationship with the centaurs and other land equines, and made every effort to ensure the success of the racino, which many of you relied on to fund your lives out of the water. Then she was murdered."

Siobhan wasn't smiling anymore, but as attention turned to her, she forced her shoulders to relax. "And you're going to accuse me of her murder too?" she asked, keeping her voice light.

I raised my voice and went on, "Shortly after Gloria's murder, Fortuna's shut down. The racino closed. The team needed not just a new leader, but a new business. And Siobhan was ready. She approached Anton Winters with the idea for a new racetrack—one out in the middle of Lake Erie. She managed to sell him on the venture, and Turning Tides was born."

I tilted my head. "Siobhan, were you always the representative to meet with Mr. Winters? Or did he speak with another authority figure at Turning Tides?"

Siobhan stuck out her chin. "I was always Mr. Winter's contact point. Turning Tides is mine, I make the decisions."

I pointed to Puck's Folly. "Puck. Did you or did you not tell me that Raichel met with Anton Winters last week?"

Puck seemed surprised to be called out. He looked to Siobhan. Her mouth flattened into a thin line, but she nodded. They couldn't afford to hesitate or appear to be hiding something. Mac Tyre was too sharp.

"I did," he said carefully.

"Raichel met with Anton Winters, behind Siobhan's back, and less than a week later she was dead. You told me that was too much of a coincidence. Tell Mac Tyre why you thought that."

"I don't recall my exact thoughts at the time," Puck hedged.

"Did you or did you not also say 'Everyone was whispering that Raichel was being groomed to take over' during our conversation?"

Siobhan was glowering at Puck now. For the first time, I wondered if Puck's taunting that had gotten me into Siobhan's office hadn't been part of her plan. Perhaps Puck had decided to do a little improv for his own amusement.

Very interesting.

"I did," Puck conceded. "But that doesn't change the facts, does it?"

Mac Tyre listened to everything with rapt attention, but his face didn't give away even a hint to his thoughts. I kept going.

"So Gloria is the head of the team, then she's murdered.

Siobhan is head of the team, rumors start going around that Raichel is going to take over, and Raichel is murdered."

"I guess I'm just lucky." Siobhan shrugged. "People who get in my way end up dead." She looked over my shoulder at Andy. "Perhaps there's a lesson there."

"Oh, there's a lesson there," I agreed. "Rowyn, what happened to the man that killed Gloria?"

"Rumor has it that Siobhan ate him," Rowyn answered. He gave the answer quick enough, but the question had caught him off guard. Not so off guard that he didn't remember to phrase it as a rumor. No sense admitting to the Vanguard that Siobhan had killed a human, when she was trying so hard to earn the right to kill another one legally. His gaze bounced from me to Mac Tyre, then to Siobhan. "Why?"

"Like so many statements that come from the lips of the fey, that wasn't a lie," I explained. "But it was grossly misleading." I smiled at Siobhan. "She only ate a finger."

I glanced behind me toward where Evelyn had parked when she'd arrived ten minutes ago after having retrieved our corrupted friend from New Moon. Gordon Larkin looked less than pleased, and I wondered if he'd tried to give the justiciar any trouble on the way over.

I pitied him if he had.

The blood drained from Siobhan's face. Shadow of Death scowled and shot her a glare, as if she'd *really* blundered. Puck looked uneasy. Charlotte's mouth quirked up at the corner.

"This is Gordon Larkin. The man who killed Gloria with an iron scythe. And as you can see, he's very much alive."

"I'm not on trial here," Siobhan countered. "This isn't about Gloria, this is about Raichel, and we have a *video* that *you confirmed* as legitimate that *proves* Agent Bradford killed her!" She swiveled to Mac Tyre. "I made my case. I want the human handed over." She shot me a cruel smile. "If he is still human, of course."

I shook my head. "I'm not done."

"Then make your point, Mother Renard," Mac Tyre prompted.

Ice slid down my spine. Peasblossom crawled onto my shoulder, striking a Wonder Woman pose of defiance as she glared around the crowd. "You've got this," she said under her breath.

I looked at Rowyn. "When did Siobhan start going to Something Fishy? Specifically, was it before or after Andy had a fight with the other kelpies, that night in August?"

"She started going there in early September," Rowyn reported.

"So?" Siobhan scoffed.

I pointed at Andy. "After Morgan told you there were kelpies at Something Fishy, did you go there every night?"

Andy folded his arms. "Not every night. But most. For a while."

"When did you stop going almost every night?"

Andy stared down Siobhan. "When I overheard Siobhan tell a group of kids that the kelpies went on Thursday nights. She invited them to come visit them on their boat. I showed up to Something Fishy to make sure she didn't abduct them or kill them. From that point on, I was only there every Thursday night."

"So Siobhan could easily predict that you would be there the night of the murder."

Siobhan growled. "And did he ever kill any of us? Was that part of his Thursday ritual? Could I have predicted that too?"

"I'll get to that," I said coldly. "According to the jockey at Turning Tides named Mickey V, you specifically ordered him to be there that night. Is that correct?"

The kelpie team leader hesitated.

"We could always ask Mr. Winters to bring him over," I pressed. "Maybe I should. I'm sure he—"

"Yes, I told him to be there. But—"

"You also gave him instructions not to go inside and not to look inside the bar. You told him to wait out front and not make eye contact with anyone but you?"

Siobhan glared at me as if she could set me on fire by force of will alone. "Yes."

"So you told Mickey to wait outside, knowing he would be dressed in his street clothes because he knew not to don his racing silks until just before an event, with specific instructions not to look inside the bar. All because you wanted Andy to think he was a kid." I raised my voice. "You stressed to Mickey how important it was that he be there, making sure he understood that you would be angry if he failed you."

"So what if I did?"

I pressed on, "You told Raichel to go there glamoured as you because you knew Mickey would see through her glamour, the way he had before at the track. You knew he'd know she wasn't who she was claiming to be, that he'd be suspicious, and that he'd fight not to go with her. And you counted on that being the scene that played out in front of Andy. A kid fighting not to be dragged away by a kelpie he knew had a history of kidnapping kids."

Rowyn sneered at me. "Your little theory of incitement only makes sense if you're admitting that your FBI partner is so full of hatred for our kind, that even after he saw Mickey was no defenseless underage brat and in no immediate real danger, he was still guaranteed to shoot Raichel."

Siobhan jumped in, "Is that what you're saying? That Bradford is a loaded gun, ready to go off at any kelpie who gets in his way? So much so that if I but put my rival in his path I could predict with certainty he would murder her?"

"Why not?" I asked calmly. "That's how you killed Gloria."

The three racers behind Siobhan tensed. Puck looked like a child who'd just figured out he'd been giving away his teeth to fey who may or may not be collecting them for nefarious purposes. Shadow of Death was angry, grinding his jaw so hard that if he hadn't had flat teeth before, he would have now. And Charlotte's Web had an anticipatory gleam in his eye that almost looked like hunger.

Even Rowyn was staring at her now, his brow furrowed. I blinked. So Rowyn hadn't known about Siobhan's part in Gloria's murder?

"A human killed Gloria, not me!" Siobhan snarled.

I pointed at the corrupted human standing beside Evelyn. "Gordon Larkin was a gambler at Fortuna's. Siobhan sent a demon called Lorelei after him—Evelyn can attest to Lorelei's statement, as well as its validity, since she cannot leave her prison."

Evelyn looked at Mac Tyre. "That's correct. Lorelei refused to give up this information without getting something in return. I believe it is the truth. She corrupted Gordon Larkin at Siobhan's request."

I nodded. "Under Siobhan's orders, Lorelei gave Gordon tips about races, let him have a fantastic winning streak. Then she abandoned him—but not before she corrupted him. Gordon started losing, and his addiction drove him to wager more and more."

Out of the corner of my eye I saw the man himself nodding along, face red.

"Finally," I resumed, "when he was on the edge, Siobhan approached him disguised as Gloria and pretended to give him a tip. Told him to bet big, that this was the only time she'd make such an allowance. Gordon had no reason to believe Gloria's word wasn't good. He bet everything, and he lost. Siobhan, knowing he was corrupted, knowing he was unstable, gave him one more nudge. She told him Gloria had joked about giving some poor chump a bad tip, that she was laughing about him losing everything and glad to be rid of him. And that's when Gordon killed her."

I had Gordon's testimony about Siobhan telling him Gloria had laughed at him, but I was guessing about her impersonating Gloria based on what I knew of her tactics. But the kelpie didn't know that.

"Coincidence," Siobhan dismissed.

I shook my head without taking my eyes from Siobhan's. "That's not all Lorelei told me. She also said it was *you* that told her to corrupt Agent Andrew Bradford back in April. You knew about his past, his struggles with his temper. You taunted him by bringing kids around, knowing he'd be here, knowing he was watching."

Suddenly I remembered something Siobhan had told me during one of our previous meetings.

"I've made a new friend. A human cop."

"Did your human cop friend tell you Andy was suspended for hitting a suspect?"

Normally I wouldn't ask a question like that when I didn't know the answer, but in this case, it paid off. Siobhan scowled. "So?"

"So you kept pushing Andy, you found out he was starting to lose control of his temper, and you saw your chance."

Siobhan shook her head. "If I were going to set all that up as you say," she said in a low voice, "I wouldn't leave anything to chance. That entire plan relies on too many pieces coming together, it's sloppy. What if Mickey had looked inside, what if Bradford didn't notice his so-called plight, or if he stayed home sick that night? What if Raichel just told Mickey who she was? Or if Andy confronted her as me but didn't shoot her, and she realized I'd set her up?"

She looked at Mac Tyre. "I wouldn't take that chance. I wouldn't move against a rival in a way that might cost me the support of the Winters. Not even if it were only a slim chance."

"No. You wouldn't. Which is why you gave Mickey a gun." I opened my waist pouch. "Bizbee, could you give me the file, please?"

I took the file from the grig and handed it to Mac Tyre. "Those are formal statements from Mickey V and another jockey, Deacon, that I got tonight, less than an hour ago. Both of them attest that Siobhan gave Mickey an unregistered gun, and he was carrying it that night. Mickey confessed to giving Rowyn the gun after the shooting."

Rowyn shuffled back, then stopped himself. Mac Tyre's gaze locked on him. "Is this true?"

"It is," the kelpie conceded. "But Mickey didn't fire that gun. It doesn't change anything."

I gestured at the paper. "In his statement, Mickey admits that if Siobhan had ordered him to shoot Raichel if Agent Bradford failed to do so, then he would have shot her. He was afraid his boss would do something to end his career at Turning Tides if he didn't cooperate with her scheme."

"Wouldn't ending his career risk alienating Turning Tides' original investor, Mr. Winters?" Mac Tyre asked doubtfully.

"Accidents can happen, with adrenaline running high for the crowd and the race participants, can't they?" I stared at Siobhan, and this time, I let the satisfaction show in my eyes, in the smile on my face. "Mickey was your plan B." I turned to Mac Tyre. "Agent Bradford isn't the murderer. He's only the murder *weapon*."

Mac Tyre nodded, but didn't take his eyes off the documents in front of him. After reading through both statements, he closed the file and turned to Siobhan. "In light of this new evidence, I'm inclined to reject your request to take custody of Andrew Bradford and punish him. If you still want to argue your case, you have that choice. But be aware, if you do so, you will need to answer for these... similarities between Raichel's death and Gloria's. And I'm sure your own people will have an interest in hearing that testimony."

Siobhan looked ready to spit horseshoes, but she held her head high. "No need. I'm dropping the charges."

Mac Tyre closed the file, but didn't give it back to me. "Then this proceeding is finished." He faced me and gestured at my waist pouch. "I'll need the rest of the file for my records."

I should have felt relieved, but something was wrong. Siobhan had put a lot of work into framing Andy, but she didn't even look mad. I chalked part of that up to her need to appear unemotional, just so her team didn't see her sweat over my revelations relating to Gloria. But I'd expected fireworks. A tantrum.

Something.

I handed my entire case files over to Mac Tyre, my nerves buzzing with awareness. I kept my attention on the equines, waiting for some sign of aggression, some hint that they were just waiting for the Vanguard to leave.

But it wasn't the equines who made the first move.

"Wait," Andy said.

I whirled around to face him, ready to tell him now was not the time to raise any complications. We'd won, but it was precarious. He had to see that.

But Andy was facing Mac Tyre with that set to his shoulders that meant he had a mission. And it looked official.

"You have something to add?" Mac Tyre asked.

"Not about my case, no." He glanced at Siobhan, then met

Mac Tyre's eyes. "What if I want to bring charges against Siobhan?"

My mouth fell open. "What?"

Andy ignored me.

Mac Tyre frowned. "What charges?"

Andy looked back at Liam. For the first time, I noticed the werewolf's expression somewhere between amused and impressed. The alpha went back to his truck and opened the backseat to draw out a large box.

"Shade said the Vanguard doesn't tend to investigate single deaths or disappearances in the human community," Andy said. "Is that right?"

Mac Tyre paused. "Not usually, no. The Vanguard steps in only in large-scale situations. City-wide safety issues, that sort of thing. Why?"

"It's my understanding that the smaller crimes you don't investigate are left up to individual societies to handle," Andy pressed on. "Specifically, the leader of a certain group or clan is responsible for keeping their people in line?"

I had no idea where he was going with this.

Neither did Mac Tyre. "I suppose," he said slowly.

"So, for example, if a vampire allowed the vampires they sired to run around murdering humans, that sire would be held responsible," Andy clarified. "I would be within my right—as an official law enforcement officer responsible for the human population—to punish that leader for their failure to control their people. In effect, that leader is responsible for the murders committed by their people."

"All true."

"So, how would the humans in that situation get justice? How would I go about punishing the leader?"

"If it was reported to the Vanguard, or discovered by one of our agents, we would send a team to confirm the facts and the leader would be dealt with."

"Dealt with?"

Mac Tyre tilted his head. "Executed."

I figured it out a split second before Liam arrived at my side. He put down the box he'd been carrying.

"Bones," Mac Tyre murmured. He looked up at Andy. "Whose bones?"

"The bones of human victims." Andy bent to take a file out of the box. "I've managed to identify the ones in this box. I have more that are as-yet unidentified. But according to a forensic scientist, these people were eaten. By equine animals. All within the last four months."

"How many?" Mac Tyre inquired.

Andy leveled a steely look at Siobhan. "Fifty-eight, so far."

Siobhan retreated, backing right into Charlotte's Web. The larger kelpie looked down at her with an odd expression. Something between censure and...anticipation.

Mac Tyre studied the file, and the bones. "Are you turning over this evidence for my office to deal with her, Agent Bradford?"

Andy shook his head. "I'd like to take care of it personally. I am an officer of the law. I believe under your customs that qualifies me to mete out justice?"

Mac Tyre looked at Andy, and there was something new in his eyes.

Respect.

"You are correct," he murmured. He glanced at me. "You, of course, are able to act on behalf of the Vanguard, as you have a history with us. And Detective Sergeant Osbourne serves as an officer of human law as well." The corner of his mouth twitched. "I assume you'd like to give Siobhan the news?"

"I would." Andy faced Siobhan, seeming to relish the

confusion on her face. They hadn't heard Andy's last exchange with Mac Tyre, and were probably wondering what the box of bones was for.

I smiled, allowing myself to savor the moment I felt coming.

"Siobhan," Andy said, raising his voice. He reached behind him and drew out a pair of handcuffs. "You're under arrest."

CHAPTER 27

"UNDER ARREST?" Siobhan scoffed. She stared after Mac Tyre as he got back into his SUV, blinking when Oksana waved at her before getting into the backseat and slamming the door shut behind her. Evelyn passed me a card, then patted my shoulder before turning away to get back in her own car—taking a silent, stewing Gordon Larkin with her.

The equines watched the Vanguard leave, their expressions a mix of confusion and something else.

"You're under arrest for murder," Andy clarified, his eyes still locked on Siobhan. He advanced toward her. "You have the right to remain—"

"Wipe that smile off your face, Bradford," Siobhan snarled. "I came ready for treachery."

The van behind Siobhan shook, the thud of something heavy against metal warning me that something was happening inside. It occurred to me then that the three racers I'd seen had all arrived in human form. Which meant the obvious weight in the van had not come from a few horse-sized passengers...but rather *many* passengers in human form.

Passengers who, by the sounds of it, wouldn't be in human form for long.

My suspicion was confirmed a moment later when three new figures exited the van on the far side, then circled around to stand by the first three racers.

The first waterhorse that stepped into my line of vision was a huge white beast with a mane of dark green snakes that hissed and writhed in the cold air. My breath froze in my lungs. She was a kelpie, but a rare breed I'd never seen in person before.

"This is Medusa's Bane," Siobhan announced with grim satisfaction. "She's come all the way from Aberdeenshire just to meet you, Agent Bradford."

Andy shifted beside me and I thought I felt the air between us grow a few degrees warmer. I didn't look at him, though. I wasn't sure how much Siobhan knew about how his corruption affected him.

And I didn't want to ruin the surprise.

A second horse creature came from behind Medusa's Bane. This one was a steel grey, with a dark black mane that fell in wet tendrils down his neck. Other than looking strong there was nothing about him to suggest he posed a particular threat.

"This is Captain's Orders," Siobhan said, reading my expression. "He's here because he won his last three races, and he deserved a treat."

Before I could respond to that, her third lackey stepped forward. This arrival was still in human form, but the shape of his irises betrayed him as a *backahast*. His dark brown skin seemed to absorb the meager light from the coming dawn, softening it into a muted velvet shine on his flesh. He wore a heavy crimson cloak with a thin chain clasp at the throat. There was something about his long dark hair that made me think of feathers, but I couldn't put my finger on what. I suspected he was not a purebred *backahast*, not with feathers in his family tree.

"Swansong is in human form for now," Siobhan said, her eyes on me. "Mostly because he has something to say to you, Mother Renard."

Liam and Scath had moved apart as Siobhan's thugs gathered around her. As if instinct told both shifters to fan out, get ready to pick the equines off one by one. Maybe they were also waiting to see which of our opponents made the first aggressive move to choose their target.

Which is why it came as a shock when Shadow of Death whirled to the side and dropped his shoulder to charge— straight into Charlotte's Web.

I stared as the *backahast* drove the *each uisge* to the ground, then wrapped his hands around Charlotte's throat. I had a split second to wonder what on earth would make Charlotte's Web his target, and not Andy—or even Siobhan.

Then Siobhan stepped forward.

"I've been waiting so long for this." She reached behind her and drew something metallic from the waistband of her pants.

My eyes flew wide and my magic roared inside me as I darted forward. "Gun!"

The roar of the gunshot made every nerve in my body spasm. Andy jerked back with a grunt, and suddenly for me the scene moved in the slow-motion of a nightmare. Blood blossomed on the right side of his belly, and he clapped a hand over it without taking his eyes off Siobhan.

"You have the right to remain silent," he hissed.

Peasblossom darted off my shoulder, sailing through the air before landing on Andy's head. Then grasping his hair to hold on as she let her magic flow over him. "Should have worn a vest!" she scolded him.

Relief washed over me. She could keep him stabilized, keep him from bleeding out. If she could hold on.

The injury didn't slow Andy down. He was already charging at Siobhan, and even in the dim light, I could see him getting bigger as he ran. That wild energy—demonic energy—swelling inside him until his body strained against his shirt. I reflected it might be better he wasn't wearing a bulletproof vest. I doubted it would tear easily, and the last thing he needed was to get tangled up in Kevlar.

Still reciting her Miranda warning, Andy launched himself at Siobhan, and his fingers wrapped around her hand holding the gun. I imagined I could hear her bones crack under the long shriek of pain.

I hadn't been expecting the gun from Siobhan, but now that I knew she was armed, I was faster to spot Rowyn drawing a weapon. This time, I was ready. I aimed at his gun, the words of the spell ready on my lips. "*Pax!*"

Rowyn's head jerked toward me, even as he pulled the trigger. But the metal wouldn't move. His eyes narrowed at his firearm, trying to figure out what was wrong. Another gunshot rang out, and Rowyn's body jerked.

I spun to find Flint approaching from around Liam's truck. He walked with his arm extended, his gun still trained on the fallen kelpie clutching his thigh. Blood seeped between Rowyn's fingers as he gritted his teeth.

Flint winked at me, the teasing gesture contrasting with the tension holding his back stiff. "Sorry I'm late."

Puck's Folly gave Rowyn a disgusted look, then fixed his eyes on me. He took a step forward, but his progress halted immediately when Scath launched herself through the space between our two groups, hitting Puck squarely in the chest and knocking him to the ground. The *nuckelavee* twisted under the press of her claws, but he didn't scream. Instead, his entire body rippled and twitched as he began the shift to his equine form, even as Scath dug her claws deeper.

A pulse of heat behind me told me Liam was shifting, and I caught a hint of his half-man, half-beast form in my peripheral vision. He opened a mouth full of sharp teeth and snarled. Then he threw himself in the path of Medusa's Bane as she reared up over Andy, ready to bring her sharp hooves down on his spine. One rake of his claws severed the heads of two snakes in the nest of her mane, but three others jerked forward, sinking their fangs into his arm. Liam growled and swiped with his other hand, claws cutting cleanly through the thin serpentine bodies.

Medusa screamed, a high-pitched equine sound that frazzled my nerves. She pivoted on her back legs, her hooves plunging through the space where Liam had been seconds ago.

More movement caught my eye, and I spotted Captain's Orders approaching Andy. The kelpie had used his magic to summon the silver bridle that his kind so often used to lure human victims closer. The morning's first light caught the silver, making it shine as the kelpie dangled it closer and closer to Andy. I lifted a hand, ready to fire another spell.

Someone started singing.

I frowned as the first dulcet tones tickled my ears, wormed their way into my brain. I shook my head, stumbled back a step as I searched for the source of the music. My search stopped on Swansong, and suddenly our gazes locked. It was him. He was singing. And I knew then that I'd been right. There was something with feathers in his heritage. *Sirin*, maybe. Or harpy.

I felt my body swaying as if I were lying in a boat on the water, being carried to and fro, up and down by the gentle swell of water. I blinked slowly, barely aware that Captain's Orders was approaching my partner, dangling his silver bridle closer to the hand Andy had wrapped around Siobhan's throat. He was trying to entrance him with the enchanted harness, convince him to release Siobhan and grab the bridle. I had the semi-hysterical thought that if Andy touched that bridle, Captain could easily swing him onto his back. It would be a fast ride to the lake after that...

I made my hand into a fist, feeling the ring of shielding on my finger, concentrating on thickening that wall of energy. I had to fight that song, get it out of my head. But the music was so plaintive, so beautiful. It echoed in my ears, coaxed me to listen. To sleep.

Andy released his crushing grip on Siobhan's broken gun hand and snatched Captain's bridle. A sharp stab of panic chased back some of my lethargy from Swansong's music, but it wasn't enough. I couldn't raise my arm, couldn't grab hold of my magic. I tried to yell a warning.

Suddenly, Andy made a sharp whirling motion with his wrist, wrapping Captain's bridle around his fist and jerking, hard. He used the hand around Siobhan's throat to yank her off the ground, and my eyes widened when he looped the reins of the bridle around her neck and pulled tight.

Captain let out a muffled scream, but froze, aware that if he struggled too hard, the bridle would come off. If that happened, it would be Andy who controlled him. The enchanted bridle was a double-edge sword.

Captain kicked out with his front hooves, battering Andy in the ribs with enough force to shatter bone. But Andy didn't seem to feel it. His gaze remained on Siobhan's face, watching her writhe in the gravel, fighting to breathe. I was dimly aware that he was saying the last words of the Miranda warning.

A flash of pink caught my eye. Peasblossom still gripped Andy's hair like the reins of a bronco, her magic still pulsing against him, keeping his injuries from becoming fatal.

I fought to throw off Swansong's magic, but his song grew louder in my ears, drilling into my brain until it drowned out my thoughts. I squeezed my eyes shut, then regretted it immediately as being blind gave my brain fewer distractions from the haunting melody.

Suddenly, the song cut off. My eyes flew open, and I saw Swansong clutching his bloody throat, his eyes wide. He made a wet gasping sound as he tried to breathe. Liam stood with his clawed hand at his side, dripping blood from where he'd raked them over Swansong's throat. He looked at me, but there wasn't time for communication.

Medusa charged at Liam, dead snakes hanging from her mane, fury blazing in her eyes. I threw out my hand, hurling a spell into the air over her head. *"Tonitrua!"*

Dark clouds swirled and gathered, writhing black masses flickering with bright silver light. I flicked my hand down, dragging a bolt of lighting from the clouds straight into the snake-haired equine. The smell of burning flesh accompanied her scream as she fell to the ground. The few snakes in her mane that had still been moving lay dead. Fried.

Flint scooped Rowyn's gun off the ground, keeping his own weapon aimed at the kelpie's chest. He stepped back, tilting his head slightly from side to side, taking in the battle with quick glances.

Scath still grappled with Puck's Folly. Her jaw hung at a wrong angle—broken by one of his vicious kicks. She was fighting to get her claws into his flesh as he lashed out with deadly hooves, trying to trample her.

Then Flint's gaze flew to Andy. Captain was still pummeling Andy with his hooves, over and over. Andy's body had swelled beyond his shirt's ability to hold, his body three times the size it had been. I didn't know enough about Andy's corruption to know how much damage he could take, or just exactly what his abilities were. But his shirt had fallen away in tatters, and the scars on his back were bleeding again, oozing as if they were fresh. It was possible that he couldn't bleed to death. That could be part of the corruption. But still, the broken ribs had to hurt. And if Captain managed to drive a broken bone into his heart, even Peasblossom's magic might not be enough to save his life...

Flint swung his gun around and shot Captain. The large equine's body jerked, blood blossoming on his shoulder. Flint's shot was true, and suddenly Captain staggered back, wheezing from his red foam-coated muzzle as if the bullet had nicked his lung.

Rowyn took advantage of the distraction and hurled himself off the ground to tackle Flint. The kelpie used one hand to push the gun away from him and the other to smash a fist into Flint's face.

A feline snarl spun me around, and I spotted Scath standing a few feet away from Puck. One look at the *nuckelavee* and I could tell her claws had severed the muscles of his shoulder. The damage was hard to look at, his right arm looking like so much raw meat hanging limply at his side. He couldn't stand, could only lie there, glaring at her with murderous promise in his eyes.

Medusa lurched off the ground, smoke rising from the bloody ends of her severed snakes, her teeth glistening with saliva as she took an unsteady step toward me. Suddenly, Bizbee poked his head out from the waist pouch. My mouth fell open as he aimed a thin tube at Medusa. He huffed out a breath, and a tiny burst of grey flakes shot over the kelpie. She screamed as the iron filings stuck to the burns all over her body.

I hissed and stepped back, then caught sight of Liam lifting Swansong's body overhead. He swung him around and hurled him at Rowyn. The airborne waterhorse struck the kelpie hard, knocking him away from Flint.

I waved my hand, sending the thunderstorm I'd conjured over the two men, then drove both my arms down. Twin bolts of lightning arced into the ground, searing through both of them in a burst of electricity.

Another gunshot rang out.

Everyone froze.

All eyes turned to Andy. He'd grabbed Siobhan's gun from the ground, and now he held it pressed against her forehead. The female kelpie wasn't moving. No one spoke. Even Scath held perfectly still, her eerie green eyes locked on Siobhan's body.

Andy shoved himself to his feet. He still held Captain's bridle wrapped around his meaty fist, and he fixed the frozen waterhorse with a murderous glare, then jerked on the tack. The bridle slipped off Captain's head, and the waterhorse let out a sound somewhere between a scream and a moan before dropping his head. Submissive.

Andy reeled forward, dragging Siobhan with him. He surveyed the area with black eyes, and I held my breath, waiting to see what he would do next. His entire body was red with blood, shiny and wet in the meager light of the new dawn.

Rowyn, Puck, Swansong, and Medusa stirred on the ground, but they were all badly burned from my lightning, and the latter wheezed and coughed up blood through the pain of the iron filings. If she could shift, she had a chance of forcing the metal from her body enough to heal, but I didn't like her chances without help. And it was possible that shifting could push some of the filings deeper into her body. Getting them out again after that would be nigh-impossible.

"You've won."

I jerked at the sound of Charlotte's voice. I'd forgotten about him and his brawl with Shadow of Death. I looked for Shadow now, and at first I didn't see him. Then I noticed Charlotte's mouth was smeared with blood. I sucked in a sharp breath. This time when I looked, I found Shadow.

Or what was left of him.

"You ate him." I hadn't meant to say it out loud. But in the silence of post-battle, my words carried.

Charlotte treated me to another inscrutable look from his dark, oily eyes that made me wild to know what was going on in his head.

Charlotte met Andy's black gaze as casually as if he were welcoming him to a summer luncheon. "You've won," he said again. He gestured at Siobhan. "Will you kill her?"

"Yes," Andy rasped. His eyes found mine. "After a trial. I have the evidence. Let her answer for it first."

The *each uisge* nodded slowly. "Then she is leader no more." He turned, looking around at his fellow teammates. "If anyone here would like to challenge me, speak now."

Flint rose to one knee, one hand cradling his jaw. "You're the new leader?"

Charlotte smiled, a soft expression at sharp odds with the blood staining his teeth and lips. "Yes I am."

"That's why Shadow attacked you." My eyes swiveled from him to Siobhan, whom Andy was now handcuffing. "He knew Siobhan would be killed or ousted or both tonight. He knew your team would need a new leader. And he knew *you* were his competition."

"Not much of a competition." Charlotte grunted toward the pile of meat that had been Shadow of Death. "He always had such a high opinion of himself. Too high, really." He shrugged. "Winning a race was never that important to me. I win when it counts."

Charlotte addressed Andy again. "As leader I will allow no more interference with children. Or almost-children. I have no desire to prey on the weak. And I look forward to punishing anyone on my team who feels differently."

"You'll still eat people." Andy's voice was such a deep, grating sound that it hurt my throat just to hear it.

"Maybe. Maybe not. There are many other options." Charlotte tilted his head. "You do know we're cannibals?"

Andy's eyebrows shot up. I put a hand to my stomach, willing myself not to throw up. I needed out of this conversation. Now.

"Andy, we need to go," I said, swallowing back bile. *Don't throw up, don't throw up.* "You need to heal."

"Go," Charlotte agreed. "I'll clean up here." He smiled at me. He didn't say anything, but I knew that look when I saw it.

It was a look that said "See you later."

That can't be good.

CHAPTER 28

"YOU'RE STUCK, AREN'T YOU?"

I leaned back in the driver's seat of my car and eyed Peasblossom where she slumped on the rearview mirror. A honey packet dangled from one hand, and the other had been surreptitiously trying to pry her dress off the plastic back of the mirror for the last five minutes.

"I am not stuck," Peasblossom said primly. "I'm just relaxing. We've been up all night, you know."

I dropped my attention back to the windshield, staring at the front of Andy's house. He was inside right now, talking to his mom and dad. Well, their ghosts. I'd offered to go inside with him, but he said he wanted to talk to them alone. And even though he didn't come right out and say it, I knew what I was there for. Why he'd asked me to be here.

Damage control.

"He'll be okay," Peasblossom said confidently. "His mum will set him right."

I sighed, pretending not to notice when she finally jerked her honey-glued dress free and almost fell off the mirror. "I'm afraid this isn't something a mom can set right."

"No such thing."

"You know Andy needs to do this himself. It's entirely up to him how he wants to proceed from here."

"I thought he was going to stay at Evelyn's church?" Peasblossom grunted and heaved herself back onto the mirror, wrinkling her nose when she sat in the sticky patch again.

"He is, but that's not what I mean. I mean, he's going to have to decide if he wants to learn to use...his new abilities."

"He doesn't have a choice."

"Yes, he—"

Peasblossom squeaked as she tumbled off the mirror. I reached out to catch her with the ease of someone who had done this many, many times before.

"No, he doesn't," she snapped, smoothing her skirt down. "If he doesn't learn to harness them, they'll come out on their own. When he doesn't want them to. His only other option would be to dedicate himself to a deity and hope they helped cleanse his corruption from him." She huffed and stood up in my palm. "And since he's not a true believer, that's not likely to happen, is it?"

She wasn't wrong. Divine intervention was the only method I knew for sure could cleanse a corruption like his. It wasn't something a magic practitioner could just wipe away. It took dedication, time, and patience.

Lots of patience.

"Evelyn will talk it all through with him," I murmured. "She'll be better able to help him with this than I am."

"Being a friend is just as important." Peasblossom crawled up my arm to my shoulder, leaving glistening, sticky footprints all the way up before sitting on my neck. "Knowing you're here waiting for him when he's done with Evelyn is important."

Before I could voice my agreement, the front door to Andy's

house opened. I popped my trunk open. After locking the door carefully he carried his suitcase to my car and loaded it in the trunk. He ran his hands down his suit, checking his cuffs and smoothing his lapels before climbing into the passenger seat.

"How'd it go?" I asked.

"Fine. I'm good." He paused briefly. "I think my mom's going to cry when I leave."

I glanced up at the window and saw Mrs. Bradford's ghostly figure waving. Her face pulled into a smile that reached up to her eyes, which looked brighter than usual for a ghost. Andy was right, that woman was going to cry.

"I'll cheer her up when I get back," Andy said. "Once I get a better hold on...this, I'll have more answers for her."

"You're a good son," I said, meaning every word.

He smiled, just a little lift at the corner of his mouth.

"And a good cop." I started the car and pulled out of the driveway. "How did you know? About Siobhan and all those missing people?"

Andy kept his eyes on the road. "When I first started hanging out at Something Fishy, Siobhan wasn't there. It was usually just a handful of kelpies hanging out on a boat like college kids throwing a kegger. When Siobhan started showing up, it was pretty clear no one liked her. They made faces when she wasn't looking, didn't face her when she was talking, and just generally seemed to enjoy themselves less when she was around."

I flicked on my turn signal, heading toward Goodfellows. "I can't blame them."

"Me neither. But I started wondering how she could be leader if no one respected her. So I started learning what I could about kelpies. Hachim answered a lot of questions for me. I found out kelpies operate a lot like pirates. For the most part, whoever can convince the rest of the team that they can improve their lives gets to be in control. And if they don't live up to their promise, someone else might make a better promise and mutiny to take over."

"Did you know about Gloria?" I asked.

"No. No one mentioned her. When I asked how Siobhan came to lead, Hachim said he'd heard it was because she had the idea for Turning Tides, and the kelpies were getting edged out of Fortuna's Stables."

"So she promised them a better life."

"And delivered, for the most part," Andy agreed. "But it still bothered me that the others clearly didn't respect her, but they were willing to play along to her face. One thing I've learned is that an employee who tolerates a bad boss with good cheer is usually doing it because that boss is letting them get away with something. They're a bad boss, but it works in the employee's favor somehow."

"And you guessed it was because Siobhan wasn't controlling them like she should." I nodded. "Very observant."

"Hachim said that a leader of any group, in any Otherworld race, bears the responsibility for controlling their people when it comes to the human world. That's how the Vanguard sees it. So if a leader is letting their people run around eating humans, that's the leader's fault. So I just needed to look for victims that would have been appealing to the kelpies."

A tiny part of me wanted to ask him why he hadn't told me about that investigation. But I held my tongue, because this wasn't about me. Andy knew I was here, and he knew I'd help if he asked. But an FBI agent was more than qualified to find missing people and investigate murders. And it sounded like Hachim had helped him—and the water spirit would have been a much bigger help searching for bodies that vanished in or near water than a witch.

Liam and Evelyn were waiting for us outside Goodfellows. Evelyn was there to take Andy to her church, and Liam was there because it was in his alpha nature to be overly cautious and he wanted to see me after I took Andy to his emotional farewell with his parents. Well, he'd said he was there to eat, but I knew him better than that.

Both of them looked a little tired, but Evelyn was smiling and Liam pulled a protein bar out of his pocket and waved it at me as I climbed out of the car.

"For all you know, I already ate," I told him as I approached. "You'd be surprised how much food I have in this pouch."

"Did you?" he asked.

"No, she didn't," Peasblossom answered from my shoulder. "But I did. Because I'm *responsible.*"

I grumbled under my breath and took the protein bar. "Thank you for all your help, Evelyn."

"It was my pleasure." She turned to Andy. "Are you ready?"

Andy nodded. I waited for him to say something, but he kept his mouth shut. His eyes were a little wider than they should have been too.

"Evelyn said you'd stay for a few weeks," I said, keeping my voice light. "We could meet here when you're done. Have lunch?"

Andy nodded again, but the tension didn't go away. If anything, he looked more uncomfortable.

Liam took a step closer, his aura growing warmer, bathing one side of my body in a low heat. He looked Andy in the eye, waited for him to meet his gaze.

"I would never let you hurt Shade," he said softly. "I'd kill you first."

My jaw dropped and Peasblossom let out a surprised squeak.

Andy's shoulders fell, and he let out a breath I hadn't realized he'd been holding. He nodded to Liam, one of those guy nods that seemed to stand in for an entire conversation. Liam nodded back. Also saying a lot with that one gesture.

Evelyn looked back and forth between them, then murmured a farewell and started toward her car, trusting Andy to follow.

As they left, I turned to Liam.

"One of the most common fears for a new werewolf is that they'll hurt someone they care about," Liam explained, reading the question in my face. "They need to hear that someone is there to stop that from happening. It's what lets them relax enough to focus on themselves, and to face parts of who they are that might scare them."

"It makes perfect sense when you say it like that." My throat constricted, squeezing my voice at the end.

Liam noticed. "You don't like it."

"It's not that. I believe you that he needed to hear that—I could see it on his face."

"You understand you couldn't be the one to do it? Or Evelyn for that matter. Hearing those words from you wouldn't have the same effect, because he would never believe that you'd kill him. And he'd never believe you wouldn't do everything you could to hide him from Evelyn if she'd made the offer."

I didn't bother arguing with that. Anyone who'd worked with me on this particular investigation would know how far I was willing to go to protect Andy. How hard I fought to believe the best in him even when the evidence didn't support me.

"What's bothering you?" Liam asked gently.

I looked him in the eye. "You mean it. You'd kill him."

"Yes. If he was in danger of killing someone he cared about, I would kill him first." He stepped closer, took my hands in his. "There are so many steps that come before that. I know what to look for. And if he'll accept my help, I'll help him. I'll do everything I can to flag him before it ever gets to that point. And I've been doing this awhile, Shade. I'm good at what I do. This is a big part of why I'm alpha."

I nodded, but swayed on my feet, my thoughts thundering through my head with the force of worries pushed to the side for too long. Then his arms were circling me, pulling me against him. I buried my face in his chest, soaking in the warmth of his aura as it closed around me, buzzing against my skin. My eyes burned, but I didn't cry.

"I never wanted this for him," I said, my voice muffled by Liam's shirt.

He laid his cheek against the top of my head, his breath stirring my hair. "I know."

Peasblossom squirmed around on my neck, her sticky arms tacky on my skin as she added her own hug to the mix.

We stayed like that for a long time. Or it felt like a long time. Liam showed no sign of pulling away, apparently content to hold me as long as I needed it. I pulled back before I was ready, if only because a lack of sleep made it a distinct possibility I'd pass out standing here.

"Do you want company?" Liam asked. "I can stay with you awhile."

I shook my head. "No, I'll be okay."

I walked him to his truck and Liam climbed into the driver's seat and appeared to hesitate. "You're not going to confront Morgan right now, are you?"

My eyes narrowed. "No. No, in fact, I'm not going to confront her at all."

"You seemed pretty intent on doing just that not long ago."

"Yes, but now I'm thinking Andy had the better idea. I let myself get too distracted by the fact that there seemed to be some sort of *geas* that stopped Morgan from telling me exactly what was on her mind. I wondered who would order the *geas*, and why. Whatever event that geas is keeping shrouded in secret took down an entire House of enforcers—a House that Morgan and her family made up a large part of. *Sidhe* chose to fade because of what happened."

Liam raised his eyebrows. "Something serious then."

"Yes, but I was focusing on the wrong thing. I let myself get frustrated because I couldn't get anyone to talk about it. But Andy took out Siobhan by doing what he'd do if she'd been human. He asked around, looked for physical evidence."

"You're going to look for physical evidence?" Liam asked. "For a *geas*?"

"Not exactly. But a *geas* can't affect the entire world. It could be that the only people under the actual magical enforcement of the *geas* are the ones who witnessed whatever happened. Or who have direct knowledge of it. But this is the *sidhe* we're talking about. They gossip, they spy, they plan. Someone, somewhere, who isn't under the *geas* knows something. And if I use Morgan as a starting point, I can find them."

"My army of spies!" Peasblossom said excitedly.

I smiled. "Indeed."

Liam considered me for a minute. "Getting involved with the *sidhe* is going to draw attention to you eventually. It's well known they don't appreciate it when outsiders pry into their secrets. What is it about this *geas* that makes it worth the risk?"

I really loved it that he assumed I had good reason, that unlike Flint, he didn't accuse me of making enemies without a thought to the consequences.

"Morgan has hinted more than once that she knows something about Scath that I don't. She makes Scath sound like a threat. But she's the one who keeps causing trouble when she tries to 'help.'" I shook my head. "It makes me think there's something going on I need to know about. And that something has been driving Morgan to interfere with my life. And now Raphael and Luna are butting in, and I don't need an oracle to tell me that's a bad thing."

"Like playing a game when you don't know all the rules," Liam said.

"Worse, I feel like a game piece that other people are moving around, and I have no idea what the goal is, or even who's playing. I don't like it, and I'm not going to take it anymore. I want answers, and I'll get them however I have to."

Liam blinked, looking genuinely surprised.

"What?" I asked.

His mouth twitched at the corner and he straightened in his seat and started his truck. "I almost feel bad for Morgan."

"But not quite," I added.

He grinned. "Not quite."

Despite my bravado, it was a little harder to say goodbye than I wanted to admit. More so because unlike Liam, I wasn't heading for bed to get the sleep I'd missed out on last night. But as much as I'd have liked to stay with him, maybe try to finish our interrupted date, there was a conversation waiting for me back at my apartment.

Fortunately, Goodfellows wasn't far from my apartment, and ten minutes later I was stepping into the blissful quiet of my quarters. Flint was nowhere to be seen—probably off to whatever safe house he hid in when he wasn't making my life difficult.

Scath watched me, her large black feline body curled up on the couch and leaving brick red smears from where her healing wounds had rubbed against the material. Her jaw was already healing, and if I hadn't known it had been broken less than six hours ago, I wouldn't have noticed the slight off-centeredness.

I stared at her for a long minute. Then I put my keys on the kitchen island and moved to the refrigerator to get a Coke.

"Are you okay? I'd have healed you if you'd waited."

She made a sound somewhere between a huff and a snort. I took it to mean she felt fine and didn't require—or desire—assistance.

"So," I said, pulling out a bright red can of soda. "We need to talk."

Tension slithered through the room. Scath didn't move a muscle, but her stillness spoke louder than words. I kept my attention on my drink, focusing on cracking it open, taking that first, burning sip. Scath hated talking. She particularly hated answering questions. And our relationship had improved drastically when I'd stopped trying to make her answer me.

But biting Liam had changed things. I needed to know what she'd done to him. I had to be able to tell him what she'd done, so he could decide how much to explain to his pack.

Scath must have come to the same conclusion. She spared a brief glance at Peasblossom as she flew to the top of the refrigerator, risking getting lost in dust bunnies to dig into an emergency bag of fun-sized candy bars I kept there. The pixie's wings twitched, and I sensed she was trying not to look at Scath.

I let my thoughts percolate as Scath stretched out her front legs, squeezing her eyes shut as she started to shift. A shiver ran over her body as she fought her way back to human form, filling the air with wet popping sounds and the spine-chilling crack of bones shifting and reforming. Not for the first time, I wondered if her natural form was a cat, and her human form was the alternate. Her preference was certainly clear enough.

I gave her a few moments to compose herself, regain her breath. She put her hand to her jaw, opening and closing her mouth a few times. The bone made a muffled clicking sound, but seemed in working order.

"When you bit Liam," I said quietly, getting straight to the point, "it wasn't just a bite."

Scath blinked, forcing her green eyes to focus on me. "No." She closed her eyes, dragged in another deep breath before opening them. "Can't talk about it."

Of course not.

It was fine though, I'd expected that answer.

"There's a *geas* on the Unseelie Court. Isn't there?" I asked.

Scath's gaze bored into mine. "You'll find there's a certain period of time no one will speak of. Small, but significant."

"Would I be correct in assuming that this event and the inability to speak of it applies only to members of a certain age?" I asked.

"Obviously those who weren't born at the time would not know of it," Scath said evenly. "Since those who were there can't speak of it."

"Makes sense." I took another sip of my soda. "Raphael and Luna are older. So is Morgan."

Scath didn't remark on that. But if she'd had a tail in this form, it would be twitching.

"I don't know Raphael very well," I added," but it seems to me that both he and his sister are warriors of some repute."

"A fair assessment," Scath agreed.

"Strange then that Raphael refrained not only from attacking you, but from defending himself when you attacked him. Almost as if he *wanted* you to bite him." I met her eyes.

One of Scath's bare shoulders lifted in a slight shrug. Peasblossom dropped the candy bar she was holding. The half-eaten chocolate bar hit the kitchen floor with a dull thud. Neither Scath nor I turned to look at her.

"He shot you in the leg earlier," I continued. "It's harder for you to use your claws when you need your good leg to stand. Sort of makes it more likely you'll have to bite him."

"That's a bold assumption," Scath argued. "What makes you think he was aiming for my leg? That's not an easy target—not compared to the rest of me."

"Maybe not for someone with less skill than a warrior *sidhe* who refers to his house as Valhalla," I pointed out.

"It's still a guess."

"Is it?"

She hesitated, tilting her head to the side. I knew that look. She was thinking of what she'd say, feeling for whether or not her answer would trigger the magic that kept her from speaking of whatever had happened. I left her to consider her answer and focused my attention on the room's other occupant.

Peasblossom's pink eyes were wide, her wings completely still. She tensed when I looked at her, hands gripping the edge of the fridge.

"You kept shouting for Scath not to bite someone. At Marilyn's, then again at that zombie property. Especially Raphael." I set my can of soda on the kitchen island. I'd been thinking about this all day. Even when I was pursuing Andy's accusers, in the back of my mind I kept hearing Peasblossom's high-pitched shriek, *"Don't bite him!"*

"You know, don't you?" I asked quietly. "You know what Morgan's talking about. You know why Raphael keeps pushing Scath, trying to get her to attack him. Bite him." I shook my head. "There was no reason for Raphael and Luna to be at that property with Andy. If he'd only wanted to get me into a contract, he could have stayed somewhere safe, waited for Flint to die. But he didn't. He was right there, pumping up our adrenaline—*Scath's* adrenaline yet again." I stared into her pink multifaceted eyes. "And you know why."

For a second, Peasblossom crouched there, frozen. I relaxed, letting our empathic link open a little further. Let her feel what I was feeling.

Her wings drooped for a split second, then she launched herself off the fridge and flew straight at me. I let out a grunt as she collided with my neck and clung for dear life.

"I'm sorry," she whispered. "I can't talk either. I would tell you if I could, you know I would tell you."

I patted her back, carefully with one finger between her delicate wings. My stomach was tight, and it was hard to muster up a reassuring smile, but I did my best.

"It's okay. I'm not mad. We're going to figure this out."

I took a deep breath and unzipped my waist pouch. "Bizbee? I need some index cards, colored string, masking tape, two pens, a piece of pencil lead, and a variety of Post-its."

Bizbee popped out of the enchanted space with wide eyes, his antennae swinging wildly. "Are ye organizing, then? What size Post-its? What color pens?" He waved a hand at me. "No, no, you'll need options. I have the very thing."

The grig's office supply euphoria eased my nerves, and I managed to smooth the furrow from between my brows. When he reappeared with the requested supplies—including two multi-color pens—I handed a stack of index cards and a pen to Scath. I also put a small pad of miniature Post-its on the floor for Peasblossom, along with the pencil lead.

Both of them stared at me as I wrote "Event" on one of the index cards and used the masking tape to stick it to the wall. Then I broke off a few pieces of purple string and taped one end of each to the index card, then spread them out like sunbeams radiating from the center card and taped the loose ends to the wall. I wrote down Morgan's name on another card, and the twins' names on another and taped each one to the end of one of the purple threads.

"Write down whatever information you can give me that's in any way related to any of those cards," I said, nodding to the wall. "It doesn't matter if it seems relevant right now or not. It could be relatives, or powers, or marriages, any kind of relationship. It could be locations where they've been, where they are. Goals, defeats, wars, house affiliations. Whether they're in good or bad standing with someone."

"You want it here, where Flint will see it?" Scath asked.

I nodded. "He offered to help. And as much as I hate letting him be part of anything important, the fact is, he could be an asset here. He's part of this world, and we all know how nosy he is. Might as well let it work for us."

I glanced at Scath. "I'm asking you to spend more time in human form than you want to. And I'm sorry. But I would really appreciate your help. I'm not asking either of you to violate the *geas*, but it can't prevent you from talking at all. It has to end somewhere?"

I couldn't see Peasblossom as close as she was to my neck, but I knew she and Scath were staring at one another. Finally, Scath nodded.

"I'll try," she said softly.

I let out a breath and nodded again before turning to the wall. "Then let's get started."

*****

Next Book

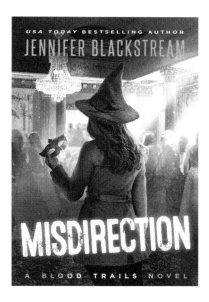

The next book is just a click away…

ABOUT THE AUTHOR

Jennifer Blackstream is a USA Today bestselling author of urban fantasy and paranormal romance. She is amazed and grateful to have made a writing career out of a Master's degree in Psychology, hours of couch-detecting watching Miss Fisher's Murder Mysteries, and endless research into mythology and fairy tales. She firmly believes that whether it's a village witch deciding she wants to be a private investigator, or a single mother having a go at being a full time writer, it's never too late for a new adventure.

A fervent devotee of cooperative board games, Jennifer sets aside at least two nights a week for team-based adventures such as Mice & Mystics, Sentinels of the Multiverse, or Harry Potter: Battle at Hogwarts. She uses games with dice-based mechanics to lure in her ridiculously lucky-rolling son and daughter in the hope that they too will develop a passion for cooperative escapism.

DID YOU FIND A TYPO?

I hate typos. Really, they upset me on a deeply emotional level. If you find a typo in one of my books, please contact me through my website at www.jenniferblackstream.com. I have a monthly drawing in which I pick a name from those who have submitted typos, and I award said winner with a $25 gift certificate.

Death to typos!

JB